A FREUDIAN TIME SLIP

"All of you should know who I am," the man said. "I am Sigmund Freud. In my time I was a doctor of medicine in Vienna who investigated the human mind. Unfortunately, I was killed by a madman before my researches could reach fruition. Now I have been reconstructed to help you with your difficulties.

"Listen to me now. The aliens must be repelled and you must do this. Caution will not work. Prayer is into a void. The lies of the administrators, those on Earth who would have you treat this as routine circumstances, will not do it."

"That's right!" the captain cried. "That's absolutely right, doctor, you tell them what they have to do!"

Freud smiled. Clearly he had their full attention.

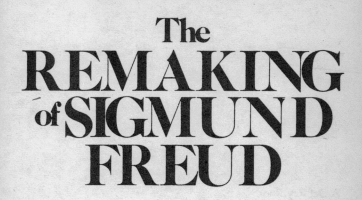

The
REMAKING
of SIGMUND
FREUD

Barry N. Malzberg

A Del Rey Book

BALLANTINE BOOKS • NEW YORK

A Del Rey Book
Published by Ballantine Books

Some portions of this novel, in far different and much truncated form, appeared in *Omni*, *Chrysalis 8*, *The Magazine of Fantasy & Science Fiction*, and *The Man Who Loved the Midnight Lady*.

Library of Congress Catalog Card Number: 85-90650

ISBN 0-345-31861-7

Manufactured in the United States of America

First Edition: July 1985

Cover art by Barclay Shaw

In memory of Celia F. Malzberg: 4/12/04−10/1/82

He gave no advice, put his faith in the insolubility of problems. You never laid a glove on the serious stuff. Disease played for keeps and though he was no expert on world affairs, he knew that if things as inanimate and impersonal and off to the side of real life as nations could get into difficulties they couldn't slip, people had no chance at all.

Stanley Elkin
George Mills

We seek to convert human misery into ordinary unhappiness.

Sigmund Freud

CONTENTS

INTRODUCTION

Frontier Life

SIGMUND FREUD, GRUNTING, PREPARES TO GO OUT UPON the dark surfaces of Venus, effortfully puts on the equipment. Boots, alternator, receiver, steel receptor, helmet, transmitter of light. Outside the mad engineer, Jurgensen, is clinging to the dome, waiting, perhaps, to utter confidences, inside the colonists are poised by this appropriated storage room, waiting for him to emerge but for the moment he is alone. A small lacunae of peace in the void. He had never imagined that life after death—if it existed at all—would be quite so eventful but this proved the worth of his theories. You never knew. That was all; circumstances were imponderable. You could never tell what was lying at the other side of the abyss.

Freud considers the engineer, the crisis, the methodological bind of the situation. He can see the humor of the situation here; Adler or Jung might be more appropriate to this assignment. After all of the tumult, his miserable colleagues might have more theoretical relevance than he. Adler would say that Jurgensen was compensating for his failures on the mission by trying, single-handedly, to demolish it; Jung, that mystic, would mumble about Venus as the plateau of dreams. There *is* something that is dreamlike (not to say primitive) about this circumstance; Adler *does* have a point about Jurgensen's loss of control. Nonetheless, it is not either of them but he who has been taken from the reconstruction banks (or so they have told him) to deal with the situation. So they must see some relative merit in his theories, as compared to the others. Or something. Whatever. It is all very difficult to understand and he is no closer to having control over this than when all of this began, some hours or days ago. Who can tell?

Puffing, Freud adjusts the equipment around him, feeling very much like the paradigm of future man which he had posited in some of his writings . . . all stimulus and response, heat and wiring, trouble and technology around the vulnerable, living cells. It is most humiliating to see his vision so enacted but at the same time, there is a certain pride to be taken; not all of his guesses were wrong. Staring through the porthole, looking at the green and deadly gases that drift over the enshrouded surface of the second planet, Freud tries to cultivate his tragic sense. This and this alone will get him through; an awareness of the possibilities and his own conclusive helplessness. In his helmet, already, he thinks he can hear the purring of the alien winds.

He perceives a slant of light, turns toward the hatch, sees them waiting for him. "I'm ready," he says before they can ask. "I'm ready." He overcompensates. "I will go with you now," he dreams he is saying in the archetypal night. "Let us go," he says. He rises. Sustained only by his belief in the unconscious, in the tragic fate of man, Freud extends a hand and permits them to ease him toward destiny.

PROLOGUE

The Trials of Sigmund

FREUD'S NEXT TO LAST PATIENT WAS A POLITICAL ACTIV-
ist and house painter. The subject had been referred by
a general practitioner; the complaint was impotence, but
quickly enough he perceived that the symptom was reaction formation against deep inner rage and that the man
was in need of extended therapy which he could neither
afford nor understand. The patient had an ordinary mind
and little insight.

"I am afraid," Freud said, relighting his cigar, "that
there is little I can do for you. A little wine before such
encounters might be helpful. It is best to encourage a
sense of spontaneity. Do not feel that you must give a
performance or are being judged." Common hedging. He
flicked out the match, put it into an ashtray, rolled the
cigar between sensitive teeth, noting tiny slivers of pain
in the lower right quadrant. Referred pain; it felt as if
cancer was blooming below the level, yet of obvious
symptomatology. Hypochondria? That was possible.
Regardless, there was nothing to be done just then.

"You are saying you will not treat me," the house painter
said. He was a bitter man. His mustache twitched. "You
have been highly recommended, however, as someone
who would help—"

"I am simply not available. This consultation is a courtesy. My bookcase is overflowing, my researches demanding, and there is the travel. Furthermore, I do not think that I am the ideal analyst in your case. I am sorry about this, but there is other help available in Vienna; perhaps you will see Carl—"

"But no," the patient said. He stood, leaned crookedly against the desk, staring desperately at Freud. Already the patient had mentioned his political involvement, the sense of inchoate, desperate rage that came over him when he thought of how common men were being exploited; this must be another of those rages. "I won't settle for this," he said. "You deny me help, just like all of the rest of them. I tell you, I have plans, I have needs—"

"We all have plans," Freud said gently. "In this society we consider alternatives, stay poised upon their existence right up to the very end. It is this necessary delusion that makes us human." He exhaled smoke, spat foul tobacco, sensation turning the jaw aqueous. Why must it happen to him? Why did he permit it to be done, over and again, and become a philosopher-fool with these patients? Nauseated, he stubbed out the cigar. "This consultation is free. There is no charge for the advice."

"I am suffering, you will suffer, there will be terrible penalties," the house painter said. "This is another example of exploitation; we cannot have it." He turned, left the room. Freud heard swearing in the corridor, and then the outer door was slammed. Looking through the window, he could see the little man trudging down the path. In the slump of his shoulder, tilt of his head, he did indeed belong with those masses who he felt were being reviled.

Freud sighed, thought of waste, pain, human folly. That patient would come to nothing and in forty years, if still alive, still impotent, would still project his insufficiency on the social condition. Self-delusion was rampant. The times fostered self-delusion as an arboretum does trees. At least that unhappy and unpleasant person was protected (by his very condition!) from inflicting his neurosis upon his children.

Freud considered his appointment book. The final patient, due in less than a quarter of an hour, in Vienna on a quick journalistic tour, was Colonel Robert McCormick, editor in chief and publisher of the *Chicago Tribune*. Freud sighed again and relit his cigar. He would die of some vague cancer of the jaw if he did not stop that; the cells themselves shouted the message, but he could not give up the habit. What could he do? So much of life, as his own studies indicated, was preordained, deterministic. At least he was fully conscious of what he was doing to himself.

So he took a further moment to rest and revive, to be properly introspective. He was a contemplative and feeling man; patients tended to run together in his mind if he did not take time between sessions to restructure and align his perception. The fifty-minute analytic hour was one of his more recent discoveries; it would be an obvious necessity as the methodology took root. Richard Strauss had reactive depression. Alban Berg, sorrowfully trapped in marriage, could not escape his dominant wife. Gustav Mahler, an hysteric, would die with (or without) his Alma. William Randolph Hearst had delusions of persecution. Alice B. Toklas was in love with her employer, a stern novelist, but dreaded her own homosexual impulses. Warren Harding felt manipulated. And so on and on. Freud was famous. He had founded a new school of mental science. From all over the world, the well-known and the obscure came to him, seeking assistance, and he could give them so little. Most, like the house painter, had to be sent on their way at once. Others, like Mahler, did show keen understanding of analytic principle and were worth some time but were too old, too pained to change their fate. A few in negative transference had been exceedingly unpleasant. It was all so painful.

Still, one had to continue. Freud's researches and profound ruminations on the human condition had imparted to him a tragic dimension.

He went to the door, opened it, and saw McCormick waiting in the anteroom. He was a florid man in sombrero and white jacket with large boutonniere. "Come in, please," Freud said politely. McCormick stood. Freud had no secretary. A secretary would only distance the patients and in addition might read the precious, private files. McCormick's self-delusion was unlike that of the previous patient, Freud sensed; it was appurtenance. If truth were marketable, then McCormick would find a way to deal with that.

His new patient following him at a respectful distance, Freud reentered his office, closed the door, seated himself once more behind his desk. He gestured to the couch against the wall and then sat there, stroking his head, as McCormick settled on it, facing him eagerly. More and more his thought patterns streamed like that, his consciousness flitted from topic to topic. Anxiety neurosis to be sure, moderately well compensated, but there was the problem that he might, well, perhaps it could lead to . . . Freud faced it—he feared imbalance. He knew that some of his estranged or rivalrous colleagues thought him mad, and he was the target of scurrilous allegations. Jung had had some very painful things to say, likewise Alfred Adler. Freud knew he was not mad, was confident of his balance and his abilities, nonetheless—

"I am not here for treatment, Doctor," McCormick said. "I know of your wonderful work and have come to make you an offer, a fine offer. I would like you to write an advice column exclusively for our newspapers in which you can give readers practical answers to their problems. Five times a week you can do this with three months off during the year, and we can offer a five-year contract at the outset. *Three* columns a week if you find this daily schedule too taxing. With our syndicate working on distribution, you would double your income immediately, as we reach many newspapers in cities throughout the country with our columnists and your work in particular would be excitedly received. You will be a most intriguing addition to the papers. Also you will be able to render help, real help to the masses, Doctor! Millions of people will read your words and be inspired. It is a marvelous opportunity, don't you agree?"

"I'm sorry," Freud said. "I'm not interested."

"But think of this, Dr. Freed," McCormick said earnestly. "Consider what we have to offer you." He shrugged convulsively, seemed to be attempting inflation within his clothing; not only the billows of his stomach but his smooth, innocent American cheekbones seeming to expand in the harsh light of Freud's office, the steamy odors of his continent seeming to come from him, America itself heating those spaces. "It would be a platform in the New World! You are already well thought of by many of my countrymen in the universities or medical colleges, but the man in the street, the common reader who we strive to reach with our newspapers, barely can be said to know you. This would make you famous; it would far expand the influence and reach of your ideas."

"My name is *Freud*," he said calmly, thinking of the lunacy of a certain kind of American, an absolute determination and unawareness of inference which was not duplicated among all the countries and creeds of the world. "No, your offer is very kind, but to accept it would be highly unprofessional. I am a researcher, a doctor, a scholar if I may modestly say so. Not an advice columnist, whatever that is you're talking about."

"But think of the good you might do! You could treat many, the masses, instead of only a selected few who can afford your very high fees."

"I'm sorry," Freud said. "I'm really sorry, but you do not understand my researches, my theories. Neurosis is a poetic malfunction, a language of the heart; it can be treated only in confidence and in a private means. There is no way that my researches can be flattened for your masses, most of whom do not suffer from anything as luxurious as neurosis." He stood, hoping that by his signal McCormick would see that the interview was terminated. "I cannot help you; what you seek is outside of my range."

"Do you know what?" McCormick said with a sneer, stroking the flower in his lapel. "You're just another intellectual, thinking you're so goddamned superior to those of us who do the real work, go on with the real tasks of this world. I know your type."

"I think nothing of the sort, Colonel."

"Well, then, the *hell* with you," McCormick said as if he had not heard that response. That had to be the case. The man had heard nothing. Only the resonances of his own voice, eternally, were fed back to him. "The hell with all of you," he said determinedly. Freud considered the rosy hue, the cast eye, the evident bigotry. McCormick would not stand. His feet fluttered in patterns on the floor. Rank projectivity was at work of course and probably self-hatred as well, but he had no time for that and the Colonel had no interior; he was as essentially untreatable as the house painter.

"Please," Freud said mildly. "Please leave."

McCormick crossed his legs. "I arranged for a whole hour. I'm paying you for this time; I'm not going to be thrown out until I make you hear my proposition."

"You bought nothing. I am not for sale. I do not wish to continue this discussion. The consultation is free." His second free consultation of the day; there was a sign of something deeply wrong. His tragic sense, unfettered, scuttled like a small animal within his breast. Really, I have made too many sacrifices, he thought. Pain, torment, misdirection, abuse, martydom, and all for what? To be a syndicated gossip columnist for Robert McCormick? He felt an uncharacteristic and dangerous flare of rage. "There is no justice," he said incautiously, thinking not only of this situation but of Jung and Adler. "You're just like the rest of them; there's no difference at all. Get out."

"Not so," McCormick said oddly. "Not so whatsoever and furthermore." He stood convulsively, removed an ancient pistol from his clothing, shakily aimed it. To his horror, Freud saw death coming. He was going to be killed. It was unavoidable. For so long he had theorized of it, strewn it through his own dreams and papers, then, unbelievably, it was happening to him. He was going to die. Richard Strauss will shit in fever and Gustav Mahler's mania will cycle ever higher, making Alma too crazy. My researches will languish, lesser men will pirate my insights, spread them indiscriminately, eventually I will become a parody, a joke, used at last against that very perception of human misery which was to be my legacy to the world—

"Please," he said, raising a hand. "Robert, I'm going to die soon enough anyway." He indicated his jaw. "I'm sure there's an inoperable cancer in there, so it doesn't matter, you see, it just doesn't matter. You don't have to do this; I don't have that much time left. Don't take me away from the little that there is. I have to work—"

"You do not have to work," McCormick said. His forehead was distended, his eyes bulged; he was a picture of the New World seeking revenge, absolutely focused upon reparation. The barbarian, free of his shackles, had come at last to exact tribute. "You have to do nothing at all. There is no need for you. You are an arrogant man, Freed; you think that you're better than all of the rest of us, but this isn't so, it isn't so at all. Everything levels out in the long run. That's the principle of mass publishing, you see, that's what has made me my fortune: *everything becomes the same*, tits and blood are the foundation of democracy. I saw that even before that pirate Hearst did, and it is going to be the face of the century."

He shot Freud in the right eye. Freud collapsed even before he felt the pain. Riven, bleeding thunderously, he saw the rose on McCormick's lapel unfurl, spout fluid. It was a splendid image, ironic and painful, and he wondered if it was merely a version of poetic truth or some deep revelation of McCormick's plans for the future.

"I don't have to take this kind of thing," he heard the publisher say. "No one is going to make me take it. Not from a kike." Footsteps receded. Freud wondered if McCormick would now go to Jung, make the same offer there. Would Carl take it? Probably, he thought. Carl had always had, whatever his pretensions, a cheap populist mentality. So he would accept the offer, save his life, redirect his life, destroy his academic legitimacy forever.

CHAPTER THREE

Emily Dickinson Saved from Drowning

EMILY DICKINSON SAT POISED IN HER BEDROOM ON THE second floor of the building at 280 Main Street, Amherst, in the state of Massachusetts, opening herself to inspiration in the accustomed way and considering her latest poem. She had finished it just that afternoon. The year was 1862. She was a widely published poet, a frequent contributor to *The Atlantic Monthly, Scribner's* and *Harper's Magazine*, and her first collection, *The Heart Seeks Pleasure First*, published the year before, had sold well with excellent reviews, but she still had a feeling of insufficiency in regard to her work.

Probably, she thought, it had to do with the long years of struggle when she worked in anonymity. She had never lost that sense of failure, even though her work had improved enormously, and, of course, long-deserved recognition had come in its wake.

The war was going badly. That was the inspiration for her newest poem; the war was going very badly for the Union. It had been her intention to contribute as best she could to the staggering northern cause with a bit of determined verse. Emily despised the Confederacy. She despised the institution of slavery. She despised, for that matter, the institution of war to which the nation had been committed, but she knew that it could have been no other

way. Harper's Ferry must not have been in vain; slavery
had to be abolished. At the center of the terrible war
guttered the flame of old John Brown's abolition—part
madness of course. But even the mad could speak true.
Sometimes, she thought, the mad are but the only ones
who can truly understand these times, can act in accor-
dance with them. It was a daring conclusion, but that was
how she felt.

Emily decided that she would send her new poem to
the *Globe*. That newspaper had been asking for her verse,
their letters becoming ever more pleading and insistent,
as if her modest poetry could really make a difference to
the editors. Still, her latest did have elements of the journalistic, and poetry in those times had to be used to take
a stand. If it did not do this, was not used to that end, of
what use would poetry be at all? Oh, she thought, in that
case hers would be an arcane and dreary art that would
mean nothing at all.

> The Heart Seeks—Pleasure First—
> And—then It looks for Light—
> The Light that will flaming lead it
> Past the arc—of—Night
>
> The Light Doth Become—a—Sword
> That Can Be Known—to Some—
> As Liberation, for the Nation—
> So at last—Freedom!

It is 1848. Kansas was bleeding, but Fillmore would
not intend. Industrialism and the fragmentation of the
culture lay decades in the future, but Emerson, her neigh-
bor, was already delivering thunderbolts to theocracy. It
would never be the same after Emerson took God from
the cycle of seasons. Emily Dickinson, unaware of all that
then, not to be aware of the shaking circumstances for
many years, regarded herself in a mirror, looking at her
red hair, intense eyes, the arresting tilt of her cheekbones

which when she entered a room struck everyone as being truly dramatic, even frightening.

She would be leaving for studies at Holyoke in a few hours. The coming year struck her as being particularly dangerous, highly exciting, and on that early fall morning she felt close to that sense of intention which had haunted her off-center for so long. "*I am different*," she murmured. "There is something special about me. I am not like the rest of them; if they could see into my soul they would know that." The explosion of purpose, almost unseemly pride, made her blush; she saw in the dull mirror the imprint of shame, and yet she would not allow pride's sister to drive her from that knowledge. I will be a poet, she thought. No, I *am* a poet, and I will use the medium to inflame and inspire. Because I want to give them the truth, she thought, they must have it, they must be led to understand what is going on.

Poetry beat within her like a bird, like a fish; she felt those hot, dark impulses moving congealed with purposes deep under the skin. Flutters of language, soon to emerge. I will write, she thought. That is my mission and my goal. First, however, I must perceive myself: this room, the world, the steeples, the churchyards, all of the angles and joints of life itself, meeting as if by skilled carpenter's hand in the angle of vision. Fully, richly, darkly; oh how they mesh. There will be much to come of this.

Blood filled her cheeks, scalded her heart. She felt an instant of giddiness subsumed in darker intention which left her drained yet full, fearful yet composed before her destiny.

Some years after the death of Emily Dickinson from Bright's disease, her brother, the Reverend William Austin Dickinson, became interested in the writings and reputation of Sigmund Freud, a German medical practitioner whose insights into the role that the mind might play in the symptoms of physical illness fascinated him. It seemed to be Freud's divination that many intelligent and creative women were "hysterical"; that they evolved physical conditions because they could not cope with the demands and restraints of their inner lives. Austin was, at that time, somewhat hysterical himself: a bad marriage, the deaths of his parents and younger sister within a span of only half a decade, had ravaged his mind and heart.

His letter to Freud, composed during a spell of discipline and lucidity, was, however, a precise and well-structured document. He began with the customary salutations of the period, then invoked his own credential and background, noted that he was a member of a distinguished New England family, explained how he was introduced to Freud's work through a mutual friend (imaginary) in the medical profession, made some appropriately self-deprecating remarks about his ability to understand such profoundly original and provocative material written by a scholar. Then, approaching the central purpose of the letter, Austin outlined the career of his late sister, who had been one of America's most popular poets in her lifetime even though that reputation in the years just after her death had already begun to erode cruelly.

"This seems so often to be the fate of those oriented toward journalistic or inspired verse and it is in many ways a cruel judgement. But this is not the issue," Austin wrote. "I am not writing you in order to complain about circumstance but only to ask you a question, a question which I believe you are better qualified to answer than anyone in my experience. What I wish to know is whether or not my sister's career was *pathological in nature*, that is to say, whether her poetry was an outcome of the *extreme isolation* of her earlier years and whether, perhaps, if she had lived a more social and fulfilled childhood she might have avoided poetry altogether. And also, concomitantly and if this is true, would it have been better for us if she were happier and the poetry not exist? Or does the work itself assume a kind of transcendent validity? These are questions perhaps more metaphysical in nature but I particularly inquire on pathology. In that regard I remain your humble servant & etc., etc." Austin enclosed a considerable sample of the poet's work so that Freud might familiarize himself with her writings and make further judgment.

Austin redrafted the letter several times, struggling for the correct voice. References to his own unhappy domestic situation seemed irrelevant; he put them in and took them out. Praise for Freud's American reputation seemed like blandishment, and he decided to excise. Certain memories of Emily's childhood did seem relevant, however, he had expanded upon them. Speculations on mortality were reluctantly removed; he was not, after all, trying to display knowledge; he was looking for an answer. At last, doubtfully and wondering if any of it had made sense at all, Austin posted the letter, wondering if there would be a reply, whether the Viennese man of science had any answers at all.

Weeks glided by, then months, and Austin came to the conclusion that either his letter had gone astray or Freud, contemptuously, had elected not to answer. The alienist was a busy man, of course, but a brief reply would have been a courtesy: it was not as if Austin were someone from the streets. But there was nothing to be done about it, certainly not a further letter, and after some brooding, Austin decided to leave the issue alone. Slowly the issue and the inquiry ebbed from his consciousness; he had other matters to concern him, including his own advancing age and incapacity. When he died half a decade later, not only his letter to Freud but Emily herself had been overtaken by time and event. Dickinson's poetry slid inexorably from popular favor. Oncoming technology and the more brutal social partitions of the swiftly approaching twentieth century would relegate her to the position of minor, sentimental poet, not atypical of so many of her time who filled the popular journals and newspapers. They reflected events, that was all.

When Freud was murdered by Robert McCormick in Vienna, his files were sealed. Years later, when his heirs at last got to and went through them, Austin Dickinson's letter was there, filed neatly under *D*, cross-referenced under *artists*. Freud had made no remarks upon it, although from the many creases and faded handwriting it would appear that the letter had been carried about and read for some time before being consigned to the files. It was not understood why he had not replied. Ernest Jones could not remark upon it in his biography and omitted any reference. (Jones was famous for ignoring what he could not properly assess to his theories.) The sequence of events was quite mysterious. Much of Freud's life remained shrouded in mystery. The alienist's motives, his feelings, his reaction to the letter, remained a matter of minor scholarly interest until the 1940s or so, by which time all of the biographies and hagiographic materials had been compiled. Freud began to fade then from attention. By the 1970s his work had been largely repudiated and his persona was virtually unknown. The issue of Austin Dickinson's correspondence, then, including so much else tied in with Freud's misguided researches, was lost.

After the initial rejections, after the bewildered or hostile editorial reactions to her first stumbling efforts to master the poetic muse, Emily Dickinson resolved to forgo the technical experiments which gained her so little and to compose in the temper of her times. She would make commentary upon issues of public interest and in that way gain the attention that she deserved. *Then*, perhaps, she would experiment. Her first appearances in the *Globe* in 1858 found good reader reception and led to new opportunities which she was quick to seize. The national magazines began to publish her. The distraction of the war, its terrible onset and equivocal conclusion, did deny her (she came to understand later) that huge earlier success which might otherwise have been hers, but delay is not denial. Not at all. By the early eighties, she was recognized as the American successor to the richly honored if unfortunately deceased Elizabeth Barrett Browning. Emily

Dickinson embarked upon a series of lecture tours which took her all through the eastern and central sections of the nation. She traveled as far west as Hannibal, Missouri, and was awed by her first glimpse of the Mississippi.

Her platform manner, alternately confidential and declamatory, was acknowledged to be thrilling. She had the gift of addressing enormous audiences yet seeming to focus with personal intensity upon every given individual. Because of her travels, Emily Dickinson had access to people and relationships that she would not otherwise have known. She met the well-known novelist, essayist, and lecturer Samuel Langhorne Clemens ("Mark Twain"), with whom she had a discreetly handled affair of some romantic and sexual import. There was the faint aroma of scandal attached, but Emily Dickinson's reputation was so unimpeachable that the consensus was that if she became involved with Clemens it was only to reform him. He was, at that time, a bitter man in a bitter condition, and some of his public postures had been disgraceful.

> To see the Stars—so—brightly strewn—
> Amidst the Corridors of—the—Night—
> Is to Know that We Live and so strictly Subsume—
> In a grander, a Wilder—Light.
>
> Someday perhaps—we will Walk In Those Stars
> In Starlight—Becoming Immersed
> But Walk In—the—Stars or Walk Out—the Night
> The—Heart—Seeks—Pleasure—First.

The year is 1873. Emily Dickinson, in her early forties, was successful. She had achieved what she sought so very long ago. In the post, she received a long communication from the eccentric poet Walt Whitman, of whose work she had little previous knowledge. Whitman wrote, she gathered, of strange landscapes in an unwholesome and unappetizing manner. She had little respect for poets of his sort whose work, rather than being an attempt to uplift, was really—and despite whatever protestations they might voice—meant to degrade. She knew that she was right about that.

"You have wrecked your promise," Whitman wrote, after the briefest of obligatory salutations and self-introductions. "You have become a vivid symbol of the wreckage of America itself. We could have transcended circumstance in this wild and beautiful country." His scrawl was childish, uncontrolled. "America might have been the first in the history of all civilizations to have *subsumed* its madness: dreams of the preachers, curses of Puritan, terror of Calvin, anguish of the slaves, bowels of the Republic, whine of machines, the great and terrible engines hammering us all, fused then in a terrible purpose which would have made our condition at last refractive of mankind since the time of the Fall but you, Emilia Dickinson, all that you have managed to do is to pervert—"

What was this? *Emilia* Dickinson? What was going on? That man, Walt Whitman, could not even state her name correctly, and yet the fool wrote a letter of insult. She should have discarded it, cast it from her and never thought of it again, but horrified, linked somehow to the words, she read on. "You with your trite and sentimental verse, your deliberate flouting of all that which moves in the embittered blood and body of this disastrous country, you express only that which is cheapest and therefore most vile in our spirit and so I hold you responsible. I hold you to blame, Emilia, because of all the popular poets you are the one with a trace of talent, of possibility; you might have done better than this. Perhaps you could have—"

No. He did not understand. She could have done nothing. Nothing at all. Didn't Whitman understand that? She had made her choice at the outset, when she came to understand the role of a poet in America. You gave them what they wanted, what they expected you to be, or you had a much harder road, and on that road there was no acclaim, only loneliness and anonymity. Amherst gave her enough of that; she wanted no more. America did not want poets; the country wanted entertainers, and it was not really so wrong—was it?—to be that.

But why was she arguing with Whitman like that; why had she made her mind an arena, given him the credence of response? It was the last thing which he deserved. She would read no further. No more of this. She would not deal with the man ever again. Hands shaking, eyes tearing, she destroyed the letter and hurled its remnants into the wastebasket. She would drag the basket downstairs herself later and empty it; she would not want Sue, who sifted everything, to discover his letter.

Whitman repelled her. He disgusted. She could not imagine why he had written her in such a manner, what he expected, what response he sought. She owed him nothing. His own verse, the very little she had read, was contemptuous and deeply, deeply offensive, flushed with images of lust and corruption. There in New England, sheltered as she might be, she knew the name for men such as he but would not speak it. She would consider this no further.

How could he have said this to her? Didn't he understand that she knew better than he the gap between the orderly and the impossible? Didn't he know what this country would do to a real poet? He was as counterfeit as she was with his blustering and self-serving odes. None of this had been easy for her. None of it. Someday, latter work, less compromised work, might come, but not because such as Whitman told her what to do.

It is 1875. At the special request of President Ulysses S. Grant, Emily Dickinson was working on a poem for the following year's Centennial. She was known as the unofficial poet laureate of America ("unofficial" only because America was not England, did not hold with titles or royalty) and in that ambiguous function had, during Grant's administration, written many poems for special occasions, but this one was summoning forth her most special powers and the height of intention.

Sometimes, even with all the compromises she had made, she was nonetheless overwhelmed by her little gift, the force which it could occasionally possess. But Emily Dickinson was resolved to remain humble in its power. She knew that she was merely a vessel used toward higher purpose.

> From force—of—all Divining—
> There came a Driving Dream!
> Of Justice, hope and—Brotherhood
> How splendid did it Seem!
>
> Be it in Boston harbor, southland
> Or wild—Chesapeake Shore—
> The Heart—Seeks—Pleasure—First
> But 'tis the Dream—Come—to the Fore!
>
> Until in all—Its—Colors—
> A Century today—
> The *Dream no longer but a Dream*—
> A great Reality!

The south had begun to fall in that eventful and terrible year. It is 1864. Amherst itself, so far from the bloodshed, seemed shaken. In the night, Emily Dickinson awakened from a nightmare that the President had been shot. People were screaming. In the dream he had taken a bullet to the temple and was carried to a small room by his advisers; then he lay drooling like an infant in the bed, the bones of his great head smashed, the blood moving unclotted through the ruined circumference of his face.

Oh, it was terrible, terrible. Why that dream? She had tried to live quietly, so peacefully. Gasping, propelled upright in the bed, Emily Dickinson saw the colors of the dream exploding against her closed eyelids; she felt like a cage struck by a monstrous, imprisoned animal hurled at the bars. Her spirit seemed to move upward, bolting from the pillow, and she sat in the darkness of her room shaking and crying. The President dead. The dream had been unconscionably vivid, and she was terrified by the persuasiveness of the forms evoked.

Oh, that was not like her. She did not react that way; certainly public events or personalities did not move her. She had always been comparatively unaffected by extrinsic political or social events, but the terrible war had assaulted her, broken down isolation. Daguerreotypes of the President which she must have seen somewhere had apparently given her apprehension. In the dream he was dying. Dying. He never regained consciousness; everything was lost in that room. The afterimage, the vivid aspect of rushing blood and blasted skull, persisted.

Emily Dickinson sat stunned in her enclosure in the New England night. Many hours passed. Time streamed by ever so slowly. Still, she could not settle. She remembered. She remembered everything as if it were an intimation rather than a dream. This cannot be, she thought. It will not happen, and if it does, oh if it does, then I could not save him. He lives, he dies, without my ministrations. It is a dream. Finally she willed herself back to sleep, murmuring *he lives, oh he lives*, evoking his form, the dancing, living body of the President as she had always imagined him to be.

It passed from her.

Awakening later, she had only the dullest recollection of the dream. He was bleeding and then he was gone. He fell over and was taken away. She could not seem to make connection, nor did she desire to do so. Later, there was only a dull wound in the heart when she thought of the President, a rubbing against the sensibility, and then there was nothing at all. Fallen from her like a discarded robe, like the leaves from the skeletal, praying trees. Fall.

In time, she forgot it all.

It is 1882. In the course of her last years as traveler and celebrity, Emily Dickinson had affairs with a few men, some of great consequence and some of less: men of the professions, political accomplishment, or learning. By the standards of her time and class she was quite open sexually, although it had been a long time getting there. She was a virgin until her thirties, until Lord captured her and with equal abruptness let her go. Of all the affairs, that beginning with Samuel Clemens in St. Louis on a summer night in that year proved to be the most significant. She had gone there to lecture, and Clemens had been invited to the dinner thereafter; they were seated next to one another, and immediately he fixed her in a stirred and private gaze. "I think you are magnificent," he said. "You have captured the spirit of America in your poetry, in the work you read this evening." She could feel the intensity, the force of the man, aspects of sorrow which also seemed to come from him as they seemed to with so many powerful American men of his generation. It must have been the strain of the war. "I think you are invaluable," he said.

"Whitman doesn't."

"Old Walt? The poet? What does he say?"

"He wrote me a letter, once." Clemens regarded her curiously. "It was a very foul letter." To her surprise she found herself telling the story, repeating the well-remembered contents. She had never discussed it with anyone. Clemens was shocked. His eyes seemed to moisten. "How terrible!" he said, touching her hand. "How could he have done such a thing?"

Observed from a distance at the brilliant dinner party, Emily Dickinson thought they would make an impressive spectacle—she the poet and guest of honor, he the novelist and local celebrity—so intensely involved with one another. She wondered what the guests were thinking. "I don't know," she said. "He seemed to feel he had the right to tell me that."

"He had no right. It is shameful." Clemens patted her brow with his napkin, squeezed it in his hand. "I think you did very well to ignore him, simply to allow the thing to die. He was only looking for an argument, for contention."

"That's what I thought," she said. Her hand was in

his; unobtrusively they were clutching at one another under the table. "So I did nothing."

"You were right," Clemens said. "Let's walk. Let's get some air." Dinner had long finished; they were seated behind uncleared cutlery. "Why don't we go to the balcony?"

"Very well," she said. He assisted Emily to her feet. Soon enough, moving through the room in a detached, dreamlike way, they were poised on the balcony, looking at the flat surfaces of St. Louis, which receded underneath into plumes of smoke. She wondered about the places of the midwest, the unknown river, the sounds of the night which came over them. Would it have been any different for her if she had lived here? "I admire your work too," she said.

Clemens shrugged. "My work means very little to me. Once it was a source of amusement, but now it is only a means of income. Have you seen enough from this balcony? Why don't we go for a walk? Neither of us wants dessert anyway."

"But this is supposedly in my honor. I'm a guest—"

"They'll do anything as an excuse for a party. Once you're here it doesn't matter whether you stay or go. Come on, Emily. St. Louis society will do just as well without us; this way we won't distract them." Clemens tugged gently at her hand.

Not at all inexperienced at that time of her life, Emily knew that Clemens was attempting to seduce her, but she was pleased by that, not frightened; she wanted him, she decided, almost as badly as he wanted her. Perhaps more. She was in her early fifties, and Clemens was a celebrity. It was an honor to know that the author of *Tom Sawyer* desired her sexually. So they wandered out into the night, the party behind them, and he showed her the river, then, later, rose above her in the warmth and dark of the hotel room upon which she had wisely insisted, penetrating her deeply. She was stunned by his need. Thunder in the room again. He fell atop her, done in. "That was good," he said.

"I needed that. Didn't you?" He kissed her once absently, slumbered, twitched his way into dreams.

Beside him, she lay alert, her eyes on the ceiling. I will never forget him, she thought. I will never forget this evening. That was partly true. Everything that Emily Dickinson thought was at least partly true. She did not forget any of it, although it lost its ability, in time, to touch her emotionally. There was no question of commitment. She could not commit herself to any one man (or even several men, serially) because the essential commitment of the poet is to her muse.

Still, and she could not deny it, Clemens did reach her for a time. "You should not worry about Whitman," he had told her, holding hands under the table, staring so intensely. "This man understands nothing, he knows nothing, you have moved far beyond him." No matter how quick and savage the latter sex had been, she would not believe that he had said all of those things merely to get her into bed. There was much depth to this man. He was sincere; there was no element of hypocrisy in his behavior. Anyone, listening to him as she had, would have known it.

So he remained with her, inside her, part of Emily Dickinson, for the rest of her life.

The year is 1862. Emily Dickinson, in the room that would be her home all her life, the room from which her poetry and dreams emanated, lay under Judge Otis Lord, staring at the plaster as slowly, confidently, he plunged through her and divested Emily of her virginity. It might have been her mortality which he was taking, so portentous were his gestures, but she felt carefully removed. "Oh my God," Lord said. "My God." He seemed to be praying. She listened to the gasps. As if from a great distance she observed his face during climax. How childish they became; how helpless. But then her own shocking culmination was upon her and she was silenced.

She thought she loved him, but she could not be sure

of that. The act was rapid, tumultuous, consequential. She would have to sort it out. Maybe, someday, she would understand all of it.

In the last year of her life, 1886, Emily Dickinson dreamed again and again of violated, martyred Presidents, not only the leader during the Civil War but of other, faceless Presidents who lay mourned in state. The dreams were savage, the recurrence unpredictable; it was far worse than it had been two decades earlier. Age and illness were fragmenting great chunks of her brain; from the oozing crevices the dreams were exploding. She saw priests with earnest features contorted by grief, riven by Eucharist; she saw men and women in black on sidings as the train bearing the coffin went by. She saw cities she had never known, gleaming metallic landscapes like half-recollected St. Louis against which the unseen Presidents were shot over and over again.

The dreams filled her with remorse, returned to her—every time by then—the panic she felt when she anticipated the assassination in Washington. If only she had responded to that warning, if only she had done something. But she had forgotten, dropped it out of consciousness until so horrifically reminded. Whitman's words had stung the more then because he seemed, somehow, to have infiltrated his way past the barrier, to have known her secret—that she had not carried warning when she might. Even if no one had listened, she could have said something, written a letter. She had credentials as a poet, and as a member of a distinguished New England family, they might have listened.

But there was nothing to be done. She confided in no one, could not; Austin never knew, nor did Sue, nor the children. Her admirers and correspondents were necessarily kept at a distance, the men with whom she bedded could never be perceived as confessors. She was always meant to be what she had become: a rich, eccentric half-forgotten poetess, once the unofficial poet laureate, who lived in isolation in Amherst with servants who were well paid to care for her and to make those last years as comfortable as possible as slowly, inevitably, she and Bright's disease mingled. Her kidneys had been failing for years, and she was resigned to the condition. No more poems were written. More and more, if she thought of her work at all, she looked upon it as childishness, affectation: that work, she now had to see, was worthless. But it was all she had been capable of at the time, and there was no way, of course, to change the situation.

"*I* did it," she said to her companions when the delirium began to set in through the last weeks, as the uremia began, ounce by ounce, to extinguish her brain. "I did it. Don't you understand? I was responsible for this, for the slayings. Whitman was right; I lost everything because I did not have the courage the courage the courage," but her voice was a mumble and they would not be likely to know who Whitman was or had been, and so her companions only plumped the pillow beneath her graying head and urged her to sleep with pats and hugs, winks and small confidences. "Hush, Miss Dickinson, you just get some rest now."

"But I *did* do it," she cried. "Everything, it was all my fault. Don't you see that?"

"No," someone said. "I don't see that. You go to sleep, you deserve a good rest now for all the wonderful things that you did, you can't worry about everything, you can't take on all the responsibilities for yourself."

The lights were extinguished.

And it was at that moment—and not an instant earlier—that Emily Dickinson comprehended how truly difficult it was for a poet to be taken seriously in America.

"I see the future," Clemens said to her in that bed in St. Louis in 1882. It was later then, he had recovered, had slid from the abscess's of sleep and sex and then touched her lightly, casually, while he filled her with his theories. "I see it, the metal poised against the sky, the grinding of the machines, the slow grinding away of purpose. What we see now is only temporary, is just a glimmering," he said, pointing at the window, at the landscape, "a twitch in the human condition. What is coming will wipe all of this utterly away."

Now, at last, all she wanted to do was sleep, roll away from it all and into a private cave of intention, but Clemens after his rest wanted to talk; he had been energized or at least impelled by connection to communicate private obsession. Perhaps it was what sex meant to him; it was an avenue toward release. "Utterly away," he said. "How little time we have."

"We have enough," she said. "Just rest, Sam. Let's sleep. There's nothing we can do to change any of this."

"I don't want to change it. You don't understand, do you? I simply want to hold on to it, prevent it from passing. What will come will be much worse than what we know now; I see us surrounded by the gleaming machinery of purpose, the knives coming in—"

"Enough. Oh Sam, I just want to sleep now."

"You're just like all the rest of them," he said bitterly. "You don't want to talk, don't want to understand; you just want it to go away. But it's not that simple, is it?"

She moved away from him. "I will *not*," she said, "be compared with anyone else. Don't tell me of the others." She struggled to rise, to find her clothing. It was a matter of principle with her; she would not tolerate comparisons.

Clemens held her with his weight. "I'm sorry," he said. "I didn't mean to do that, it was just something I said, something that came out. You must forgive me for this."

"It's not right," she said. "It isn't. You can't compare any of us to the others; how can you do this? We are ourselves."

"I'm sorry," Clemens said. His voice had a pleading cast. "I meant nothing by it. I have very bad dreams, Emily, thoughts I cannot control, fears I cannot mention, dreams that overtake me—"

"So do I. So do more of us than you think, Sam Clemens."

"But then you know. You know what it's like to live this way. You understand how it can be."

"Oh yes," she said. "I know how it is."

"But *they* don't know," he said intensely. "Those without the dreams, I mean; they don't understand, not any of it. They only go on, reacting from moment to moment, working in a kind of reflex, reflex all the way to the grave." Clemens, despite his reputation as a humorist, did have a brooding view of human nature. "This will only get worse the further we go," he said. "Out against the stars, if we get to the stars, it will be awful. We are not equipped for it."

She huddled against him. He put his arms around her once more. She sensed his necessity. Calamity, necessity, stunning conjoinment. "Oh my God," the atheist Clemens cried, "my God!" They fell heavily to the floor, humping. Cataclysm. Atop her he plunged, she rose to meet him, he fell in descent. They devoured one another.

Through their passage, America itself moved hugely. Later—much later, in fact—she thought that she might write a poem on the matter, but she could not do it, she could not find the language.

It is 1886. In her last moments, Emily Dickinson's relatives grouped in a ghostly way around her, leaning toward the bed, observing closely. The dying poet had a moment of clarity, then. It seemed to her that she had an answer at last for that demon, Whitman; he would not leave her alone, had pursued her to the lip of the grave. "Bring me pen and paper," she said urgently. "I faint, I fail, I am dying. Bring them to me immediately." The relatives twittered. Margaret, her niece, was pushed off to comply.

"I will tell him we changed nothing," Emily Dickinson said. "I will tell him that we made no difference, that we have no effect at all, bad, good, dense, patterned, trite or grace, doggerel or archetype, whatever it must be listen to me, *the world must remake itself before we can.* That is what I want to say." But before the frantic Margaret returned, Emily Dickinson had lost speech, then reason, then purpose, then breath, sight, distance, and was borne at last to a place where she lay with the faceless Presidents of her dreams, all of them perfectly reconstructed for the purpose of dialogue, and there they discussed much throughout eternity, but then again they might have talked for a much reduced period of time, but of that duration, unfortunately, very little can be known. The facts are not available to provide evidence. Nothing may be known of the machinery. Clemens intimated this.

It is 1853. Slowly the alteration came upon her, deep in the cells, then moving outward. Emily Dickinson trembled with the slow force of it. What had happened to her? In the New England night the sound of insects was hard against the heavy air. The landscape trembled. Within, she felt the slow gathering.

Emily Dickinson looked at her desk. It was littered with paper; she pushed it aside, found a fresh sheet, began to scribble. Light beat within the room, light was a bird, its spokes wings. The sounds consumed her:

> He fumbles with you Soul—
> Like Players on the Keys—
> Before they drop full music on—
> Then—stuns—you—by—degree—

She stares at the page for a long time, trembles.

> Prepares—your—brittle Spirit—
> For the Ethereal Blow—

The ethereal blow.
Lacking intimation, lacking understanding, only knowing that she must proceed, her hair a firmament, her work a crown, redheaded Emily Dickinson continued, reconstructing her life, reconstructing, as it were, all of time.

CHAPTER FIVE

The Heart Seeks Pleasure First

THE LETTER FROM WILLIAM AUSTIN DICKINSON, WITH
its remarkable enclosures, created in Freud unexpected
(but somehow inevitable) consternation. Dickinson wrote
that he was the brother of the deceased American poet
Emily Dickinson, samples of whose published verse he
was including. "What I want to know," the letter said, "is
whether or not there is pathology here, whether or not
her very condition might be said to have been pathological. Your reaction would be appreciated. Your reputation
on these highly judgemental matters is already accepted
on these shores and your opinion, then, would be highly
important to me."

It was a bizarre request. Of course, Freud had seen
many such since his researches were, against his will,
publicized, but this was disturbing since both Dickinsons
appeared to have attained prominence. The poet herself
died of Bright's disease, uremia, in 1886 when only in her
mid-fifties; trouble with kidneys, bowel, or colon seemed
to be so characteristic of a particular kind of creative type
in America. Her brother was a minister of some apparent
notoriety. The poetry itself was dreadful: delusive and
contrived, sentimental to the point of obscenity, it was
truly hard to assimilate. That Emily Dickinson professed
in verse to believe in everything was, to Freud's reck-

oning, proof that at the center she believed in nothing at all. He knew this to be true of the inspirational poets.

Nonetheless, she was widely published in all of the better journals of her time, was as close, with Whitman, to an American poet laureate as might exist in that egalitarian country. Or so Austin Dickinson said and the enclosed obituaries indicated, and this information filled Freud (as he contemplated the verse) with profound despair. How could Americans be so misguided? What did these people think they were reading? Was self-delusion that condition which would forever characterize and isolate the New World? What was there to say about work like hers?

> The Heart Seeks—Pleasure First—
> And—then It looks for Light—
> The Light that will flaming lead it
> Past the Arc—of—Night—

And yet he found himself struck by some quality there, some intensity, perhaps a monomaniacal insistence which could emerge only from a weak poet. Bad poets have their purposes and effect too. Their work can penetrate like a fist, touch emotions that good poetry cannot.

Freud did not know why this was the case; he simply could not explain it, and he would have liked to communicate that subjective confusion to William Austin Dickinson, but he did not quite know what to say or even why he found himself compelled to reply. The letter should be treated as merely another piece of crank mail. A man in his position received many such communications and ignored them all: why could he not ignore this one? That would be best; it would be the most sensible way to handle the problem. He had seen a great deal of crank mail.

Well, hadn't he? Any alienist known for dealing in an area as explosive as intellectual malfunction should have been accustomed to letters like that, particularly if he had jealous and antagonistic colleagues like Adler and Jung, traitors who once worked at his side and later would do anything to embarrass him. There was too much pain and treachery in the world, not to say dysfunction; not only those who actually suffered but relatives and friends would attempt to justify their own positions. The surprise, really, should be that there was not more crank mail, that he was not pursued on the streets by the relatives or friends of sad, decompensatory Viennese pleading for just a chance, just a touch, just a random bit of advice which might somehow set the afflicted free, redeem them, provide the illusion of another chance.

Already he felt targeted on his long walks, and embarrassed in public. Strangers seemed to be pointing at him, conferring on his identity, engaging in hasty speculation behind his back as he strode by. If the researchers were to continue in their current direction, he thought, would a time come when there might be absolutely no peace at all, when he would have been wholly overtaken by obsessives. What would he do then? He would no longer be a scientist; he would be a public figure. Any public figure in his field had to become a charlatan.

At the time when Austin Dickinson wrote, Freud was undergoing a professional and personal crisis in Vienna. His careful studies had brought him, he saw, to the periphery of awful conclusions about the true nature of human conduct and its motives, but he did not yet have enough evidence to conclusively publish, and he was terrified at the notoriety that publication might bring upon him. There would be no peace whatsoever when those researches came out. His personal life had already become more barren then he would have liked to admit, and his colleagues struck him largely as fools. Furthermore, he was surrounded by dry testimony from professional societies whose conclusions were no longer acceptable to him. What was going to happen? How would he deal with all of it? At the end, he might be cut off from all faith and conclusion and have only one piece of knowledge in exchange:

that there is no soul. That was the discovery he feared most, that the soul would prove to be merely an extension of the ego and therefore of no transcendent quality at all. What would the world of his forebears make of him, what would he make of himself, when he stripped the soul and therefore God from the universe? It was a question which disturbed him unduly; Freud was no atheist.

And Dickinson's communication and enclosures were disturbing because of their very irrelevance. That might be the key. What would the man have him do? What was being sought? There simply did not seem to be anything to say; he could hardly tell Dickinson that the principal interest Emily Dickinson held for him was not her pathology but her ineptitude. This poet was awful beyond any question of neurosis. Indeed, a certain kind of mental health had to be present to create verse like that. A true neurotic would not have had the patience to be so self-deluding.

If anything, then, he might have discovered rebuke to his own researches in Emily Dickinson; he seemed to have found a human being, a poet no less, without an unconscious. The issue was interesting, but he did not have the time or will to apprehend; as always, his concerns lay restlessly elsewhere. Perhaps it was the brother who merited study. He took poems seriously.

Dear Austin Dickinson: Let me tell you this: there is something about America. There is a quality to your wild, beautiful and tormented country which makes debased art possible in a way that my own wearier, more precise civilization cannot. You are free of the past and thus able to create your own possibilities. We are sunk within history, move confluent with the past, and the difference can be seen. I believe that your Walt Whitman is trying to say something very much like this.

Although not a literary critic, I have thought deeply of these issues. They are important and relate to the larger political context. Bad art, as much as good art, requires energy. In fact it requires more energy since the "artist" must shut off his own perceptions of the ugliness of his work. This is difficult since even the least sensitive creator has some sense of the material. The energy comes from your insularity, then, the sheer profound disorder of your country as I have come to regard America. In that case, assuming these conclusions are correct, I must tell you that Emily Dickinson strikes me as compelling proof of this theory, in fact a splendid exemplification—

But to come to the point. This is some of the most appalling verse (how can it be dignified by the term "poetry"?) that I have ever read. It is typical of your culture, it reeks of sentiment while at the same time denying those very qualities of torment, passion or sacrifice which are the essence of that very "love" of which it speaks. It angers me, does this poetry, there is something dead about it, dead at the core, and because I find it hard to tolerate the ambivalent I must tell the truth which is simply

Dear Reverend Dickinson: Over these months I have given much thought, personal and professional consideration alike, to these writings of your late sister. I thank you, however belatedly, for having turned them over for comment and apologize for the failure to acknowledge more promptly.

But what would you have me say? What judgment is there to render? What, in God's name, do you seek? I am no critic but a doctor, a foreigner to you, one who has struggled to assumption of your language painfully and with difficulty. Your devotion to this poetry (you think of it as a "cause") and your efforts to keep the material alive even in the face of those killing, necessary questions you raise must be praised. You are truly devoted and I can respond *to this, having had so little devotion in my own life, being exposed to the treacheries and calumnies of certain once trusted former colleagues who have proved to be extraordinarily treacherous. You cannot imagine what I have lived through in these times.*

Nonetheless, I am faced with a mystery. Do I judge the writer or the work? Which is to prevail? Your question is obviously clinical and yet, not having known your sister in any way, I would be most presumptuous to attempt any kind of summary or diagnosis. Still, let me say—

—Well, say what? I have considered the matter at length (doesn't that sound suitably defensive? to say "at length" is to give an indication of vast attention but can mean nothing at all) and from many perspectives, sometimes thinking of these poems in one way, sometimes in another, coming to this poetry with a variety of moods and possibilities, and I have been able tentatively to conclude after so many bemused readings that most alienists of my acquaintance, perhaps even initially myself, would be tempted to classify Emily Dickinson as falling into a peculiar middle ground of symptomatology, a condition of some morbidity which might be put under a classifica

Dear Reverend Dickinson: I have looked over these poems and I do not know what to do. I do not know what you want of me, what anyone *wants from me. The intrusion, the assault upon my time and privacy, increases; less and less do I feel like the old Sigmund Freud. Progressively now I feel betrayed. Perhaps you can empathize with this feeling of betrayal, have known something similiar in your life when trusted colleagues and friends turn upon you, turn out to be utterly lacking in those qualities which had been ascribed to them and to the contrary appear to be of the greatest untrustworthiness; perhaps you know*

*Reverend Dickinson: One has a sense of helpless-
ness, it can overtake even the most skilled and
professional alienist in this difficult field; the best
way to explain this helplessness is*

Reverend Dickinson: I do not know what to do

Shortly after these difficult and abortive attempts to
render a judgment which by its very nature had to be
incomprehensible to all outside the frontiers of his new
science, Freud was accosted by Gustav Mahler, a conductor and composer of some note who came to his quarters, seeking assistance. Freud's reputation had spread
through all of Vienna; Mahler and he had mutual acquaintances, and the composer risked a direct contact, as auda-
cious as that might have been. Now, standing at the door,
his head bowed in a penitential way, Mahler claimed quietly to have gone beyond the gossip to have studied Freud's
publications most carefully, to have spoken of them with
mutual acquaintances. "Oh, they are remarkable," Mahler
said expansively. "They are absolutely remarkable! They
propose a new theory of behavior just as my music itself
has attempted a new kind of statement. I think of us now
as spirits united in the forefront of our time."

"Not exactly," Freud said. He was frightened by the
composer's demeanor. Mahler appeared hysterical.

"May I come in?"

Freud stared at him, weighing the invitation. Little
clots seemed to pulse under Mahler's cheekbones. At the
time of Mahler's visit—and a certain perspective must be
given these memoirs—there were unpleasant and unexpected intrusions into the alienist's life; he had tried at all
times to work within a serious, scientific context, yet
inaccurate reports of his studies reached outside the
profession, reports which attributed some kind of magical
austerity or property to Freud's researches. Mahler's reputation was creditable and Freud did not think he had

much to fear from the conductor, who he recognized, but there had been embarrassing instances of strangers at his doorstep in the past year, some with strange confidences or requests. There had been some ugly scenes, and he little wished to tolerate this.

But he could not so easily turn away Mahler. There was the matter of professional courtesy for one thing, and for another there was the damage that a complaining Mahler could cause. Freud needed all of the goodwill he could find. He had enough enemies in and around the community. Jealous colleagues were out to undo him. "Very well. Come in, but only for a little while, please; it *is* best to make an appointment for an interview because I am trapped in a network of obligation. There is so much to be done, and thus I find myself very busy. It is not so easy to impinge upon an afternoon like this. The public tends to think that it has a call upon our services, but this is not quite so; we can best serve by protecting our privacy, keeping our integrity—"

"Oh, I understand that, Doctor," Mahler said, stepping quickly through the door. His slender frame trembled with energy, but there was an element of ill health to his aspects, those peculiar facial clots, a series of irregular tremors in the limbs which might be of nervous or organic origin. "I do understand and I assure you that if the circumstances were not such, I would have called for an appointment, would have sought your counsel in more regular fashion." He pushed the door closed, lumbered determinedly toward the center of the room, turned, faced Freud with hands on hips. "I am in such terrible pain, you cannot conceive—"

Mahler looked longingly at the couch. Freud shrugged. Mahler sighed and subsided upon it convulsively. "Oh yes," he said almost luxuriantly. "Oh yes, that feels so much better. I could collapse with the pain of this—"

These romantics. What Shelley and Byron committed could not be undone. Freud thought sometimes that this was part of the neuroses he saw. The imposition of artistic

sensibility without capacity, posture without talent, it was
one of the follies of his time, legions of burghers swooning
and fainting and trembling upon their couch of passion,
arising from this blight not to write poems or commit
battle but only to plead with their wives and mistresses
for fellatio. The vision was appalling even though Mahler
was a famous composer and conductor—Mahler acted
like a fraud, even if he was not.

"I can understand pain," Freud said. "Do not tell me
what I cannot conceive." He stood by the couch, looked
upon the stricken Mahler. "It is easy to be presumptuous,
but there is consequence—"

"Pardon me, Doctor," Mahler said, less emotionally
than before. He removed his glasses, wiped them on a
corner of his frock coat. "I did not mean to give offense
of any sort."

"I am not taking offense."

"You stare at me with anger, there is anger in your
eyes. I know that you are furious for having your time
usurped. I would feel the same way. But you will hear
me out, you will understand my condition and see how
seriously things go with me. I assume that you are familiar
at least with some of my symphonies, with the *Songs of
a Wayfarer*, *Song of the Earth*—"

"*Das Lied von der Erde*, I know that well." He had
heard it once at a concert he could not avoid. The symphonies he knew only by hearsay. They were supposed
to be heavy and insistent, bloated, wallowing creations
with the thick and unpleasant harmonies of Wagner but
much overextended and without scenery. All were far
from the trim incision of Bach; beside the pretentious
Mahler, Freud found even the unpalatable Brahms a relief.
"And I have heard some of the symphonies," he said
cautiously, "and find them most interesting."

"You do not have to flatter me. It is not necessary; I
know that there are many who do not like my work, and
we are in different fields anyway."

"I do not flatter," Freud said, which was partly true.

"I am not much of a concertgoer, but I have heard some of your work and know that it is admired. Also your conducting."

"Many dislike the concert hall. That is why I have always tried to program lighter works, the more accessible classics. Not only the difficult is good."

"Surely you are not here to discuss music or the conductor's responsibilities. I do not know much of it and can hardly advise you."

"No," Mahler said, trembling on the couch. "No, of course, that is quite true. I merely asked this in order to determine whether you did know of my work." He sighed, twisted his head, leaned back into the dull fabric as if he were trying to impress himself upon it. "I will be absolutely frank," he said after a pause. "Nothing will come of this otherwise; it will be absolutely futile and I could not bear thus to take up your time."

Mahler leaned toward a seated position, confronted Freud with an expression so fixed yet so curiously open and childlike that, against himself, Freud was fascinated. Dedicated to professional detachment, committed to the sanctity of the confessional in what he thought of as his mission, he was nonetheless easily reached by some of his patients, found himself struck by their disingenuousness and internal squalor. This might explain his attachment to the Dickinson situation. Mahler waved a finger absently in the air, made tight little circles of compulsion. One, two, three of them. "I am suffering from a terrible depression, Doctor, a sapping of the heart which is so profound, *profound*—"

He broke off, cleared his throat, looked down at the floor. "May I explain this if I can?"

"You must. You can obtain little without explanation."

"Very well. Oh that is so true, Doctor; you have touched my heart. I thought that it would be simple to make glorious music, music dedicated to the service and glory of God, that all I would have to do, once having opened

myself to His spirit and the spirit of that which was created, was to sing—"

"Opened to the spirit?"

"Opened to *His* spirit, yes, knowing then that He would
utterly sing to me, grant that as if I were only there to be
the receptacle of His grace. But something happened; it
went wrong. It was not as I thought at all. I found myself
less able to give voice to that meaning because I was no
longer able to hear His voice; something blocked it, but
by then I could not admit the truth to the others, those
who listened for my music and depended upon me, so I
misrepresented, I lied, I did not say that He had departed.
Instead, I allowed them to believe He was still speaking.
Oh my, Doctor, the pain, you cannot know the *pain* of
this—"

The composer stopped. His face expanded in distress
and he began to cry. Freud regarded him steadfastly, not
responding, allowing the patient to ventilate. This was
one of the keys to his technique. He had to withdraw,
allow the neurosis to articulate and enact itself, be detached
so that the miracle of transference, the beginnings of
catharsis, might occur. Or so he believed, even though
he would reach out to touch Mahler, if only to cut off
those tears. It was distressing; Freud had thought he would
become accustomed to this, but he had not. It was embarrassing and difficult.

He waited, carefully neutral, detached, uncommitted.
Little bolts of light played at the corners of his peripheral
vision. After a time, Mahler recovered and began to floun-
der into gesture, pathetic simile, simplistic comparison,
as he explained himself. Freud sighed internally, did not
respond. The story was already familiar to him by virtue
of his researches; he could not, however, indicate that
familiarity or betray boredom. It would block release.
This might be familiar to him, but to each patient, like
sex, it was eternally fresh: orgasm, death, distress, all of
these emotions were uniquely fused to the persona and
were undertaken as if for the very first time.

So he merely listened to Mahler, witnessing the story which underlay the mania and fixated religiosity. There it all was: sexual panic, impressions of futility and loss, subjective hopelessness coexisting as they must with grandiosity and a religious sense of mission to allay the guilt. It was the guilt which made the symphonies ever longer, bloated monstrosities because "they will survive me, transcend all of us, they are what matters." *Is that so?* In a way, although not as Mahler meant it; he thought of himself as the vessel, but of course he was the perpetrator. For the symphonies were clearly narcissistic, Freud perceived, and this confluence of the grandiose and the desperate, the stupendous and insane, was a consequence of the composer's fixity at an oral infantilism.

It was classic, this symptomatology; it exhibited the truth of his theories in a pristine, almost beautiful way. But of course none of this could be shared with the damaged and anguished symphonist; those insights derived their power from the code of secrecy. Offered outright, they would shrivel in the daylight of consciousness, assume horrid shapes, become repugnant to the disturbed Mahler, who would be unable to accommodate. As now, as ever, the patient could be led toward insight only hesitantly. The magic, the dazzling acuity and compression of unconscious motive, are not to be shared.

"I will tell you this," Freud said when at length Mahler had purged himself, had left nothing unsaid, lay on the couch, breathing out his pain: "There are ways to deal with this sadness, ways to accommodate and to make yourself whole once more."

"I want to believe that, Doctor. Truly, I want to believe this. But it seems so hard, so hopeless—"

"All things are possible." Freud felt pity for the man; as clownish as he might be, the pain was real. "Come, let's go for a walk, let's get some fresh air. There is a pretty lake down the road; we can enjoy ourselves looking at the swans."

He could not explain his offer; such generosity was

unaccustomed as was the rupture in his schedule. Perhaps Mahler had reached him, too, in ways which could only be intimated. "Let us take some air."

Stricken, Mahler nodded. "That would be good if it is no imposition upon you."

"Everything is an imposition. Nothing is an imposition. Everything matters. Nothing matters. Let us take a walk."

Mahler acceded, stood, took several deep breaths to avert an obvious panic reaction, then moved with Freud toward the door but having reached it hesitated; a sudden, wavering panic seemed to overtake the man. "Perhaps we should stay in your offices." Looking at his features, Freud could see the blight, the entrapment. None of this, after all, could be easy for Mahler. Locked within himself for all of that time, he was not yet sure that there was release. At the door he trembled, wavering on the still.

"Perhaps another day will be best, Doctor?"

"*Nein*," Freud said positively. He put a hand firmly on Mahler's back, propelled him toward the open air. In the doorway, some aspect of the composer's ambivalence caught him, mirrored his own condition. This is not easy, Freud thought. He had moved in parallel distress within his own obsessions throughout. He could have spilled this to Mahler; it would have been temptingly easy, but he dared not. It would gut the pattern he was trying to establish. "We will get some air."

"Whatever you say, Doctor," Mahler replied weakly, staggering into the street. "I came to seek help; I am at your mercy—"

Mercy. Is that the word for it? Freud waved the composer toward silence, propelling him toward the street. Oh, this meekness, the submissiveness, the hint of fanaticism, all mask deep hostility, Freud mused reflexively. But he should not be concerned with this at the present time, nor should he use it to further advantage. Often enough a cigar was merely a cigar. It was sometimes best to take matters precisely as they seemed. Complex outcomes had simple beginnings. Infantile needs might prevail, but they did so only subtly. Behavior was a lush and tangled foliage.

"After you," Freud said to Mahler at the gate, and "After *you*," the composer said, and there was an awkward moment, a *danse profane* of arms and legs, hands and feet, which seemed on the verge of disastrous and embarrassing conjoinment before, at last, they slipped safely into the weather. Freud, with an explosive sense of relief, closed the door, feeling little giggles push to the surface of reflection. Mahler was having the same reaction; he backed giddily against a fence and began to laugh, his teeth exposed, rotten and gleaming in the sun. Freud leaned against the door, waiting for Mahler's fit to ease. The near contact of flesh with another adult male (as in the past) shocked and faintly disgusted him; it indicated a component of the personality with which he must deal. But that would be later, at some self-analytic point far from there; he should not, did not, have to worry about it then. A cigar was merely a cigar.

"I'm sorry, Doctor," Mahler said, subsiding. "Everything is fine with me now. Shall we walk?"

A cigar is a cigar. Tremors of his own design swept from some nether region as from far below, and Freud found himself momentarily discommoded. He wanted to toss objects into the air and sing and dance. He wanted to shout with conviction into the heavy Viennese atmosphere. He wanted to tell them all that his discoveries had at last proved out.

But he did not do that. Instead, he began to walk. His stride carried him firmly, and Mahler joined him at a determined waddle, needing to extend himself to stay abreast. Submerged in crowds and commerce, Freud began to move rapidly.

"Doctor, I want to say—"

"Later. Let us get to the park now, let us walk."

"But if I could only explain now—"

"There will be time later to explain. Enjoy the crowd. Enjoy the air, the walk, this circumstance."

Mahler submitted, shrugged, accepted, as it were, this proper medical judgment. Breathing through his mouth with determination, he stayed close. Freud took in all of the surroundings with curiosity and interest, wondering how much of it would survive, if it would be known in the next century. Already it looked like a Munch painting to him, a kind of anarchy better controlled in retrospect. His countrymen appeared vaguely misshapen, extended in one detail or the other: their faces were enlarged, their limbs swollen at one extremity or the other. Their eyes were enormous, staring.

One simply does not know, he thought. That is the point. One can predict nothing whatsoever; it simply occurs. In space and time a cigar will fill its own perfect design. Sometimes there is less to this than meets the eye (sometimes more), and that is the only knowledge to which to cling. Mahler momentarily came ahead of him. Freud let him do so, watched the musician's hindquarters, thinking, We are anachronisms, we are impositions, impossibilities. We are already dead and preserved as artifacts in memory. Here is the point so many of us would otherwise miss: now is temporary investiture.

No. This is an aspect of depression, this thinking.

He allowed Vienna to propel him forward on the crest of all possibility.

At length they arrived at the lake which Freud had mentioned, Mahler still slightly in the lead, Freud following, and they began to traverse the winding path laid around its sticky, green secrets. Children crouched by the murky water, investigating as if for origins; their nurses and mothers sat at some remove and did not complain. Mahler stood hesitantly over the brackish waters, hands in his pockets, looking curiously removed and out of focus now in suit and tie. "Is it all right to talk now?"

"Yes. You may do that."

"You wanted me to wait. I know this. But may I talk now?"

"Yes, it is all right. I wanted to wait until we got here, allow you to walk off some of your tension, that is all. But now you may talk."

"It is difficult," the composer said, "so difficult. All the way here I was thinking of what I wanted to say, what I wished to impart, and it is very painful. There are things I have done, thoughts I have had, which are difficult to share. *These* are the reasons, I think, that God has turned His face from me, and I have said to myself all the way here, yes, I must tell the doctor, I must tell him the truth, but it is so difficult to find a way to let you into those corridors of the heart, my heart is so riven, Doctor—"

It was as he had expected. It could have been no other way, he knew. He had seen it all before; everything was predictable, and nothing ever changed. Oddly, this gave him comfort, to know that there was a certain precision, a certain predictablity, to the heart as well as other qualities. "You will find it easier if you talk," Freud said. "There is nothing about which you should be concerned, judgments are not being made here; you have nothing to defend. Just talk if you will."

"Oh, Doctor, oh Doctor," and then, overtaken by need, or perhaps it was merely the ambience of the lake (which might invoke an aspect of the womb, those greenish, brackish depths the waters of the placenta), Mahler began to impart certain rather shocking intimacies, aspects of behavior which the musician took to be unique and frightening but which of course had little such effect upon Freud, who could have anatomized all of this, who knew the dimensions. The confessions saddened but did not surprise. Nothing surprised anymore. Mahler talked of his marriage, the state of the marital relation, his fantasies, the images which flooded his mind at moments of conjoinment and orgasm. "Frighteningly, I seem to have similar images when I am in the act of composing. Have you ever heard of such a thing?"

"Oh yes, I have heard of such things."

"You are not saying this to comfort me?"

"No, I am not." How could Freud explain to Mahler that he had, in his brief time, *already* heard everything? Confessions had crossed his desk that would have undone a spoiled priest. His notebooks would have exploded the faith of a spiritualist. "I am telling you the truth."

"Then let me tell you of this image," Mahler said, emboldened. "It is always the same. It is that of a distorted angel, Doctor, an angel with limbs of fire, limbs consumed by fire and the face of a beast, that beast seeming to descend as if from the heavens with fire shooting from the lower appendages. I can grasp it for just a moment and then—"

And then, indeed. Mahler had reconstructed the Book of Daniel, but it was merely scatology in his version. It is always the same, Freud thought, the same circularity, the same unconscious puns, and yet the force of human pain is almost overwhelming. One can see the humor in this grandiosity and obsession, but this does not in any sense cover the anguish which Mahler feels. What is there to say? What can be done? Angels with the face of beasts, fire shooting from their limbs—what does Mahler think is going on here? Doesn't he understand?

Probably, he did not. One had to be trained in Freud's new and terrible science truly to understand such things. Mahler's fantasies proved some of Freud's more daring formulations. The sacred and profane mingled, one seen as rationalization of the other; there was really no shading between these two other than what the sufferer would himself impose.

Abstract, terrifying. Freud stared at the green surface of the lake; little filaments of algae fluttered beneath the surfaces like fish. His theories had proved again to be effective; it was nothing that he could share with the subject (Mahler had to struggle through to knowledge of his own or not at all), but it would have granted some enormous satisfaction if he were a different, a more prideful man. If he had not felt the force of the revelations so keenly, if only he could have taken a pedant's pleasure in his pursuit.

"Go on," Freud said automatically, "just go on." The lake was fascinating; how could something so luminescent be so putrid?"

"It is embarrassing, Doctor. I do not know if I should proceed, if this is truly necessary—"

"Do you feel it is?"

"Well, yes—"

"Everything is necessary, so then you must go on."

"I am taking too much of your time."

That hasn't concerned you to this point, Freud wanted to say. He dared not. "You are not taking my time unreasonably. Just go on, tell me what you will. It's too late to stop now."

This was not proper technique. The analysand should be encouraged to articulate only when he desires, there should be no forcing in the process, but Freud was eager to learn what would emerge next, and this was no conventional analysis. Mahler nodded, sighed, began to talk of subsidiary creatures in the images, creatures of fire and flesh in the form of religious symbols, which likewise descended after the visitation of the larger creature. Apparently—Mahler was almost ready to admit this—he needed the images to urge himself toward orgasm on those diminishing occasions when, driven by fury and remorse, he attempted to make love to his wife. The sexual act, the carnal possibility, was, to Mahler, infinitely degrading; he saw it only as a debasement, so deeply implanted had been the guilt. But if sex was a bottomless humiliation, what else was to be said? How could the issue be approached?

No, in this way the composer was little different from any other middle-class, repressed Viennese. The condition was epidemic, the prognosis absolute. This group would never change.

But they had to be provided the illusion of change; that

was the purpose of all these transactions. "I do not know why these creatures assault me so," Mahler said. "I only know that there is no way that I can keep them out of mind, no matter how I struggle, how I try—"

"This is nothing of which to be ashamed, you know. It is the kind of circumstance which occurs often enough."

"You want me to go on? To hear more of this?"

"I want to hear anything that you have to say."

"It is not fair to you, Doctor. I am taking up too much of your time, this is true—"

"Say what you want to say, that's all."

Mahler shrugged, continued talking. He went on and on; at last he approached specifics of copulation. Freud, unwillingly, blushed; he, a stranger, was being told matters that Mahler would not give the most intimate confessor. On nothing other than reputation he had come to Freud's doorstep to remainder the most terrible of all confidences, yet he did not (nor did Freud, really) seem to comprehend the absurdity. How could this be? What gave Freud the right to the revelations? What put him in the position of auditor, Mahler of speaker, when the positions could arbitrarily have been reversed?

It was not a question with which he could contend at all, but it was probably the heart of the issue.

Freud sighed. Children's cries drifted across the lake, whimpers of babies, tag, innocent torments. There is so much pain in the world, he thought, so much and so little annealment, nothing to be done really. And because of this harshness, the insights that he could grant the anguished Mahler were slight. There was almost nothing of use there, nothing of significance. All was peripheral to the unspeakable center. For the irony of the journey was this, he knew: chronology is geometric, knowledge only arithemetical, and the years overtake far before understanding, trudging lamely in their wake, can possibly catch up.

"Do you understand my dilemma?" Mahler said, gesturing awkwardly. "I would be at one with the gods but feel entrapped, impotent."

"Yes, I understand that."

"Do you really?"

"Yes." He really did. He understood. Grandiosity and paralysis had become fused as in the most infantile fantasy: the child Mahler lay amid the lights and the dazzle, the terrific force of a world which he could not comprehend, and waited to be fed. Fed, he believed it to be his screams that brought on result, and so the cycle was enacted over and again. He lay fused to that condition of infantile omnipotence and entrapment, and it would have taken years of hypnosis and regressive therapy to free him toward uncertain outcome. Analysis would have been even worse because analysis would force confrontation that the man simply was not ready to make. What could be done? Mahler was frozen. He was trapped.

"I feel helpless," Mahler groaned in a voice so wretched that the words might have come from the deepest abyss of self. "Absolutely hopeless, it all seems so worthless, futile, pointless; there seems no way that I can possibly deal with these forces—"

"Well, of course it would," Freud said. "You make too much of these burdens; however, you should not make such demands upon yourself."

Demands upon himself! Here was the last thing that Mahler would understand. Freud paced, kicked at stones, watched ducks skim the surface of the lake, and thought how peaceful it all would have been if somehow this were taken from him and he were allowed researches without the necessity of his confronting the results, the symptomatology, the human misery which the case load represented. Would any of it have made a difference? Probably not, he thought. It would not have touched him.

"Hopeless," he repeated. "Hopelessness is subjective as you must surely know, Gustav." The composer's name hung between them. "This is largely a creation of your own consciousness." So it would have to be, of course;

the condition of the infant as described by the adult. *Helpless baby, hopeless baby*, the usual dismissives. But this was nothing that he could discuss, the concept was entirely too sophisticated for Mahler, and he would not be able to get hold of it. This would lead to profound conflict.

Instead, Freud had an inspiration so perversely sudden that it caused him to smile. He saw a way, perhaps harmless, possibly efficacious, to deal with this and that methodology, arriving whimsically but with enough force to make him stumble, changed everything. Mahler fixed him with an expression of fleeting concern, but Freud flailed it away absently.

"Well, now," he said. "There is, of course, the matter of poetry."

"Poetry?"

"Versification, the creation of metaphor. There is this American poet who died some years ago, 1886 I think it was, by the name of Emily Dickinson. Have you heard of her? Does the name mean anything?"

Mahler stared at him. "This is not a familiar name. Have any of her poems been set to music?"

"Not that I would know. So you have never heard of her?"

"Never," Mahler said defensively, spreading his arms. "Not at all, not ever. I am sure of this. I know many Americans in the musical community and their works, of course, but of poets nothing; this is not a community which I understand. Should I have any knowledge of her? Should I seek to know her?"

"She's dead. I told you that; in 1886. How could you seek to know her?"

"Well, I don't know, I suppose—"

"Anyway, it does not matter. She wrote poems of simplicity and inspiration."

A herd of ducks, as if in emphasis, darted from behind a tree and scrambled across their path, squawking busily. Mamma bit Papa, admonished little ones, grumbling, urged them across. Freud stared at them with longing. At this level, everything was so simple. Little brown and black ducks. Creatures of nature.

"Aren't they beautiful?" Mahler said. Reaction formation.

"If you say so." The ducks jumped gracelessly into the lake, tumbled away.

"But they will not save us either. I do not think anything can save us from the common doom."

"Who is to say? No one can be sure. You must face the situation as it has been granted and not be unduly pessimistic."

"I do not understand this. I don't see what Emily Dickinson has to do with matters anyway. Why are you telling me of her?"

"I have my reasons, and you can attend to them." Freud guided Mahler along toward the lakeside. "They are interesting poems of their sort, written for the inspirational journals and magazines of their time, having a special appeal to those who feel themselves to be downtrodden."

"Are you saying this of me?"

"No," Freud said hastily, seeing the suspicion in Mahler's features, an archness that could well have become unpleasant. "I don't consider you downtrodden at all. Your condition is different, but there is much quality in this work, quality of a universal sort. These poems might indeed speak to the very conditions that you feel you so deplore, that is all."

"How can poetry help me? Music, all the forces of the divine which move within, they cannot. So how could poetry?"

"Because," Freud said with an elan of which he was proud, "it is something that does *not* emerge from you and for that reason can be said to have special value."

Before Mahler could ponder this, Freud reached in, took a packet of the poems from its hiding place in his pants. Recently he had taken to carrying the damnable things about, simply so that he could stop at some private point of the day to consider the work with disbelief, shake his head at the cast of mind capable of such work. He handed Mahler a sheet. The ducks chattered and dived, then emerged from the lake greatly refreshed, the children beating their wings at one another. "Look at that," Freud said encouragingly. "Read it now. You might find it rewarding."

The sheet flapped loosely in Mahler's grasp. "Are you sure that this will help me?" He sounded doubtful.

"It's certainly worth trying, isn't it? You trusted my judgment, sought my advice. What damage can there be in considering this?"

Mahler scratched his head, shrugged, read the poem, weaving back and forth. His mouth slowly opened to an expression of astonishment, and he looked up from the paper shyly, like a schoolboy caught in some inexplicable, unmentionable act. "Poems?" he said. "This is poetry to cure disquiet, is that what you said to me?"

"So some feel."

"But that is impossible. I have never seen anything like this. What can it cure?"

"Have your symphonies not those expressed purposes?"

"But they are profound. *This* is doggerel; it is atrocious."

"How can you make that judgment? What makes you so confident of yourself, that you can say something like this?"

Mahler raised an eyebrow, his forehead creased. "But that is different. It's not the same thing at all. How can it be?"

"What do you think?"

"But look, *look*." He extended the sheet, began to read aloud, the words coming out awkwardly, without a sense of phrase, as he tapped the extended sheet, his fingers hitting the page at every word. Freud could understand the consternation; not so long before, he had felt that way.

From force—of—all Divining—
There came a Driving Dream!
Of Justice, hope and—Brotherhood
How splendid did it Seem!

Be it in Boston harbor, southland
Or wild—Chesapeake Shore—
The Heart—Seeks—Pleasure—First
But 'tis the Dream—Come—to the Fore!

Mahler was silent. He shuffled his feet, slowly folded the paper. He seemed to be without words.

"Do you see?" Freud said.

"See what?"

"What do you think?"

"I think—" Mahler paused for a long time. "I think that it is very intense. There is much intensity, I will testify to that."

"My researches have carried me into areas exploring the curative value of poetry, you see."

"I once felt the same way about music. That it could heal, that it could make a difference of some sort. I do not feel that way anymore."

"Maybe," Freud said gently, "that is your problem then, the root of the pain here, that you have lost faith in the music, in the ability of art to heal. Couldn't that be so?"

"I don't know." Mahler's shoulders slumped. "I came seeking advice. I simply do not know!"

"Music, you see, is abstract." Freud felt perversity infusing him, but this mischief had a serious core, and in any event Mahler sought him, not the reverse; there would be no blame for any of this. He held no responsibility because the composer had sought him out, initiated the contact. Surely this was one of the most crucial aspects of analysis. It must be voluntary. This allowed the analyst much freedom.

"So that is my problem?" the composer said, "that I

have been trying to make an abstract medium take on concrete purpose? Is that the core?"

"No, I don't think that this is the problem at all. It goes much deeper than that. But it has been found that poetry has some relevance and use. For instance, in England the works of Lord Byron and Wordsworth have been found most efficacious in cases of depression."

"Depression? Is that the diagnosis?"

"That would be the inference."

"Then there is a name for this condition," Mahler said with relief. "It is not because God hates me or I am being punished but has to do with illness. I am not a well man—"

"Depression," Freud said. "It is a name for this." The invocation of Byron and Wordsworth was most convincing, he thought. He would have to keep that in mind for the future; it might even be an analytic technique of sorts. He considered the sky, various parts of the landscape. Soon enough it would be time to return; he had gone as far with this as he dared or needed to go. "Dickinson has proven helpful with some conditions as well."

"This poet that I have been reading. You say that this has been found helpful for cases such as mine."

"Absolutely." Freud nodded vigorously, drew a circle in the air for emphasis, then added an imaginary box and pyramidal structure to make the point more certain. "There have been successes throughout the continent. Secret successes to be sure; the results are not publicized. It has been requested that the matter be kept private for now, until we are ready to publish. But poetry has yielded some provocative results, Dickinson's among them."

Mahler's face smoothed, radiance appeared. It was as if he were composing. "If that is so, I would very much like to read some more of this person's work."

"You may."

"Perhaps even to meet her on my next trip to America."

"She is dead. *Dead*. Must I tell you this again? She died in 1886."

"Oh. That is embarrassing. Of course you told me. The work should be read on a regular basis, is that correct?"

"Exactly. That is what I would advise."

Two solemn, ponderous Viennese gentlemen standing by a lake, ducks clattering and scrambling around them, little rays of fading sunlight framing in haze: who, watching this pastoral scene from a distance could imagine the content of this conversation, judge what is going on here? Yes, mine is an impossible profession.

"You will have to familiarize yourself with this work, expose yourself to it on a regular basis. Fortunately, it is widely available in America, where she appears to be quite popular."

"It is fortunate, then, that I can read English to savor her in the original?"

"Very fortunate."

"Would you give me a preferred list of her poems?"

"If you would like that. I have many with me. Perhaps I could give them to you and you could arrange for a copyist—"

For the first time on this difficult afternoon, the composer smiled. It was beatific; he looked like a waif. Freud could see how he could be considered attractive, how he might well be able to make his way through this society despite his dark moods, bleak interior. Even the depression could be part of his charm, a vulnerability inviting assistance. He was not as simple as he appeared.

Freud searched through his pockets, removed other samples, extended them. Mahler grasped the sheets, opened one of them, and stared at the words as if they held the key (perhaps they did) to all the secrets of his life. They began to pace again, finishing out the circle of the lake. Mahler scanned the poetry, mumbled quietly. On their second circuit, by some unspoken understanding, they walked toward Freud's domicile. Clearly the analysis had been concluded.

To signal this, Freud thought of putting an arm around Mahler, being almost companionable as he drew the man to him, but he did not dare such a gesture. Surely it would have been misinterpreted, and he did not want to breach professionalism in that fashion. Mahler hummed brokenly under his breath, patting his pockets absently where the poetry resided. Freud could make out little atonal fragments which were doubtless part of a contemplated symphony. He did not like it very much. He wondered how, if at all, he would write this up for the journals. What would he say? How would he render this comprehensible for his colleagues?

The answer was obvious—he would not write anything. This interview with the composer would have to become part of the apocrypha, the detritus of the profession, along with so much else that he dared not commit to the record. Decades would pass and the sense of this interview would be obliterated, and yet somehow it would exist at the borders of the profession, the edge of credibility: they would argue as to whether Freud and Mahler really walked around this length, whether Dickinson's terrible poems were part of this transaction. It amused him greatly, the possibility of squabbles by his colleagues. Of course he would not be there to witness any of it.

He felt, for the first time in hours, the stabbing, familiar pain in the jaw. He had been free of it just long enough to be deluded into thinking that it might be gone, but no, that was not to happen. It would always be with him. He was a very sick man and he would die, was dying, of cancer of the jaw. He was convinced of this. It was not hypochondria. His medical training gave him unswerving insight. But he would not plead for pity.

"You will keep all of this private, won't you?" Mahler said.

"Of course."

"It would be most embarrassing, most personally threatening to my career, if it was to emerge somehow that you have been consulted. I promise to read these poems diligently and to pay any fee which you consider reasonable."

"That is not necessary. You need not pay a fee. All of this will be kept in confidence."

"I *will* read the poems."

"That's perfectly all right," Freud said comfortingly. "Do what you wish." His jaw hurt. He wanted to go back and put cold towels on it, try to draw the pain through distraction. It was terrifying, this intimation of cancer, and there was nothing to be done about it. "None of this matters," he said to Mahler, "none of it." And that was true, was most remarkable; it did not matter at all. Thinking that it did, thinking that there was a difference to be made, *that* was the illusion. Words in the air, limited transaction.

He would say nothing, would leave even the most secret of his journals blank. This said more of him, he suspected, then it did of the insistent and tormented Mahler. It said more of him even than the science he had created—but he would have to deal with that. Here he was, here was Sigmund Freud, concealing information which might be of the most vital use to posterity, and he did not care; his purposes were more benignly serviced in that way. Oh, he should have known that. He should have known that it would be this way.

"I do feel better," Mahler said. "It's the strangest thing, but things do not seem as bad. I appreciate what you have done, Doctor, more than I can possibly say. I feel at this moment that I am possessed of myself."

Possessed of himself. Oh yes. Freud let the patient babble on. There really was nothing else to be done, no way to end this, and it did not matter. That was the insistent point with which he had to live: that it did not matter. It had no reality.

"Thank you," Mahler said, "thank you, Doctor."

It had no reality at all, this darkness, this dream. It was cobbled on the margins of possibility. The man beside him, the day around him, the torment swaddling them, made no sense at all—but then, Freud thought, this aphasic principle was to be expected the entire pursuit; his ambitions were wrong. Demented.

Futile.

The Honorable William Austin Dickinson: I take pen in hand at last, somewhat apologetic about this long delay but with some news which, perhaps, will lighten the load of uncertainty which has been placed upon you. I have obtained interesting results by sharing your sister's poetry with M—, a composer and symphony conductor who consulted me in recent clinical context.

I trust that you do not object to my having used the samples for that purpose. When you learn of the salutary results obtained I am sure that you will understand. Given samples of Dickinson's poetry (conventional methods of therapy seeming inadvisable and overextended) the patient began almost at once to exhibit a more positive and cheerful attitude. From the first moments, M— exuded an optimism and positiveness of spirit which he seemingly had lost and began to come to terms with crippling depression. His changes in demeanor and attitude were marked and you would have been pleased, deeply moved in fact, to see the effect that this had. M—, whose grandiosity and delusions of persecution were savage, appeared charmed and comforted by the verse which spoke profoundly to his own delusions.

Now, I realize that you did not send your sister's poetry to be used in therapuetic context; other purposes were involved. You wished me to deduce whether a pathology was indicated. I did indeed consider the work in that context but, of course, it is difficult, unethical, to diagnosis an unseen patient and therefore I refrain from that harder judgement. But I can assure that Emily Dickinson was able to reach a patient as distressed as M—. Clearly, here

*was an outcome toward which your sister devoted
her working life.*

*So I must stand silent on your provocative ques-
tions. A clinical relationship would have been necessary; it would now be a perversion of a process
which I have evolved only through the most labo-
rious mea*

Freud decided that it would not be a good idea to send
the letter. It would only offend. Dickinson would not have
understood, and he would have read the letter as mockery.
Perhaps it *was* mockery. This had to be considered. His
jaw hurt often now. He knew he should seek a diagnosis,
but he had a deep and abiding distrust of doctors.

Mahler sent him a brief note of thanks and enclosed a
substantial check. Freud brooded about this, destroyed
the check, put the card away unanswered. Mahler
attempted to reach him at his quarters, but Freud left
instructions everywhere that he was never to be in for
the composer; he even hired a male secretary to protect
his privacy. Mahler seemed to get the idea and ceased the
attempts at contact. Freud consigned the remainder of the
Dickinson poems to the fire. He could not bear further
contact with them.

*Dear Reverend Dickinson: What you ask is impos-
sible. I am in an impossible condition myself, clearly
a dying man, certainly a misunderstood man; I will
be able to do nothing with your communications at
all. They are a violation of my privacy. How can I
make this clear? I want nothing to do*

Freud sent no letters, made no statements. He did
nothing whatsoever. It would have been improper. In the
night, now and then he heard Mahler's voice whispering
that his work was futile, infinitesimal, that it would come
to nothing. Fleeing in sleep the terrible accusation of that

voice which had a power he had never known in life, he plunged deeper, streamed through constellations, the burning fragments of stars. In the dawn over and again he thought of a paper which would make use of this, would make some kind of final statement, but he did not get around to it. He could have; he had, after all, a conscience, but McCormick, hugely, came first.

And last.

CHAPTER SEVEN

Sigmund Fraud

IN THE BRUTAL VENUSIAN ATMOSPHERE, PEERING through the vile gases behind shield of helmet and wire, a thousand yards of the most sophisticated insulating equipment which the twenty-second century had been able to devise, Freud began to sense the dimensions of the trap into which he had been led. Now men had been swaddled in consequence, consequence had become the huge ship that had taken them to the near planets, but even less than in his own time are origin or motive understood. This was pernicious. It could lead only to the deadliest of circumstance.

"It is wrong," he said aloud. "This is all wrong, I tell you." But there was no response. He had turned down the transmission device, shut off their silly, clamoring voices, needing to be free of them. He would have no dialogue with the dome until he chose.

Now, he only wished to make a point of them, somehow retaliate for his passivity back there, assert his own legitimacy and control. "Deadly, do you understand this?" He supposed that they did, that they knew it only too well, but it gave Freud some satisfaction to be rhetorical. This declamatory aspect was an important part of his personality, just as was the need to establish control. He had always wanted control in any circumstance. That explained his profession.

"Don't worry," they had said. "Don't think too much about how you're here or what caused this or what the reconstruction process means." And then he had been sheathed by steel and wire, pushed from the ship to the surface. "There's no time for any of that now, no need for it either. Just concentrate on the task at hand; that's what should concern you." They had been an undifferentiated mass, undifferentiated hands and voices behind the implacable sheen of their faces; he could not discriminate among them. "We know what concerns you, what you want."

Oh, it had been easy for them to say that. Debacle could be controlled by language, by their devices. But perhaps they were right after all. In any case, they had him at a severe disadvantage.

These technicians of the future, he had already come to understand, had contempt for those ironies, shadings, delicacies of implication, which had controlled his own functioning. Torn from the abyss, restored to flesh, given so little time to prepare himself for the voyage to the surface of this murderous second planet, he suspected that determination alone could not perform the conditions of his craft; intellection would not lead him through this. Not that they cared. They had, he was warned, more immediate concerns.

Still, he would do the best he could. He always had and would again; that was the shell within which he functioned. In Vienna or out of it, through all the partitions of his life, he had been a believer, a man secular in his practice but committed to faith. This reconstruction process, they explained, was a means by which historical figures judged capable of giving assistance could be brought to life. The process worked, and it had had numerous successes. He would be another of them. They had trust in his bearing. Otherwise, they would not tell him anything. No time, they said, no time for explanations until later. He did not believe it. They were clearly holding back information.

They promised that when circumstances permitted, when the crisis was over, they would give him all the information he could want; for the moment, however, he had to take on faith the existence of this remarkable process. He was a key subject; they approached his reconstruction with awe, and he would surely not disappoint them. It had been vindicatory to learn that he was still considered, centuries later, to be an important historical figure, but it had little to do with what was being asked of him now.

Also, he was not the first choice within his profession, and that had to be mortifying.

Conondrums, paradox, were Freud's specialty, not the solution of more practical problems. "We must turn human misery into ordinary unhappiness," he had warned . . . but this was a practical difficulty, not spiritual. This small colony on Venus, only fifty souls, the highly qualified and brave technicians who were elected to settle Venus, taken from a pool of thousands as the very best, this sturdy colony, this representation of the best of human hope and possibility—the colony was overwhelmed by disaster of sudden and potent force. Poisoned atmospheric gas had seeped briefly into the compound, sickening all of them, threatening lives. Supposedly invulnerable hydroponics equipment had failed, threatening the food chain, and the holographic transmission system had collapsed, cutting off not only realizations of Venus but all communication with a frantic home base. They could not locate the cause of the failure.

Strange words, strange concepts, these: "hydroponic," "holographic," "video," "home base," and it was due only to the energy of the technicians, his own diligence and application, that Freud had been able to comprehend the dilemma. What was clear, he was told, was that the mission was being sabotaged, and that the saboteur must be the engineer, Jurgensen, who escaped to the surface of

Venus and was clinging to the dome, threatening ever more terrible consequence. He had explosives. Jurgensen had lost control and was bent upon the destruction of the colony. Freud's mission was not to analyze motive so much as it was to contain the man, get him safely inside.

"Tell me," Freud had said when, senses restored, hot liquids and conversation battling the stupor, he had marginally come back to himself. "Are you sure it's Jurgensen? Maybe you're blaming him for something that isn't his fault. How about aliens? Are there such things as Venusians? Are there creatures who live on this planet? We considered the possibility, you know."

"There are no Venusians," one of the implacable faces had said to him. Surrounded by these people, he had felt like a patient on rounds, exposed to probes and terror. He could not individuate them. "Absolutely no evidence of them at all."

"Are you positive? Has it been verified in every way?"

"It doesn't have to be proved. All life within the solar system is confined to Earth."

"You seem very positive."

"This is science," the face said. "Science is something that you must be trained to respect. Jurgensen got out of these quarters somehow and is on the surface; you're going to have to bring him in because we can't. Perhaps you have a methodology which we do not understand. We are hopeful."

"Why did he go out?" Freud asked, leaning toward the speaker, feeling slow waves of illness tearing at him. He was still very weak, had been warned to lie back until the restorative processes had had a chance to function, but there was no denying his wanting to seize control.

"We don't know. We just know that he's out there on the surface and he's waiting for you."

Waiting for you. How quickly they had shifted the focus, taken it from explanation to demand. Trapped in the aseptic spaces of the reconstruction room, Freud had found himself succumbing to incredulity, but they had given him no time, no proper measure of this, had only maneuvered toward his accepting obligation.

And now it was he, clumsy in the massive gear, shaken by the dimensions of what he did not know, who was sent to talk to the escaped engineer and recover him whole for the possibility of vengeance.

And vengeance was clearly in the offing. The circumstances were serious. Home base did not know specifics, only that communication had been cut off, and if they ever found out they were likely to break the colony. Freud had come to understand the risk, the expense, the tenuous nature, of this errand: it had been accomplished at great political cost, and any conspicuous failure in the program was apt to end it. The administrators were nervous and extremely vulnerable; they dared not take the chance of a lunatic on the surface of Venus, committing sabotage. The publicity alone might set the program back decades.

Lunatic had been their phrase. Freud had protested, with all the credibility of a reconstruct. "He may not be that but only a man who cannot cope with the situation. Do not be so quick to judge."

"What's the difference?"

"The difference is profound. You cannot treat any malfunction or personality disorder as madness. It just isn't that simple, and you know the consequences. To me, Jurgensen sounds as if he is suffering from agoraphobic grief."

"So be it," the face had said. "Call it what you will. Motives are of very little interest to us here; the fact is that they're looking for any excuse to shut this colony down."

"But why?"

"Why? Because it's costing fifty million dollars a day and they're under increasing pressure to bring it to an end. They'll seize any excuse at all. We can't permit this, I tell you; we're trying everything, even reconstructs, in order to stop this. We have to make it work."

"But what if it doesn't work?" Freud had asked. "What

if you can't save the situation? If the colony is abandoned, is it so terrible? There must be plenty of problems on Earth. What is the point of a colony at all if it causes such resentment?"

"You don't understand any part of the situation. Of course there's no way that you could. You're just a reconstruct."

"How could anyone understand?" Freud had felt almost genial, considering the consternation that this question had caused. "Matters are hardly balanced here."

"Look here," the implacable face had said, radiating a frantic kind of earnestness. "We need this planet, we need it, that's all, we have too much invested to abandon now. Treasure has been expended; we can't withdraw."

"Go on."

"What?"

"That is all very interesting. Just go on."

"That's psychiatric methodology."

"Why do you think that?"

"If we lose Venus, the course of colonization itself will be set back a full century."

"Will it?" Freud had been inclined to ask then what difference a century would make. He had been dead or in the reconstruction tank for some multiples of that period, and it did not appear to have made much difference to anyone. The time had passed in fire, in emptiness: it would be similarly easy now if he were returned to the tank to find, emerging, that the colony had been abandoned for a century and then restored for another; *another* century or two gone, what was the difference? Of course, this only betrayed the difference in perspective between the living and the dead, a complicated subject which had not been answered in his own time, either.

There was that difference between contemporary perspective and the forced longer range which had been thrust upon him. He could understand that as well as the disconcerting effect Jurgensen's sabotage would have upon this colony. Also, there was obviously no point in arguing with these technicians or taking issue with them because it was within their means to return him to limbo, and for reasons which he was only beginning to understand Freud preferred this not to happen at that point.

It was interesting if nothing else; it was another chance at life, this reconstruction. What a surprise to find out that immortality, in a sense, did exist! If McCormick had stolen time as he had, then the reconstruction would give it back to him in small pieces, and he felt committed to that. Curiosity more than anything else had dragged him through his years; curiosity would take him through this new place. He had been given lots of equipment, many advantages. It could have been worse. Grave, where was thy sting? McCormick had been defeated.

"I promise nothing," he had said. "I cannot guarantee that I will be able to do anything at all."

"But you will," he had been told. "Oh, you will." There had been utter certainty on that point. It went beyond threat into utter positiveness.

So there was no doubt: there he was, all reality swaddling him. Freud stood on the surface of Venus, breathing insistently through the awkward respirators, looking for the treacherous engineer who (he had been assured) was hiding somewhere near the dome, thinking of all the complex patterns and consequences of his life, which, however irrelevant to these times, was the only life he had ever known. Here was some satisfaction and dismay: the decision to send out a psychiatrist (their term for "alienist") had come from the highest levels of command, and they had first selected not Freud but Carl Jung to deal with the situation. Carl had failed utterly, disgracefully (they were ashamed to give the details), and only then had it been decided to go with the founder. That was their word, "founder," and it had filled him with pride, however base the circumstances might have been. "Oh listen to me," he had said. "I could have told you he was a renegade and a fool, completely fraudulent. The man was half a charlatan. He attempted to convert reality to his views, but his grasp was so uncertain that he could not make it work. They will always fail, people like this will never understand."

He could have told them a great deal more about Carl; it still infuriated him, even then, what the man had done to him. Carl had been if not his first then his greatest disciple, and Freud had seen enormous promise: had he not given Carl everything? Had he not taken him utterly into his confidence? And then at the end to be turned upon, betrayed, just like everyone else in Carl's life (he saw the pattern too late), but there was a reckoning. That reckoning stretched on and on, went beyond the grave and so would have been the case here. Even on Venus, even in the amazing year of 2176, it had been given to him to atone for Carl's failure, rectify wrong done in Freud's name.

They would not tell him what Carl's mistake had been, where the misapplication had centered, but watching the evil gases boil, standing rooted on the surface of the second planet, Freud could picture it in his mind, apprehend what must have happened, and little giggles interfered with the rhythm of his breath, danced through the tubing. Oh he could see Jung all right, see him on Venus just in this posture: the man must have panicked. The malodorous swamp, the vile landscape, must have unbalanced the rigid and unbending Carl (already unbalanced from the fact of reconstruction and what it did to all of his precious ideas about spiritual immortality). This desperate terrain must have undone the man, much less being turned loose upon the surface of the planet.

No, Carl had, for all of his pretensions and seriousness, his rich fantasizing, and the lechery, only a tenuous grasp on the world and its flesh; without fragile ego to interpose against the situation he would have been unable to confront any sudden threat, and that is what must have happened. Carl must have collapsed at the sight of Venus. *Mons veneris* certainly but Venus never; Carl must have screamed and when they had dragged his treacherous disciple back to the ship and stuffed him again into the chambers, they must have known then the extent of their folly, how wrong they were not to have dealt with the founder himself. Oh yes, Freud could envision all of this. It had probably happened that way, and even though his reaction was not of the most defensible sort—he would have to work this out later; his self-analysis was an ongoing process—he could not circumvent feelings of triumph. He was entitled to them. If he succeeded with Jurgensen, he hoped that he would be given explicit details of Carl's shame. He would enjoy that. He would make a point of asking.

In the meantime, he was conscious and functioning once more and was there to deal with the engineer who was very close, he had been assured, to the dome. It was the efficacy and assurance of Freud that they were seeking, they said. *Efficacy and assurance.* He could expound upon those qualities; there had been ample opportunity in the last years of his truncated life to consider all of this. Assurance was only in part posture, but technicians could relate to it. The Viennese always enjoyed a man of action, and so did this committee of the future. His jaw hurt. That too has been carried within him all these centuries, the defect within that would bloom to metastasis. But surely by the twenty-second century they had evolved a cure for cancer. He would discuss this with them.

He was still the activist Freud, he thought, wobbling his jaw determinedly to make the pain recede, a gesture which worked as well then as it had in 1898. The old fire was still there. "Consider the pointlessness of this escapade," he could have said to them, "the pointlessness of the evasion; you technicians are trying to conquer Venus because you cannot conquer Earth or yourselves; this need for conquest emerges from inadequacy. But why do you use the word 'conquest'? Why has that sexual metaphor been the prevailing means by which humanity has always escaped the conditions of mortality?"

Oh, it would have been an interesting speech, all right. It would have astonished them. It was unfortunate, perhaps, that he did not take the opportunity to discuss the issue, but he had felt it best to repress it for a time. "The same futility, the same mystery," he had wanted to say. "You live, you die, you procreate and perish, fuck and fight and pass from their time, id reigns and superego chains and superego cries and the ego lies and it just goes on and on, nothing changes." But if he had said that—

Well, if he had, they would have reacted in disgust, scuttled him through the chute with the same disdain that had finally dismissed Carl. And that would not have been right; he would not have appreciated being treated that way because above all it was interesting being on the surface of Venus, looking at terrain that had never been seen or properly imagined when he had last walked under the stars. When he had written of Venus it had been metaphor, but look now, look at what it had become. Metaphor does not have in its power and implication half of the force of circumstance itself, Freud thought, and if I had had the wit to understand this in my own time, it might have been different.

It might have been different, but perhaps not. It was all very difficult. There were no easy answers; matters devolve toward complexity. He stood in the midst of equipment, poised as if for activity in those gases, the gray compound looming above, the broken surveying equipment mindlessly tracking him. It was not their suggestion that he be sent immediately to the surface. They had wanted him to stay in the dome and work by remote, trying a different technique, but Freud had said no, that was impossible, Carl had had the right idea anyway, just the wrong execution: you had to get into the field to accomplish anything. They had deferred as he had known they would. Sighing, he had donned the gear with much nagging and had stumbled through the various pressurized zones to seek a madman. They had resisted this until the end. "Listen, Freud," they had said. "We'll get this equipment working soon and establish a communications band; you can talk to him over the radio. Repairs can be made. There's no need for you, a reconstruct fresh from the banks, to brave this surface; we're not asking that. The physical strain could be dangerous alone, and there are other problems—"

But Freud had refused, adamantly. He was a machine now, an organic device, he had pointed out to them, and besides, it was necessary to do the field work. "If you want therapy, then let me work within a therapeutic context; anything else would be fraudulent."

"But why go out in the field as a first step? Why not use it only as a fallback device?"

Well, why not indeed? He had been given the choice. It was his decision, not theirs, to be out there. Was this a serious mistake? But the basic mistake had been scheduling McCormick for an interview without knowing anything, anything whatsoever, of the man's background.

Too late to be concerned about that. Here he was, clinging to the surface of Venus, stumbling through the mud like a reluctant explorer. He had not dared tell them the real reason he wanted to leave: he had to get away from them, to escape the unctuous, frantic pawing attentions, that hint of panic which he knew lay under the dogmatic and persistent statements.

For they had not been in control. That was clear; they had absolutely no idea what to do next. One would have thought a civilization so technologically advanced, a colony so sophisticated, would have on hand specialists who would have been enlisted for just that purpose, to identify psychological malfunction and contend with it. Wouldn't that have been reasonable? But he suspected that the twenty-second century (or so they represented it to be; well, he guessed that he would take their word for it, there were limits to suspicion) was cannibalizing the achievements of history, that this was not a culture with collective intelligence or humanistic philosophy. Certainly the role of alienist, he would have thought, should be as important in the colonization of Venus as it would have been at any point in the intimidating twentieth century. (Oh, what a horrid time it had been; they would not speak to him of those years, but the inferences were there to be made.) But there were no alienists in the colony, he had learned. Space was at too much of a premium; skills were marginal. Still, it made no practical sense. If they had taken the time and trouble to call upon Carl and then him, the function was still accepted as important.

Why would they *not* have their own?

Well, an explanation was buried there, and perhaps he would find it. At this point, however, it did not matter. The question was for later. Underneath their cool, technological jargon, behind the rhetoric which had been evolved to deal with circumstances, it was clear that the colonists were as neurotic, intimidated, frightened as any of the old case load. Their explanations was armor. At the core they had lost control, and that awareness of lapsed control was extraordinarily disturbing: it led to the darkest speculations on the nature of human destiny. Was it the technology which had done this?

Under the dome, it was impossible to deal with these questions, to work out answers in some privacy and peace. No, they would not understand or tolerate that; they would not allow him a cubicle or some space of his own where he could confer with them one by one, obtain testimony, work it through. They would not permit him to interview sequentially in a clinical context, would only see him in groups. No, they did not want to deal with the issue of their own psychic incompetence, making his only escape the surface.

So he had been compelled by his own desire to go upon the surface of the planet; there at least, seeking Jurgensen, he might find some key to the mystery. He would be able to interview the man alone, simulate an analytic situation. That was an attractive possibility.

Within his helmet he heard the sound of the whispers once more. They were faint, barely perceptible, sound as a schizoid might report hallucinative "voices," but they were intermittently seductive and fascinating, just as those voices were purported to be. One could indeed imagine himself in communication with stranger powers. *Ship*, he heard faintly, *all the ship*. Call the ship? *All the ship within without*. No, it was almost impossible to establish location, to relate to this. He had to resist the sounds for the sake of his own difficult balance. *Call the ship*. No, he would not do it. How easy it would have been to accept special powers, how truly narcotic psychosis might be. Venus was a trap, an invitation toward dementia.

Tracking not for sound but, as they had suggested, the trajectory of the dome itself, moving on the sight lines in the fog, Freud saw the engineer. It was all much easier than he had thought it would be. The figure was crouched against the dome, wedged tightly there, frozen in a posture so intent that it could have been fixity or death. There was the doomed Jurgensen, exactly where they had expected him to be. Certain matters were predictable after all; surveying was a science. The engineer had been out there for a hundred hours, Freud had been told, with only the minimum rations strapped in the gear itself. He had been alone all of that time within the capsule of the suit, mingling with his waste, shocked to that condition: surely he would be in a weakened and vulnerable condition now. The minimum rations in the equipment must have been gone by now.

Jurgensen had strapped himself into a spacesuit off-shift. There was no security in the barracks at that time; it had been easy for him then to ease through the hatch and go away, leaving the faultily designed hatch ajar, allowing dangerous leakage of oxygen from the dome, bleeding into the gases. When he had turned on the transmitters then, shouted his departure through the gear, he had meant only to accuse, but he might well have saved their lives. There was no way of knowing how long that leak might have gone undetected. So it had been a good thing that the engineer had been crazy, had sought the craziness of a final statement: everything had worked out for them.

The engineer had screamed that he could not take it anymore, had had enough of Venus and its lies, was going to destroy all of those in the colony because he was now the resurrection and the light. His voice had been so vengeful that it had been traumatic. (That was when the cries began that an alienist was necessary: they had run frantically toward the banks.) While they worked desperately to bring Carl to functioning, their mistake, others had pleaded with Jurgensen, made desperate efforts to talk him back under the dome, but the engineer had resisted all of it, furiously. Jurgensen had made it clear that if they attempted to bring him back inside, he would use explosives to wreck the dome. No one was sure if this was possible or if Jurgensen even had such explosives in hand, but they had decided that it was not worth the risk.

On the other hand, they *had* sent Jung to the surface and then had permitted Freud to go. So much for stability and consistency in the twenty-second century.

Precisely why he was being sent to attempt what they had been warned against doing themselves was not clear, but it must have had something to do with their own incapacity. They were willing enough to let reconstructed alienists deal with the madman. This was not, apparently, the most rational group that ever had been drawn together. "Be careful, come upon him quietly, make no sudden gestures, try not to instill fear, keep calm, be brave." This had been the sum of their advice. *Be brave.* They liked generalities at that time.

But that had been all right with Freud. He had no objection, was glad to get away from them. Dragged from the banks, exposed to so much information, granted the full, horrifying weight of circumstance, he had been numbed. He had elected to cooperate with them out of a despair which, for all he knew, had persisted until this moment. He was not himself but a machine; that had to be kept in mind. He was a simulacrum of the actual Freud, a crafted organic duplicate and not necessarily a perfect copy. Perhaps he was entirely different from the recollected Freud and was not acting or thinking like the famous alienist at all. Submissiveness, he had decided, would at least free him, move him from this unction and their demands; everything else could be aligned if he was only given that chance.

"Just be careful," they had warned at the end as he stood on the rim of the hatch. "Don't try anything dangerous, don't take risks, respect the difficulties, there is too much at stake." As if this bunch had to tell *him*, the founder of what was now known as the psychiatric school, the creator of the unconscious, to be careful. *Be careful?* His life's work, his orientation, the science itself, had been founded upon the necessity to take utmost care because the unconscious was always there, ready to lunge, to reach through barriers and defeat all rational purpose. How could he not be careful, knowing what lurked behind the arras?

"We have nothing else," he had been told. "We have no other ideas. We must trust you, depend upon your ability; that's why you have been reconstructed." What an appalling statement. He, Sigmund Freud, had been yanked from limbo, laved to terrified consciousness, given this fragmentary information, impelled to the surface of Venus, which he had never seen or imagined: he was the last hope of the colony? A simulacrum, an organic machine, torn from history to perform as these could not? It was preposterous. What manner of conditions had these colonists evolved? What did they think was the meaning of their lives?

Nonetheless, this was what had been presented, and there was nothing to do but accept the terms. He had no doubt at all that had he objected, they would have disconnected him as mercilessly as they had brought him to life, and he was yet reluctant to extinguish a consciousness so perilously gained.

Curious to know what it was truly like, what this new century might bring, what lasting effects if any he had

had upon the human condition, how he might bring further ignominy to the memory of Carl Jung, Freud had made what was taken to be a choice; he would function, go on, attempt their bidding, elect to survive within these difficult terms as long as he could.

Why not?

Jurgensen imagined himself to be a vine. That was part of the symptomatology. They had been very specific on this; the engineer took himself to be entwined powerfully against the dome, locked to it as a kind of vegetation. This had been the sense of latter communications, just before everything had been cut off, and it had been suggested to Freud that he might have some success by himself pretending to be a vine, insinuate himself upon the damaged Jurgensen in that way. "Hello, I'm just another Venus vine here, another part of the resurrection and the light, just come to share with you," and so on. Well, it was just a *suggestion*, they had said, abashed at his stare; he didn't have to do it if he felt otherwise. He was the expert after all; perhaps he had other approaches. It was a technique Freud could acknowledge but hardly support. Pretend in his extraterrestrial garb to be a vine? It had very little credibility, even with a lunatic.

What he had to do, he supposed, was to win Jurgensen's confidence, establish a mutuality of trust if at all possible, try to ease him back to the ship without demonstration or struggle. Perhaps Jurgensen could be led in this way to reason. Keep it all from home base, that was the essence of the assignment; conceal it from the controllers because otherwise the colony might be lost. If they could get the engineer back inside safely, he could, at the least, be given palliatives and tranquilizers, placed into sleep or numbed toward a kind of cooperation, whereas left outside to broadcast his lunacy or play with explosives, anything might happen. This was monitored occasionally; some of the rhetoric might be happened upon and the situation, already intolerable, would then be out of control.

This had obviously been the advice given Carl, they half admitted, but Carl had not been able to deal with it, had lost control and mishandled the operation badly. More than that Freud could not determine, they would not tell him, but the mishandling was obvious in their stricken expressions, in the hostile aspect which the engineer projected. No one so withdrawn could be lacking rage.

"Why don't you tell me what happened before?" he had asked. "It seems to me that you would want me to know, want to avoid a repetition of error." But they had been insistent that this could not be, that for some policy reason, all news of previous reconstructions should be denied later reconstructs. There was some kind of powerful taboo, and he was disinclined to pressure them for fear of penalty. But he could make deductions, certainly; knowing Carl as he did, he could speculate that his rival had spent too much time evaluating and then, stupidly, had attempted a long consultation. Yes, that would have been his style; such was the vanity of the man, to want attention focused on methodology. How foolish all of it would have been, but to Jung it would have been a tour de force; the first analysis conducted on Venus! Such would appeal to the child in him.

But Freud knew differently. He had maturity and wisdom. Treatment would have to be conducted under the dome. Therapy—even crisis therapy—was an attenuated, difficult process, littered by traps, false steps, endless recapitulation, tiny, poisonous misunderstandings. It could never be used as a palliative . . . but Jung, being himself, had sought dramatic cure, a sudden reversal of the situation. It was so much like him. Even on Venus, pulled from machinery, he would have sought reverence or acclaim.

Well, Carl was a fool. Freud had known that in Vienna and knew it now; it would always be that way. Nothing really changed, nor would it ever. This was the fundamental insight to be disclosed.

"Whatever you think, then," he had been told. "Do

what you will, we cannot interfere; this situation is desperate."

"Maybe," he had essayed mildly, "maybe this is so only because you *think* it to be desperate. Perhaps it is not as bad as you think, controllable in fact; if you would approach it that way."

"Oh no, that isn't so at all. It is of the greatest importance that he be brought back inside before something catastrophic happens. Against this everything dwindles; you must accept this."

Well, perhaps he should. It was their culture, their colony; he had to take their word for it. The terms and conditions had to be accepted for the moment; their urgency was palpable, and it would have been dangerous to dismiss it out of hand. Still, urgency or otherwise, insistence or not, harm should not come—how could it?— from a brief investigation. He would circle it for a while, try to make some kind of evaluation before plunging. A wisp of memory extruded. He thought, unreasonably, of Gustav Mahler, of that day at the lake, of the intensity of the conversation. There was a man who seemed unreachable, yet Freud was able to bring some change to the situation. Could he do the same here? Offer Jurgensen some of Emily Dickinson's poetry? The thought, even under the pressure of the situation, made him smile. There were limits to perversity which not even he could explain.

The heart seeks pleasure first. Whisper this to Jurgensen, whisper to him of unions and sacrifice. Oh, it would be profoundly helpful, would bear upon the entirety of the situation, would it not?

He began to see how Jung could have perpetrated such an utter disaster. It was not a terrain conducive to reason.

Freud stood some yards from the engineer, centering on the figure, listening to the tortured sound of respiration streaming through his helmet above the faint and clamoring voices in the background, tracking in that breath the dimensions of the man's anguish, the keening of the soul. The soul must still exist: reconstruction had proven

what he could never doubt; even on this subterranean,
swampy horror which they had told him was the surface
of Venus, the soul remained a commodity which had to
be worked into the eventual equation. If there were no
soul, he could not have been reconstructed; it was the
core of Freud inserted into the mask of flesh, or so he
had deduced. If it were not so, there would be no purpose;
he would be a disconnected fragment wandering without
memory through the mists of the unknown. Considering
this eschatology, sifting it through but not allowing it to
interfere with nearer purpose, Freud moved slowly forward, balancing in the ooze, holding himself perilously
upright, pleased against all rationality at his ability to
negotiate the surface. It was as if the process of reconstruction had given him a new body, a stronger version
of himself; he could not imagine having been able to do
it otherwise. Really, the deftness and grace astonished for
what they were, and if they could have observed him from
the dome, they must have been delighted with how well
he was functioning. Surely Carl could have kept on like
this if he had only possessed control and discipline. But
he had not.

> *The light that will flaming lead it*
> *Past the Arc of Night—*

Past the arc of night, into the arc of night, Freud moved
to within just a few feet of the engineer, observing the
fluttering gestures, the tremble of sheathed limbs. Like
the vine which he took himself to be, Jurgensen was arched
against the dome, clutching the dome, his body poised
against the gray, transluscent surface. Tense as he might
be, Jurgensen's attitude seemed penitential, a clasp of
prayer in the arch of posture. He might have been kneeling
before the gods of Venus themselves, trying to make a
case to them.

Oh, it is impressive, atavistic in its ferocity, Freud
thought. His own breath came through the helmet in little

purrs and burbles. There was water in his breath and thus a hint of tears which flowed against that harsher underlay, giving an aspect of illness. His lungs did not seem right, deft as he might be, accomplished as the machines; reconstruction seemed a shoddy affair. His body had been assembled casually, splinted rapidly. Freud's breath was like Cheyne-Stokes. He had heard the sound before, of course; it was this which he had heard in the seconds just after McCormick had fired, and that clinical, detached part of him which had always observed from a distance, taken account of behavior, made proper comment of necessary, avoided distraction, that voice had pointed out, *Sigmund you are definitely in trouble now, you are dying, he has killed you*, and he had known from the moment of impact that the wound was mortal. So quickly had this breath carried him past consciousness and to the oblivion of the reconstruct banks: what happened then did not seem to have been centuries but only a few days ago, before arousal, and McCormick enormous, ready to rise before him. Would McCormick have been enlisted as a reconstruct, too?

He shivered inside his gear, struggled with the controls to elevate the temperature slightly. The sound of his breath filled him with revulsion, brought back all which he would not consider, and yet how could he erase the sound of his mortality? He could not do it; he was doomed to the shell of self like Jurgensen, like Carl, like all of them: willingly or not he had to replicate his own condition all of those centuries later on the surfaces of Venus. There was simply no way out of this, nor was there ever. In your time or out of it, you irrevocably lived only that one circumstance you had been given.

And this, of course, was the soul of his science—that you could never get out. This was all that he had been trying to learn (and then to teach) in the various postures and confrontations of his life and to pass on. However one felt about emergence, one was only emerging into the *self* under the guise of extension.

But he could not probe these surfaces indefinitely; he could not do this at all. There was no way around the matter, and he had to establish communication with the engineer. Circumspection only up to a point and then activity: so had it to be. He sighed, cleared his throat, tried to lighten the sound of respiration so that it would not remind him of death. There had to be some reasonable way to approach this. But then—as it had been with his very research—there had been absolutely no precedent. He was unequipped to deal with any of it.

"Jurgensen," Freud said. "Hans Jurgensen, is that you? Hello, Hans; I am your friend."

He paused, checked gear to make sure that his voice was projecting. The figure was locked into place. "My name is Sigmund Freud, and I have come here to help you. Do you hear me? I am your friend. Don't you want a friend out here, Hans? Surely you must; it is very frightening, and you are brave to be so much alone, don't you think?"

The engineer's limbs flailed at the dome. He seemed to be attempting to crawl upon those surfaces, but of course he fell back. Oh, it is cold inside this damned suit, cold with all of the centuries of accumulated death, Freud thought. He clutched the thermostatic control and yanked it all the way over, feeling heat stream across. Decades, centuries, in limbo, unloved, untouched, barely mourned, much forgotten, extinguished through the passage of all the years; how truly cold a man became lying in a jar, vital cells computer-generated for restoration. They did not understand it, the damned technicians; they thought not of entombment, the mortality of the flesh and its corruption, but only of their computers and reconstructive code. Having died and lived again, though, he knew differently. He knew that flesh was all. The flesh screams and chatters, cavorts inside its own insistence. The surface of Venus could destroy his new body, freeze him in this suit, and all of their computations would be worthless;

he would be a piece of equipment that had failed. Was there any way they could understand this?

No, he thought. They cannot be led to understand. Of this they do not know.

"Hans," he said again, "I'm here to help you. My name is Sigmund Freud. Signal that you understand, that you are hearing this, that you know I am your friend."

How bizarre. Signal systems on the surface of Venus to indicate friendship. The systematic intelligence is perhaps the most delusional. Freud heard nothing but a slight alteration in the rhythm of his own breath, *huff-chuff, chuff-duff*; he was breathing differently once again. It was encouraging; the rhythms of death had shifted, and it meant that he was more acclimated to the situation, but it did not speed communication, had nothing to do with that at all. "Hans," he said with determination, "I want you to talk to me. There's no time for silence, no reason to be coy; we've got to work on this together. I'm here to help you, to make it possible to deal with this situation."

He paused, tried to think of the best way to put a point on what was, essentially, a difficult abstraction. "There's just no reason for this. Don't you see that? It serves no purpose at all. So you have to come back in with me and we'll discuss this in a reasonable way."

Get him back to the dome, they had said, and let us take care of it from then on. Get him inside the dome. Well, Freud was trying. Most certainly, he was trying. It was a monument to obedience from one who was once the most defiant of figures.

But there was no response, not even a flutter, from that dim figure now.

Coming from the banks, clawing for light and life, he had not believed that it was happening to him, that such a thing was possible. He had thought at first that he had been dragged off to hospital after the gunshot, and somehow they had saved him from what he had known to be a mortal bound, but one look at the apparatus hanging a mortal wound, but one look at the apparatus hanging above, the machines, their faces, the strange landscape glimpsed through the oddly shaped window, had convinced him differently: these were not people of his time, and he was in a place which could not have been known. Even before they had told him anything, as he was squalling through the helpless, infantile streams of the reconstruction, he had somehow known this, known that every possibility dimly glimpsed in the *fin de siècle* had come to be and that things could be done, somehow, that had then been at the rim of the fantastic. Restrained, bolted, strapped, half gagged so that he would not swallow his tongue while screaming, Freud knew before having been told that all of the possibilities of the century had come to pass and that with their machines it was possible for them to do anything, anything at all; there was nothing that could not be done by their technology and their devices. He had known that at once, and everything thereafter had only been in confirmation.

And they spoke in his idiom; there was no difficulty in understanding these creatures, even if they gave every indication of a destroyed affect. It all made a mockery, that was what it did, mocked everything that he had believed of religion and prayer, mortality or transcendence. But then again it validated Jurgensen, didn't it?

There was a resurrection and a life. If not a light.

They had advised him that the engineer was stubborn and uncommunicative, qualities which seemed at variance with the grandiosity described, but so be it. Engineers were known to be taciturn. There were many contradictions, little confluence there. After pointing out through the transmitters that he was the resurrection and the light, Jurgensen had had very little else, really, to say. He would not respond to questions or demands. And then there had been the catastrophe with Jung about which they would not talk.

"Damn it," Freud had asked them finally. "Why not just go out there and drag him inside?" And the simple exasperation in his tone must have for the first time impressed them with his validity. They had conceded then, not without some embarrassment and humility, that this just might not be an intelligent way to handle the situation because Jurgensen just might have incendiary devices to break down the dome if he so desired. They were not sure of it. No inventory had been kept, it seemed. But it was possible that the engineer had accumulated those devices. In any case, his help was needed as never before had a reconstruct been. "We need your skills, your services, your ability to control the mind," they had said.

"Oh yes you do," Freud had said later, infuriated as they stuffed him into gear, gave instructions, took his temperature and pressures with monitoring instruments, left the monitors in, impelled him on his way. "Oh yes, this is the future that you're telling me about, the future which is to impress me so. This is the future! You don't log explosives, you allow a lunatic free access, you allow him to leave the ship undetected, you pull dead creatures into the land of the living because you cannot deal with it yourselves, and you begin with the wrong alienist. What kind of century is this? Haven't you heard anything? In all of these two hundred years hasn't there been any change at all?" It was impolitic, injudicious, to address them that way, but he had finally lost his temper; it was merely one staggering example of folly piled atop the others, all the way to the end.

But worse than that, they had had no response. His language was perfectly assimilable, they all spoke in the same rhetoric, and two centuries had made no difference there, but they could not answer him. Abashed, they had stared with cold and yet curiously vulnerable eyes. He had shamed them, that was clear, had said something to them which had no reply. And so much the worse for all of them then, so much the worse because they could only have accumulated resentment. It would have been better

if they had argued, ranted, resisted the accusations. That
they had not—

—Well, it was too late too worry about it. All was in
the past, and there was simply nothing to be done.

It was in the past, and he could work it through over
and again; reconstruct that he might be, Freud had to
move forward. He had to deal with Jurgensen, handle the
situation as it had been given. "Listen here," he said now,
leaning toward that figure draped across the dome, leaning
as if reducing the objective distance might in some way
subjectively fuse them. "You have got to know, Hans,
that I am here to help you. Your friends have sent me to
make you feel better, and I am your friend too, Sigmund
Freud, here from two centuries ago to give you special
care. We're all very concerned for you; we want you to
be happy and to enjoy your new life here. So the first
thing that all your friends are going to ask you to do is
give all of this up, give up the posturing and come back
inside where it's warm and friendly, not like the hostile
atmosphere here, and once you're inside it's going to be
nice because we'll discuss all of this rationally in a very
friendly way. We know that we can work things out
together. All of your friends are waiting for you to come
in now, so why don't you do that? It's going to be so
much fun for all of us inside. We'll talk about everything."

Freud swayed in a sudden gust of Venusian atmosphere
whose effects he could only infer; perhaps it was imaginary and he had but externalized his sense of doubt, but
he almost lost his balance anyway, had to scramble for
control. It occurred to Freud that if there were indeed
aliens, if in contradiction to insistence there were in fact
Venusians, inhabitants of this planet who had scuttled to
the outskirts of their settlements to see what these peculiar invaders were doing, if this group of Venusians (Freud
imagined them to be greenish in cast, reptilian in aspect,
built solid, close to the mud) were trying to make sense
of this, absolutely no distinction could be made between
him and the engineer. Oh no, there would be no distinction

whatsoever; he and Jurgensen, lunatic and alienist, menace and healer, would be there, welded to the landscape, two aliens on a jaunt. The thought, foolish as it might be, that to hypothetical Venusians he would be indistinguishable from the patient was enough to ease Freud toward a kind of gravity, even grief. In other circumstances he might have found it comic (one of the saving virtues of his insight was that he had always been able to see the humor in situations of his own devising), but now it all struck him as thunderously depressing. What Venusians? Where were they? Why were they not considering all of this? Could such a thing be permitted to be on their once inviolate planet?

Oh, they had assured him that there were no aliens. No Venusians. "No Venusians," they had said. "The planet is uninhabited. There were no forms of life whatsoever; the atmosphere is carbon dioxide, conducive to no form of life as we know it." *Life as we know it,* that was the key. It was an odd formulation and left lots of room for life as it was not known, but they had been ever more strident on the issue when Freud had mildly pointed that out. "There are no aliens, no Venusians; we know that you are a nineteenth-century man and this was once believed possible, but there is no such thing. Darwin was wrong; there are *no* fittest here. We are the Venusians, the only living beings on this planet in all of the twenty million years since it was thrown into orbit by catalcysm." They were so certain on this issue, so unbearably certain, but how could they be sure? To Freud's nineteenth-century perspective, that same point of view which they derided, it all looked very suspicious. They could not control there own colony but would make positive pronouncement on the issue of Venusians.

Could they really know? The state of their knowledge, the standards of their science, might well be far advanced over the astronomical ken of his own time, but one could not be sure. For that matter, he might have a surer, swifter perspective than all of them, having come awake unarmored by prejudice. He was only 72 hours old, after all; that was young enough to know that anything was possible. Consider the purposes of reconstruction: to those of his time it would have been resurrection, an affirmation of prophecy. What would Paul of Tarsus have made of it? What would Jeremiah have had to say? Zephaniah, seeing all things on the face of the Earth being comsumed, would have had no difficulty fitting reconstruction into his lexicon; he would have known that there would be another chance. They defeated all reason here, yet insisted upon it; that was the irony of their condition and his. Confluent but paradoxical, fused but shattered.

"Come, Hans," he said patiently. "Come back with me. Give all of this up; it's pointless and it must be difficult for you anyway. What are you waiting for anyway? What do you expect?"

And Jurgensen answered him.

He did so in a fashion so routine that it denied a sense of drama; it was as if the engineer had simply been waiting for the proper conversational point to be made before he would join the discussion. "Expect?" Jurgen said. "Waiting? I am waiting for everything."

His voice was bland, controlled; he did not sound disturbed at all. Freud did not know exactly what he had anticipated, what he had thought he might hear, but the voice was so resolutely ordinary, refined further by the metal of the transmitters, that it might have been the voice of anyone at all cruising through the wire. There was a casual plausibility, a centrality which defeated all expectation. It was merely another version of that inner voice to which he had listened all of this time.

"And I will obtain everything," Jurgensen said.

"What *is* everything, though? Explain that."

"*Everything* is the resurrection and the life. I am the giver and the light. I will dwell that I may receive. Surely, you can understand all of this, that resurrection, this light;

you know of matters like this if you come from the nineteenth-century."

Freud supposed that this represented progress of a sort. It was an enormous step, really; contact had been made with the defiant engineer. That contact might have been equivocal, but matters clearly could have been worse (and had been for Carl); futhermore, Jurgensen's responses were relatively balanced. His speech was not all *that* irrational, taking the situation into account. One thing about all those years intervening which Freud could praise; accents and language did not seem to have changed that much. Communication, at least, was adequate. The changes were technological, but he could converse with these descendants. That was an advantage. At least it was not a disadvantage. Everything was relative, here.

"The giver," he said. He addressed the engineer as if he were in a therapeutic office, a therapeutic situation, dealing calmly with a new patient. "The giver and the light. Very well then, if that is what you want." He blinked against the green, effluent light, halftones which flooded the landscape in a fashion which Tintoretto or Vermeer would have appreciated. One could imagine a half-crazed Vermeer under the dome, palette draped perilously, trying to simulate this landscape. *The heart seeks pleasure first*. He wondered if Vermeer was on the list of reconstructs, an emergency painter as it were.

"That is an understandable position," Freud said. "You're due a lot of sympathy. But you'd be even more of a giver of light, perhaps, if you were to come back inside? Don't you think? You'd be a lot more comfortable and we could discuss this at our leisure."

"Why?" Jurgensen sounded flat, skeptical, but utterly sane. His helmet seemed to be cocked in a position of attention. There was no question of interest being engaged, anyway. "Why should we discuss it?"

"Because you want to."

"*You're* the one out here, bothering me," Jurgensen said reasonably. "I didn't start this."

"It's an alien environment," Freud said, trying to shift ground. "I don't have to tell you that. Very dangerous, poisons all around; we need full gear in order to survive here. It isn't at all conducive to rest and discussion, but that's what you need if you're going to be the giver of the light, Hans. You know that I'm right."

"Peace and calm."

"Absolutely."

"I *had* peace and calm until you came out here. What do you think of that?"

"I don't think it's logical. The question, though, is what *you* think of it."

"I don't think anything. Why don't you go away and leave me alone? I was doing fine until you showed up."

"Can't do that," Freud said. "Besides, the Venusians might come here at any time and attack." He found himself delighted with the audacity of his approach; he had not even thought of it, and here was an answer. "There *are* Venusians, you know," he said confidentially. "Have been all the time and they're just waiting for a good opportunity to strike."

Jurgensen made a sound as if he had spat within his helmet. "Your name is Sigmund Freud?"

"Yes."

"What manner of troll *are* you? Who have they sent out here to prey on me? What do you want?"

"Hans, I'm just trying to help you. I want you to understand what could happen here. Come, we'll return and discuss this safely inside. Free from the possibility of alien menace or sudden attack. Think of me as your friend. I'm here to help you in any way possible—"

"There are no Venusians."

"Oh yes there are, Hans."

"I've heard all of their lies but not this one yet. How can you say that? Why did they program you?"

"I'm not programmed. It's the truth; they didn't think you were ready for it all along; they didn't think you were strong enough to handle the truth. But there's no time, no room for secrets anymore; you've got to deal with it."

"Secrets? There are no secrets." Jurgensen's voice was flat, level; it betrayed no affect. That might have been the transmitters screening out all emotion, and on the other hand might have been symptomatic of schizophrenia. There was no way of knowing. Nothing would ever be certain again. "I am the resurrection and the light," Jurgensen said with splendid calm. "I am the giver and the life. I hold within myself all of the secrets, all the strands of time."

Oh, the grandiosity! The megalomania of it all. There were certain constants in behavior, it would seem; here was yet another. Even in this era of steel and light, colonies and transmission, holography and the cold, sad gleam of stars, there was need within the neurotic to extend himself beyond the borders of ego, to appropriate an identity which he did not truly possess. To this necessity, Freud knew that there was no reasonable response. He could not address the condition directly; as the eye cannot see its own movement, as the ego cannot confront its extinction, so the neurotic cannot face the nature of his behavior. This is a constant; it cannot change. Freud had to avoid confrontation of this sort.

For these people, these truly courageous if troubled descendants were entitled to generosity and respect. They had, after all, spanned the stars, brought Freud back to life, conquered the spaces among the planets, restored Carl Jung too, staked out Mars, prepared the Book of Reconstructs, sent their probes to the Centauris, given life to noted figures of his time, proved the colony on Venus, brought Freud to help the colony on Venus, and begun the careful exploration of the sun. Their lives were filled with uncommon wonder; in their capacity to deal with these circumstances they had been marvelous if troubled. Despite all of the embarrassments and difficulties, they were not to be dismissed, not lightly, not at all. If they were disturbed it was because disturbance had been bequeathed them; there was nothing of these people that was not an outgrowth, a true consequence, of what had happened in his own time. This had to be accepted; it was part of the common legacy, and there was no understanding without it.

No, he thought. No. In the presence of this time one had to hold a certain kind of humility. He had to respect Jurgensen for what he had done, for what role he played, no matter how dangerous the engineer might be. Not doing so was what undoubtedly had destroyed Jung, made him so inefficacious under the circumstances. Carl had been filled with intellectual contempt; that was always his problem: he would not have granted the credit that was due under the circumstances, would have treated the colonists like patients. Freud knew that Carl had condescended to them, simpered on the borders of the situation, denied true explanation, had tried to treat Jurgensen himself as a routine paranoid schizophrenic suffering from some simple delusions.

That was it; the temptation was to approach these people as if they suffered from the delusion *that they lived in the future, lived on Venus.* How easy it was to consider the matter from that perspective; all training had been framed to that. Their lives would have been a single, enormous delusion, then. But this case was complex, maddeningly so; the reconstruction banks worked, the future could be verified on the calendar, and all of this was happening on Venus. Hurled the millions of miles from Earth through the sky, should not the engineer think of himself as the giver and the light? For so were they all, now. These men were as gods; they stormed the heavens, traversed the skies, used their machines to control all uncertainty. The framework was not hallucinatory, it was real, and this demanded then the most careful, the most respectful, of approaches.

No, the engineer, even in his anguish and his fury, had powers that Carl could never have apprehended. This was inhospitable Venus after all; the spreading terrain was of green and awful implication. This was no hermetic enclosure in old and damaged Vienna, and Jurgensen was not a spiteful, brooding *Burgermeister*. Carl would not have had the wit to grasp this; that was all. But without that understanding, there could be no prophylaxis.

He had been shocked to hear from them in brief outline what the shape of the century had become after his demise. The twentieth-century had been a slaughterhouse, had confirmed every view of the worst potential of human nature allowed escape; the charnel house of this century, the war, the executions, the brutalizations, the *auto-da-fé* which had led them to the stars, perhaps as an escape from all of this, had made him shudder. If he could have summoned emotion, he would have wept for the millions of dead, but it was too late for that; *all* of them were dead, he could no more weep for the slaughtered Jews than as a young man he could have wept for all the nameless millions of history who had died before he had been given consciousness. Certain events, as he had been fond of pointing out in his writings, were beyond capacity for outrage, even pain.

"If you say so then," Freud ventured pleasantly enough, "perhaps you *are* the resurrection and the light. Who is there to say that you are not? You make quite a convincing case for yourself, Hans."

He sidled closer to the engineer, moving downrange, closing the gap now to only a matter of feet, slants of the dense Venusian light infiltrating the space between them, granting their figures, from a distance, an aspect of fusion. "Hans, you are as you wish to be. Never forget that. Essentially, then, it must be your decision from this point as to what you will do. No one can make that decision for you; you stand on your own."

"Ah, yes," Jurgensen says. "That is right."

"You accept this."

"Yes I do."

"Then this represents progress. You should be very pleased."

"Of *course* I accept it," the engineer said with some irritation. "I am the vine of all purpose. That is why I must hold on to the dome."

"Is that the reason that you must stay here? To hold on to the dome?"

"Something like that. If I let go of the dome it will collapse. That will be the end of the colony and the end of exploration; we won't get out here for another two thousand years and what do you think of *that*, Mr. Freud? There are no Venusians. You just made that up to frighten me but if I let go of the dome then it will fall and we'll be wiped away and there will be room for the Venusians to develop. I understand all of this, it took me months to figure it out but now that I have it's too late to let go now."

For a figure who was so completely uncommunicative, the engineer had had an entire personality shift; now he was conversational in the way that only an unstoppered neurotic can be, but Freud wondered if he was not the more dangerous because of this. Every word seemed to further confirm neurosis. "None of this is easy, you know," Jurgensen said, confidentiality flooding his affect. "There's got to be some respect for my condition here. Going out and taking responsibility for the planet, that's a very big thing. Most people wouldn't be able to do it. I don't see that *you're* doing it, you're just coming out, trying to make trouble."

"It is a big obligation."

"Of *course* it's a big obligation; what are you talking about? No one but me thought to come out here and do this, no one knows what it's like. It's a little frightening being in this position, you know; I don't mind telling you that I'm a little scared. *But it has to be done*. I have no choice."

"And why do you think that?"

"Because this is the case."

"But perhaps you do, Hans," Freud said gently. "There are always choices after all; if you relaxed and did not feel under such terrible pressure, looked past this situation that you find so intimidating, perhaps you would see some of those choices."

"That's easy for you to say."

"No it isn't. It's the therapeutic truth, Hans, and there's a lot to be done if you would face up to it."

"No there isn't. If you're saying that, it's because you're a reconstruction, a toy, and you don't *know*, you haven't lived through this. There are no choices, Sigmund Freud. None at all."

Well, Hans might have a point, Freud thought. It certainly could look that way from his perspective. A reconstruct somehow was not real; what kind of advice could one take from a creature that had clung to limbo all this time? Hanging on to the surface of the dome in the darkness, awash in greenish translucence, feeling the winds of Venus shudder through him, driven by megalomaniacal compulsion to enact the darkest drives of his spirit, Jurgensen might not have found his situation signatory of choice. It was a long and difficult siege; it had enacted terrible penalties. What would a toy know of the terrible passions of this time, even if the toy had once been the center of an intellectual community? Freud must have seemed as frivolous to the engineer as the poetry of Dickinson had initially appeared to Mahler. What could these truisms have had to do with human pain, human life?

It is all pointless anyway, Freud thought, looking at the dim form before him. It just did not matter. He could not force Jurgensen to leave the surface. How could he possibly persuade him to do this? The engineer could hold out on this terrain indefinitely. He should not even have been trying; he should have defied the colonists, as Jung had not, and given up. Freud was collaborating with a crew as alien to him as the imaginary Venusians.

In its own way, the century and its tormented engineer

drew integrity from the same force: they suggested that
matters not be forced, that they must arch to their own
design. Whatever Freud did, whatever happened, Jurgensen would not be moved; Freud, like the colonists
themselves, would be surrounded by hostile forces, ringed
in by that which he could not understand. None of this
would be easy. The methodology was utterly out of place
here; it could only invite ridicule. How could he create a
climate of analysis on the surface of Venus? How could
he make this determined figure an essentially passive
object?

So this, he mused, this is what must have happened
to Carl—except that his colleague would never have faced
the situation. Deluded to the end, his old rival would have
made excuses, would have tried to manipulate the situation into perceptions that would leave him free of guilt.
He would not have dealt with the situation, and that was
what must have undone him.

"See?" Jurgensen said. "You can't answer me. You
have nothing to say; you only know that I've told you
the truth."

"Truth is relative," Freud said. "But tell me this, was
there another man?"

"What's that?"

"The other who came out to talk with you. What did
he say?"

"Oh, that one," the engineer said casually. "He was in
the line for resurrection a long time ago, but I offered him
nothing. He did not want to listen, only to speak. He was
worse than you."

"What did he say?"

"What did who say?"

"This other man. Did he tell you his name? Did he tell
you what to do?"

"No one tells me what to do; no one would dare. There
was a man with big hands who tried to hit me when I
would not obey. Then he went away after I hit him. I
hated him."

"Because he hit you?"

"He didn't like anything out here at all. He said that it wasn't good for him to be here."

"How long was he with you?"

"I don't remember. So much has happened since then. I've been very busy. What does it matter? Are you working with him?"

"No."

"Maybe you're the same man behind all that equipment you're wearing. You're trying to make this some kind of joke."

"This is no joke."

"How would I know? You're wearing the same gear. How could I tell? You don't want me to know what's going on."

"I'm not that man," Freud said, trying to be reasonable. "If I was, I would tell you."

"But you are. You could be. You're all the same. He talked to me about Venusians too; he said that there were aliens here. So how do I know that you're not the same?"

"Carl said there were Venusians?"

"I'm not so stupid or crazy. They have reconstructs; they took you from the tank to come here and talk with me. Say it isn't the truth, what do I care? I know what's going on, what they're trying to do, but I don't have to go along with it. Yes, he talked about Venusians too; he tried to scare me just like you did. But there aren't any; I know better than that."

"It isn't easy," Freud said. "I didn't want to do this. They made me. I had other ideas, plans, they insisted that I go out—do you think that I want to do this?" Learning that Carl had also invoked aliens upset him. He had thought the idea to be his own; it was vaguely humiliating to learn that all along he was merely replicating other work. Of course the man *had* been his disciple; he had only applied a technique which Freud had understood earlier and better. There was that much, at least, to hold on to.

"Leave me alone," Jurgensen said. "Just leave me alone

now. I've talked enough; I don't want to talk anymore. You don't care what happens either. You're just like the rest of them, like that Carl Young."

Well, Freud thought. Maybe I am. From a certain perspective this could be seen as true. There was no reason whatsoever why Jurgensen should go along with this, nor should he. It was all observation in these spaces, all fudging and deduction, intimation and possibility: pointless. It was meaningless, just a brief period out of the tank anyway. They had used him just as Carl had been used; he should have known that all the time. There was never any regard whatsoever. To the crew, the two alienists were indistinguishable; try one, then the other. He should have known that all the time, would have if he had considered the matter.

Never had he been granted real option; it was all obligatory. What could he know of Jurgensen? What could he comprehend of Venus, of this planet itself? The engineer made a kind of sense here, had acquainted Freud with the absurdity of the situation, had taught him more, perhaps, than the others. In a sense they had become collaborators against the fools inside who only wanted the situation covered and hidden from view.

"You don't have to go along with this, Hans," he said. "You can do anything that you want. No one truly controls you. We're in no position to do so, and it's never happened that way."

"That's *right*. Right for the giver and for the light. Now at last you're beginning to understand. If you keep on that way, you won't even have to leave, you can stay with me and reason this out. You're beginning to understand what they've done to us."

Perhaps he was. Perhaps indeed they had done something. In or out of the dome, in or out of the banks, there remained the possibility of education. Even locked unconscious, stripped of flesh in the dull preservative waters of the reconstruction process, Freud must have felt the weight of the centuries, felt the slow, turning edge of his own psyche shifting. He would trudge back, then, would remove the gear and look at these inhabitants, in the tiny rooms and fetid little halls and laboratories which had become their domicile, and tell them the truth, that they had failed unspeakably, that nothing could be done, that he should not be their messenger.

That they should not *have* messengers but should take responsibility for their own situation. "This man," he would say, motioning to the deeps where Jurgensen still stood arched against the shell of the dome, "is as possessed of reality as any of you; he understands the truth and has made the rest of you indistinguishable, then. You stand separate from him. How could you think otherwise? What possessed you to ask Sigmund Freud to make judgments? Why would you turn to the dead instead of the living?"

Oh, it would be futile; they would stare at them through their bland, bleak twenty-second-century eyes, the dull frames of their countenances without comprehension, and he would seek to batter himself against them without possibility, without return. "You just don't see this," he would tell them. "You lied to yourselves all this time, but there was never that chance at all, never that possibility.

Oh, it was hopeless, hopeless then and now; he should have known that from the first. Would have if he had only properly faced it. Freud turned, put one foot in front of the other, slid in the ooze, balanced himself, positioned himself in relation to the dome which now lay massively before him. He took another step. I must open distance, he thought. I must separate us. There is nothing more to be said; truly this is the only way. Circumstance must be abandoned now. There must be another way to handle this, and it will be flight. I am going to go away; this man has beaten me. He did not mean to do so and it was never a competition, but that is what has happened.

"Where are you going?" Jurgensen said. "What are you doing now?"

"I'm going away."

"You haven't even tried to help and now you're leaving?"

"Do you want me to stay? You've done everything to make me go away, so what is the difference?"

"I don't even know why you're *here*."

"I'm an alienist," Freud said. "I was detailed to help you."

"You're a reconstruct. A toy."

"Yes, that is right. I am a reconstruct. But I am not a toy. I am earnest; I have real purposes."

"What purpose?"

"The other man tried," Freud said. "Everybody tried. But it doesn't work. So let the Venusians eat you. Let them take over the dome, what's the difference? It wouldn't matter anyway."

"I don't remember," Jurgensen said slowly. "The giver of light doesn't have to know everything, remember everything—"

"Hans," Freud said as he began to move again in the mud, "I have to go back to the dome now. I don't stay here indefinitely; I'm weak, I lay in limbo for two centuries before they sent me here—"

"So go back to the dome. I'm not stopping you. I knew that you would abandon me, just like the rest of them."

"No one is abandoning you, Hans."

He began to walk, as briskly as possible under the circumstances.

In the dome they had conceded one amazing intelligence: he was not necessarily the only reconstruct of Freud. Some of the large ships were equipped with reconstruction banks, and so were the colony on Mars and certain selected reclamation centers on Earth. He was only one version of what might be many, some in limbo, others perhaps conscious at this moment, all of the Freuds connected to their one avatar who lay in the ground of Vienna, long departed. This realization, that there were so many of him that he could barely apprehend their number, had made Freud gasp; the multiplication, the replication of these parts of himself filled him with awe. Nonetheless, he had been assured, there was no intersection possible; he would be but this one Freud indefinitely; there was no chance of spilling over into the others. This restriction, that multiplicity, had been a concept which would have undone a personality less balanced than his, he decided, but he would make the best of it. They must have had some reason for telling him.

"Stop!" Jurgensen cried. "You were supposed to help me. That's why you came out there, you said. So that I could be helped."

Freud stopped, pivoted slowly, gracelessly, held himself from tumbling in the mud. "It doesn't matter, you see; there's *no* way to help you," Freud said. "You've made your position absolutely clear, and there's not a thing that can be done. Your air supplies will run out."

"No they won't."

"Yes they *will*, they told me that—"

"Reconstructs don't need to breathe anyway. Why are you asking about air?"

"I need to breathe," Freud said. "So do you. You're not facing the truth here, not dealing with the reality. You've got to contend with it."

"I'll keep on breathing all I want," the engineer said aggressively. "What does it matter to you?"

"I don't know. I don't know what matters. It's not something with which I can deal. This isn't easy, you know; I didn't ask for this. It wasn't my decision at all. I was shot in Vienna a long time ago by a criminal publisher, I never had a chance; it wasn't given to me to control this situation. They never consulted, they never cared, they made me come naked from the tomb—"

"Now don't you complain to *me*," Jurgensen said. "Don't tell me what they did to you; they did worse to me and I was supposed to be one of them all the time, not a goddamned toy, a plaything like you. I hate them more than you do; you have no idea, none—"

"You don't know," Freud said. "You don't know what a reconstruct is. There's no playing with us, we're not toys—"

"If you cared," the engineer said, "if you really cared, you'd stay out here, you'd talk to me, not turn your back like the other one did, that Carl. You'd *stay* here, help me, show me why they are this way, wouldn't you? But it's all a lie, you don't want to take the time, make the effort—"

Oh, it was impossible. The craftiness of the man was not to be denied: just at the point when some understanding had been reached, he would turn, lurch; all understanding would cease. It was a scatology of the soul, this, an impossibility. Futility overwhelmed. Freud shuddered with disgust, turned, stared at the shrouded figure. Greenish plumes of mist rose, obscuring his view. He could well have been in a greenhouse, not on Venus; how would he have known? All of this might have been invented for his benefit, some demonic scheme of futuristic technicians or even the technicians of his own time. Perhaps there was no Venus at all.

"Listen to me," he said. "I tell you, there has got to be an end to this."

"I know that. But do you?"

"If you want to be a vine of purpose, then be that vine. Crawl on the dome. If you want to be the resurrection and the light, come to terms with it. You'll just have to accept the situation, as will I. But if you do this, then you must accept the penalties as well. I am. I can't even attempt to treat you, Hans."

"How were you treating me?"

"I did what I could. I listened, I tried to change matters. But it didn't work, you see. The Venusians—"

"What Venusians? There are none. You don't know what you're saying anymore, you're a broken machine. Just like the rest of them."

"No I'm not," Freud said. "I'm not broken." He felt a dangerous, lunging certainty, almost delight; he was coming to terms with the matter after all. He thought that he might understand. "The penalties of paralysis, that is what I mean."

"Whose paralysis?"

"Yours, mine, all of us." At this juncture he could say anything; nothing would make much difference—the dialogue could be pushed toward the edge of possibility and still have a fundamental kind of sense. He felt pleasure in the loss of control, however; this plum alienist centuries out of his element had obtained a kind of liberation. "You will stay and stay, Hans; you will remain on the surface of this damned planet clinging like an insect to the dome; you will remain until your rations are gone and likewise your oxygen, and then you will freeze into stone. You will lose all powers of mortality and conviction, will blend irreparably, like a figuration, into the dome and the landscape of the planet, and when the Venusians come to finish the colony, they will find the metal of gear over your remains, a remnant that they will never ascertain or understand."

"I told you there are no—"

"Oh Hans," Freud said patiently. "It doesn't matter whether you listen or not; it's all too late for that."

"How can you say this? You're a reconstruct, a toy, a machine, a piece of garbage pulled naked from a tank: you know nothing at all, have been floating for all of these centuries. I'm just an engineer, but I know what you things are; I've looked at the Book of Reconstructs and I know the truth—you're breaking apart, Freed."

"Freud. My name is Sigmund Freud."

"Freud, Freed, Fraud, what is the difference? Sigmund Fraud. You're wrong about the Venusians, you're just completely wrong there," Jurgensen said with great agitation. "I know that for a fact. Is this expedition yours or mine? Ours or theirs? Humans or reconstructs? Who would know the truth? There are *no* Venusians, never have been, you're just saying that to unsettle, make me unhappy, but—"

"But it's true. You're all wrong there, you see, there *are* Venusians; it's confidential information which was given when they took me from the tanks because that's the only way that reconstructs can function, we have to be given the entire and absolute truth you see, but since it looks as if you're going to be here permanently and die outside and you're just a dumb engineer to whom no one listens anyway, I might as well give you the truth. They sent me out with those instructions, you see, that I could tell you this if nothing else worked and that's what I'm doing, I don't care anymore, there's no reason to protect you. The landscape is *filled* with Venusians, hiding from sight, watching us. There are a hundred million staring at us."

"It's just not so—"

"Ah," Freud said, "it is, it *is* the truth, they're watching all of this and mocking you because you can't see them, can't protect yourself at all. They've kept their distance because it's to their advantage to hide away, hide their presence—but they're aware of everything that you've been doing and soon enough they're going to attack. Attack, Hans! They'll drag you off to the forests of Venus and then return to sack and loot and burn the dome."

Freud was entranced by his words. This portrait that he had given of vengeful and maddened Venusians was so convincing that it seemed to complement the situation. He pivoted in the ozone, confident, feeling in control as he had not since McCormick had shot him. "They'll come in the dark and drag you away," he said confidentially. "And it's a *long* night on this planet. They're vicious, alien creatures; they can do anything they want."

"Impossible," Jurgensen said, wavering. "There couldn't be any Venusians, not any; if there were we would have heard of them a long time ago. They would have negotiated with us, defended the planet."

"That's what *you* think. That's why you're an engineer,

because you have no imagination, accept what's said to you without thought or challenge. I've tried to help you see the situation but no more of that, then; I've done enough and there won't be any more."

Freud turned, peered at the horizon, looking for the Venusians. What was interesting was that he appeared to have convinced *himself* of the presence of aliens. There just could have been Venusians in the slime, lurking, waiting, staring. It would have put them in a terrible position. "I'm going back."

"Now wait," Jurgenson said intensely. "Just wait here. How do you *know* there are Venusians?"

"Because they told me everything."

"What did they tell you?"

"I won't repeat myself."

"But that's crazy! Venusians! It's impossible!"

"It could be," Freud said offhandedly. "But that's something for you to explain, not me."

"But why wouldn't they tell us?"

"They had their reasons. There was contact from the start, you know. From the moment of first disembarkation, contact was made. Actually, they were very helpful at the outset."

"They cooperated?"

"Completely. Before they knew the true purposes of this mission, thought it was merely exploratory, they were quite helpful. They didn't learn until later that there was going to be a colony, that conquest was planned. They didn't like that at all."

"Well, I can understand that. If there were such a thing as a planetfull, which I don't believe."

"They were very cooperative. It was uncanny how willing they were to get along."

"This is insane. No one told me, no one told any of this. It's inconceivable that it could happen; they wouldn't do it."

"The crews don't know. Only the administrators. And the reconstructs. And now you because I told."

"Son of a bitch," Jurgensen said intensely. "Son of a bitch."

"It won't be long now," Freud said. "In the meantime I'm going inside. I hope you don't feel too much pain when the paralysis begins."

"Paralysis?"

"So they can come in and scoop you up. Good luck."

"Now wait, wait now. I don't want to be out here when they come to get me."

"Who would?"

"I don't want to be here."

"It's your choice. You could arrange to return with me at once. We could go back there together. Of course, I'm not sure if they'd allow you in; you might be considerably contaminated because of the length of time that you've been on the surface, and that could be dangerous."

"I am the resurrection and the light," Jurgensen said desperately. "I am the giver of all light—"

"Well," Freud said comfortably, "that would be your decision, wouldn't it? Whatever you want to be. Whatever you make of the situation. I've had all that I can do with it."

He eased the thermostat a little higher by force, pushing it past the safe point, felt heat billowing merrily through the tubes, escalating against his uncomfortable flesh. Truly, he had never felt as cold as this. Inside the helmet, he could hear the tinny resonance of giggles as if they were trying to reach him from the dome with some fresh hilarity, but the switch was down and it would stay in that position. He would not grant them access; from the very beginning of this tour on the surface, he had made it clear that he was going to handle Jurgensen all on his own, without intervention. This to be sure was the fundamental principle of analysis, was it not? He had been reconstructed to administer analysis, or so, at least, they told him. If there were other alternatives, he did not know them; he had been granted nothing else.

"We'll check with the Venusians on your condition," Freud said. He raised a hand. "They'll let us know."

"There are no Venusians!" Jurgensen said loudly. "No Venusians! None!" He paused, seemed to strangulate. "All right," he said, "I'll go back with you."

Freud turned, his aspect nonchalant. "I don't know if that's permitted now. You may have lost your opportunity."

"Don't tell me what's permitted. I am the resurrection. I am the resurrection and the light." Jurgensen lunged, lost his balance to slide in the ooze. "Oh my," Jurgensen said helplessly. "Oh my."

Freud leaned toward him. The mud was treacherous; it shifted under his gear as he stumbled toward the fallen engineer, reached out a hand. "Here—"

"I can't stand," Jurgensen said. "I can't *move*. I can't get out of here, I can't get up now—" Losing his purchase on the dome seemed to have forced him to lose everything. Jurgensen was suddenly frantic. "I must get out of here!" he shouted. "The Venusians—"

"Wait," Freud said. "Hold on now. Don't panic." He attained a grasp on the man's gear; Jurgensen was floundering, not sinking, but could not seem to tell the difference. Disorientation was clear. "Don't panic," Freud said again. "We'll get you out of this."

"Oh please. Please—"

"Come now," Freud said. He made contact, seized Jurgensen's wrists, attempted to pull him to a standing position, but the man was floundering, and so, with a sickening lurch, Freud began to feel his own balance in a state of equivocation and collapse. He knew that he was going to fall and felt his own clutching panic. Was he indeed doomed? Would he go over as well? He tried to locate himself, root in the mud so that he would be protected, but the flailing of the engineer was so frantic, so insistent and corporeal in its despairing energy, that it discommoded, and suddenly, sickeningly, he was on the surface, collapsed wholly against the resurrection and the light.

Oh, the slick feel of the mud was nauseating; it was horrendous. He felt his nostrils beginning to fill with the scent of blood, and even though this was all reactive, intuitive, psychosomatic, he could feel the revulsion, feel himself approaching an edge of screaming panic.

"I should never have come," Jurgensen murmured underneath. "I should never have done this, it was not for me at all. I am the resurrection and the light, the giver of all life—"

His arm tightened; Freud felt the pressure. He was being dragged toward juxtaposition. *The heart seeks pleasure first.* The man wanted them conjoined, to perish in the ooze together. Dragged toward immersion, brisker contact, suffocation, Freud awaited drugged and slick death on the surface of the second planet. Beyond all the rhetoric he now faced extinction. His skills had failed. They had failed everything, and none of his knowledge, of their effortful attempts at reconstruction, would protect him now. Stripped of all possibility, he could do nothing. He had died once, he had dealt with it; he awaited his second death with resignation. Perhaps this time it would be easier and when he was next summoned he would have somewhat better command of what to do. He would try not to make these mistakes again.

"Oh, help!" Jurgensen shrieked. "Help! You must help me now!" And Freud tried to choke back the panic but too late, too late; he was going the same way as the engineer. They had become, at last, what they were meant to be from the beginning: they were indistinguishable.

"Help!" Freud cried. "Help me!" his voice in sum becoming all of the others that he had heard in the various compartments and partitions of his life, the voices pleading, mingling, begging for assistance—

"Help!" they cried together. "Oh help!" and Freud's fluttering, stricken hand found the knob of the transmitter locked to his hip, his limbs thrashing, convulsed. He turned that knob. There was nothing else to do. Abandoning isolation, reaching out at last, he opened it to full volume, and the chattering voices that had been so long withheld flooded his helmet, flooded his mind, the deranged chatter of the natives screaming. He heard the sound of the Venusians, who were, of course, to be found in the dome.

That is what he should have known all along; he should have dealt with that imperative. But it was too late. It was too late for all of this. Locked in dreadful collision, Freud and the damaged Jurgensen rolled on and on, they rotated on the slimy and barren surfaces of the second planet, the sound of the Venusians overwhelming. "Report!" the voices cried. "Identify yourself!" and in slick and deadly embrace they were urged toward completion as, immersed in the gases of that landscape, they surged toward that first hard and rigorous contract between man and alien. Between alien and man.

"Help, help!" he and Jurgensen shrieked, intertwined amid those voices, but of help there would be no sufficiency nor in time.

He would be stuffed into limbo for centuries again after this failure.

To await the resurrection and the light.

CHAPTER NINE

Waiting on Sigmund

FROM THE OUTSET OF EXPLORATION, THE LARGER SHIPS and the major colonies were equipped with reconstruction banks, archetypes, and instructions. The reconstructs were deemed vital. Early experiments on the space stations, disasters on the L-5, had been felt to be avoidable difficulties; the presence of reconstructs was declared essential to the probes. With all the risks of exploration, the obligations involved, why not have immediate access to the best minds of the most vital century? Why not allow those minds to interact freely with the crucial events of exploration? This more than anything else would show the commitment of history and circumstance to the future. Every aspect of the probes was crucial; every small advantage had to be sought.

So the equipment which had been worked out at such enormous theoretical difficulty and expense was produced wildly, multiplied so as to amortize those costs. That was the wonder of technology; it could be cheaply replicated. All of the referents and masks, organs and specifications had been locked into the computers, the proper alterations had been made throughout the other various equipment, crews had been briefed in the situation, and then the craft were sent on their way. On the colonies and in the ships the famous lay huddled in code, ready to be summoned at any time to render what aid might be necessary.

The history was complex, riotous, not without surrealism and elements of darker relevance. It was a story of color and dimension which would someday be told (although it cannot be in the context of this simpler, more pointed narrative) and in its irony and implication would have much to say. But this is the narrative of the end of the reconstructs, not of their origin or their functioning, and any true understanding of this narrative must begin with the madness which swept through the *Whipperly*; space madness they called it, although actually it was nothing of the sort. The madness was palpable and dangerous, and the executive officer, Daniel Hoffman, and the ship's doctor, Alice Wyndham, met to confer on the situation in Hoffman's quarters; they did not know, as they conferred, that they were embarking upon a series of events which would end the reconstructions, indeed end all circumstances, as they experienced it. If they *had* known, perhaps they would never have had that conference, but then again it is impossible to be sure. There are no certainties in this narrative; there were no certainties in the life that they had created.

One considers the *Whipperly* and the subsequent events with compassion. Compassion alone will serve where recrimination would only fracture the situation earlier.

It was serious and they were frightened. The fact that the exec and the doctor elected to exclude their captain from the conference would in itself have made that clear. The captain was quite mad: Wyndham and Hoffman had reached that conclusion, and in those circumstances they had to shield their discussion from him. This was not a matter of mutinous intent. They knew that the records would support them on that, to say nothing of the ongoing history of the fleet which bit by bit was being traced through the starpaths of the twenty-fourth century. Nevertheless, they had to protect themselves.

For there would be no way to delay, they now saw, what had to be perceived as inevitable. They would have to utilize one of the reconstructs, probably Sigmund Freud, in order to bring prophylaxis to this very difficult situation. But there was a problem: the Freud had not been used for centuries; it was a version which, according to records, had failed on Venus a long time before and probably should have been refurbished at that time. Instead it had been stuffed, forgotten, into the banks, transferred along with the detritus and equipment from one ship to the next, and had ended on the *Whipperly* still uninvestigated. It might well have been a damaged or defective model; nonetheless there was nothing that was more likely to work in the circumstances. The necessity for Freud seemed clear.

That was one reason for the meeting, then: to evaluate the extent of the damage and evaluate possibilities. Wyndham was responsible for the final selection but needed the concurrence of a senior officer, and although they were trying to work this through in the most civilized and courteous manner, there were undertones of strain. Hoffman was doubtful about all reconstructs, afraid of the Freud in particular.

He was a determinedly simple man, this executive officer... it was that absence of complexity, he felt, which shielded him from the madness racing through the *Whipperly* just as Wyndham was helped by her own superior knowledge. From this simplicity, Hoffman was prejudiced in favor of Wilhelm Reich instead of Freud. Reich certainly seemed the way to go; he was an intriguing figure with some dramatic and revolutionary ideas, but Wyndham had already told him in the bluntest terms that Reich would not be possible. Reich was not to be considered. "No orgone boxes," she had said. "No negative charge, no entropic lure, no mechanical transfers of sexual energy. These are catastrophic measures to be associated only with the aftermath of disaster."

He pointed out to her that they already had a disaster,

but Wyndham was not amenable to this argument. They had words about it, but now, looking at her calmly and lovingly, Hoffman felt in a different, more generous frame of mind, hardly obsessed by conflict. "We are in trouble here, you know," he said gently. "We're going to have to reach a decision quickly."

"It's not as bad as all that," Wyndham said. "The expedition continues, all is uninterrupted, we remain on course—"

"Only because of the automatics."

"We travel through automatics," Wyndham said, "and we are on course."

"Reich *is* my favorite, you know," Hoffman said. "Radical, dramatic treatment; that's what is needed here, and he would certainly apply it, there would be some very definite alterations—"

"Entirely *too* drastic," Wyndham said. "I've studied the records, and the one time he was used there was almost a civil war on the ship before they could stuff him back inside. I tell you, there are no secrets."

"I'm not a technical person," Hoffman said. "That's not my specialty at all; I leave that to you. It was just an idea."

"Everything has been checked through," the doctor said. "And although I don't have the time to go into details, I can tell you that Reich failed when called upon, failed so spectacularly that there can be no question of ever using him again. In eighty-six years no one has even thought of using that reconstruct. I just want you to understand that at the outset."

Hoffman looked at her lovingly. He was at that time— had been for quite a while, long before the present crisis— locked into a state of profound sexual and emotional longing for Alice Wyndham. It was a circumstance which he found profound, perhaps his first such involvement as an adult. He had kept it to himself; it would have obviously been dangerous to share these feelings, but he found Wyndham the only woman among all of the crew who met minimum standards of attractiveness, and she did so easily, so surpassed what might have been asked of her that inevitably Hoffman somewhat exaggerated her qualities. Now and then he had considered cutting down on the required dosages of sexual suppressant, libidinal block, and making an appeal to Wyndham's better nature and obvious compassion, but so far he had dismissed the idea: Alice had always been pleasant, and she had been properly forthcoming within their context . . . but she had also always been masked, part of her concealed. Beyond that, it seemed inconceivable to Hoffman that a cold, highly trained professional such as she could be interested in a man of his relatively modest attainments. It was crisis which united them, but how long could the crisis last? And then either it would be resolved or some fundamental disaster would bring all of this to an end. Clearly, their relationship was not fashioned for permanence.

Sitting next to her, however, in the sudden and dense enclosure of the lounge, the exec succumbed momentarily to an innocent passion, a sense of possibility cleaving him as utterly as the *Whipperly* cleaved the distances (such was his imagery) among the stars. Hoffman thought that a reduction in their distance could be accomplished in an instant, with a simple touch, and what might happen next fell into the area of the imponderable. But it was not only professionalism which kept him in place; he was also rooted by dread. The situation was perilous, and sex and sexuality would have to wait; furthermore, he knew that emotional entanglement would be the price of union, and it was emotion, consequence, implication, which had already rent the ship. There was lunacy in the corridors and the bulkheads, the compartments and the assembly halls of the *Whipperly*, and he did not want to add to it; perhaps he and the doctor were the last sane members of the crew, and it was desperately important to keep it that way.

Implacably, professionally, Wyndham laid out the alternatives for him. "Discarding Reich as impossible," she said, "and stipulating that Freud is the best possibility, there is also Jung, Adler, or Harry Stack Sullivan, all of whom have been used in earlier situations to no particular effect. Freud has been used only once, two centuries ago, but there are special circumstances, I think, surrounding an obvious failure."

"What circumstances?"

"It was a first reconstruct and it was on the planet Venus itself. It must have been quite disorienting, and it was never made clear to Freud exactly what he was supposed to do. In any case, none of the others here have experience with rampant madness; they have been utilized only for isolated cases of breakdown whereas Freud, a theoretician, would seem to be best qualified to deal with a general syndrome."

"This is all very technical to me. I don't know if I understand it."

She nodded as if he had confessed erudition rather than ignorance. "Of course," she said. "That's well understood. Nonetheless, because of the factors that I've enumerated, I think we have to go to the source, the founder, the founding influence, the essential originator of the school. Only after the Freud has been given a proper chance to fail should we go with disciples or offshoots."

"What happened on Venus?"

"It's all very technical. A colony failed. But it probably would have failed anyway; the situation was already lost when he was summoned. He was never given a chance."

"What can Sigmund Freud possibly do that you cannot?"

"That's a difficult question," Alice Wyndham said. "That's perhaps the central question here."

"So maybe I have no right to ask that."

"I didn't say that, Daniel. I just said that it was a difficult question. You're entitled to an answer. You may be the last one on the *Whipperly* to force me to answer that question, and it should be done before we go ahead."

Some aspect of her eyes, some scent of her flesh, disoriented Hoffman. It must have been that; he would never have asked a question like that otherwise. It was entirely outside his professional experience or his sense of the role that he would play. But by forcing her into professional persona, challenging her in this way, he hoped, perhaps, to reduce this subtle attraction and retain control of the situation. No good would come of trying to reach her emotionally; he would only disgrace himself.

"Look," he said. "You're more familiar with the situation than some kind of play-Freud. You have your own skills, your training, which is far more contemporary and of this era than Freud's could possibly be. What could he know of this?" She was really a devastatingly attractive woman, Alice Wyndham. Her blonde hair, the inquiring fixity of her eyes, the fine poise of her features, the suggestion of sexual promise underneath the utilitarian clothing—well, he would never know. Secrets unrevealed do not exist. "It doesn't seem very practical, that's all," he said weakly.

"Do I have to explain theory of reconstruction? Surely it's too late to take the time for that now, and you should know a little bit of it by now—"

"I know some of it. Some of it; we've had our own training, you know. I'm not ignorant, it's just that the circumstances here are, well, so filled with risk and uncertainty—"

"The reconstructions, it has been found, can work from the outside. They have a kind of objectivity; locked to circumstance as we are, we lack that. We don't have the ability to understand the issues because we cannot get outside of circumstance to define. The efficacy of the reconstructs has long since been demonstrated, and there have been some striking successes." She stopped, looked at him with something close to amusement. "Are you testing me?"

"No."

"That's reasonable, Lieutenant. I mean, you have that right. But I'd like to know."

"I don't have the authority to test you, and I wouldn't

know what I was doing anyway. I just want to know what's going on here, what the reasons are for digging up these old figures."

"That's kind of a test, though, isn't it?"

Hoffman shrugged. She was remarkably stubborn and persistent for all of her education and irony. A complex woman in many ways, she was simple and predictable in others. "There's a little of everything. You learn that on the starflights, if nothing else."

"Enough theory, Lieutenant? I don't think we have much time left, and we must give Freud a chance to fail."

"Like he did on Venus?"

"This is different. You can read the charts if you want, there's no secret there. I don't see the similarities."

"If it's the best decision," Hoffman said, "I won't overrule you. I'll go along with what you want."

"If it's not the best decision," Wyndham said, leaning forward, "you *can* overrule. You have the right in the chain of command, and I'm not protesting your application if you desire—"

"Stop it." Hoffman stood, began to pace in the confines of the small lounge, hideous, dazzling light bouncing off the fixtures and the tables, the sound of screams quite palpable, he imagined, through the otherwise soundproof doors. She folded her arms, looked at him calmly. Alice Wyndham was a strong and determined woman; there was no doubt of this, and he wondered—but did not feel that he had the authority to ask—why she had to anticipate failure as an inevitable outcome of the reconstruct. Why did she stipulate Freud's *right* to fail? He kicked a chair leg absently, seated himself facing the back, his legs spread to accommodate the seat, leaning forward on his elbows. "I won't override you."

He thought of putting his mouth against her blonde hair, so close to him now, whispering terrible secrets, telling her of his immersion in the darkness, his fear that he had been stricken by the madness too, and that need was so palpable that he felt himself trembling . . . but he resisted it with great effort and leaned back slightly, easing his back, stifling a grunt. Wyndham stared at him, then seemed to smile. "You think you can hear them too, don't you?"

"Yes. I know the room's soundproofed, but it's like I can hear them running and shouting."

"Me too," she said. "Of course it's an illusion. We're both very concerned here; considering our position, we ought to be. I don't want to see you upset."

"I'm not upset."

"Your respiration is terrible."

"Well," Hoffman said, noting that he had been breathing through his mouth, "maybe I am; I don't know. It doesn't matter, Alice, as long as I can function." I must reclaim control, he thinks. I must control myself, for if I do not I'm going to be like the captain; it's going to be the same thing all over again with me. Of all of them, the captain's breakdown has been the most undisturbing— his chatting with himself in the corridors, drawing little circles in the air, lurching through the corridors of the ship peering for aliens—he was such a *resolute* man. I had such trust in him.

"You are functioning, Daniel."

"I'm more than functioning. I'm running the ship." There is nothing, he thought, between me and the *Whipperly* and the void now. It is a responsibility that I never wanted, but there it is. "This ship is doomed," he said suddenly, shockingly. "There is no hope."

"Why are you saying that?"

"Because it's the truth, Alice. It's a truth which has to be faced; it's got to be said. There is no hope for us now unless something changes; we cannot save this ship ourselves."

And that knowledge, this statement, brought focusing urgency to their talk, he thought, an urgency that Hoffman had now to admit. The *Whipperly* has gone mad, he thought. It is filled with palpable lunacy. It may be the rumored Vegan probes, it may only be some subjective

arc of space, but the madness is so real that the craft
literally seems to be trembling in space: this is yet another
illusion, but it is most dangerous. The automatic drive
will work only up to a point; eventually the ship must be
guided, it must be given power, it must be brought to
descent. Our flight is on the verge of dissolution, it is
quite clear now, and it is impossible to tell whether this
is an effect of travel among the galaxies or whether those
Vegans, rumored manipulators of the mind, have had
effect.

"What do you think?" he said.

"About what?"

"About everything, Alice. The Vegans or space itself;
what has done it? Or is it all just an unlucky coincidence.
Are there Vegans? They must be using deadly rays to
drive us mad." That's what the captain has been saying,
he thought. That is exactly what his statement has been
as he goes running around the deck; the difference is that
he doesn't know what to do about it and I'm trying to
take action.

"I don't know," Alice Wyndham said. "I can't analyze
origins, only outcome; you know that."

"But you have to have an opinion on this."

"Must I? We don't have to have opinions on *anything*,
Lieutenant." She looked at him coolly. "We think we do,
that's the training, but opinions are largely reflex. Actually we're just functionaries here trying to get through
this; that's all and no more to it."

He saw that her features, tight and closed as they had
become in the last moments, were no longer quite as
seductive as he had thought. Underneath she was as
frightened as he, as limited as the captain. She no less
than he was indeed a functionary. Who was to say that
the ship's doctor would be able to deal with this any better
than the rest of them?

"Tell me about Freud," he said. "Let me look at the
record."

Slowly the consternation passed from Wyndham's face;

she looked bland once more. But underneath he could see the tension, the anguish. Taken in the wrong direction, he knew, she would break on him too, and then only he would be left. In her element, however, she seemed to assume a tenuous kind of control. "It's all in the book and the charts," she said.

"Let's look at it together. You can explain things to me. I'm just trying to learn what's going on here."

Information, he thought. Information is her proper function. Keep it on that level, ask for nothing else. And so it was information which she gave to him, talking slowly, tapping her finger on the heavy, incomprehensible charts as she told him as best she could what had happened. Just one prior reconstruction for the Sigmund Freud, she told him, that being on Venus 220 years before. Sent into the landscape to retrieve a crewman who had broken down, he apparently had collapsed and had to be brought back by the expedition. The crewman was never found. Freud was in an aphasic state; he yielded no information whatsoever. The memory tapes were ineffectual, blank or chaotic. He had been placed back in the banks with a cautionary signal and left alone.

"And we want to use this now?"

"Don't worry about Venus," Wyndham said. "It's not relevant. All of that was checked through carefully, investigated, verified before the cell was placed back in service. If the problem on Venus was felt to have had any longterm implication, the Freud would have been removed. There have been many other uses of the archetype in other situations and never difficulty."

"But why take the risk?"

"The cost. Reconstructs are enormously expensive. But the tests are all negative; clearly this is functional. Venus was felt to be a special circumstance anyway, not typical, not to be applied to anything else that might happen. The charts are open for you to consider if you wish."

"But you tell me that there isn't enough time. I can't understand them anyway, so what is the point?"

"There really isn't," she said. "It's up to you, of course, but there isn't really time at all."

"So you say that the Vegan invasion, the *Whipperly's* situation, aren't Venus, that it's entirely different."

"They are," she said. "This is deep space, a disorienting, fragmented situation, exactly right for his kind of therapy. The Venus detail was a trap; it concerned disorientation; there was no fluidity whatsoever. Freud should never have been placed there. The investigation made that quite clear. Still, they were hesitant to bring him back after that. One can understand that, the reluctance to use a failed reconstruct. But there should not have been."

"But how can we be sure?"

"You can evaluate the charts if you want, Daniel. Everything is open, to be considered. The problem is that you weren't trained to interpret, and you'd just have to let me talk you through them anyway. So you'd still be listening to, accepting my opinion."

"And there's no time."

"No there isn't; there's no time at all if the situation is as dangerous as we think it is."

"I'd still like to know what happened on Venus," Hoffman said. At any moment pounding could begin on the bulkheads, maddened crew members could pour into their enclosure demanding answers. It had not happened yet, but anything was possible. He hunched his shoulders, moved closer to Wyndham. "You're not giving any specific details here."

"It's complicated," Wyndham said, running a hand over her forehead, staring at the papers in front of her. "To state it simply, Freud misjudged a situation for which he was completely unprepared. He might have panicked. The colony was abandoned subsequently, and several colonists were lost in the confusion, but that wasn't his fault. He had already been decommissioned. It was what they did after Freud was brought back to the dome that resulted in the damage. They appear to have utterly lost control.

Freud was not to blame; the researches were exhaustive, and they were clear on that point."

"Could the same thing happen here?"

"Not that way. No, definitely not; it's clearly impossible. It was an atypical failure, never to be duplicated. Furthermore, there's a feedback, a learning effect; the problem was programmed back into the decommissioned Freud and it will be integrated into his functioning, therefore not to repeat the error if error it was."

"But no one has used that Freud for two centuries." The awesome weight of the chronology descended upon Hoffman, the span of the years, all of that empty time in which the reconstruct, empty, had been in limbo. "How useful can it be? What can it do?"

"It can do anything that we ask, within this context."

"All that time locked away—"

"It is a passage without sensation. They emerge with no sensation of time having passed. If they didn't, if they were at all conscious during that period, then it would have been abandoned, that program, at the very beginning. Do you know why?"

"I think so."

"Of course you know," Wyndham said. "If it had been that way for them, the reconstructs would have been insane, all of them. They would have been unable to function at all."

He looked at her, admiring the lovely intensity of her bearing, the fixity of her stare. "You make me feel good, Alice," he said irrelevantly. "When I listen to you, I believe that someone is in control here, that we know what we're doing, that we're not just stumbling through moment by moment trying to keep the crew away from us but are really working on this. That's why I like you most of all, because you make me believe there's some kind of control."

Almost, she smiled at him. He saw the intimation of something amused and infinitely touched beneath the resilient, placable protection of her features, but then it was pushed away. "Keep on thinking that; that makes me believe in myself too."

"Hopeless psychotics, the reconstructs. If the process didn't work. That's what you say they'd be?"

"That's what they'd be, Daniel."

Psychotics, he thought. Mad reconstructs, like mad crew. But of course that would be expected. Centuries in limbo, centuries locked, psychically shrunken, in the cells with all of that time to consider: what would happen if something went terribly wrong and the reconstructs were indeed aware, all the time, of their imprisonment, of the slow and terrible passage through the underside of time? It would be unbearable; it was hardly to be conceived. He did not know what it would do to him, could not imagine what his aspect would be. Released, the reconstruct would be evidently mad. No, the passage would have to be instantaneous; there was no other way whatsoever. It was too terrible to think about.

"Are you sure that the failure on Venus has no bearing?"

"None at all."

"And even though he hasn't been used for two centuries, there would be no sensation of passage."

"None at all. The process would not permit it; it's utterly inconceivable."

Utterly inconceivable. "Certainly." Certainly, he thought . . . well, perhaps. Decades and decades after, stretched through the centuries of emptiness, floating in the abscess of one's own memory, one's recollected impulse, trapped within the wires, tubes, and interstices of the preserving machines. What would it be like? He simply could not grasp this; the thought made him tremble, and he felt a shudder of profound revulsion. If nothing else, it worked—as it must—as a distraction against desire.

He stood, began to pace, oblivious to Wyndham's stare and concern. He had been shaken, there was no doubt of it. When I die, Hoffman thought, and it may well be soon now, we are out of control, let me *die*, leave me not to be a potential reconstruct. Let there be no chance of such happening to me, for the technicians of the future venturing to exhume a twenty-fourth-century starship executive officer and making him part of newer equipment. Oh he could see it, he could see it now: fanned by the waste and breezes of the ship of the fourth millennium, lying stretched to their devices, the faces peering. There seemed little likelihood of this, perhaps; none of the reconstructs were later than twentieth-century origin for reasons of tradition and belief, but the administrators had been known to lie (they could lie about anything; that was one of the constancies Hoffman had come to understand), and in the future the policy would be changed and reconstructions from later eras would be negotiated. STARSHIP EXEC: 24TH, LEADERSHIP POTENTIAL. He could visualize it. "Be quiet," they would say to him as he struggled to consciousness. "Be quiet and rest. Later your time will come; you are needed, you are going to run to the stars in this ship." Those faces, staring, were patient, solemn in the void. "We have no alternative to this, you understand," they would point out. "We are compelled by simple circumstance now."

Hoffman tried to distance himself from the vision. It was dangerous, humiliating, but it came in with the force that unseated the stars themselves: what would he be able to do? He would do nothing, of course; that was the point. He would be in that position of fundamental helplessness which characterized the reconstructs. They had always known that he would be in that position.

So he would lie there, docile head against restraining cushions, his humiliated, submissive little eyes blinking against the light as the monsters and apparitions of the fourth millennium closed upon him. They would look like men and yet again they would not; their features would be stretched and distended in a fashion which went beyond the anatomical limits that he thought he understood, and he could feel the churning of the engines, the more accessible of those urgencies, stirring beneath.

"You don't want me," he would try to say, his tongue caught by six centuries of paralysis and dreams, the dry ridges of his mouth, sucked clean by six hundred years in a vault, barely able to sustain movement. "You cannot possibly want anything from me at all." But the monsters and apparitions would stare with terrible patience, and looking back at them Hoffman would come to understand that they knew exactly what he would do, and this was the reason he had been summoned. Outside, there would be forces in witness for which he did not even have the language. Oh let me up, let me up, he thinks, struggling against the bonds and lashes which cross his body. Courteous but implacable, they put their hands on his shoulders and eased him back.

"No," the voices said. "Not yet. The time will come when you will have to run this ship for all of us; we will be utterly in your hands, but for now you must gain back your strength."

And he saw then; he had a moment of utter and terrifying insight as he struggled from the abyss of sleep. This indeed was what had been meant for him from the start, all of the decades of his life this had been waiting for him, and the disastrous Vegan mission was but a prelude to what would be asked of him now. It was as nothing, an irrelevance, a circumstance, and he should not have even been concerned and fought them... but there was no way that he could retroactively flee to the twenty-fourth and make all of it different. If I could recapture those moments, he thought, I would handle matters differently, pledge myself to Alice Wyndham, tell Alice that I love her, want her desperately, will dare the restraints which are imposed; oh yes, I would tell her that and be done with it, tell her and take the consequences. But he could not. At that time of resurrection there was no way back; one could only move forward in this sterile abscess of the fourth millennium to what is called destiny, and so he only flailed against the bonds, the apparition of bondage so great that he could feel the cut and shackles of wire. Shocked, he opened his eyes, gasped, found that he was not there at all but was instead at the point of origin, facing Alice Wyndham in the *Whipperly* lounge, and that nothing had changed. All was as it had been, and her face, luminous, met his gaze; he could literally fall atop and die for her . . . but among the things that had not changed was his incapacity: he could not talk to her. He could say nothing at all.

I want you, Hoffman struggled to say, but the words would not emerge. *I want there to be possibility, some chance*, but there was no change whatsoever; nothing could be said. It could never have been any different. Hoffman thought. The cold and freezing aspect of the fourth millennium dwindled against his interior vision; ineluctably, indelibly he was there, and that was where he was going to say. His fate was not to be reclaimed; it would always be this way for him, and there would be nothing else.

So what had he been saying? Something about Venusians and Freud, that was it, it did not matter, go on with it, though, give her what she wants, act as if the situation were tenable. *I want you*, he struggled to say, but the words would not emerge. It never could have been different. Venusians and Freud, yes. Stick to the issue. "No resemblance?" he said. "You're saying that there is nothing at all between the matter on Venus and what we face here?"

Beautiful, as she had been in imagined recollection, Alice Wyndham stared at him. "No," she said. "There were no significant resemblances at all. There was a possibility of Venusians just as there is a possibility of Vegans, but it is all profoundly unlikely. You are talking of supernaturalism, Daniel, not logic. None of the resemblances are significant."

"Daniel or Lieutenant?"

"What?"

"Sometimes you call me Daniel and other times you call me lieutenant. I can't understand what this means. Does it show that you look at me as two different people?"

For perhaps the first time through all their acquaintance, he saw a slight shift in her composure, a slight fissure through which he could peer to enormous depths. "Would you prefer me to call you lieutenant?"

"I'd prefer you to call me Daniel, I think, but I wish you'd settle on one or the other. It is disconcerting."

She looked downward; the fissure already appeared to be closing. "I'll call you lieutenant."

"How can you be sure?" he leaned toward her intensely, resisting an urge to seize her by the shoulders and begin shaking. "How can you be sure that Venusians and Vegans have nothing to do with one another and that the Freud won't break down again? What will happen if he does? We'll be in a mess here."

"Who can be sure of anything?" Wyndham said forcefully. "There are no easy answers, no positive outcome."

"Then it *is* indeterminate after all. You're just trying to protect yourself by saying that the likelihood is the other way, but you don't really *know*." He looked away from her, stared at the aspects of light pitted deep through holographic process in the walls facing him. "I don't know much of anything at all, myself," he said in what he hoped was a mollifying way. "I want to depend on you. Don't you see that? I'm a simple man. I believe and trust; there's nothing else for me. Consider me simple to the point of stolidity, a man of action, essentially, rather than introspection or contemplation—"

Wyndham smiled disbelievingly. "You're not all that simple. I don't think of you that way, and you can't believe what you're saying. But the records on these reconstructs are clear; they are well established, and I feel secure in what I'm telling you. Of course there are no guarantees, but—"

"I'm not complex," Hoffman said. "Really, this is true. I have one of those systematized, programmatic intellects which are helpful on prolonged flights because I can perform simple tasks and I don't think much. They grant preference to minds like mine, you know, skew the tests toward us because we can deal with the subtleties and terrors of threatening situations by ignoring them while more intellectual types would go mad. Even the captain turned out to be a shade too introspective, and now it's too late for him."

"Not necessarily."

"It's too late for all of us, I think. Alice," he said hoarsely, "it's just impossible here, you know it, maybe one or two in the crew can still function even a little, it's just the two of us, but I'm going on because I won't grasp the implications; I'm just immune to their damned probes, I think." He was babbling, not fully in control of rhetoric, not even sure what he was saying, but Wyndham seemed to be impressed by it, as well might she be. He could reach her on that level, he thought; she had not expected that intellection from a self-described simple man. "Maybe you're still sane because you aren't that complex yourself," he said wryly. "We're in a hell of a situation, Alice."

"Who's to say we're sane?"

"That's right. And who's to say that they're crazy?"

"Freud, that's who."

"We're in a hell of a situation," he said again. He tried to mimic the captain's tones: how would the captain have said this if he were there? How precisely would he have evoked his own concern? Portent would expand the words, lend resonance to the statement; the captain would been impressive here. "We're talking about the survival of the expedition, perhaps the survival of humanity itself." How did that sound? It didn't sound bad at all. "We're just the beginning; they've intercepted our minds, looped them; they'll make us carry them back to Earth and take over the government."

"You've been playing too many adventure tapes, Lieutenant."

"But why wouldn't they do that?"

"I don't know. I can't answer that. We're not getting anywhere; we're not making progress here. Freud's reconstruction is a fact, then; it's settled. So there's nothing else to say, is there?"

"No there isn't."

"You concur in the reconstruction?"

"I said that I would. I have no choice but to accept your judgment."

"Of course you do. There are always choices. Don't you understand that? Even when you think you have no choice at all, that's another kind of decision in itself, don't you see?"

Well, no. He did not. He wished that he could say that as bluntly, but it would be best to defer. Daniel Hoffman had never lived in a universe of choice; options were no consideration for him, not ever. He did what he was supposed to do, that was all; following orders at the beginning, internalizing the orders later on so that he would imagine what they wanted, and then do it. Granted any choice at all, he would not have been there, not have come to this. Nonetheless—

Nonetheless, you had to act as if there were options, as if a difference could be made. That was the illusion by which you measured survival. "All right," he said. "Let's reconstruct."

"That's an official approval, I take it."

"Official. Absolutely. If you are saying that it's necessary for us to proceed, then you have it. Go on, perform the procedures. I assume that you know how to enact them. *I* don't."

"If I didn't, this would have been a foolish conference. I know what to do."

"But it's your first reconstruct, right?"

"Except for training, yes. But it's simple."

"If it's so simple, why can't I do it?"

She shrugged. "It's mechanical. You could do it, anyone at all could. Any one of those poor, crazy people out there could do it; it's just a matter of following the codes."

"I don't want to do it."

"No one is making you. It's just a mindless process; this whole thing has been mindless."

He supposed that this was so. In another environment, another circumstance, Hoffman thought—while considering the issue of mindlessness—he might have asked Alice Wyndham right at that moment if he could take her to his quarters, place her like a jewel on his pallet, and make desperate love to her. Libidinal block or not, he felt at the rim of performance, would find some way toward connection. She had never been more attractive than at that moment, conceding the ease of the reconstruction process, the essential irrelevance of her own function. She had in effect handed over to him any advantage her profession might hold. Mindless indeed. Hoffman had heard reports of this, that there was nothing to the reconstruction process but the performance of machinery, but she had been generous to have so quickly conceded the simplicity of the process. She had yielded herself, in effect, to him.

Yes, he would have liked to test her sexually, to seek knowledge of himself in that way. Risky and dangerous as it might have been with the crew lurching around through the corridors, the captain himself likely to pound on walls and interrupt their tangle, it would have been worth it. But to do so in the lacunae of these difficulties would be to create an entirely new circumstance, a set of alternative possibilities with which he was not yet ready to deal. There was simply too much menace. He had to admit this; the situation was dangerous.

How much longer, after all, until the crew emerged from the shells of their individual collapse and turned upon one another, experimented with the brutality which was there at all times? They had journeyed too far, found too much risk; anything was possible. He and Wyndham were, he thought, the last sane people aboard, and they had to capitalize on that strength. If some ordering of the situation were not quickly imposed, there would not be enough sane crew to maintain a command presence, and what would happen then? What would become of them all? Chaos, that was the answer, that void of streaking light and possibilities which had always been feared on long expeditions; the crew would lose control, the captain himself would take the station, and the aliens, with their mysterious probes and lights, would overtake. There *were* aliens; the Vegans were closing in on them. That would be the end of the *Whipperly* and all that it represented, and he was not ready to make that concession, not just yet.

"Very well then," he said somewhat ponderously, noting the officiousness in his tone, which was of course a reaction defensive to the situation. "Begin the reconstruct. Let's get started on this right away."

"Perhaps," she said, "you'd like to consult the biography. If there's anything relevant which you seek—"

"I don't think that's necessary."

"Take a look," Wyndham said. She put a hand on the sheets, turned them around, placed them in front of him; reflexively, Hoffman stared. Murdered in 1905 in Vienna by Robert McCormick. Shot in the right eye at close range, brain destroyed. Famous alienist whose researches into the so-called 'unconscious' mind had created great excitement in professional circles. Married, no children. McCormick at a spectacular trial claimed that Freud had "deeply offended" him but offered no further details. Insisted upon the role of sexual repression and fantasying in much human conduct. A man of some humor and intellectual range, author of some popular expositions of his theory. Much influence at the time, subsequently dispersed through disciples and colleagues for decades to come.

Interesting enough and—like all of those selected for potential reconstructions—clearly not ordinary, yet with all of this range of abilities, what could Freud, dead for four and a half centuries, have conceived of the circumstance that was to follow? It was that which bothered

Hoffman most about the theory of the reconstructs, his feeling that they could never grasp the situation. The theory went the other way, of course, that they had a clarity of thought, purity of approach, which had been lost and that they could make contributions which were beyond contemporary abilities, that they were archetypal, in short, but he simply did not believe this. Something else was at work, something which limited the administrators' selections to those who lived in that narrow period between 1800 and 2000, but he did not know what it was and had never had the enterprise to find out. Nor, he suspected, did Wyndham really know the answer either.

He looked up from the spare outlines of the material, saw that he was under Wyndham's spare, cool gaze, which with convulsive, contrived lack of attention then flicked away. Was it possible that she was appraising him sexually, that she was interested as well? But that would be impossible, and in any case it did not fit into the circumstances. "This just didn't mean much to me," Hoffman said. "These things never do."

"Is there anything you want to ask?"

"You?" he said. "No, I don't think so. Not really."

"I don't mind telling you what you want to know."

"Do we have the time for this?" Hoffman said. "I'm a simple, practical man; I'm just trying to make this work. I told you already, I'm not interested in theoretical material. I can't handle it, and perhaps we shouldn't be taking so much time now. Maybe I'm just a stupid man—"

"No you're not."

"So I'm *not* a stupid man, perhaps, but I have to leave this in your hands. What do I know of reconstructs? What do I know of anything?"

"More than you think."

"I just can't understand why he was murdered then. This isn't explicit. How did he deeply offend this McCormick?"

"That's the best available information. It's been looked over very carefully, and the answer isn't clear."

"How about the Freud itself? Has the reconstruct been asked?"

"No, the records don't indicate any such thing."

"Then perhaps it should be questioned."

"You'd probably find selective amnesia, a complete block. The eye can see everything but its own movement; the ego cannot imagine its own death. That's one of his own statements, unfortunately. All that we know is that McCormick looked him up in Vienna, imagined some grievance, and shot him."

"A pity that McCormick can't be reconstructed then. We could ask the question of that one."

"You utterly misunderstand the process if you can say something like that. Do you know the expense, the risks, the involvement?"

"I wasn't serious," Hoffman said, although perhaps he had been. "I told you, I'm a simple man. It would be interesting to know, that's all."

"So we'll ask Freud. Maybe you can get some kind of answer; there's no prohibition, you know."

"Maybe," Hoffman said, without wit, "maybe I'm *not* that interested, Alice." Indeed, he was not. He could feel little hints and intimations of lack of interest; it seemed to move through him in a fashion almost palpable; he felt the scene literally dwindling, Wyndham herself seeming to shrink in proportion. He could reach out, contain her in a hand, could squeeze, fondle Wyndham, feel her little body, shrinking rapidly, crushed tightly against his palm. What an odd illusion, what strange practice. The Vegan probes had to be working after all if he was entertaining such bizarre fantasies.

She stood. "All right, I'll make the arrangements."

"Go ahead and do that."

"You're right, we're wasting time."

"Yes. Yes, we've wasted a lot of time, Alice. I hope we know what we're doing."

Momentarily, he declined to stand with her. Even at that angle, from that perspective, he felt overwhelmed, enormous; he felt as if he was literally looming over the insubstantial and reduced psychologist. The reserve in her aspect was profound. Even her breasts seemed shrunken in withdrawal, but underneath he intimated little fickers of psychic yielding, abscesses of need such as he had never known. If only—no, it was not to think about. Hoffman put his hands flatly on knees, heaved himself to a standing position. The pity was that she must call upon Freud. If she really loved, really trusted, perhaps she would have called only upon *him*. How bizarre all of this was, and yet it made a kind of sense. "Do you want to go to the reconstruction banks?"

"Yes," she said. "I think we'd better get started."

"Or do you think that we should wait awhile and—"

"There's nothing for which to wait," she said.

"So we'll walk to the banks."

He put a hand on her elbow, guided her from the small enclosure which had been called a lounge, moved her into the corridors of the spacecraft. They were vacant. This was an unused portion of the craft; the crew were in their quarters toward the anterior end, which also was where the devices were . . . but pulled into the sudden axis of light of this tormented craft they could hear, as it were, the sounds of the madness, hear the clangorous, demented music of the ship. So much was going on there that was beyond their control: the Vegan probes were sunk deeply into the minds of the crew. The screams and cries, numbing cackles and shadows, of the demented fleeing forms were only illusory, Hoffman knew. He retained a strong purchase on reality (they had not gotten to him), but the illusions were compelling indeed. Walking swiftly with Wyndham he imagined that he could hear the crazed laughter of the captain over the speakers. "To arms, to your battle stations, the aliens are coming!" he thought he heard the captain cry. "Take your positions, repel them at all costs!" Was that what the captain was shouting? The *Whipperly* had become a ship filled with illusion, mockery and portent were throughout, interstellar flight was a dream. Under crisis the hold itself seemed to buckle. It was almost impossible to separate that which was to come from a sense of possibility; potential was fused with circumstance. That was the message of the century. The hot light of the constellations, glitter of the stars, refracted through the portholes into shimmering holographs which split into a riot of color. "Look at that," he said, pointing distractedly. "Look at it now."

"Look at what?"

"The space," he said, shaken by the holography. "The light, the form, the color if it all—" He dragged them to a halt, pointed to a prism in the shape of a pentagon, spitting the spectral range at them, washing the deck. "There's never been anything—"

"It's always been this way," she said. Her elbow was poised in the cup of his hand; she leaned against him. "This is nothing unusual."

"It's just so—"

"Daniel, do you feel all right?"

"It's so uncontrollable," he said. He wondered if this was an insight or only the concealment of something more disturbing. "We're beyond ourselves in space," he said. "This is not for us."

"You're a pilot."

"It's beyond us, Alice."

"This ship is going to be saved." Wyndham touched his elbow, urged him forward. "Don't stop now, Daniel."

He stumbled, balanced himself against a hatch. Momentarily, an aspect of the craft seems to shift; it was the holography which had so discombobulated him. He closed his eyes, willed himself to disciplined focus. "He failed last time, and he's going to fail again."

"Freud?"

"Yes. Don't tell me it's different. It's the same thing, all the time." He stopped, moved her slowly against a wall. From the far edges of the ship he thought that he could hear the shouting; it might have been illusory, but the crew were shrieking in their madness. "All the time," he said. Her mouth opened, she was transfixed; he could grind himself against that mouth, could perish. "We all fail," he said. "It's all we know, all we understand, the failure, just goes on and on." She would be soft, dark, dense against that wall. "I'm trying to understand, but I know that he failed."

"Please, Daniel. Don't succumb, don't be like the rest of them. For all I know we're the only ones left here—"

"I'm all right. Everything will be all right. I'm just trying to learn something here too, Alice?" She was open, yielding to him; he sensed a vulnerability in her then that he had never before suspected, it would be easy to do something in the dank hallway that neither of them would ever forget, that would blight lives, and yet it was only by the hair of circumstance that he was able to hold back. "I'm not immune to disturbance, to possibility. Even a pilot can have an interior—"

"I never said you didn't. I never said anything like that, Daniel, please, you're frightening me, you're so close—"

He was. He was so close. Shaking, he backed away from her. She followed his movement, her eyes refracting, then concealing, distress. She was afraid of him, he saw, and it was the madness on the ship that had brought her to that condition; she did not know, any more than he, what could happen there. "I don't want to frighten you Alice. I'm sorry."

"It's all right, it's just—"

"It's just what's going on here, we don't have control, we simply don't know anymore, the sounds, the lights, the probes, there *are* aliens, Alice. We're sure of that now and we're just not prepared for contact."

"We don't have to stand here. We have to get to work; there's so little time, just as you said—"

"All right," he said. Ponderously he moved away, opening space between them. It is going to be all right, he thought. I came up to the brink of this but I did not go over, and now everything will be under control because

I have confronted the worst and have yet remained in control. The control is real; it is not an illusion but something which has been given.

He took her hand. "Let's go," he said, and they commenced to walk.

"It will be all right, Daniel."

"I know that. I know. I'm trying." He was vaguely embarrassed. The holographs, colors shifting under the subtle atmospheric change induced by their breath, revolved slowly before them and to the sides. Some sudden new formulation of the stars cast ornaments, strips of bannered light, across Alice Wyndham's thin shoulders. In that posture she was stunning to him, so intertwined was he with fresh desire for the woman. He had never found her so beautiful as at that moment, and the effect was not only anticipatory but reminiscent; he felt that at some time he might have possessed her. Like a reconstruct, he had a whole arc of memory locked within, to be spilled out at the proper insistence. Was she oblivious to this? Was she oblivious to the effect that she had upon him? Her hand was limp within his, slightly damp; he did not know. There was no way, then, to know everything. Just as the *Whipperly* in its ruin cleaved the stars, so did he seem to cleave all purpose.

"Faster," she said, moving ahead of him, exerting pressure, leading him. "There's not enough time." It was as if she wanted to open distance without giving the impression that it was so. He followed, his limbs feeling smooth in the traction, the joints blurred by the sensation of fluidity. He was finding a new sense of himself, a loose, disjointed simulacrum emerging from the cracked shell of the old exec; like a reconstruct in the banks, he was giving birth to himself. He squeezed her hand, the new man, trying to show her the sense of his recovery, but obtained no reciprocal pressure. She was intent, but slightly, speeding before him. "Faster, faster," she murmured.

In concentration he trotted along. Little purls and gasps came from him. The reconstruction room was about a quarter of a mile down through twisted, jagged corridors, past curves whose machinery jutted to the surface, closing some access so that they had to, however unwillingly, move more cautiously. She slowed, dodging protruding steel, unclasped her hand from his, signaling that she needed both hands to work her way through. "I'm practical too," she said, pointing out an emerging obstruction. He wanted to kiss her.

That was what he wanted, to put his lips against her cheek, feel the rising pressure of her flesh, feel the moist planes of her face slide to intersect, that suggestion of expansion which always accompanies the act. Oh it had been so long ago, but he has not forgotten. They could take function but not memory from him: oh yes, that slow yearning slide past dissolution into a kind of meld—

No, he would not do that. He must not show it; like the crew, then, he would have succumbed. It was remarkable that of all, he and Wyndham somehow held on to their sanity while the rest collapsed; he did not know why this was the case. Perhaps they were supporting one another, each preventing the other from sinking. They moved at a tight amble, abreast now. He was still clutching her hand. "Tell me that we're going to get there," she said. "Tell me that one of our friends isn't lying in wait to brain us."

"It won't happen."

"What if the captain was there? He could hide anywhere in the dark. I never thought of that before."

"I don't think that's possible, Alice."

"He would smile. I can see the smile on his face, that slow, maniacal, doomed grin as he closed in on us, a kind of triumph—"

"He's not violent."

"Everyone can be violent, given the right circumstances. How would we protect ourselves?"

"I'm armed."

"But can you be trusted to deal with it?"

"I'm not afraid, if that's what you're asking. No, that's

not quite true, is it? It's not fair to say that. Of course I'm afraid. I'm afraid of everything, but I'm not ashamed of that; you don't try to deny the fear, you just work with it. I'll handle the situation."

"He's crazy, you know."

"Alice, they're all crazy except for us, and who knows how long we can hold on here."

"Maybe we're crazy ourselves and we just won't admit the truth."

"What a thing for a psychologist to say. You're supposed to lend stability and hope."

"Who can be sure of anything?"

"Not me. I'm just trying to listen to you and do what you say. Do the best I can."

"Daniel, you're hurting my hand. Every time you say something you squeeze, and it's beginning to be terrible—"

"I'm sorry." He relaxed the pressure, then dropped the hand, reluctant to let her go but facing up to that necessity. They had emerged into a slightly more open area; he allowed her to take the lead again, followed at a distance of a couple of paces. There were no holographic exhibitions here; it was easier for him to manage a sense of control.

"We could decline to do it, you know," he said quietly. She did not respond. "I said, we could not do it," he said more loudly.

"Not do what?"

"Not have a reconstruction, just give it up, try to make the best of everything on our own and hope that things will settle down."

"Settle down to *what*?"

"Well," he said, pulling them to a halt once again, "that is an interesting question. In fact, Alice, maybe that is the central question. Back to what?"

She looked at him. "You know something? I think that if you don't protect yourself, you're going to be like the rest of them, Daniel. You're not in control."

"That's a central point."

"It's my responsibility to raise central points."

He supposed so. It was as good a way to look at it as any other. They should have been scurrying along, hands locked, rushing toward reconstruction. In the distance he thought he could hear the rumble of the machines. Awaiting those tapes, the machines would cue to that set of codes which would recreate Sigmund Freud. Did he only imagine those sounds in the distance, or had she already started the machines? He leaned against the wall feeling stunned, feeling the impact of circumstance come upon him. Through the wall he felt the shuddering of the probes as they moved ever nearer, targeting on his soft and quivering core.

"I'm afraid," he said. "I don't want to go any further."

She looked at him, oddly tolerant. "Why not?"

"I don't know why not. I just fear what they're going to do to us. I'm afraid the reconstruct will hurt us."

"Oh, Daniel—"

"How long can we last? They're all crazy, you said that yourself; now I'm going crazy too. I can't deal with it anymore, Alice. It's leaching away, palpably, right to the core."

"Daniel, I can't continue this way. We've got to get work done."

"Yes." It was comfortable against the wall. Maybe he would stay there for a long time; he seemed oddly suited to it. Here at last they could get him; he was no longer preventing conquest, rushing toward reconstruction, he was only an object. "Get work done, that's what we're supposed to do. Was there ever a choice? I don't think that you offered us anything at all, Alice, not ever."

He had nothing else to say. Let her stare at him, her eyes afire, her expression fixed; he had nothing to add. If she wanted to take over, so be it on her own ground; she did not have to implicate him. Within, Hoffman felt the sinking weight of imbalance, but it was not really that with which he had to deal. Was it? Was it now? Replicated, confident, let Freud stroll from his cocoon, wander through the *Whip-*

perly, do the best that he could so that, repaired and restored, they could move on with the further conquest of space. Conquer the Vegans. Run them to the source, take away their powers. That was all right with him.

"We were made for conquest," he said. Wyndham seemed beyond comment; she merely looked and looked past him. "This is the issue, that's at the heart. That is what had undone us now, that we have lost our way. What other purpose could there be? What else could we do?"

"You don't understand, Daniel."

"I understand enough, now." The wall was comfortable. He could stay backed against it for a long time; it had no promise, but there was no menace. "We must overtake the Vegans as someday they will overtake the universe, carry out their deadly but necessary mission to the stars. Mission to the stars." There was a good phrase; it had the right authoritative ring. If the administrators had put the issue to them that grandly at the outset instead of talking about "exploratory probes" or "investigatory balance," it might have been different. *Seek and kill Vegans*, that's what they should have said.

"Get up, Daniel. It won't work. You can't hide; you have to come with me and deal with it."

"Conquest," he said. "That is our circumstance. That is what has been thrust upon us from the first, our hereditary obligation."

"If you say so."

"I *do*. I do say so."

And indeed he did. Because it was this which he had been trained so assiduously to conceal, what all of the restraints had been fused to mask, but at that moment with Wyndham nodding and blinking above, with the Vegan probes making the walls tremble, with the image of holographs dazzling, he could not evade that fundamental truth. There was no alternative. The holographs had resonance; they conveyed the sense of a circumstance which had to be conquered, that was stretched through the canvas of eternity for conquest. He took Wyndham's hand in both of his, stared at her like a child. "I wish it could have worked some other way. I wish that it hadn't come to this, that it could have been different."

She allowed her hand to rest there, devoid of pity, torment, or the desire to move. "We all wish it could be different now, don't we? Isn't that what we go scraping through to the end, trying to believe?"

"It could have been different. If there had been a chance..."

"But if something like that had happened, that thing of which you dream, it would only have been the worse for us, and I know that too."

"I don't understand," Hoffman said. Her hand was warm. He would grasp it like bread and draw sustenance, draw from all of her, the blood in its passage. "I don't know what you're saying; I'm breaking, too, Alice. I hurt. I think they've gotten to me also and that you're the last one left."

"But you do understand," she said. "I know that you see this just as I, and it's what is going to make you able to get up and go along with this. Because it is passion, passion that is fracturing this goddamned boat."

"Oh my," he said. "Oh my."

She had been so flat and forthcoming as to be at variance with what he had long come to expect; this was not the Alice Wyndham, then, with whom he had so long conferred. She had become someone else. But even as he thought that, he gathered the centrality of what she said: *Passion fracturing this goddamned boat.* "You're right," he said quietly, deep in his throat, "you're right," all of it spilling out of him, "you're right, you're right," more and more loudly, and here was something at last that they could share, "you're right, Alice, it was passion that broke us, if we had been able to go to the stars without that, everything would have worked, but always, always we carry ourselves to those spaces, that is the terror of it, that we carry ourselves—"

"And the good part too," she said. "Maybe the better part, that we cannot be different, that we cannot forsake."

"But maybe it is worth the risk either way, maybe this is the price we pay for what we will become." And he turned toward her urgently, hands on her now, moving them up and down her arm, and slowly he rose just as she fell, heavily, against him, and they were in an embrace. That embrace, clumsy and necessitous, assumed spontaneity as their culpability increased, and then at last there seemed nothing to say. He was holding her; at last he held her against him; deeply, forcefully, he pressed their bodies together.

Soon enough they would enter upon the reconstruction and all would be done, but for that moment, that abscissa in time, there was something else to do. He felt. He knew. They were standing tight against one another, psychologist and officer, for whatever moments would be there in the glinting dazzle of light, and it was as if, clutching so, they were waiting for Freud himself.

How hastily he tugged at her clothing, how desperately she reciprocated. They made small bleating sounds against one another, mouths locked, crying confession into each other's throats as bit by bit the clothing was slowly removed, as the deeper disarray began. Of Hoffman's passion, of Wyndham's consummation, of the motions subsequent to this, nothing need be said; they are a familiar and thunderous set of occurrences. But as Hoffman drove against her, as he felt that first and essential opening, as he gathered himself for that plunge which to his surprise would be more effective than he could have thought, he thought of Sigmund Freud, that rumored and trapped redeemer soon to come forth enormously and to show them the way at last toward conquest of that oldest, that least known, that most instructive of all the barriers.

"Oh Daniel," she said. *"Oh, Daniel."*

She held him.

They entered together.

CHAPTER SIX

Mark Twain Full Fathom Five

FOR IT WAS THE PSEUDONYM THAT HAD APPEALED TO the dazzled captain from the first. It was compelling. "Mark Twain" resonated with the mystery and force of history; dark rivers flowed wildly in the syllables. Someone who had elected to be known as "Mark Twain" would know how to deal with the simpler matters here; also, the photograph from the book had been very imposing. That Book of Reconstructions was certainly interesting even though it was hard sometimes to make sense of all the parts of it.

But that just went to show you, all right, showed you how much you could trust the research, the technicians, the book itself, because this "Mark Twain" had turned out to be something of a fraud. From the moment Samuel Clemens had burst from the reconstruction chambers he had been in a rage, a rage partly directed at the captain. Eyes afire, limbs trembling, he seemed to find everyone at fault, but the captain came first because after all he had been responsible for bringing Clemens here in the first place. Only anger seemed to work with this Clemens; there seemed to be nothing else inside him.

"Oh I knew, I always knew it would be this way," he said again as he had said so many times before; this reconstruct seemed to have an overly repetitive mechanism. "I had no doubt of it, that the fires of hell were always waiting and anything else was a lie. A lie, don't you understand!" The captain stared appalled, dismayed by the unleashed, shuddering energy. "I always knew it would be this way, always knew there would be no peace at all, that they would not let you rest. Theology had other plans for us!" The captain had not thought that reconstructs would truly be so lifelike; he had had no idea whatsoever.

Prior to starting the machinery, which was his perogative because he still was in command of the ship and everyone had better know that, the captain had checked out the records, as was only sensible, and had been pleased to discover that this would be Clemens's first reconstruction. That was very good because it meant that the reconstruct would be cluttered with no other material and could be educated properly, in the most explicit fashion. The captain looked forward eagerly to the job of familiarizing Clemens with the conditions. The manual had warned that some particular disorientation might be expected with a first reconstruction, which was also reasonable, although nothing at all had been said about anger. But then again and perhaps, this only indicated how poorly familiar the captain was with the situation. Perhaps Clemens was not the typical reconstruct and this was a very special reaction. But if so it proved only that his luck once again on this abominable voyage had run out: the crew out of control, defying him, plotting his overthrow in the corridors and now his select reconstruct useless. It really was not fair to him at all.

"Everything's all right," he said soothingly. The manual had been specific: establish a dialogue at once, make friendly overtures to the reconstruct to allay the confusion, do not be remote but keep a certain distance, emit an atmosphere of calm and control until the personality has had a chance to reassert itself. "I'll explain everything in just a little while, just be patient." Do not grant the reconstruct too much information at the very beginning; it will not be assimilated, will only have to be repeated.

Don't try to do this all at the outset; feed the information slowly. "Be patient," he said again.

In the event, Clemens did not respond. His impressive face with flaring mustache twitched, he considered the aspect of the chambers, his glance taking in as it were not only the bulkheads, the sterile abscess of the room, the gleaming, dangerous machines lined up against the walls but the century itself which had created such detritus as the *Whipperly*, the captain, and attendant circumstances. "Oh my," Clemens said thinly. "This is beyond me all right. Who would have known? I should have known that it would be this way." He made a gesture obviously meant to encompass the circumstance. "I knew that it would be strange, different; I knew that it would be bad, anyone could have had a good sight of that by the end of the war, known that it would all come to no good, but this, *this*—"

He coughed, choked. "Am I dead or alive? That's all I want to know." He shuddered on the table. The spools and hypnotic devices might have granted superficial hold on the situation, but clearly it was still beyond him. The manual had of course pointed that out. "God damn it anyway," Clemens said. "It's really not right, then, doing this to a man, yanking him from the coffin—"

And he stopped, his head swung up, his fine, glaring eyes taking in the captain as if for the first time. Those eyes, curiously removed emotionally and yet avid for information, passed across the walls, the machinery, toward the bulkheads. "What's going on here?" Clemens said, more calmly. "Where am I and who the hell are you?"

"You're on a starcraft," the captain said hurriedly, intimidated. "I'm the captain—"

"Captain of what? Of a star craft? You mean something that flies to the stars?"

"Give me a moment. Just give us time, I'll tell you what I can."

"There's no time. You'll tell me now or not at all."

Loosely held by the restraining straps, Clemens fluttered, lifted his arms, looked at the bonds with disgust. "You've got me *tied down*."

"Please," the captain said. "Keep your voice down. Be quiet. I don't think the walls are soundproof, and I don't want to be overheard."

"By whom?"

"They're all outside. They're looking for me all of the time; any moment they could come in here. I've got the doors locked, but who knows—"

It was not easy. That much was fair to say; it was a very difficult situation for both of them. He should have kept all of that in mind from the start. Clemens was, after all, coming to the situation unbriefed. "Let me tell you to begin with why you've been reconstructed."

"I know a little something," Clemens said, his eyes glittering. "It's kind of coming back to me. Dreaming and then waking, yes. That's what has happened here. I was dreaming, and now I'm awake."

"Something like that, yes."

"You built me up in some kind of machine from information that you had; this is the far future, and you have the machines to bring some of us back to life. You want me back here for some reason; we're supposed to be able to give you help in certain ways. What century is this?"

"The year is 2372. We're on the *Whipperly*. En route to the Vegan system, far from Earth."

Clemens leaned back supine as if all of this had momentarily overwhelmed him; he gave a luxuriating, fading sigh. "And what made you go through all of this time and trouble and expense? And who are you?"

"I told you that, too. I'm the captain. I have to tell you the truth now; you've got to be prepared. It's all a plot, don't you understand? A plot against me. The crew is conspiring against me; every one of them has been turned that way because of the deadly Vegan space probes, and now they've reconstructed a doctor, someone named Freud, who has been told to find me insane so they can make confinement official. It's *all* the plotting of the Vegans. They've worked out this whole thing but there's still a chance, a chance for me to reassert control over the crew, and that's the reason why you're here, why you've been brought to the situation." He stopped to catch his breath, gasped. "We've got to work quickly, though, there's so little time—"

"Wait," Clemens said. "That's quite enough for now, if you please." He stared at the straps. "Please untie me."

He was right, of course. No reconstruct, no one at all could work under restraints; practicalities had to be observed. Hesitantly the captain reached out, began to struggle with the bindings. They were curiously slick under his hand, machine-made, machine-adjusted of course. They came free.

"Good," the reconstruct said. "That's much better." He arose with effort.

He was naked of course, and observing him from his position the captain felt embarrassment for the first time: supine, Clemens was a device; seated, he had become an individual. The captain motioned toward the corner where there was a valise filled with items, the name CLEMENS imprinted on it. "That's for you, I suppose," he said. "It came from the machine."

Clemens shook his head, stood, seemed to balance himself in the cool, barren surfaces of the room, then walked cautiously over to the valise. His bearing seemed capable; his footsteps, only slightly cautious, had a certain spring. He bent, began to struggle; there was the sound of mechansim. The bag unfurled and fell open. Clemens inspected the contents: clothing, little notes, books. He shrugged, winked, came over dangling some white items of clothing. "I'm the one who has come out of the machines," he said casually, "but you seem to be really unable to get hold of yourself. You've got to stop being panicky, reacting to situations like this, if you're the captain."

"Well," he said, as Clemens sorted through the clothing, selected something attractively off-black, a top and bottom, and, gestures becoming progressively assured, began to dress. "It's more or less of a ceremonial function; it isn't what it must have meant in your time. Virtually everything here is automatic, run on remote, by programmed devices, you see, but there always has to be someone who assumes the command function."

"Oh, there's always got to be a commander. You're quite right there."

"Actually," the captain said, "I don't know all that much about technology, about astronomy; that's not quite the command function as it has evolved, but someone has to take responsibility. When you get into the kind of situation that we've reached now, with Vegans attacking and controlling minds, when the whole crew turns against itself, that's when the kind of command function really pays off. Someone has to take the responsibility. I guess that sounds stupid."

Clemens rubbed a sleeve across his cheek, wiping away little spots of water. "Everything always sounded pretty stupid to me, son. Your business with the Vegans certainly sounds serious, though. These are aliens, right?"

He had not taken into account how primitive was the astronomy of Clemens's time or how little a man of his background would grasp of it. "That's right," he said. "Aliens from another star. From the Vegan system. I could give you the specifics, but they really wouldn't help."

"No, I guess they wouldn't. Now the question I have to ask you is what *I'm* supposed to do. This reconstruction process, it sounds dangerous and expensive, but beyond that, what is the point, the practicality of it? What am I supposed to do for you here with your Vegans or crazy crew or like that?"

"Plot," the captain said. Clemens did have a way of getting to the center of an issue; in certain ways it was an admirable characteristic. "We have to plot together."

"I'm not what you'd call real good on plot. Dialogue

was more or less my speciality, Captain. Why don't you just tell me now what you have in mind?"

"We have to work things out together," the captain said with some urgency. "You have to help me; we have to decide how we can best seize power from the crew, let them know at headquarters what is going on here." He cleared his throat. "We have to plan right now. There really isn't a lot of time to do this: Freud is seeing the crew right now one by one, taking testimony, creating some kind of dossier. My executive officer mutinied and in collaboration with the ship's doctor brought Freud out of here, and they're working to create a dossier, then there will be some kind of diversion—"

"Freud?"

"Sigmund Freud. He's a reconstruct. He was apparently a psychologist or psychiatrist of his time, very famous. I tried to read about him, but I don't really have the time."

"You don't have the time for anything, do you?"

The captain sensed the asperity in Clemens's tone; it was difficult, but he had to face the truth: he was being patronized by a reconstruct. It might indicate another level of his humiliation. "I have time for *you*," he said. "I worked to get you out of the machines, to bring you back to life. I'd think that you would be grateful for that—"

"You know," Clemens said almost genially, "I had no belief whatsoever in the afterlife, not until the very end. I knew that there was no such thing, that it was a device of the clergy to control the masses and instill fear in their hearts, the biggest, broadest swindle that was ever perpetrated upon humanity in the name of love and possibility, the whole question of God being another lie. Maybe at the end I weakened because I missed Lavinia so much, wanted so badly to join her, but you can excuse an old man's ravings, and by that time I was weakened; I know now how much. I think that I was positively reconciled to death, in fact, I was eager for the prospect, but look now, *look* at the surprise that was waiting for me all through eternity. You know, you people must be bigger fools than the people of my time. It is an unutterable consolation to me that all of them are dead except me and maybe this Sigmund Freud."

It was infuriating. In all of the materials on reconstruction, all the discussions of their function (this being his first direct experience, as the process was rarely used and only under the greatest of emergencies, or so they were instructed), it was never indicated that reconstructs were anything like this Clemens. The impression was that they were docile, easily manipulated, impressed by the fact of resurrection, cooperative, eager to serve, highly responsive to any expressed needs. The captain had had no conception, absolutely none, that a reconstruct could be preoccupied, self-willed, even defiant. Had he failed to obey instructions, not properly regenerated the machine?

"Please," he said, trying to calm Clemens. "This is all very interesting of course, but we have to *plan*."

"Plan what?" Clemens brought up one leg, balanced on the heel of his right foot, then reversed the procedure, balancing on the left heel, flexed his wrists, wrung his hands, obviously trying out the various parts of his corpus like tools. "Just what kind of nonsense is this anyway? Mutiny, Vegans, plans, actions, it's all crazy. Crazy!"

The captain stared helplessly, then walked to a bulkhead and suddenly, furiously pounded on it. "You must *listen* to me. There's no time for this because soon enough they'll find you, enlist you to their own purposes, and what will happen then? I can't control them, my word isn't accepted anymore, they've stripped me of authority—"

"Maybe they'll take me out of this," Clemens said. "Between you and me, I'm quite ready to die again. I hope they do a better job this time."

"I have work for you to do."

"Work? You're dragging me from the tomb and putting me to work?"

"I want to make a proclamation. You're a writer; you know how to do these things. I want a firm statement, something that will really take a position, give indication that I stand—"

Clemens put his hands behind his back, faced him in a magisterial posture. "This is utterly bizarre. You're just throwing words at me, concepts. The last thing I remember is McKinley—I have a very good vision of him, the poor bastard—and then the Mississippi at twilight. I guess you don't know what I'm talking about. You're going to have to help me piece this together."

The captain looked intently at the reconstruct and saw that it was so. He would find nothing unless he cooperated, worked in the way that Clemens advised. No other approach was at all sensible. The instruction books had carried that warning: that the disorientation of the reconstruct could block any utilization unless it were dispelled.

"All right," he said. "We'll do as you say. The Vegan probes destroy minds. The aliens are sending messages through space which warp the brains of the crew, not *my* brain, somehow I'm exempt from all of that—it's because I'm stronger than the rest of them, invulnerable to the assault—but the rest of the crew are not. Under that treacherous executive officer of mine, Hoffman, they've deposed me, taken away my command function. The Vegans have implanted a message that *I'm* the enemy but that isn't so but the crew is completely under their control—"

Clemens raised a hand. "Stop. Just try to be calm for a moment. You're running ahead of yourself."

"I'm trying to tell you—"

"I know, I *know* you are, but you're so excited and it's pouring out of you so rapidly that it's difficult to sort out."

He came over to the captain, put a hand on his shoulder. The contact was exactly as if the captain had been touched by one of the crew, as if human hands rather than those of a machine had been laid upon him; no difference whatsoever. Perhaps there never was, and the schism between humans and reconstructs which the administrators had built to such proportions, insisting upon the secrecy of the banks and reliance upon them only in the most extreme instances, had never existed. Perhaps, like the split between humans and Vegans, it was all merely a function of the administrators.

"You know," Clemens said quietly, "there's not really much that I can do to help you in a situation like this; I'm a writer and lecturer. Now what you seem to be looking for, son, what would help you out the most, perhaps, is some kind of military adviser."

"Military adviser?"

"Like Ulysses S. Grant, someone who can advise you on how you can deploy against those Vegans. Not a busted-up old journalist like myself." He winked, shrugged, squeezed the captain's shoulder. "I really think that would be best, son."

"I'm going to be eaten away," the captain said. He felt the panic coming upon him again, the panic he had felt when scrambling around the ship, running from the disorganization and the chaos until the idea of raising a reconstruct had momentarily calmed him, diverted him from the more terrible concerns. But the panic was there again, coming in close and hard, assaulting him in the way that the Vegans would assault him when the planned attack began. It could not possibly be long now; he did not have much time at all. "Paralysis," the captain mumbled. "Fear, death, paralysis, Vegans, that's all there is."

"Now wait a minute," Clemens was saying. "Wait a minute, maybe I didn't quite have this right, I'm *new* here, everything is new to me, but you've got to understand that I'm at a disadvantage. You're just giving all kinds of information so quickly, overwhelming me, and it's hard to come four centuries from sleep and know what to do, what to tell you—"

"I have nothing more to say," the captain said, struggling with the hatch. "Don't you understand? There's nothing more to be done here, nothing!" He flailed away, somehow sprung it, forced his way through. Light from the outer corridors hit him intensely, like a blow, made him contract from this sudden assault from the fluorescence. Grunting, he felt himself in descent, as naked as Clemens delivered from the banks. Somewhere behind— as he grasped his belly, attempted to ambulate—he could hear Clemens making further dull protest, but he could not respond, could listen to it no more.

Staggering through the corridors, darting through the odd and receding spears of light which were thrown by the stinking, hidden lighting, feeling the resilient padding underneath which seemed to firm his stride and grant direction, the captain experienced, hesitantly enough, a sensation of freedom, a pure wide arc on which he could ride. It was still his ship, this one, still under his control; he had yet the right to walk through it. They could not take that from him, and as long as he possessed it there was a kind of control.

He felt an odd, bracing bounce in his lurching stride, felt himself momentarily, that younger version of himself who had so confidently prowled those spaces in the private time, checking upon the splendor of the voyage for his own satisfaction, seeking evidence of secret misdeeds committed by his crew. How the holographs would dance, how the galaxies would beam cold implication through the viewplates! The sudden sense of power, the isolated grandeur, which this gave him were terrific; he had recovered the irreplaceable. Nothing can be lost if regained, the captain thought. That is the lesson, the truth of all these struggles.

Hoffman stepped from behind a bulkhead and confronted him.

The executive officer stood there solemnly in full regalia, hands poised as if to strike. "There you are," he said. "We knew that you'd be along soon. And look who's behind you!" His eyes flicked over the captain's shoulder. "I see that you've been busy in the tank just like the rest of us. Well," Hoffman said with enormous satisfaction, "that's fine. We've been waiting for you, you see. Hello, Clemens," he said to the following reconstruct.

"Go away," the captain said. "Don't let them trap you. You can still flee."

"As you can see, it's very difficult. Why don't you just leave?" Clemens said to Hoffman.

"The aliens are going to be vanquished," the captain said. "Me and Sam, we're going to take care of things here."

"Oh," Hoffman said quietly, as if he had had pointed out to him some routine history of patrol, as if the captain were filling him on routine information necessary to conduct a watch. "Oh, all of that business with the Vegans, you're still concerned with that. That's why you think I'm here."

"Traitor," the captain said. "You lied about everything."

"Come along," Hoffman said.

"Conspiracy, that's what it may be, but it won't do you any good at all. Mutiny if you want, but you're fools. I still hold the power, hold command position, have all of this in my hands as much as ever, and I want you to know—"

It was infuriating. Just at the moment when he seemed to be reasserting control, when there seemed to be some order to the situation, Hoffman would find him. It was probably due to the influence of the aliens, who were keeping careful watch on all of his movements. Clemens, at least, came along. There was that much defense. "Get out of my way," he said. "Submit yourself to my command; that's the only way that you can save yourself, the only chance—"

"Well," Hoffman said mildly. "Well then, good enough, if that's the way it has to be. I thought that cooperation would have been easier." He put a hand gently on the captain's wrist, but it was a hand with fire, a hand made brutally, swiftly efficacious given external power, and he pulled at the captain. "Why don't you just come along now?" he said. "This won't take long at all."

Oh, the treachery of it! The pressure became savage. The captain found himself yanked, propelled forward in his inferior's grasp. Clemens was there beside him, loyally rendering accompaniment. "You know," Hoffman said, "you're really looking quite well considering what we've all been through here; it's quite surprising the way that you've come through an ordeal like this. You should be very satisfied with yourself. Most wouldn't do as well, but we've always felt that the captain, *our* captain, was highly qualified, that there was nothing space could hold for him that he wouldn't be able to transcend—"

"There is indignity."

"Oh sir," Hoffman said, guiding him along. "Don't worry about it; you're just too concerned for all the rest of us. No one is going to pay for anything; it's all going to work out for the best, you see. You'll see how this situation is being brought under control."

"No control," the captain said. "No *control*."

"I can't keep up," Clemens said. "I'm just out of the back rooms, you know. Slow, give me a chance—"

Hoffman brought them to a halt, stood blocking the corridors, stared with desperate reasonableness, his features tense with culpability and guilt. "There's just no need for these threats," he said. "I heard you talking to yourself in there before; we all have, and we know what it must be like—"

"Wasn't talking to himself," Clemens said. "The two of us were talking together. We were having quite a nice conversation, as a matter of fact."

"It's the same thing. Whether you talk aloud or talk to a reconstruct, we heard what you were saying, we know what's going on, and it must be a strain for you now: the suspicion, the pressure. You think of yourself as surrounded by enemies all through the *Whipperly*, but it isn't so. You have friends here."

"Got no friends."

"Can you walk now?" Hoffman said to Clemens.

"What's the difference?" Clemens said. "I don't even know where you're taking us."

"We have to get there."

"Get where?" said Clemens.

"Where we want to go," Hoffman said, obscurely enough. He pressed the captain's elbow painfully, urged him into motion. Clemens came up behind them; the three moved clumped, almost in a defensive posture. The captain thought of the probes, burning, burning into them. Somewhere in the distance the crew, the Vegans, all of the denizens of this situation were evaluating everything.

"I was talking to Sam Clemens here," the captain said. "Not to myself." It seemed important to make this point; he wanted the exec to know it. "I brought him back, we were exchanging ideas, I was telling him what was going on, that's all. I don't talk to myself. I'm not crazy."

"That's true," Clemens said. "I want to make that point. He was talking to me. Some of it was very interesting."

"All right," Hoffman said. He came abruptly to a halt; they bumped against one another, almost sprawled on the deck. "That's enough. I've heard enough from you. Go back to the reconstruction room."

"Me?" Clemens said, "You want me to go back?"

"Right now. I can't take you along. I shouldn't have let you come. Go back."

"Don't go," the captain said harshly. "Don't leave me alone with him. Stay here. Protect me."

"No," Clemens said. "He's right, you see. I'm going to go back." He moved away from them, his eyes fixed, burning. "It will be all right. I know the way back." He turned, began to move with arching little steps. "I'll wait for you. I know you'll be back." Quickly he was out of range. The captain struggled in Hoffman's grasp, tried to free himself, to pursue his reconstruct, but he could not; Hoffman was powerful, and the captain felt reduced in his grasp.

"You'll get in terrible trouble," he said, "letting a reconstruct roam around the ship; what if the crew finds him?"

"Enough," Hoffman said. "Let's go." He forced them into a pace once more. "Now we'll be able to deal with this. I should never have let him come along. I thought I'd humor you, but there's no humoring—"

"I'm still the commander, Hoffman. I'm still in control no matter what you do." He stumbled against a wall; the clout in the shoulder almost sent him down, but he righted himself, watched Hoffman carefully as he found his pace. "You're going to pay for this, you know," he said mildly. "You'll know sanctions."

"No threats, sir," Hoffman said, slapping him on the back, flicking dust off the surfaces of his full-dress uniform, straightening him as if he were an errant bolt in the machine room. "Please don't make any threats; it's not becoming and there's no point to it."

"You were fooling around with that Freud, getting him ready to work with the Vegans, that's what."

"No," Hoffman said. "I'm not saying anything at all."

Nor did the captain. There really was no point to any of this; let Hoffman be apologetic, let him be accusatory, let him rationalize, let him lie about the matter, it would change nothing nor excuse the hideous misapprehension at the heart of this. The misapprehension that the Vegans were at all benign. It was all beyond discussion.

He was at the center of a mutiny, that was all, under restraint in his own craft. The mutinous circumstance was evident, had been out in the open for a long time, but he had nonetheless to make decisions carefully before he decided what to do, how best to protect himself. How to protect them all. The ship looked dreary, unkempt; the corridors never seemed narrower and more depressing. An aspect of shabbiness had come over his gleaming, mighty starcraft.

"Far enough," Hoffman said.

They stopped. They were standing in the middle of an anterior level in the far port of the ship, facing a large, sunken abscess, an implacable hatch shuttered like a closed eye. Perhaps he was wrong, the captain thought. He might never have been here at all. The *Whipperly* was two kilometers in length, half a kilometer wide, with all of the interstices and crannies that a complex starship might hold; a commander could not be responsible for having visited every section of his ship. Hoffman pointed to the hatch. "In there," he said.

"What?"

"Someone is waiting to see you in there. Just walk toward the hatch; it will open."

"It's that Freud in there, isn't it? You have him waiting for me. No."

"We're not here to quarrel; we're making the best of a very bad situation as you know by now. You've got to cooperate."

"You mean cooperate with Freud."

"Please go in."

"But I want to know why," the captain said. Somewhere within him, even after this ruin, the command function persisted; he did not have to be submissive to Hoffman. There were still options, possibilities; he was not a functionless, manipulable reconstruct. "How do I know what's waiting for me in there? Your Freud might assassinate me. Or there might be mutinous members who won't even let me get to see Freud. Why should I believe you? Why should I believe anything you have to say?"

"Oh Captain," Hoffman said. "Just go in there, please; don't make any of this more difficult than it is already. It's not easy, not easy doing any of this; there's a great and catastrophic strain upon all of us, and we don't like it any more than you."

The captain was hurled toward the door; the shutter fell before him, and he staggered into that enclosure, struggling for balance. Behind, he heard the clanging of the closing hatch, and then, in the dense, sharp odor of the small room, an odor which he had known nowhere else in the ship, the captain was staring at an elegantly bearded man behind a metal desk, dressed in a style that none of the crew could possibly adopt. The clothing was black from shoulders to ankles and immaculate, immaculate as was Clemens before he began to run through the corridors; so was the tie, the beard. The slightly misshapen jaw was the only indication of imperfection.

The man raised a hand in greeting or signal. So this is the Freud, the captain thought. This is what has been resurrected to cure us.

"You're the Freud, aren't you?"

The creature shrugged. "Who else would I be? What do *you* think I am, however?"

"A reconstruct, some creation from the banks that Hoffman dreamed up. *He's* the one you should be treating, you know."

Freud—surely it was he, there could be no doubt of it—looked away, reached into his clothing for a cigar, and put it into his mouth. A repellent habit; now the creature was going to light and inhale it. The captain had heard of such a thing, had reviewed it in training courses, but it was indelibly repellent. With extreme care the Freud produced flame from a small clump of sticks in his hand, lit the cigar, blew noxious smoke, then delicately extinguished the match. The captain had visions of the ship's imploding, a massive *whump!* from overconcentration of ozone, and that would be it, all of the walkways and steel plates buckling, the entirety of the craft coming in violently upon itself. The Freud spread smoke from its mouth.

"Go on," it said. "Tell me what you think. That I came out of the machines? What an interesting image. Go on."

"I don't care," the captain said. "I'll tell you anything." A sensation of risk swaddled him. He indeed did not care; it did not seem to matter to him at this moment what he said. What would the difference be? "The Vegans are taking us over. They picked us up with their probes in space as we approached them and they've established contact, they've made us mad. That was always the threat, that they could control our minds from a distance. We had warning, but it was decided to send the expedition anyway, to take the risk. It doesn't look good for us now, though, I have to admit that, what with the probes making the crew mad and all of them opposing me because I'm the only one immune to the effects, but as bad as it looks at this moment, it hasn't been settled yet. That's what they teach you in the command academy, not to give up until the last battle has been lost, and we're a long way from that last battle now."

"What academy?"

"The space academy." Keep it simple; it was not quite so, but it was good enough for the purposes of this interview. What would Freud know anyway of space academies, training, or Vegans? "I still have my weapons. And I'm going to use them to make the fight; they're going to pay for this, for what they've done to my crew—"

"Who?"

"The Vegans who are the purpose of this voyage," the captain said in an explanatory way. "They're the reason that we're here to start. Now you consider them for a moment. They're an apparently humanoid race of greenish hue; we've seen transmissions and there have been reports from the previous expeditions, with an advanced technology and a mighty propensity toward violence, a desire to conquer all of the galaxy . . ."

"My friend," Freud said with enormous calm, "why are you so convinced that there are such creatures?"

The captain stared at Freud speechlessly. "Of course there are Vegans! We've seen them, dealt with them, succumbed to their terrible powers. We're in a death struggle for the galaxies with them—"

The captain paused, looked at the gray face of the machine, the alert, shifting eyes, the cigar in the restless hand, saw the intelligence behind those eyes and, within, the deeper intimation of wire and circuitry, that circuitry making interconnections, carrying programmatic implication, all of those synapses at the speed of light, the Freud walking, talking, gesticulating, carrying forth, with horrid credibility, and he felt a calm descending upon him. "Ah," the captain said, "aha. Now I see."

"What is that?"

"They've affected your mind too," the captain said contentedly. "They can control reconstructs obviously; you wouldn't be any more immune to it than the rest of them. Well, it's of no concern to me; I can't be responsible for that. You're not a part of the crew, you're just a machine."

"This concern you say you never feel, this lack of involvement. Is this of such importance to you? To be free of the situation?"

"I know their maneuvers," the captain said bitterly.

"There are no Vegans," Freud said with superb calm. "No Vegans at all. This is illusory."

He ejected more smoke, flicked an ash from the cigar, little spatters of ash dancing in the air, being sucked through the respirators, the clear, high odor of the cigar melding with the stink of ozone; then Freud looked at the captain in an attitude which was obviously meant to indicate great and forthcoming frankness. "It has all been investigated carefully," the machine said, "And there are only a few uninhabitable planets circling an arid and burnt-out sun. The purpose of this voyage has been merely to investigate the terrain . . . it has been proved conclusively that there are no Vegans, and you must free yourself of this delusion."

The captain leaned forward, plucked the cigar from the reconstruct's hand. The motion was so deft and unexpected that there had been no opportunity for preparedness. Freud stared stupidly at his empty hand as the captain put the cigar on the floor, rubbed his heel over it. There was an expiring, extinguishing hiss, as little fragments of dust and ash welded to the deck. "I will tell *you* something. It's your perspective that has been destroyed, and you're at the mercy of their probes now. Either that or you've listened to the crew, believed them and the lies they told you, listened to that traitor Hoffman."

"Not Hoffman," Freud said. He looked at the crushed cigar with longing and regret but made no effort to retrieve it. "Your ship's psychologist Alice Wyndham and I have conferred; she's briefed me most thoroughly—"

"She'll pay for this too."

"Nothing," Freud said. "Nothing has changed at all. They were right; you're stubborn. You do not listen, you seem absolutely fixated—"

"She's without any credibility. I tell you," the captain said. "This is my command, I know them, I know them all, and they're the easiest victims for a clever, manipulative group like the Vegans. They're created to be tools of their circumstance."

"If only I had the time," the reconstruct said, "to work with you through all of these convenient delusions. I would envy the opportunity to be in an analytic situation of that nature. I could take the time and trouble to lead you through toward proper insight and it would be so much more efficacious—"

"For you too," the captain said. "If only you could be shown what has happened here, everything would be changed."

"But there's too much urgency," the Freud said, unheeding. It cubbed the cigar back and forth, back and forth, convulsively under its shoe, the stinking embers spreading moistly on the deck. "Let me tell you something now. I will tell you that this of which you complain is merely an extension of your disturbance, an expression of neurotic outcome or perhaps even psychotic reaction. I must give you the truth of the matter: there are no Vegans, no probes or rays, no mind control, intervention or stalking of the craft, but merely the warped and pitiful channels of your own misapprehension. The misapprehension! It is so profound as to be unsettling on every level. But I want to be encouraging; I don't want you to feel that the situation cannot be mended because ultimately there are real possibilities of cure here, of a means by which you can come to terms—"

"Oh stop it," the captain said. He flailed out irritably, struck the reconstruct on the chest, sent it back reeling. There was a satisfying *thunk!*, a whine of machinery. "Enough of this. What can you possibly know? You're scaled from the twentieth century; that's a long time ago. Your techniques, insights, approaches, are completely outmoded. Meaningless."

He closed in on the Freud, hovered threateningly. What a powerful feeling it was to assert control, to feel himself at last taking proper control of this. The reconstruct seemed to shrivel in the full glare of his personality; he wondered what they would make of it outside. Hoffman would be shocked to see how the situation had been reversed. "We don't need you," he said, "not any of you; that's what I brought Clemens out to prove, that none of you mattered, would make any difference at all, even the writer. We revered the twentieth century for reasons that had nothing at all to do with its value—it was the last century before the missions began, and maybe that's why we romanticized it, made it something that it was not, but we were wrong, we were so completely wrong in that regard." Oh, he felt triumphant; he had never been so articulate. He was in control once more. "It was our weakness, you see, our unwillingness to come to terms with the real necessities. I don't have to stay here anymore. I don't have to listen to you." He gestured vigorously; the Freud backed away in a fluid motion, as if it were rolling on invisible wheels. "There's no need for me to stay at all."

"Well," the reconstruct said after a long, uncertain pause as if it were feeding new tapes through its sensor—they did not work that way, of course, but it was a pleasant illusion—"that *is* your decision, you know. You have to make up your own mind about these things, take your own responsibility, and if you truly feel that there's no reason for you to stay and get the help you need, then there's no reason—"

"Oh stop it," the captain said. "Stop this nonsense, this telling me it's all for my own good or I can do what

I want. I just don't want to deal with it anymore. There's no need to continue, Freud, you have nothing to *say*—"

Freud leaned against a wall, his poise not yet fractured but obviously damaged, obviously shrinking; he clamped his hands against one another and slowly, slowly squeezed. "Everything is relative—" he said.

"Oh come on. Stop repeating the words you've heard from Alice Wyndham. That's one of *her* lines, everything is relative. I know Alice, I know everything about her. It's a captain's responsibility to know the crew, and I understand everything about her. She's a hysterical woman, a cold, cruel, terrified woman who needs to hide behind words. That bitch would try to convince you of *anything*."

"I'm sorry," the Freud said quietly, "but your condition, I can see this, it is more advanced than I originally thought. It is progressive, certainly deteriorative. Nonetheless, we must have courage. We must move forward. We must attempt to treat because that is our oath, the obligation which has been given us, that under which we must struggle. I accept that obligation; I know now that there is nothing to do but to go on—"

"Oh I tell you now," the captain said with satisfaction, looking at the reconstruct carefully, observing the shaking, the slight giddiness, the whirl in the eyes, the clear evidence that he had smashed something crucial, broken the delicate machinery within, that there were things awry inside of this mechanism that were terminal and that it no longer had to be taken seriously by him, by any of them. "I tell you, it's too late for any of this. I'm going to deal with those Vegans now, those aliens." He backpedaled, swaying. The reconstruct followed his motion with luminous, stricken gaze but made no attempt to halt him. Not that he could have. No reconstruct, no machine, nothing would stop him from what he had to do. "I tell you," the captain said, "I'm not frightened by any of you now and you can see that. You don't intimidate at all. I will not be dominated. I am completely in control, absolutely, right up to the moment when I make command decision—"

"Our oath and obligation is to treat," Freud said, running the words together in haste, stumbling over them in a musical, liquid way. "In any circumstance for any reason that is what we are given to do. Still, what is to be done? What is to be done, I ask the bastards, what can we possibly do? One can after all come to terms only with the known, we cannot take in the unknown—"

The machine was broken. That was clear. It would never work properly again; the captain had battered it into malfunction with the sheer force of his will. "It is a disaster," the Freud said obscurely but with absolute conviction. "A disaster, I see that now but it must be done, always done—"

"You can do nothing. You never could. It was all a lie. Go back to the banks, go back to your sleep, span the centuries..."

The captain stepped to the hatchway, leaned on it, found the handle and pushed it, grunting convulsively, to the side, then staggered ambiguously into the corridor, ready for fresh and final battle.

"No," the Freud mumbled behind him. "You cannot do this, you are not ready, not cured—"

Nonsense. Move on, the captain thought. Assert oneself toward the process of adversity itself. Having vanquished the reconstruct, he was now ready for more valorous battle. It was a proud and necessary claim for a graduate of the space academy, the commander of this voyage. "I'm going on," he called back to Freud. "I'm going to deal with this finally, now."

But he had forgotten Hoffman. Maybe that was what Freud had sought to remind him; the treacherous exec was still very much there. The captain found himself pinned suddenly in the man's grasp, those enormous hands, those remorseless features, fixed upon him. "No," Hoffman said. His mouth opened wide to frame the simple word; it emerged from the very depths of him. *No.* The captain was dazzled by that clutch, the sound, lurched, tried to dodge the exec but moving to the side was pinned again and backed into a bulkhead. In the officer's maddened eyes, those eyes which fixed him with intensity, he could see then the Vegan light, the dazzle of treacherous Vegan constellations. *Hoffman is one of them; he has been fully taken over*. Not satisfied with invading minds, the aliens had settled for the full possession of personality; they left nothing to chance, had permitted them almost no options. "All right," the captain said. "All right, let me go by, let me pass, I must pass, must plan," trying to appeal to that sense of command responsibility which might still be felt by this dangerous Vegan clutching him.

"Wait," the enormous Vegan said, restraining him. "Just wait; you're not going to go anywhere at all until you have permission—"

"You're not *really* a traitor," the captain said earnestly, stricken with a new thought. "Hoffman, you're not responsible, you're just a tool in their hands. I appeal to you, appeal to your sense of humanity, that buried part of yourself beyond all of this which they cannot touch. They can't take that away from you; I know that you're not responsible for any of what's happening here."

He put his hands on Hoffman's elbows, pushed downward, but the aliens had, as would be expected, fused the limbs. He could not be budged; the force locked them. Deadlock, the captain thought, deadlock in the corridors of the stricken *Whipperly* as the heroic last survivor of the Vegan probes and his *ur*-alien antagonist struggled with one another for purchase. If only he could be seen now, if only proper account were taken of what was happening. How headquarters would admire him! Of course headquarters was not to be reached; they were cut off from the bureaucracy forever. It was another part of the sadness.

Freud said behind him, "Let him go now."

Hoffman, clamping the captain, shuddered. "What?"

"Our oath and obligation," the captain heard the reconstruct say. The speech was again forced and rushed but seemed to have a certain assurance. "It is to treat under any circumstances. He cannot be persuaded, he cannot be moved, he can only be released. *That is the treatment.* Let him go."

Hoffman, the Vegan control, looked at his Vegan master. "Are you sure of this?" He shook the captain. "He's only going to do something terrible."

"Let me go," the captain said. "You heard him. Those are your orders."

"I'm sure," the Freud said. "It is that upon which my researches are founded and my science. It would be for the best. Let him go."

"The best, then," Hoffman said, "always the best." Convulsively, it dropped its hands.

"I'm free," the captain said. "I'll remember all of this. It's too late to recant. I know what happened."

"Oh, we'll deal with you in just a while," Hoffman said furiously. "We'll settle this later, you're not going anywhere—"

"Let him go," the Freud said. "There is no point in threats. Threats amount to nothing. They have no standing; they have no efficacy. Let him do what he will now. It does not matter."

"It's not over," the Vegan-Hoffman said. "I tell you, this is not at all finished. I have to listen, but only for a while."

"No," the captain said quietly. "That is correct. It isn't finished; this is only the beginning." He felt poised and dignified, in control of himself once again. Admirable the restraint that he demonstrated; he was entitled to felicitation. What he had done under these provocations was remarkable. The academy would approve that also.

"You'll see," he said, and propelled away, moving now toward his destiny, a destiny which might be his undoing. What after all would there be to say? What could he add to this? He understood now what had happened. For the reconstruct there might be excuses—it was, after all, merely a machine, a device taken from the bowels of the ship, incapable of will or implication—but Hoffman was a graduate of the academy, bound to the ship as its second in command, and for him there could be no equivocation or apology. No excuses could be made for him; a terrible judgment would be rendered.

So the captain turned then, raised a hand as if for the last time, and addressed the reconstruct. Freud at least was wired for understanding; one must grant some credence. "I'm leaving," he said. "Good-bye."

The reconstruct looked at him sadly, intensely. "I know," he said. "I know that you must."

"Good-bye," the captain said gently. "Good-bye." Enough. He dropped his hand, turned, began to move slowly toward the quarters where Clemens waited for him. Hoffman extended a hand; it fell away. There was no way that contact could be made. He was going to see Clemens.

Oh yes. Clemens was a faithful reconstruct, a machine designed to assist, one to be counted upon then, one with whom all of these thoughts and possibilities might be properly shared, one with whom true compact might be joined. Clemens would be very interested in all of this as the captain provided the full, the shocking facts of what the Vegans had done to them, and this would change Clemens's position on everything. It might lead to a confrontation of the most serious definition. Clemens would not permit this kind of cruelty and barbarism.

For the reconstruct Freud was the traitor, Hoffman the tool of the furious Vegans, but the captain had Mark Twain, the immortal and never to be forgotten spokesman of his time, and together—ah always, always together!—they would conquer not only these damnable Vegans but the reaches of the expiring universe itself.

And they would together prowl the tired and contracting limbs of the galaxy, as they would enact their destinies on far-strewn, dying stars.

CHAPTER FOUR

Full Music

BECAUSE HE WAS IN THE ROOM WITH THE OTHERS, because Wyndham (who seemed to know) had told him that it would be easier for Emily Dickinson if he were there (but who had ever made it easier for him?), because there was no way out of it, Clemens saw the poet in the first instants of her emergence. It was a frightening thing to witness, awesome in its capacity to shock: her face was palsied, wiped clean in that first clambering toward consciousness of all emotion but terror, and it was the terrified face of the infant that he saw then, squalling for some purchase on reality. She needed only, at the outset, to find out who and where she was.

He could see as he stared at her, horrified yet involved, that memory came upon Emily convulsively, inch by inch here, hammering away, each small bit of recollection as it entered knifing at her, and she jolted in reaction, mewling. It was almost unassimilable to him. Without language so far, language coming in later, she whimpered, clawed at the air, heaved underneath the straps. Language would return, but in its absence there was only the fear. There was nothing whatsoever that could be done about it; she must suspire through.

He looked at the face of this woman he might once have loved, who was to know about this, appalled by the obvious effects of the process but fascinated too, as well as he might be, because what was being done here was somewhat miraculous, and he had to accept that too. He thought of her gently fluttering against him in those rooms of possibility. Oh, they had constructed circumstances for themselves; it had not all been lies. He had loved her in his way, certainly loved her enough for understanding. Clemens thought of this difficult and terrible process that had brought them together once again. It involved rekindling versions of themselves described in that grotesque book which lay closed now under the seals in the case, versions and photographs of historical figures of his time who were declared capable of rendering assistance in future situations. It was absolutely bizarre, a madness, but they seemed sure that this kind of thing would work. What did this say of them? What did it say of the century to which he had been spliced?

"She needs the context you can give her; seeing you in the first moments will make her feel familiarized now and integrated as if from the outset," Wyndham had said. Oh, my, what jargon! What battle it all was! How they had tried to make it sound clean and controlled, but it was none of that. At the time he had only thought of how good it would be to see Emily again, even in these circumstances, of the new confidences that they might exchange against the panorama of stars. But Wyndham had said nothing of the drooling and the blood, the screams and the nonsense syllables, the frantic, unladylike thrashing against the restraining bonds. "It can be a little disturbing," Wyndham had said, but this was only after they had locked themselves in the room and the whining of the machines had signaled the beginning of the process. "It's a brutal and abrupt process which simulates the birth trauma, but she'll get over it. Everything will be all right." But this small admission had not properly foreshadowed the matter at all. Clemens had not expected anything like this. It was almost unbearable to witness, particularly when his own situation was so perilous. He had not been out of the machines so long himself; he could not account for his own responses. What they had done to him was wrong.

Nonetheless, witness it he did; he had a responsibility toward the situation, and he had been well implicated. They appeared to know everything about the affair; there were no small areas of secrecy left. Also, there was something fascinating and disturbing about this process which would have been inexplicable to any of his time. It was to Clemens's credit, he knew, that he had been able to absorb this. Starships, Vegan probes, reconstruction banks, crew distress, obsessed captain, stars shuddering in the corridors, whispers from the ship's doctor, the extreme light of the constellations: none of this had been easy to absorb. He deserved credit, Clemens thought, for having been able to deal with it so well. So he was locked to witness, impelled to give this the closest attention so that he would be able, somehow, to make a record of it, carry testimony against the future.

So when Wyndham came over, her face grave and drawn, and said, "It will be better soon, this is normal, it is all part of the process," he shrugged off her touch, made a gesture of denial. "No," he said. "Just leave me alone now." Some horror, his revulsion, must come through. He thrashed at her, and Wyndham looked at him with pity. "Go away," he said.

She shook her head. "It's all right," she said. "Listen, you can talk to her now, you can talk to her yourself." She guided him over to the table on which Dickinson moaned and thrashed.

Clemens leaned over hesitantly, trying to find the Emily whom he had known in this stunned creature, took her hand, feeling all the cold of the centuries passing from her glazed fingertips to his. She trembled in that clutch, reciprocally squeezed. "Do you recognize me, Emily?" She muttered something deep in her throat as if from the furthest recesses. He repressed an urge to pour out terrible confidences, whisper innuendoes to her, tell her of

the times they had had; it would not help, it would only
incur a kind of disgrace. He was appalled by his emotional
reaction to the situation; he would not have thought that
he could be so moved.

"Emily," he said quietly. "Emily, we're in the twenty-
fourth century. You've been reconstructed, that's their
name for it—"

"You do not," Wyndham said quietly, "have to work
on the disorientation this way. The information is already
implanted—"

"Let me tell her," Clemens said fiercely. "*Let me talk
to her*." He clutched her hand more tightly. Smoothly her
eyes fell open; she seemed fixed on his gaze. "They took
some of your cells, scraped at your body somehow and
stored, and were able to somehow regenerate from them,
through their machines. We're in some kind of spaceship
a billion miles from Earth, and they need a poet."

Round-eyed Emily Dickinson stared at him; whether
she recognized him or not was problematic, but she granted
a fixity of attention that he remembered dimly from her
in another time. "They need a poet," he said again. "They
thought that you could help. There are problems here,
very serious problems."

Credulous Emily Dickinson listened. She nodded her
head stiffly, mechanically, indicating a kind of comprehension. Perhaps it was more the soothing tone of his
voice than the words he was saying, but she appeared
relatively calm, did not flutter in his grasp now, but reciprocally squeezed with some firmness and began to croon
deeply in her throat as if soon enough words would burble
forth.

"You're doing very well," Wyndham said quietly.
"Really, this is very helpful now, what is happening. She's
coming back much more quickly than we could have hoped
under the circumstances."

"Just don't rush this," Clemens said.

"We're not rushing anything; we know what we're
doing."

"But I know *her*. Let me deal with this, let her take the time. It's the twenty-fourth century, Emily," he said, stroking her hand. "Just try to accept that; believe me, you'll be all right. I'm going to be with you."

Her eyes were round and full, credulous and accepting. "I said I'll be here with you," Clemens said. Would he really? He did not know, but he had to give her what she so badly needed to hear, what they would have her know.

Soft, vulnerable, open to the bone, she listened. He began to whisper confidences to her, told her what he could, leaning close, talked to her of warps and time, aliens and paranoia, the invasion of outside forces, and the oblivion of the reconstruction banks. He was not so much concerned with the sequentiality of this information, only with keeping up a flood of recollection with which she could identify. Wyndham discreetly turned her back, let him talk uninterruptedly. The circumstances were irretrievably bizarre, compounded by the known fact of their relationship; everything was in the books.

They *knew*, these technicians; Clemens was exposed, and in a way it was unbearable. Did he love her? Did it matter what went on between them? Wyndham and the executive officer were in hard conference in the corner, talking to one another intensely as Clemens stroked Emily's hand, remembering all that she had murmured against him, compared this bland face to that which he had held between his hands, kissed, knew, whispered against, but as he tried to focus concentration he felt his mind skittering away much as had the poet's in the initial circumstance of recovery. He stopped talking. She heaved in his grasp, seemed to slide under again; diminished, she was retreating from him.

"Don't," he said. "Don't, Emily, stay."

She looked at him, stricken, seeming to be on the verge of words.

"Better," he said. "This is the worst it will ever be. Stay with me; something will happen."

"Better," she said weakly. "Better?"

"Yes."

"What is better?"

"I don't know," Clemens said. "But we'll see."

Wyndham, hearing the light sound of Dickinson's voice, came over, handed him a cup of greenish liquid, indicated that Emily should drink it. He raised the poet's head, showed her the cup, helped her slowly to take it down. Her breath was coming irregularly, the gasps heaving and convulsive; she seemed to be trying to find some proper rhythm of breath as if this were some shocking experience, but her face was beginning to reorder, piece by piece, into that countenance which he had known. Age and knowledge slid into the panels of her face. He took the empty cup back and handed it to Wyndham. She nodded.

"She's better now," Wyndham said, kneeling. She put her hands on Emily's wrists, squeezed, clamped for pulse, raised an eyelid. "The recovery is normal, ahead of schedule in fact."

Hoffman came over and looked at them, touched Wyndham on the elbow. "Must you stay?" he said. "I want to talk to you."

"Later, Daniel."

"Tell me," Emily Dickinson said, more insistently. "What do you want? What is happening here?"

"Not now," Clemens said. "Just wait. There will be time for that."

"But I want to know now."

"You can tell her," Wyndham said. "It's not as if there's anything to hide. None of this is a secret."

"Everything's a secret, Alice," Hoffman said.

"Is that why I'm here?"

"*You* tell her," Hoffman said to Clemens. "Tell her anything that you want; this is between the two of you. Let's go, Alice," he said. "Leave them alone for a while. We don't have to stay; there's no need for us to be around."

"What do *you* want, Daniel?"

"You'll see," he said. "You'll see."

Clemens noted then the glances that passed between them, and with a shade of his old ferocity he thought things were not so different after all.

Wyndham looked at Clemens, and it was as if she could infer his rumination. Awkwardly, she smiled. "All right," she said. "All right, I don't care then. What do I care? It's out of my hands. Leave them alone." Hoffman guided her away from the table and toward the hatchway. "We'll be back in a little while," she said.

"It won't be so long," Hoffman said, guiding her through the exit. "Don't worry about this, just talk." They left.

It was highly unprofessional conduct, Clemens supposed, but then again, no less than the others, Hoffman had to be thinking of the aliens, the Vegan probes. How much time was there? Clemens kneeled at Dickinson's side, put his hands on hers. "Hello, Emily," he said. He touched her fingers. They were warmer; slowly the familiar blood cruised through the surfaces. "Hello." She pressed his hand with surprising strength. "You see," he said. "You're coming back to yourself after all. It isn't that bad. I thought it would be terrible for me, but everything worked out."

"I want to know why, why I'm back here. Tell me."

"Does it matter?"

She closed her eyes. "Everything matters. I—"

"Don't talk," he said. "You're still weak."

" I *have* to talk. Why me?"

"Because of your reputation, because of how you were thought of in your time; they felt that—"

"Nonsense," Emily Dickinson said gravely. "You're lying to me. Whitman was right you know. Everything he said was right. I took that to the grave with me; he was right, I ruined everything—"

"No he wasn't," Clemens said angrily. No one could ever oppose Emily when she sought self-deprecation; that core of revulsion seemed to have survived the centuries intact. Nothing ever changes, he thought; we carry ourselves forward in any circumstance. "Who cares about

Whitman anyway? We have no time for this; he's gone,
our time is gone, there are things to be done."

"What is to be done?"

"This is a ship in trouble. Terrible things are happening;
they've brought three of us back to try and save them."

"Which three. You and me and who else?"

"I'm in trouble," he said. "I'm in serious trouble."

"Sam, that's no different from the last time or any of
the other times I knew you. Who's the third they brought
back?"

"An alienist named Sigmund Freud."

"I've never heard of him."

"I'd never heard of him either. But this is what's interesting, Emily. *He* asked for you. He was the one who
decided that you should be brought back; I had no vote
in this."

"And when will that be? When will he see us?"

"Whenever he chooses," Clemens said. "After all, *he's*
the doctor here."

So he tried to tell her in the time they had of the history
of the reconstructs, of what all of it meant. Much of what
he had to say was based upon confidences given him by
the captain, but Clemens put in his own assumptions as
well as certain remarks which from time to time both
Hoffman and Wyndham had let slip. Overall, he gave her,
he thought, as workable a portrait of the twenty-fourth
century, the nature of this voyage, the condition of the
crew, as seemed possible under the circumstances. As a
man of letters, he retained the ability to organize his insights
and premises.

Emily Dickinson listened to all of it without comment,
absorbed it slowly. Now and then the monitors clicked,
the lights dazzled and shifted, there were other indications
that they were being observed, but no one came into the
chambers. Specific instructions, it would seem, had been
left by Wyndham; they were not to be bothered. Clemens
did not know to what degree Wyndham had their interests

at heart. It might only be a matter of concealing the reconstructions from the crew.

But then again, whether this was observed or not, a lot of autonomy had been given. They could do as they wished here; this was not precisely imprisonment. The question was what they had in mind and whether Sigmund Freud would be in soon, what Freud's position on all of this would be. It was surely complex and confusing, but Clemens could see the ironic aspects of it, not to mention the fundamental outrage. Some of it he communicated to Emily; other parts he decided to retain. Through all of it, however, Emily Dickinson, even under restraint, maintained her posture of rigid attention, focusing upon him, absorbing everything that he had to say. Her complexion improved; she began more and more to resemble the woman whom he had known. Clemens decided to release the restraining devices, allow her movement of less restricted nature. Her color was really quite good; her face had recovered the mature outlines that he remembered; she was stronger, obviously, than she had ever conceded that she could be. Clemens admired her, the resilience, the courage. But then he always did; the remarkable aspect of this woman was what she might have done if only she had asked more of herself, not settled for the easier demands.

Submissively, she rose from the table, put her feet on the floor, sat there for a while, her mouth open, the breath curling in and out, then cautiously brought herself to a standing position and began to move shakily forward. Clemens reached out a hand, but she signaled it away, continued on her careful, straightforward amble. He watched her judiciously; for someone in her condition, after so little time out of the machines, she had done remarkably well indeed. Emily ambulated delicately, maintaining an even, swaying pace around the hermetic enclosure, grabbing the bulkheads only for temporary purchase and then beginning to move with increasing confidence. Once again he moved over to lend assistance but was balked; she slapped a hand gracelessly away, and he retreated. It was stirring to watch her, stirring to observe what was happening here; it somehow renewed his faith in the very process of reconstruction itself, in the continuity of men that they would be able to preserve and rouse themselves and function so remarkably. He had never believed in an afterlife, but the permanence, the totality, of the human condition was another issue, and looking at this, he could intimate a little of it. They had possibilities, after all.

"Now," she said, standing before him, looking quite secure, rubbing her hands against one another, "now I seem to be able to deal with matters to your satisfaction. What's going on?"

"I don't really know—"

"You as much as told me that if I cooperated you would explain what's happening here. Well, I've cooperated. I've done everything that you could ask. Now it's your turn to tell me."

"All right," Clemens said. He really did not want to enter into dispute, and he owed her what information he had. "Keep on walking," he said. "Get your strength back."

"Only if you tell me—"

"I'll tell you. I'll tell you while you're moving around, but it's very important that you do this—"

"All right," she said, "I'm not arguing," and began to toddle around the enclosure, becoming perceptibly stronger with every small circuit of the room, the robes which had been draped around her flowing and billowing so that she looked like a madwoman buffeted by the wind, although such was not the case at all. She made circuits of the room while Clemens told her what little more he could, that she was the third reconstruct to be aroused on this ship, Clemens having been the second, the first a European alienist named Sigmund Freud who had been brought to deal with a crew which had been manifesting symptoms of mental illness. There were factions in this crew, it would seem, and although Freud was reconstructed, Clemens's own reconstruction had been the idea of the captain, who appeared to be suffering from symptoms of a bizarre nature. The captain had brought Clemens around to give special advice. Meanwhile, it was Freud's decision to awaken Dickinson, since at some crucial point in his life he had apparently used her or her work successfully.

All of this, Clemens went on, he had learned from Wyndham and Hoffman, psychologist and executive officer, with whom he had consulted confidentially. They had enlisted his cooperation even though he had said that his first loyalty should probably lie to the captain who had, after all, brought him back. Hoffman and Wyndham had informed him, however, of the danger of the situation, the multiplicity of risks, the depth of complexity with which they were forced to struggle. Now some kind of apocalyptic confrontation with the aliens seemed to be at hand; soon enough the fate of the ship would be decided when the Vegans were contacted. "And that," he said, "that is all I have to tell you. I know no more."

Emily stopped pacing, leaned against a wall. "This is the strangest thing I have ever heard."

"This is a problem we've all had," Clemens said. "I want you to know I'm very glad you're here."

"But you didn't ask for me."

"I have no influence! It was all Freud's decision. But I told them how glad I was to learn you would return."

"For what purpose? You told me there is no love between reconstructions."

The bluntness of her response touched something equally brutal in Clemens. "Then I'll have to test it out for myself. What do you care? All you ever thought a man was good for was procreation or self-abuse."

"You're a cruel man," she said bleakly, pushing hair from her forehead. "A truly cruel and vindictive man. Nothing about you has changed in all of these centuries; you are exactly as I remembered. I don't believe anything that you've said to me, I don't know how I can."

"You have no choice."

"We're not in a ship at all. Nothing is as you say it to be. You've just done all of this to torment."

"No, Emily." Clemens found himself trembling with unrepentant, unassimilated rage; it was like all of the other times brought back again. "You're all wrong," he said to her. "You understand nothing." He stumbled to the hatch, flung it open, looked into the solemn, poised face of the young crewman standing there. "Get the hell out of my way."

The crewman stepped aside, astonished. "I didn't think—"

"Never mind," Clemens said sharply. "None of this matters." He plunged into the corridor, pushing the stunned crewman to one side, strode furiously into that abscess. "Get away from me," he said. "Just get back. I don't want to deal with it anymore. There's only so much I can deal with." Infuriated, he charged toward the control room.

Emily Dickinson felt rage too. The feeling of betrayal was absolute; if it had not been for Sam Clemens's lust and selfishness, she never would have been exposed to this. She believed nothing about Freud; it was Clemens who was responsible for her being in this terrible situation.

It really was all his doing, dear Sam's, not hers at all, and they should put her back into the chambers, let her sleep once more. Upon their return to the room where she stayed, alone, she told them this, tried to make clear that she wanted no part of anything that was happening, but they would not listen. Once released she was not to be returned for a long time, they told her. Something to do with shattering the rhythms of the process. Also, she had a role to play, a function to fulfill; they had plans. She was out and must stay out. They could, however, move her. And so, kindly by the crew, she was taken through the ship most rapidly and given rather luxurious space in a room which Wyndham said had been reserved only for her. These would be her quarters for the duration, she was told; she would be safe here. No one would bother her, least of all Clemens, who, she was assured, would be kept at sufficient distance. She might, however, observe.

So, fair enough, she thought: she would observe. Sulking in the darkened spaces of her room, watching the dazzle of stars in the viewplate, staring at holography for her amusement, nibbling on the copious selection of foods they left her, she decided that this was what she would do: observation had, after all, always been her central ability. She was a miserable poet, Whitman was right, and she had to accept this, but she could see with acute and forceful eye if she truly wanted; she could have been more than this if she had had the courage to make things possible. Was it entirely her fault that she had come to nothing? She was not sure of this. It was hardly so simple. She wanted to see the alienist Freud, having heard only rumors of him thus far, but this would have to wait until they were ready. They would give her nothing, otherwise.

So she observed, kept to her quarters, talked now and then quietly with Wyndham, who dropped by to see how she was doing, contemplated the spray of stars she could see through the viewplates, tried to make some sense of what was going on. It was absolutely bizarre and did not properly codify. Much time passed. Her strength, such as it was, returned. There were no problems with her kidneys; they seemed to have been fixed by the machines. She asked Wyndham now and then when she might see Freud, but Wyndham said that there was plenty of time for that, meanwhile there were some more urgent conditions. In due course the alienist would be around. Right then he was trying to obtain some measure of the situation. Clemens would not bother her anymore, she was assured. They were keeping him very much at remove. The captain seemed to believe that an alien race, the Vegans, had taken steps with the minds of the crew, had inserted dangerous probes which were making them mad, and an argument seemed to have developed between those who sided with the captain and those who thought he was mad. Freud was at the center of it, trying to make adjustments as best as he could. The important thing, Wyndham advised her, was to understand that the situation was well under control and to have trust. She would have her own role to play eventually. Are there truly Vegans or not? she asked. This was an issue which was not easily answered, Wyndham replied, although the weight of evidence would indicate in the negative. The captain appeared to be quite mad.

It was remarkable, all of this. Nothing in her history or this drear outcome seemed to connect. Hours passed, days passed, ship's time crawled as it did so often at 231 Main Street, and still she found herself not entirely believing in the situation. Who would have thought such a thing possible? Who could have conceived it? At the root, she was a simple person with routine needs.

Nonetheless she would, she decided at length, deal with this. That was her obligation, after all; here as anywhere else she had to come to terms. The heart seeks pleasure *first* but not last. Therefore, when Wyndham came by the next time, she told her that she wished to see Clemens.

After a time, submissively enough, just as she could have predicted, would have wanted, he came to her.

"Listen Sam," she said, "this is not at all what you think it to be. It is something else entirely. You misunderstood."

"No, Emily," he said. "*You* are the one who misunderstands, I think." He might still be angry at her—how could he not be?—but she could see that Sam had resolved over this period of separation to be calm, to deal with her in a pleasant and temperate manner. "You are the one who does not grasp what has gone on here. You must accept. It is in any case another chance at life, not to be taken lightly. How many of us thought there would be another chance?"

"This is not life."

"What would you call it then?"

"What did you expect of me, Sam? You knew that there could be nothing between us, that it could not work."

"I didn't bring you back, Emily. That wasn't my idea. Freud advised it. Soon you will see him and he will tell you so."

"Why hasn't he seen me already?"

"He's had other things to do. I loved you, Emily. Can you accept that? I think I truly loved you."

"I never believed in God, Sam. Whitman was right when he accused me of that. I mean, I wrote all that drivel, but it didn't have a thing to do with how I really felt; I knew it was drivel as it was coming out. I wanted to be well liked and famous, and that was what I chose. But I never believed a thing I was writing."

"Who does? I didn't believe that crap I was turning out either, most of it. That was why I was interested in you; that's what attracted me in the first place. I knew that you believed nothing too. We could share the emptiness."

"Really?" She felt her estimation of him shift. It was a strange thing; after all these centuries, Emily felt that she was just beginning to understand this lover, and it was surely a contravention of everything she had known. "You suspected that?"

"Even before I met you. Only from reading the material. Emily," Clemens said calmly, "why do you want to see me now? I know it's impossible, this ship is doomed, whether there are aliens or not the voyage is over, Freud knows that—"

"Why hasn't he come to see me?"

"That's for later, Emily, after he's come to understand what is best, what he really wants to do—"

"But why hasn't he come to see me? He brought me back, he must have something to say to me, I can't believe that he wouldn't talk—"

"He doesn't know how strong you are, Emily. He thinks that you may panic, that you'll be unable to deal with any of this, that you'll collapse when you hear what is going to happen, even though I've told him—"

"Oh my," she said.

The laughter built within, almost uncontrollably. She shook with the sound, trembled with little gasps and peals, ripples, and shudders. The fault had to be in this process; they built her wrong, she had never laughed like this. "I must be defective," she giggled. "A defective reconstruct, that's all, something that doesn't work."

"I want you to stay with me," Clemens said. His expression was embracing, sorrowful, damaged. "Can't you see that? After all of this, don't you grasp that this is what I want?"

"I'm never with you. I wasn't then and I'm not now. Freud, madness, Vegans, reconstruction: none of this touches us, Sam; it has nothing to do with us at all. They've involved us in something that is entirely outside us. But I don't have to take it, I can face the truth, I want to get back into those machines because that's where I belong. Tell them."

Clemens leaned against the wall, ran a hand across his lapels. "*You* tell them, Emily. If you have anything to say."

He stared at her and in his eyes it was as if she could see all of America, her vanished continent, all of space, time, destiny itself refracted. "You think you know best," he said. "You think that you're the only one who understands this, but do you really? Do any of us? Can it be said that any of us, even Freud, even the crew, know what has happened?"

She shook her head. "It's enough, Sam."

"Go back then," he said. "You tell them what you want; you work it out. Summon them, tell them what the situation is and what you want done. Abandon me as you have all of those times before."

"Oh Sam—"

"Be done with it! Just be done with it—"

Portholes opened. Alice Wyndham was in the abyss,

staring at her from sad, stricken eyes. "Emily, you are wrong," she said. "We're all here to help you."

"I'm just a malfunctioning unit, isn't that how you would describe it? A broken-down machine, something that doesn't work. Put me off right now."

"Failed," Sam Clemens murmured. "It's all failed. We tried so hard, worked on it, wanted to make it be—"

"You don't know what failure *is*, Sam." Emily Dickinson pounded the steel with her fist, felt the resonating shock, the good pain traveling up the pistons and tendons of her arm. Wyndham came over, seized her arm, as Clemens backed away, appalled. In the doctor's grasp Emily felt rigid, metallic, but then something broke within and she was weeping. She felt Wyndham's own fierce, bitter tears fall upon her. Hands grasping were sudden, enormous, and she felt herself locked against Wyndham as the walls wavered.

"You've failed," Clemens said. "We all have. It is a failure of condition."

"No," she said. "Not that way, not like this. You don't understand; you're not giving us credit—"

"It isn't the way you think it is," Wyndham said, an edge of desperation to her voice, "it just *isn't*," and leaned forward, gently touched Emily's face. "Oh no," Wyndham said. "Not that way." *Failed*, Emily thought. *Failed*. Clemens shouted something, the voices murmured, the lights flickered.

She heard the music.

The music was of the ship, of space; it came on full and resonated, permeated her being with that high whine, and she found herself sped by it toward an imponderable, an unmentionable destiny. Was that it? she thought. Is that what Whitman tried to tell me, what Clemens knew in Hannibal, what all the voices of the night cried in America, toward the Amherst dawn? No, it could not be this. Whitman didn't know, he didn't know what was coming for any of us; he saw but did not see, could not do anything with the conditions.

She felt Clemens's hands upon her, his arms around her. "Emily," he said hopelessly, "Emily—"

The music rose, it was burning; she heard it as it mounted ever more crudely against the bulkheads, and then the light itself was shimmering. It had to be only for her, she was a reconstruction, the mechanism had failed ... but Emily Dickinson knew better than this, she knew better by far; the disaster was general, and nothing would come of it. "Oh Emily," Clemens said. "If only it could have been different, if we had but known—"

Failure. Yes. It has been contrived for that all of the time. The merciful wedge of darkness came down upon her like a hammer, and for that moment, as that hammer plunged upon her, she felt that she was beyond this, did not have to deal with any of it; free from the binding mechanisms which turned her this way, she was untrammeled, was free, knew that it had been taken from her, yes, and oh oh oh what a relief it was finally now as—

—*As they come upon her*

CHAPTER EIGHT

Sigmund in Space

FREUD WALKED THE ANTERIOR CORRIDORS OF THE *WHIP-perly*, meditating on the situation. The captain suffered from schizophrenia, paranoid type. The executive officer was a manic-depressive with fantasies of aggression which he had subsumed by excessive deference. The ship's doctor, a humorless woman at best (although there were intimations of passion), manifested indications of catatonia, and at least half the remainder of the crew, by all standards of early twentieth-century Vienna (which must of necessity be his touchstone), was neurotic to the point of dysfunction: depressive reactions, conversion hysteria, bizarre sexual urges, and the like. Clearly, this Wyndham and Hoffman were in desperate condition to arouse Freud from the reconstruction tank, rely upon his judgment. The alienist hardly knew where to begin. What could he do? What psychotherapeutic techniques (which by definition require patience and isolation) could possibly prevail in this emergency? If Freud had not been so ambivalent about his abilities, so protectively despairing, he would have been entirely undone. As it was, professional detachment threatened descent into woe. He had to be enormously careful. He had to remain in control.

The rhythm of his pacing increased. Freud risked greedy little glances at the huge screens glinting around him, seeing here a disorder of constellations, there a smudge of stars. Here in the middle of the twenty-fourth century, space exploration was not routine; the *Whipperly* was on a dangerous, visionary quest toward the theretofore unprobed, threatening Vegans. This refracted view of the universe from a distance of so many light-years (a term he had had explained to him) was astonishing. Freud would not have dreamed such things were possible. Furthermore, he would not have thought that as technology advanced, the common neuroses would remain obdurate, would in fact prevail. Of course that was foolish, to think that way; the pain, the schism, the older ironies would indeed persist. They would in fact widen as the differences between subject and the technology increased. This crew exhibited symptoms that would have astonished no one at a routine Wednesday-morning presentation.

Freud shrugged. He reached inside his vest pocket for a cigar, struggled for matches, lit the cigar with a flourish, and watched smoke whisk into the ventilators as he turned into a corridor and returned to the small cubicle he had been given as space. In his mind, he littered the desk with papers, the wall with diplomas, to feel at home; actually it was a stark and gleaming enclosure, but he did the best he could with it. Within their limits they had done everything possible to grant his credibility and a sense of domain; if he was unable to cope, Freud knew, they would be free to blame him for everything. Everything here.

Well, he thought, they will decide what will be done. When it is over they will shrink me again and put me back in the dreaming space, and it may be centuries, it may be never until I receive another assignment. But then again and fortunately I will have no knowledge and therefore my entrapment will be unknown to me. That last time with Jurgen, no, Jurges—

Freud struggled for recollection. *Jorenson? Joralemon?* He could not seem to recall. He scuttled frantically through the tunnels of memory; it would be a terrible thing if he could not remember this case. *Jorson?* No, that was not it. *Jurgensen*, there it was, Jurgensen, the mad engineer who thought he was a vine. He remembered it well; all of it came pouring back to him. Jurgensen had some very bizarre ideas, I didn't handle that too well I guess and got derricked for centuries, but then again here I am and none the worse for it. Their sanctions did not put me away permanently. He supposed that he should take some satisfaction from that. He did, however, not.

The recollection, however, impelled Freud toward his next act, which was to use the communicator on his desk to contact the captain and summon him to the office for a further interview. Of all the technological wonders of this time to admire, Freud admired the communicator the most; it was a simple device, a compact telephone. He wondered idly whether they had given it to him to make him feel at home or whether the twenty-fourth century was simply less sophisticated than that slick and dangerous twenty-second which had given him some difficulty. The aspect of the planet, the shielding and wire, the insulation with which they had packed him for the descent to Venus, had really been quite marvelous. While waiting to see the captain again he also thought of his old rivals, Adler and Carl Jung.

Doubtless they had considered reconstructing that miserable pair before electing Freud. There was grim satisfaction in knowing that. Still, he would have hoped (even in light of the Venus situation) to have been reconstructed more often. Only one assignment, this, after all that time. Not good. It did not speak well for their opinion of him.

Well, there was really nothing to be done about that. Here he was and here the responsibility for the mission reposed. The captain entered his office, a slender, ashenfaced man dressed in fatigues but bearing a full-dress cap. He looked slightly less demented than he had the last time, but the aspect was still not promising. One thing was sure, however: deference oozed from the captain's postures, the captain's gestures; he would do what he could to comply with any directives or procedures given.

Freud could not control the fate of the mission or bring the captain back to equilibrium so quickly, but he had some kind of authority and scholarship, and the captain had been properly intimidated. Removing the cap, wrenching at it with both hands, he took the chair across from Freud and stared earnestly, eyes slowly igniting under searching gaze. "Have you completed all of the interviews now?" the captain said urgently. "Do you understand the situation? Wasn't I telling the truth about all of this?"

Freud said nothing. He would allow the captain to ventilate at the outset. This was for the best. Gravely, he nodded.

"We've got to combat those Vegans," the captain said. "They've taken over everyone now except you and me. They've got all of them in their control. But they'll never have me. Never. Isn't that so?"

Freud took an exquisite puff on the cigar, stubbed it out. Discipline. "Let us hope not." Little reeking fibers glinted at him from the receptacle. It was a pernicious habit; it would have destroyed him if McCormick had not.

"You know that, of course. You know what's going on here; you've checked out the situation, right?"

"Absolutely. Why don't you tell me a little more about those Vegans if you will?"

"Absolutely," the captain said. "I'll do that absolutely." He put his dress cap carefully over a knee, clutched the desk with both hands, leaned forward. "They're a green, humanoid race," he said hoarsely, "essentially primitive in their civilization and technology but with great mystical force and power which they can turn into energy, hostile waves which come from their planet to selected targets. They've warped the minds and souls of all of them, everyone, that is, but the two of us. Of course we're going to deal with them while we still have a little time." The captain's voice began to waver. "I have plans. I have such plans." He pulled himself into an expressive crouch. "They can't get away with this." Exhausted by this confidence, he leaned back, seized the cap, drew it across his forehead. "Goddamned Vegans. They can't get away with this. The plans that I have—"

"Of course you have plans." Freud looked at the captain with what he hoped was impressive, dependable serenity and control. "I knew that from the first time we spoke. You're a purposeful man."

"I'm the captain. I *have* to have plans."

"Absolutely. But why do you feel the Vegans must be destroyed? Wouldn't it be enough simply to evade them?"

"Because otherwise, in less than a generation, they'll be in our system. They have the technology to get there already; all they have to do is suck the information from our minds. Don't you understand that? It's just pouring into them, everything we know; that's why they've got the deep probes into us. They're out to get us."

"If you think so—"

"But don't worry. I'm aware of the situation. I'm completely in control of this, I really am; I'm a highly trained man. Together, we are going to defeat this bunch."

Freud had read the capsule reports on the crew which were kept updated by the psychologist, working through the powerful computers. The captain's condition was clearly deteriorating; he was more dramatically bound to his obsession every time that Freud saw him. Still, this was understandable in terms of the background; pure obsessiveness was one of the qualities prized by the academy. It had to be instilled within the command.

Freud wanted to say to the captain, Look here, there are no Vegans whatsoever. You have imagined all of this, it is a complex paranoid fantasy. There are three silicon-based planets circling an arid star in that system; in three centuries of star missions, life has never been found anywhere, let alone intelligent, purposeful life. Of course this would have constituted a direct attack upon the captain and would have led into most dangerous territory; he did not dare do it. Still, it would have been interesting and certainly would have forced matters toward a conclusion.

"I *know* you're trained," Freud said gently. "As a highly

trained man myself, I do respect that. Still, I have a question if I may."

"Ask me anything." The captain tugged at the cap, coughed, cleared his throat, concealed the coughs behind a hand as if they were small, explosive secrets being slowly discharged. "I am prepared to deal with any questions, any eventuality. I am eager to do so."

"That's very good," Freud said supportively, "always to be on the alert, ready to deal with situations, that is to say. Still, what if there happened to be *no* Vegans out there?" He locked the captain's gaze, looked into the small, tormented eyes, pierced now by knowledge and implication. "Is that a question which you have at least considered?"

"I've considered—"

"Of course I'm not saying this is the case. Very likely there are and everything is as you have said it to be. Still, what would happen, what would be the case if there were not?"

"But there *are* Vegans, Doctor. Several hundred million of them, huddling on the three planets, sending out the probes, warping and controlling our minds. They've been waiting for this; they've got us tracked closely. I'm going to save us, though. Single-handedly, if necessary, or with your help if you will cooperate. If you'll join me in this effort. I am still the captain—"

"Ah," Freud said, wondering if he was pressing the matter and yet finding it irresistible. "But what if there were *not*? Just as a speculation—"

Emotionally labile, the captain's persona switched, predictably, to rage so quickly. "You're just like the rest of them." His face was mottled. "You damned toy, you mechanical, you reconstruct. You're just like the rest, and they brought you back to warp *my* mind. Don't humor me. I'm going to save this ship. Now I must return to the bridge."

Freud sighed, leaned back. He could have predicted this; nothing was to be done. Still, the force of the obsession, its centrality and force, were most distressing. Even more distressing to the captain, had the man a shred of insight. "Deadly, cancer-causing Vegan probes," the captain said, pulling himself to a standing position, swaying unevenly in the light. He clawed at his legs, slapped them. "They could encircle us at any moment. We have almost no time left. There is so little time left."

"How long have you felt this way?" Freud essayed mildly as the captain turned, dragged himself away, leaving the hatch open, stumbled into the corridor mumbling about treachery, only some words of which Freud could deduce. He sighed, stared at the wall for a while. The captain was clearly out of control, but then everyone there was out of control in some way. It was an intensely difficult situation, defying any mandated, single approach. Really, he was without precedent of any sort, or methodology. When he had thought about the futility of it all long enough—it was a futility not without humor, though, as he was careful to see—he used the communicator to summon the executive officer, Hoffman.

The exec took considerably more time and trouble to reach than the captain—apparently he was concerned with certain duties and shipboard obligations—but at last he appeared. Hoffman showed considerably more rationality, significantly less affect, than the captain, but after some gentle probing disclosed that he was obsessed with Alice Wyndham, the ship's doctor. (Freud could have well suspected that already.) It was her coolness, her arrogance, which involved Hoffman. He wanted her desperately, and if the price of having her was to assume command, to displace the captain, then he would do so. Of course the captain was crazy; that was the major reason why Hoffman wanted the command post, the captain could not be trusted with any aspect of that . . . but having the prestige of command and the ability to work more closely with Wyndham was certainly a subsidiary benefit of these events. He wanted her on every level.

She had, indeed, become a fixation; Hoffman confessed that he had, secretly, stopped taking sexual suppressants recently in order that he might be able to function if he ever found himself in the position to do so. This was risky behavior, and the exec knew how it might jeopardize his position. But it was coming upon Hoffman slowly and distressingly that he was in thrall, that all of the events which possessed the *Whipperly*, the breakdown of the captain, the polarization of the crew, had functioned as little more than backdrop for his more basic, even unalterable, obsession. He could not bear the possibility of losing her.

Freud could pursue this only up to a point. Hoffman was less interesting, less ambivalent, than the captain; also, he was not poised on the center of the dilemma as Freud took the command officer to be. Essentially, the exec was a simpler man with circumscribed desires, although in his way he was no less mad than any of them. Freud thanked Hoffman and sent him away and then, after thinking about it for a long time, summoned Alice Wyndham, who responded immediately, said that she had been virtually hovering around Freud's quarters hoping to have the opportunity for professional consultation. She had done the best she could with Daniel Hoffman, but she thought that the man might be losing control. Also, she did not know if Freud was aware of this, but certain patterned irregularities in the *Wipperly*'s orbit, indications from the holographs, clued into the fact that there might be Vegans after all, not the cancer-causing, mind-probing Vegans of the captain's deranged imagination, of course, but nonetheless an intelligent culture that had somehow become aware of the presence of the ship in their sector and was taking protective action of some sort. "Do you see how interesting this is? What it might mean?"

"No; you can explain it to me, though."

"If it's true, it may mean that the captain isn't completely insane, that he *does* understand something."

Not necessarily, Freud thought. Subjectivity and

objectivity are different phenomena, to intersect only occasionally. "Not precisely," he ventured.

"If this is so," Wyndham said, "we're all doomed. You're as doomed as the rest of us, but at least in the interim, you can help Daniel. Can't you? He's very much in need of help, Doctor." She courteously offered her hand, said that she would of course do everything she could to help in the interim, and then left.

Freud, in the wake of this, put his feet on the desk and pondered the situation for a while. It simply became increasingly complex; the longer the pondered it, the more exquisite and dangerous the ramifications. He decided to talk to some selected members of the crew. The captain thought they were all crazy, Hoffman thought that the madness was restricted to the command post; Freud would attempt to make his own determination. Messages once again passed through the communicator. Events, as was the case so often for him, accelerated. The crew—unimaginative, functional types all of them, technologically sophisticated but seemingly without interior—were neutral on the subject of Vegans (although they believed that there probably was something out there), but they were positive in their evaluation of the officers; they were convinced that the captain was out of control, that Hoffman was not entirely stable himself, that only Wyndham could be trusted although not very much. Of course, protocol and the chain of command forced them to phrase matters far more delicately. From the crew, however, Freud found enormous respect. They were impressed that an alienist so famous and historically revered would actually have been reconstructed for the purpose of helping them. Reconstruction was an exceptional feat; it had occurred only a few critical times in most of their travels. So he *was* known in this century after all outside the profession. The fact that his reputation seemed almost legendary gave Freud some comfort. One of the crew whispered, exiting, that she was particularly happy to have Freud on the *Whipperly* because there had been rumors that it would instead be Carl Jung, who did not have the kind of aura surrounding their own alienist.

Freud sent the last of them on their way, decided against further interviews of any sort, and after much consideration lit another cigar. The symptoms evinced were extraordinary in their consistency, yet that consistency could not put him off the point which Wyndham and others so misrepresented: *Everyone* on the ship was evincing symptoms of madness, and that was probably a consequence of the mission itself. This at least had to be the logical inference. Long probes—their stress, isolation, boredom, and propinquity—must tend to break down the crews. He had been called from the banks not because of special circumstances but because of ordinary stress, magnified in the captain who had lost control. What they wanted him to do, it would seem, was to patch over matters in order that the mission might somehow conclude. There had been much difficulty and expense, the captain had been embarrassingly deposed and then became a seedy lunatic lurching through the corridors; other indications of the breakdown of function indicated that the mission might have to end. It was too close to the prospective end for this to happen; they wanted Freud to patch as best he could.

Patch. He needed to patch himself. He stood, groaned, neatened the desk marginally, extinguished his second cigar, and brought the chair compulsively into alignment with the desk. Everything had to be brought into place. Then he went into the corridor and resumed a more restless and extended pacing, staring at the holographic representations of constellations which flooded the corridors. This welter of light stunned and discommoded; Freud adjusted the angle of the projections as they taught him so that he could evade the thin and stunning light. Space, for an early-twentieth-century Viennese, was overwhelming, shocking: it must have had less of an effect upon these custodians of flight, but several months in this environment, he thought, would undo anyone. It was absolutely unnatural. The administrators tried to routinize these missions and drain mystery, just as with the reconstructions they tried to routine, make sympathetic a terrifying if qualified immortality. But in neither case had it truly worked out.

Centuries in a cube, he thought. Centuries locked away. All of that time trapped, dreaming, for no reason other than that he had failed with Jurgensen, whose psychosis would have defied any methodology. They should not have done it, he thought; they should have allowed his residue to commingle undisturbed with the stars, should have left him with the less noted and obscure of his time. He should have been spared this difficult and humiliating afterlife. They did not need reconstructs aboard the *Whipperly*; they did not need a doctor, a writer, or a lady poet but a priest or perhaps a Talmudic scholar. Like the hapless Clemens, like Dickinson, Freud could offer no solutions at all; at best he could take them further into their unspeaking, resistant hearts, at the core of which outrage had been transformed into the various paradigms of response. It was not the Vegan probes that the doomed captain feared; it was instead the perception of his own desires which had been destroyed by the command function, by the ship, by the century itself. That was the problem and the eventual test.

Clemens and Dickinson had not even penetrated that far. He had misjudged the lady poet—she was not quite as stupid as he had thought—but she was unable to deal at all with what was going on, whereas Clemens, a distraught pessimist, could deal with it all too well. It existed in confirmation of his bleak view of all human outcome.

This line of thought, however, did give Freud an idea. It was the first useful idea, he intimated, that he had had thus far, possibly better than any idea since McCormick. (Venus had been a thoroughgoing mistake.) He strode through the holographs and returned to his cubicle, used the communicating devices as they had been explained to him, and summoned officers and crew to an emergency meeting in the largest lounge immediately. Then, refusing questions, shutting off access, he strode into the corridor, where, just as he had expected in the wake of this, he saw Wyndham and Hoffman waiting for him, their faces bleak with concern. "A meeting?" Hoffman said. "There was no call for a meeting, at least until you had referred its content to us, obtained permission—"

Freud raised a hand, silencing the exec. Wyndham touched Hoffman's arm, but he shrugged it off roughly and she stood in place, stricken. Hoffman reached out, but this time it was she who rejected him, pushing the hand away. The byplay was subtle, fascinating; it could have gone on endlessly.

"Listen to me," Freud said. "I'll talk to you before I talk to them, but I want you to know this: your twenty-fourth century is a fraud, your deep-space probes are finished. Your Vegan mission is done, and you had best understand this now, rather than later."

"And why is that?" Wyndham said.

"I will tell you."

"You're overreacting," Hoffman said. "There's a lot of stress here." He looked at Wyndham in a pleading way, but she ignored him.

"Soon all of them will know; I tell you this first because you are responsible, because you brought me back in the beginning and must hear this first."

"And what is the truth?" Hoffman said. His expression crept toward anger. "What are you trying to tell us?"

"I am telling you this," Freud said, and poured all of his conclusion out at them then, knowing that it would make no difference, but they were entitled to the material whether or not they could make use of it, "because you have pushed limits, you have violated circumstances, you have misunderstood the human spirit itself. You have lied your way through the circumference of the planet, out to Mars, Venus, and the rest of the solar system, but you cannot do it among the stars," Freud said, and so on and so forth, spewing it out, giving it to them, not concerned with controlling his language or feelings, expressing his persona, because it simply did not matter. It was too late for all of them.

He permitted a raving monologue (in a detached way he could admire this) of several moments during which he accused the administrators of all the technological barbarities he could call to mind, blamed Wyndham and Hoffman and the rest for an unwitting and destructive collaboration which had put the mission in the worst possible circumstances. "The captain is not the maddest among you," he said. "He is only the most visible."

"You had a terrible time on Venus," Hoffman said. "It was all on the record. I didn't pay sufficient attention. It must have done a permanent kind of damage, then—"

Freud ignored this. "I have found, in spite of all of this, a one-time, stopgap solution to the problem."

Hoffman stopped talking. They stared at him. He supposed that they were utterly intimidated; that was not surprising. It was the only way to function under the circumstances.

"It can never be used again, but I will invoke it just this once for the sake of all on board who cannot discern their right hand from their left and also much cattle."

"What cattle?" Hoffman said weakly. "We have no cattle here."

"It's a figure of speech."

"Where did cattle get into this? I don't understand."

"Stay calm," Wyndham said to both of them. "You're becoming florid, overexcited. There's nothing to *solve*, you see. Not everything is a problem which has to be approached in that way."

"*I* don't have to be calm," Freud said. "That's what brought you to this condition, the fear of emotion, the feeling that you had at all times to be strong and to control your feelings. I'm not going to be that way; repression is not going to work. I'm your last hope and you know it. If I fail, then this mission is finished, it's going to break apart in this cluster, and you can't deal with that, you don't want to die any more than did the people of my time. You are monstrous in the clean, aseptic nature of your passage, yet unconvinced of your monstrosity: that is the centrality of your condition, and it means that you are separated not at all, not in the least, from those conditions from which I came."

Ignoring the issue of Venus—which he would—it was a good statement, a clean, high ventilation. The two officers were obviously impressed. They stared at him, had nothing to say. He had stripped them of speech. Feeling as triumphant as the damaged captain must have felt when he settled the issue of the Vegan probes and knew what they represented, Freud walked away from them, gestured, nodded, thus dismissed himself and descended to the brightly decorated lounge where the 53 other crew members sat uneasily staring at him, waiting for him to speak. Deferential mumbling ceased. Freud acknowledged their attention, moved to the front of the lounge, where he found a small podium had been set up for him. How cooperative they were; they appreciated his work after all. He stood before them, swaying unevenly in the wafting, odorous breezes of the ventilators, staring at the painted figures on the walls so much less distressing, more natural than the holographs of the stars in the corridors. This was more in keeping with the traditions of his time.

Well, he thought. There is no reason to wait. Nothing to be done but to go on and finish it.

"All of you should know who I am. I am Sigmund Freud; in my time I was a doctor of medicine in Vienna who investigated the powers and potential, the illnesses and the damage, of the human mind. Unfortunately I was killed by a madman before my researches could reach fruition, but I was closing in on many important issues. Those studies were seminal. I liked to think of myself as an artist of the mind; I sculpted and arranged the various models of the mind with exquisite care. Maybe it was arrogant of me to think of myself as an artist, but that is the way I felt about my work. Now I have been reconstructed to help you with your difficulties on this Vegan probe, and I was enlisted to give you assistance. I am going to do the best I can; the matter has received my most serious consideration, and I come before you with the solution to your problems."

They stared. At the rear of the room Wyndham and Hoffman appeared inconspicuously, ignored the glances as their entrance was heard. Freud smiled. It did not matter anymore; there was nothing they could do to him. He wondered if the captain would also enter or if he was taking the occasion of the meeting to perform secret acts of grace or sabotage in the corridors. Just as he considered that, he saw the captain enter quickly, surreptitiously, to crouch behind Wyndham and Hoffman to glare at the podium. So be it. Clearly, he had their full attention.

"Very well, then," Freud said. "Listen to me now. Understand the solution I give to you. The Vegans must be repelled, and you must do this. Caution will not work. Circumspection is not possible. Prayer is into a void. The lies of the administrators, those on Earth who would have you treat this as a routine circumstance, will not do it. Only your own courage and integrity will accomplish this difficult task."

Chairs shifted. "That's right!" the captain cried. "That's absolutely right, doctor, you tell them now. You tell them what they have to do!"

"I'm telling them," Freud shouted back. "Understand," he said, beginning to pace now, making their glance swing, distracting them deliberately from the captain. "Your administrators have lied to you. They have always lied. Space flight is not the routine transference of human cargo. Space itself is not the ocean; a star probe is not a battleship. Vega is not the Azores! Conditions are new and terrible; monsters lurk behind the curtains of space. Your holographs reduce rather than expand the territory; they do not show the cold and enormous spaces between the stars. Everything is frozen."

"Oh yes," the captain shouted, "Yes, yes, that is true!

Everything is changed, nothing is as we had taken it to be. That is the lesson you must give them; I tried to, but they would not listen—"

"It is too late to tell them," Freud said sharply. "Words will no longer function, nothing I say is sufficient. You must *act*, all of you. You will land upon the Vegan planets, you will prepare for debarkation, rig the computer for entry. You will advance then, upon that debarkation upon the Vegan's cities, and *you will kill every one of them*."

"Yes!" the captain shouted. "Every one."

"It will be done," Freud said. "It is the only meaningful climax to our mission. Until the landing has been accomplished, however, you will remain quiet and you will plan. You will work this out. I will see some of you individually, the self-appointed leaders that is to say, to give instructions and to tell you what roles must be played in the great conquest of the Vegans. For the moment, I thank you and wish all of you well."

"Bless you too, Sigmund!" the captain cried hoarsely from the back. "Bless you for all your help!"

Freud acknowledged this with a wave—it would have been impolite not to do so—and then bowed. To his surprise, applause began. At first it was only the captain, but others joined in one by one; soon the vacant hand claps turned into a rustle and then at last a mild storm. The applause swerved toward him in deepening waves. Freud was humbled. He felt the tears come. It had not been this way for a long, long time indeed, certainly never on Venus, where he had failed so disgracefully, nor here. It had just been beginning in Vienna when McCormick had so cruelly aborted his mission. He had not been used to praise.

He basked, momentarily then, in the applause. Even a reconstruct might be permitted vanity. He was still human: breathed, ate, slept after a fashion. This century permitted all forms, all possibilities; he felt no less deeply than any of them, was more human than most. He stumbled from the podium overcome, moved on the ramp into the darkened corridors above.

Getting there, taking the hidden exit from the room, he felt himself beginning to calm, the emotions of the moment slowly draining. He had to return to function. Matters had not ended; they had, in their own way, only begun.

Pacing once more in the hidden corridors he had found, oblivious of the crew for the moment, sequestered from them, Freud adjusted the viewscreens so that he could stare at the dark constellations which he no longer feared. He had conquered implication. Holographs danced at his shoulders. Freud thought that there in that strange circumstance, almost five full centuries from Vienna, he had found some qualified answer to his own problems. Those problems had proved, after all, manageable. Yes, it was possible for him to concede this.

And it was possible to say that these moments were happy for him or at least as happy as one of his dark turn of mind could sustain. But all of this came—as did the circumstances on Venus—to a startling termination. He was really luckless in this regard; it was impossible to plan. The mission was finished.

Not by the captain, by Hoffman, by Wyndham, or any of the crew. Not by the distant administrators perhaps monitoring this, listening and fearing what he had had to say. For all of these—tortured representations of steel and power—Freud had found perilous respect. They created the mission; they would not undo it.

It was the Vegans.

The Vegans with their mighty space probes at last unleashed which do not bring cancer (the captain here at least was wrong) but the fire.

CHAPTER ONE

Bedside Manor

AGAIN AND AGAIN, FREUD HAD EXPLAINED THE SITUA-
tion to those demented Vegans. "Listen here," he had
said. "I am *not* capable, I am simply incapable of performing procedures of an orthopedic nature. Although my
degree is in medicine, my specialty is treating diseases of
the *mind*. Also, I was schooled in treating humans, not
aliens, and finally, I have lost virtually all of that training
anyway. I cannot help you. I cannot give what you
request."

Nonetheless, the Vegans were insistent. They were
precise in their demands. In their execrable German, fun-
neled through the ominous translating devices that they
brought aboard the seemingly vacant and distressed
Whipperly, they made clear that they would take no protests, that they had carefully defined their needs and
Freud's capacity to meet them. " I cannot help you," he
had said again and again to the implacable, insistent, tormented Vegans. "You utterly misunderstand my skills,
the background, what I am capable of doing. You have
not considered this at all."

"Nonsense," they said. "This all foolishness denial is.
We assistance need hard, we assistance for fusion which
you restore will. Nothing done can be undone; nothing
proper can be improper riotous." Or something like that.

It was difficult to make out their voices through the roar of the machinery; the scatter of words seemed synoptic and fragmented. At times the voices were so indistinguishable that they might have been addressing him from their star.

Sigmund Freud felt as a broken man. Matters since the Vegans had overtaken the craft had been disaster. Earlier, this had been a bizarre and doomed mission; he had known that he was in difficulty from the moment of reconstruction. Objectively, he should not have been reconstructed, and the manner in which he had dealt with the situation had proved worthless. But now it was immeasurably worse for him; there was no sense of control at all. The crew was nowhere to be found; he had gone through the ship with tracking devices and on his own paddling, reconstructed feet, searching for any of them, but they had been utterly removed from the *Whipperly*, possibly dispatched to some retaining facility, perhaps murdered. The reconstructs were gone too; he could not find Dickinson or Clemens, not that they would have had anything to add to the circumstances. Now these aliens were asking him to be their orthopedist. Their bone and joint man! Nightmares given flesh: multilimbed, multitentacled, angularly unstable Vegans of various hues and sizes appeared before him with crushed appendages, seeking assistance. It was as if this shipload of cripples had incurred some common disaster in space which had undone all of them. He could not understand it. There was not a Vegan who did not appear malformed. Were all of them that way?

Ah, but Freud was no orthopedist. Not at any level; there was no such training in his background. He had pointed this out repeatedly to the Vegans. The miracles of latter centuries' diagnosis and reconstruction were not available to him. He knew nothing of the peculiarities of their construction, nor would they provide him with charts and indications. He knew nothing of *human* bone construction; all of this had been dealt with in different seminars. Nonetheless, these Vegans sought assistance. Many had been damaged on the voyage, they explained (others, then, had not), and it would be many years, or perhaps they were talking of centuries, until they were able to return to the alien equivalent of home base. In the meantime, Freud was beseeched to make repairs as best he could. "We have no time," he had been told. "Time not is, you must best you can do as soon as possible." Oh, how the translators hummed as they sent out the garbled messages, those tubular extensions like weaponry which the Vegans so proudly disdained. They had other means of control, they said. "Soon now we propose you us cure, there not enough time for that is not is."

"But where?" Freud said, gambling for information, for an explanation of some sort. "Where then are the crew of this ship, my fellow victims, the survivors of this invasion? Surely you can tell me this. You cannot ask for help and give no information at all. What have you done with them? What has happened?"

"This not your response," the aliens informed him. "Need not to be concerned with this as you will; later for a certainty but perhaps not now, not here as we would like. Later is."

So they would not tell him. All of them gone, scavenged away from the *Whipperly* while Freud was in some kind of narcotized state, coming to consciousness to find the ship cleaned of human presence and himself surrounded by Vegans. Freud tended to group these aliens, think of them as speaking collectively or in chorus, but this was not truly the case. They utilized a series of delegates who addressed him at various times. He had come to individuate and identify only by the various injuries or malformations: the one he called the Professor had a mangled left tentacle, the Athlete a crushed interior foot; the Actress made her way to the room favoring an exquisitely splinted anterior claw. Each of them in turn took on the burden of communication although none seemed pleased to be so occupied. It appeared that the dialogues were incurred, then, by obligation rather than desire, but they had to convey if nothing else an expression of intent, which they did colorfully and at extreme length.

But the aliens would tell him nothing of the whereabouts or fate of the crew. They were mute on that issue, gave ground of no sort whatsoever, much as if Freud had hallucinated captain, Hoffman, Wyndham, the other, grayer functionaries who made less impression on him (he knew now with regret that he should have gone among the crew and gotten to know more of them; he did sequester himself) . . . as if Freud had invented these people and had actually been alone on this huge craft. If the Vegans could get him to belive this, if they felt he was credulous enough to accept that information, he had no doubt whatsoever that they would try. They had an exquisite contempt for the man whom they asked to splint or cure them.

But they did know differently, he knew differently, he grasped the situation. The crew had been real, their condition perilous, and he, Freud, had been reconstructed to help them, to somehow save this mission. He had pleaded, railed, demonstrated their mutual impotence before the stars, invoked the presence of the Vegans, until, to his dismay, the Vegans had indeed come. It was something like Venus when he had dazzled Jurgensen with the imminence of Venusians in order to get him to return; Venusians had not been manifest, but Vegans were. Here they were. And in the wake of the invasion and appropriation of the *Whipperly* there had been only silence, solitude, remorse, contemplation, those few rooms in which Freud had eaten, imbibed, paced, meditated, consulted with Vegans, considered his history and desperate condition. None of the rooms provided evidence of human presence.

So, all right then, he had to face the possibility, concede the necessary truth . . . it was likely that they indeed perished in the invasion, were massacred to the last of them. All but Freud, that is, who had been wrongly identified by impatient Vegans as an orthopedic physician and retained for the purpose of repairing mangled aliens. That seemed to be what had happened. There seemed no other premise on which to base his understanding of the circumstance. He had to accept, there was no crew. Then again—because the aliens would concede no information at all—perhaps the crew was alive, if not on this ship, then in some quarters which had been prepared for them. Maybe he had merely been isolated in order to better concentrate upon his work. There were a *lot* of tormented, misshapen Vegans out there, absolutely no flawless examples by which he could even measure the severity of their conditions. It was all very puzzling. He did not know (and who would tell him?) how he could deal with it.

Freud had always been humble. This did not sit well with rivalrous colleagues who controlled the journals of his time; he knew that to be the case, but it did not make it any easier to assimilate. Still, how could he have changed? His humility was the basis of whatever modest accomplishment he could still hold; it was that quality, he suspected, which had evaded his biographers, evaded even those who created the Book of Reconstructs, raised so many false expectations, sent him to the tank from which he had emerged twice now to fail. He would never have envisioned the process of reconstruction, of course, but more importantly, he could not have imagined himself a reconstruct.

Who would possibly select him? What scholars of the future would want Sigmund Freud to preserve or resurrect? He had been a medical doctor with a few interesting and highly unsettling insights into a theory of unconscious motivation, that was all. Who would have thought it could come to this? But unbeknownst to him, utterly unprojected, his researches seemed to have had great effect, had landed grenade after posthumous grenade in the battlefields of the twentieth century. Now a force after his time, he had twice been recreated, exposed to an impossible condition, and then confronted with the imponderable. It was a circumstance best laughed at, and he could see the absurdity, but laughter was difficult. One day you strolled around a lake with an agitated composer, centuries later you found that it had assumed the proportions of legend. Who was to know? Who could have seen? Who could judge any of this?

He had never made claims for his ability; he could not. To know that wicked instrument, the unconscious mind (although no one could know it; this could be barely intimated), was to understand all too well how uncontrollable it must be, how tentative all conclusions. How rich, how deep, how sheerly perverse that unconscious was, of what strange and terrible connections it was capable! And how much less, consequently, he must know of aliens. He knew nothing at all. That was the premise from which he had always functioned, that all but the simplest truisms were beyond his grasp. Nonetheless, this accumulation of injured aliens lurching around what had been until so recently a human ship, this gathering of horrors, seemed to admire Freud. They demonstrated a kind of protective reverence. He saw awe suggested in their attitude, submission in their demeanor. Never had he obtained this from the haughty and recalcitrant Viennese. Jurgensen on Venus had spat and raged; all with whom he had dealt had been somehow condescending. But these Vegans were certainly different. They would measure themselves, it would seem, through his own judgment. He saw awe in their attitude, submission in their posture, respect in the dreadful syllables that came through the translators. Clearly they took him to be a healer, and so, however reluctantly, he had to be charged with that task. He had to try to do something for them even if he could not.

And there was another reason to feel this way: Freud knew that it was only the anticipation of his orthopedia that kept him in the aliens' favor. Once they learned how truly incompetent he was, it would be all over for him as well; he would be consigned to that dreadful fate found by the others. But if he could jolly them along, maintain the illusion of function, he would be preserved. Past the routine protests then to protect himself against their eventual rage at his failure, Freud had not elected to refuse them. He, no less than the departed captain or Hoffman the exec, had become cunning. He wanted to live, even in those circumstances.

He wanted to live.

He retained his survival instinct; he was not at all that curious to face a final oblivion without this time the swaddling of the banks or the hope of reconstruction. In the abstract, through the theories that he had propounded, the death wish might be quite powerful, but in reality he knew it was surprisingly easy to keep it at a fair distance. Who, after all, wanted to die except when subject to the greatest trauma? It was not as simple to let go as the easy theoretician he had been might have thought. Oh no, it was quite difficult. One wanted to hold on, one had plans, and Freud had learned much in this incarnation. Reconstructed, he wanted to go on; reconstructed, he elected to continue. He did not want it to be all over for him again (and for a last time) so quickly. He did not want the oblivion of the shafts, for he was still curious, and vital. Intellectually, one's death wish might suspire, but emotionally—and it was the emotional in which he lived—Freud wanted to go on, retain consciousness, not be blocked yet again. The captain would understand this. If he was given the opportunity to confer with the man, they would reach an accord about the necessity to go on.

Endlessly curious, still a scientist, still the researcher, Freud wanted to confront the remainder of the century, the startling denouement of the Vegan probe, even though he would never have imagined in his youth that he would be able to conceive, let alone control, the matter.

Oh, there was plenty of evidence of id rampant here, but Freud did not care to inspect it deeply. He would not ponder it all that much. Thoughtful as he might be, his own self-analysis had been—he was willing to admit this—highly suspicious, often self-serving. As all self-analysis had to be. As most human transaction is compelled.

* * *

Once, on Venus before they had sent him out to the wastes, he had asked, "Am I the only Freud reconstruct or are there others?" The question had a rather plaintive, egoistic edge although he was actually more interested in the paradoxical aspects. They had told him (in that less sophisticated, less protective time) blur y: no, he was not . . . reconstructs serviced many of the expeditions and colonies, reconstructs could be replicated, and other verions of Freud at that moment were locked in the banks of ships or hidden in the colonies. And there was a cache of prototypes back home. No, they could not tell him how many; every ship had its own records and none other's. To the best of their knowledge there were somewhere between forty and fifty Freuds available.

The thought of these other versions of self carrying on, living through other eras, had obsessed him for a while then. In their multiplication, these other versions were also capable of experience; some were in process and some were shut down, but he felt that he could intercept in dreams their own adventures. It had been a frightening phenomenon, almost unbearable to think of, but later the calming thought had come to him that the dreams were counterfeit. The versions could in no way intersect. How could they communicate with one another, and how many were functioning at any given time? Each was separate and alone, alone and separate, used only for emergency conditions, locked to his disparate condition, soldered to his individual Fate.

So on Venus, even before the events which had led to his embarrassing end, Freud had put away any hope that he could find a qualified immortality. The other versions were invariably separate. They had nothing to do with him at all. They did not matter. Each of the Freuds was alone and locked bitterly to his own condition; the multiplying, refractory versions of self were of no significance whatsoever. It was at that point only, the point at which he freely internalized his condition and came to understand its uniqueness, its barrenness, that Freud found himself able to contend with the larger circumstances awaiting him on Venus, circumstances which, alas, had worked out in unconvincing fashion.

At length and as he had known would happen, the blank and isolated period ended and once again he was faced by necessity. "You will Freud surely with us come now and intended," a friendly Vegan with dangling anterior tentacle said to him, standing deferentially at the access to quarters. "It most important is, we are needing you." There was a straightforward aspect to this summons; Freud could feel a thrill of utter certainty: *this* is where it begins. Well, it was the time. He had known, had he not, that the period of isolation could not possibly last and that at some point he would be confronted by demand.

"In just a moment," he said, trying to contrive some task, some aspect of busyness which would put off the alien. Of course it would not work, but he was exceedingly confused, he needed time.

"No," the Vegan said. "Come." It beckoned with an undamaged tentacle. "You to us come I say," and Freud sighed and moved toward the door. These last hours— he dared not call them "days," for there was no sensation of day or night aboard the ship, and the first thing of which he had to disabuse himself was the notion of any normal cycle—had been very difficult. He had spent some time in troubled sleep, some in troubled thought, a little less in troubled eating and staring through the portholes, feeling the slow knife edge of doom pressing in: now the cutting had begun. He did not know how to deal with it. Freud moved slowly into the corridor, subjectively feeling the floor moving in thin waves underneath. The Vegan held out an undamaged tentacle encouragingly as Freud succumbed to a wave of giddiness, felt the panels shifting underneath. Oh, it was conversion hysteria to be sure; it was symptomatology of the most classic sort, but it was painful, so painful, to be humiliated in that fashion. He had hoped for better; he had hoped to become immune to his own perceptions.

"You well are?" the Vegan said. "You to proper showing be done?" Its face, of course, was expressionless; Freud had not trained himself to read human emotion into those flat and blank features. Anthropomorphism was certainly not the answer. "Well are you, this an interrogatory demand it must is."

Freud remained impassive. There seemed no point in giving information of any sort; also, he was not sure exactly what they wanted. What did they want? What were they seeking? He did not want to take a position, risk antagonism. What would they do to him? "I don't know. I guess so."

"You must be well are."

"If you say so. If that's what you want."

"Is of importance highest." The translation device, glinting, was brandished before him in a ruined tentacle. "Report as suited."

"Oh yes," Freud said in a mollifying way. These aliens must not be antagonized. "I well are. I well be. Of highest possibility I am." Mimicking their speech pattern was not difficult, and it seemed to please them. He had done it before, hoping that it would be taken for mockery, but it was seen only as compliment. He had lost any desire to defy the Vegans. He took them as seriously as they wanted to be.

"That is good," the Vegan said. "You with me come, then. With dispatch that is; there must be things are."

It was an unusual request, the more so because they were already slowly on their way. The Vegan limped along, Freud at its tentacles. There was an aspect of irrationality, then, to this. But he wanted to cooperate. There were certain absolutes, he knew, and this must be one of them: hostility bred hostility, defiance when in a vulnerable position would lead only to pain. He indicated to the Vegan that he was already walking. "I'm coming along."

The Vegan nodded in an easily assimilable gesture of

satisfaction, brandished the translation device. "We going, going. We going along." Freud felt the pace increasing. He had to come through this, had to do that for its own sake. It was a matter of principle as well as survival. Perhaps the crew had merely been taken to a safe place; perhaps the administrators at home base were monitoring all of the events on their powerful, instantaneous transfer viewscreens and were at that moment in the process of planning rescue. Oh, it was vital to maintain those delusions: if nothing else they would keep up his spirits.

Moment by moment, regardless of all circumstance, Freud wanted to live. At the end of all this, he knew, no good at all awaited . . . but curiosity had impelled him through all of these travails and would do so, he knew, right through to the end. It is the primal scene, he thought, that is at the heart of all, the child's fascinated need to catch a glimpse of that reenactment. In all guises, in all of Freud's struggles and researches, it seemed that he had been doing nothing but peering through the bedroom doors of his childhood, the doors equipped with mirrors, throwing back at him then the imperishable and endlessly replicated images of the self. That was all it could do for one, this was the final outcome of his researches, that endlessly and in all postures what one found thrown back was—imperishable, eternal, endless—that huge aspect of oneself, one's inquiring eye, one's sullen and boyish face seeking out, nonetheless, some answer.

When they had dragged him in finally, separated him from Jurgensen, torn him from the layers of gear to stand winking and blinking in the intense focus of the terrible lights, he had almost said all of this to them: that it was the simple and terrible exercises of sex and birth, death or disgrace, which all human acts merely replicated, and they should not be angry at him for what he had done; in his crumbling, he had merely expressed their common necessity. But he had not dared say this to them because they were so angry; their faces were so filled with peril and driving accusation that Freud feared that anything at all he would say could precipitate the most immediate of acts. So he had said nothing, merely standing there naked under the lights, and at last, with an enormous gesture of repudiation they had turned the lights off and left him there. At first he had sensed decay, but then there had been a dismal and stunning obliteration as final as what he had felt from McCormick, and that had been the end of it.

So what had started with Jurgensen had ended once again alone, and sinking into the Jungian ooze he had allowed himself the hope that this time at least there would be finality and he would not be unfolded and forced to deal with all of it yet again.

Toddling behind his escort at rapid clip, puffing in the thin air and ozone of the alien-converted *Whipperly*, Freud strode through the vacant corridors without hope or anticipation of any sort. The sounds of space, the watery hum of flight, the dark hues of space spattering the viewscreens, overtook. The ship was still mindlessly probing the constellations at constant acceleration; he knew that much at least (Hoffman had taught him a little crude astrophysics), although no longer in which direction it might be going. Through the unmasked portholes he could see the spin of constellations, gray lurch of stars, dazzle of filtered light. Here Hoffman had pointed out the greater clusters; here too the captain had pulled him aside, warned him hoarsely that those effects were false. "The holography mimics the stars, gives an illusion of location," the man had said. "But it is a creation. Oh, these spaceways themselves are slick, fast, and empty; the drive carries us through places where no stars shine." The captain's manner had been utterly convincing (as why should it not be? he had the expertise), but Freud cherished his illusions as he had once treasured the probability of the unconscious. He would not sacrifice any of this. Not yet. Not until they were ready to decommission with finality.

The Vegan similarly seemed transfixed, slowed, halted amid the clutter of the projection. "Space," the Vegan said, flexing an inside tentacle. "Space is impressive very. Space most expressive is. *Big* outside, big ship, many stars." It was not technological jargon, not sophisticated, nothing advanced or even alien about this, but Freud could sympathize. For these Vegans, a cryptic and inarticulate group if he had ever known one (they reminded him of *shtetl* Jews in their insularity, the parochialism from which they regarded all situations), this was virtually a poetic statement. The Vegan had been moved.

"Yes," he said. "It's very big."

"You about this know?"

"I know nothing," Freud said. "Nothing at all. Maybe a little bit about the unconscious mind, about neuroses among upper-middle-class Jews in Vienna. But I'm not sure how relevant this is."

"You about limbs things know. You fix good, you cure."

"No," he said. "I don't know anything about that either, friend. You misunderstand the possibilities here."

"We go on," the Vegan said. "We go to change all of that." It gestured vigorously. "No stop now, must move on we."

"I didn't stop. You did."

This reasonable point seemed to leave the Vegan non-plussed. "Now go, and now do not look at stars. Look at self, look at *legs*." It began to move again at a rapid clip, and Freud following as best he could. For a damaged race with many injured appendages, the Vegans did seem to move most expeditiously.

Stumbling through the corridors as best he could, alternating his gait between a waddle and more determined scuttling when distance opened, Freud coaxed his mind, that panel with uncontrolled internalizations, to remain smoothly blank, tried to wring out vestiges of panic, warned himself that introspection should be limited. It led absolutely nowhere; there was no point to it. *I must be a circumstantial creature and accept these events without* comment. What is the point of it otherwise? I am not even myself, I am a replication of self, the real Freud lies four and a half centuries behind, mingled with the fumes and earth of a forgotten city; Earth is a rotten and declining planet, they have told me; it is impossible to take myself seriously, and I should not. I must not.

But ever since McCormick shot him, ever since his "death" was accomplished and even more than had been the case in what he thought of wonderingly as his "previous life," Freud had been unable to close off these inward verbalizations. "How silly, how mundane, how utterly without point or vision, relevance or meaning, are most of the patterns of our consciousness," he had written or had soon meant to write at some point in this voyage. "They are mere lisping chatter, empty reflections of the present, refractions of the past or self." The primal scene, yes, sought in the bedchambers of the mind, and now he, no less than any of his miserable patients in Vienna, of the tormented Jorgensen, of the wretched crew of the *Whipperly*, was unable to block this musing, empty commentary upon his life, the sound of that idiot auditor expanding and replicating that which must be compulsively enumerated. His researches, his studies, had been filled with bemused acceptance of human vulnerability and shared plight; nonetheless it was still depressing to understand truly how little control there is.

Perhaps this had always been the secret at the center: there was no control at all. Nothing would change; the *Whipperly* made cargo of them all, staggering through the mindless galaxies to some indeterminate outcome. Nor—and this despite the attractive lures of hypnosis, auto-suggestion, dream therapy, regression analysis, reconstruction, reconstruction banks, the removal of the blocks, the replication of archetypes in an expanding universe—was there control of any sort, ever. It was a possibility.

But even if this was so: what then? It changed nothing

for him, this insight; he was utterly paralyzed before the implications of his knowledge.

This was a possibility in failed analysis.

Even for a reconstruct there were sleep and dreams, and in some of those dreams McCormick rose enormous in the room, leveling the gun while Freud tried to find some way to stop him from completing the act. In some of the dreams he pleaded for his life, in others he propelled himself at McCormick and tried to spring the gun loose, but in all of them he failed; over and over McCormick pulled the trigger, and he felt the slug tear into his viscera, the riotous explosion of the blood leaping within. He could not evade the feeling that there was some word, some gesture, some combination of circumstance, that would stay McCormick's hand, give him another chance, but he never found it.

In at least some of the dreams he had acceded to the request. "All right," he had said. "I'll *be* an advice column, I'll give advice to the masses, I'll tell them what they want to know if not what they fear." But that had not worked either; it had led to no better conclusion.

"I'm sorry," McCormick said in these dreams. "It's too late for this, Sigmund. Your time should have come before, but now it is ordained that you must die. There is nothing else, you see, no other possibility," and then the gun abysmally had been leveled at him, the hammer struck. So at length and through all of the dreams Freud had been forced to the conclusion that history was immutable and that nothing could be done, but that never took away the pain; the pain was always there, and the sense of futility. If McCormick had not shot him, he felt that he would not have been reconstructed, he would have had a completely different outcome, his researches would have come to fruition and he would have found a way somehow to stave off this future, but then again, perhaps not. Perhaps it was all truly as complex as he had originally taken it to be and utterly beyond his ability to manipulate. That was most likely under all of these rediscovered circumstances.

At length, the Vegan escort led him through an unexpected exit and into a bright, electric enclosure which Freud had not seen before, a luminous enclosure so large that he would not have believed that it could exist on the craft. This was an amphitheater, an arching, vaulting enclosure: enormous, ill-fitting ceilings jutted against one another at a height of a hundred hands, dim beams of light competed and intersected. Struck from unknown sources, the intensity of the light had the effect of a prism. Slightly beyond this, half concealed by the light, were Vegans, hundreds of Vegans poised in naked rows, leaning forward, staring at Freud with what he took (anthropomorphism again!) to be terrible yearning. In front of them, on a table, lay a Vegan in what seemed a severely distressed posture.

Unlike all the others, the condition of this alien seemed acute, and it appeared to be in much pain, thrashing and flapping upon the table, restrained tightly by a fine cord. Little purrs and wordless moans escaped this Vegan; it seemed unable fully to control itself, the pain as palpable then as the restraints themselves. The aspect of all this is mysterious and powerful, powerful and mysterious, thought Freud, metaphoric in the extreme if I can only move past the terror of the situation and the obvious anguish which the alien expresses.

Moving closer to the table unescorted, he could detect mottling of the skin, a twisted aspect to the features indicating torment. This was not a situation which could be dismissed in any way as symbolic. Here was real pain, genuine fragmentation of the soul and spirit, and even so, Freud could feel pity.

"Him help," his guide said, considering the situation, then making a gesture and moving deferentially to the side. Lights seemed to dim as if in preparation. "*Him* help," the escort said, putting the emphasis this time on the first word, which intimated to Freud some kind of connection which would have to be worked out later. *Him* as opposed to *me*? Or *us*? "Away go now," the alien said and passed in front of Freud, moved to join the others indistinguishably in the naked rows. The lights dimmed further, and Freud found himself even more sharply the concentrated focus of their attention.

He had not wanted this. Clearly he had not wanted notoriety, but now he had it. Everything human was gone; he was their cynosure. He had hoped to slide through, to move toward the periphery of their attention and then perhaps out of it, but this did not seem destined. He wiped a hand across his forehead, felt the sweat, felt the slow congealing in the limbs. No less than ever—and credit the technicians for this; they must have worked hard to produce the effect—he was a physical creature. He was tied to the corpus.

In his few contacts, stumbling efforts to manage communication with these Vegans (did he dare call himself an alienist among the aliens? that turn of phrase would amuse all of them from the old days although, unfortunately, it could not be shared), Freud had learned, if nothing else, to distinguish various levels of function. The aliens with whom he had dealt had been damaged, all of them, but this Vegan seemed not only in pain but disastrously crippled. No orthopedist, let alone Vegan orthopedist, he could clearly see that. Moving closer to the table in a kind of clinical thrall, Freud saw the creature's eyes blinking against obvious pain, the small, involuntary tracing movements of the uninjured limbs as they struggled against the restraints. The anterior limbs appeared to be wholly crushed. They were not functioning at all. This alien had suffered a disastrous trauma, that was clear, a trauma as it were beyond the initial trauma of dysfunction which they all possessed.

He came to the edge of the table, smelling the high dense ozone which seemed to drift from the trapped form. Slices of light met at the fine, abysmally concave head with the small crest perched off-angle above. Avian beings, these. Unwillingly, Freud bowed his head against the light, found himself in a posture of involuntary submission, shocked by the force of what he had witnessed. He was not made for circumstances like these. No man was. Nothing in his earlier life had shaped him for transaction of this sort; now he found himself in worlds, among creatures that were wholly incomprehensible. Something like this had driven the captain to destruction. And yet—for reasons that evaded him, that he absolutely could not comprehend—these creatures were insistent, expected him to take measures of some sort. Truly, he could not understand it. None of it, none of it at all, made any sense.

"What is going on?" he said. The words were pulled from him slowly and uncertainly, from the absolute center. "What is happening here, what do you expect? You must understand that I can do nothing—"

He stopped. His words, exposed to surprising amplification, rolled out, thunder in the amphitheater. Behind them was the silence of the void. There was nothing at all.

And in this moment Freud felt, not for the first time on this terrible expedition, but certainly never more strongly, a flicker of real apprehension, vaulting fear. They could do anything they chose to him; they could disable him like the device that he was. If McCormick himself, boutonniere aflame, were to burst through some unnoticed arras in this space, screaming renewed vengeance for Freud's failure to agree to an advice column, if McCormick were to burst in brandishing his weapon and threatening immediate juxtaposition, Freud could not have felt the consternation that he did then. The helplessness was appalling; it filled him with some utter sense of doom. "No," he said. "This is impossible. It cannot be done."

The alien fluttered against the restraints, emitted little peeping noises that, apparently untranslatable, would not become words. "Impossible!" Freud said again. He did not want to hurt the alien, wanted to hurt no one, but he had never felt more incapable.

A heavy Vegan in the first row stood, struggling on crutches to an upright position. "This," it said, pointing at the table. "This now. Cure. Make well. Make better." It balanced on the crutches, fixed Freud with a long, ominous gaze, and then reseated. There were shuffles and sighs in the background. Freud heard a very human cough. The lights flickered, then brightened marginally as if encouraging rapid surgery.

In the distance, he heard a series of dull thuds as if, somewhere in space, an armada were coming in for closer observation. It was absolutely silent in space, he had been told that, knew all of the theory, but the sound was as if the *Whipperly* were being attacked at close quarters. Purely illusory, it had to be. For the thuds, he now saw, were taking place in the amphitheater itself; some of the aliens were bringing their tentacles together, rubbing them urgently, patting in place as if simulating applause. Was this what was happening? Were they applauding his presence?

How could such a thing be, what did they want? It was madness, that was all, and he felt the laughter bubbling like lunacy within him, the urge to spring from his elevation, run among the aliens giggling, hurling little objects at them. "I can do nothing, you have got the wrong alienist," he wanted to shout, and the vision of himself perching amid these Vegans, declaring his unsuitability to them, was momentarily hilarious, but even as he thought of this the alien on the table peeped again. The sound was much like a human cry.

And so Freud found himself brought back to the reality of the circumstance that he inhabited. The situation, truly, was terrible: it was so serious that laughter had to be annulled before it could begin. He had to confront this situation then; no matter how hallucinatory it might seem, it had a reality of its own, had to be taken on its own terms. Wasn't this, after all, the thrust of his science? *There are no hallucinations.* Everything taken on its own terms assumes a complete, a terrible reality.

"Cure," the same voice said. Freud peered through the dazzling light. From this angle he could not differentiate amid the rows, but he sensed a greater fixity of attention, a gathered and ominous quiet. In that various light he could not ascertain what was happening; here the best that could be deduced was that a clinic of some sort was being staged and that the gathered aliens served the function of observers. Perhaps the ship had become a hospital vessel for Vegans, had been given all of the malformed and he had been enlisted, as the *Whipperly*'s doctor (or so they thought), to conduct a demonstration. But what of Wyndham? She was a far more credible doctor than he. Why had they not used her? The point was that there was no precedent whatsoever for this situation, not at all, not in Vienna, not on Venus. "Ambulation he cannot," the voice pointed out serenely, "and therefore you cure will, this is absolute, necessary it most is."

Most is. Ambulation cannot. Necessary must. But how, and to what purpose? What was really at issue here? The voice had nothing to say about this; the aliens had in effect abandoned him. Seated at a far distance, they now compelled him to deal with the situation on his own. He peered through the intersecting slants of light, but there was nothing, nothing whatsoever; no one out there would help him. He was entirely on his own, and the situation continued at its state of ominous, unformed menace.

He sighed and looked more intently at the Vegan on the table. He would have to confront the situation whole, on its own terms. Now he could see how large the Vegan was; the supine position misled, but this alien was eight feet, perhaps, the curious, ropy tentacles glinting dull in the light, the tentacles fanning in various directions, the terrible injury to the rear hanging brokenly on the side. The restraints were fierce; on inspection they were made of a luminescent, metallic substance which he did not recognize, and they must have been very strong indeed for the circumstance, some alien material. The Vegan paused in its irregular, broken rhythm to cry out with pain, murmur indistinguishable syllables every now and then; as Freud stared, the gaze was broken, averted. The Vegan would not look at him. No one on this voyage would meet his eyes. He had had the same trouble with Wyndham, Hoffman, Clemens; only the captain would confront him directly, but the captain was mad. Freud extended a hand to touch the corpus, felt a thrill of revulsion, shuddered, brought the hand back. He could not bear that intersection; there was something elusive, fabricated, in the feel of the alien, and to touch the Vegan was to feel drawn past that hold to stunning collision. No, he was not qualified to do this.

He turned to face the audience. Perhaps he could make the issue clear to them. "Listen here, I have something to say."

Something to say. His voice boomed out, the translating devices which the aliens brought, every one with his own little box, reproduced his voice in their guttural language a half syllable or so behind him; the enclosure filled with roaring sound. "You have got to listen to me, please; you have got to hear this. I am not a specialist of limbs or the skeleton; I know nothing of joints or splices; my specialty is otherwise. I have told you this again and again, but you do not seem to understand. I treat diseases of the *mind*. In my own time, I would have been called an alienist, that is the term for my specialty, and I have to tell you that I am not qualified—"

"Alienist," one of the Vegans said from the rear. There was a long, portentous silence. The three syllables— *ay-lyen-ist*—seemed to hang palpably in the recycled, purring air. "*Ay-lyen-ist.* That is proper, the specialty, no?" one of them said mildly.

"Well," Freud said, heavily. "No. Not at all." He listened to the translator's squawl, wondered how he could possibly put this now so that they would understand. On the table, the alien was whimpering. "This is a *semantic* difference, a semantic problem, you have raised. It comes from a misunderstanding, from the translation. An alienist in my world, in the time that I lived you see, refers to that specialist who treats disorders of the mind, mental illness, that is to say, profound disorders of function—"

He broke off. It was not working at all; he was only getting in deeper; meanwhile the alien on the table was whimpering in pain. The pun had absolutely trapped him as had the damnable language itself, as had his condition here. The pun was bizarre, appealed to his own sense of irony. So much humor, after all, was composed of puns—visual and psychic if not precisely linguistic. Wit came from absurd similarities and juxtapositions. It would have been worth an essay if he had had the time, more than that. But he had to keep it as simple as possible and address the issue directly. "I cannot treat your race." He had almost said *your people*; he felt a reflexive embarrassment. "I cannot treat Vegans. I'm incapable of administering any kind of procedure to you. This is not my fault, it is a condition of training itself. You misunderstand."

Well, didn't they? Wasn't this fair to say? Surely, they had to misunderstand. If they did not, then surely *he* did, and there would be no hope, absolutely none, if this were the case. "You must have medical personnel."

Med-ic-al person-nel. The sound of the translators was horrorific; it buried him in amplification of his own voice. "You do not have to resort to me," he persisted, "unless there is some experimentation involved, some attempt to evaluate, but this is cruel, it is not proper." He gestured to the struggling, anguished alien. "He is in terrific pain. It is not right to force him to struggle in such pain as this—"

"We medical personnel do have," an authoritative voice said from the middle distance. It spoke with more confidence than the others; the timbre of this statement was absolute. A judicial figure might sound like that, some Vegan official responsible for the ordering of all equity. "Positively do medical personnel have but this not of concern is. This outside is."

"But surely your own personnel, your medical advisers—"

"No. No personnel, no medical advisers. None of this at all. Only you, Freud; *you* to do."

"Come forward," Freud said desperately. "Stand, address me, let me see you, deal with this respectably—"

"No. This is impossible now. Does not matter. He ambulating cannot, he on table pain is but ambulate cannot? Assumption is wrong. Difficulty is of a psychotronic nature, Freud."

"A what?"

"Psychotronic. Is your word, not? We displease."

" I don't understand—"

"Maybe psychiatric. That is it. Psychiatric problem."

"Trouble of a psychiatric nature? The man's limb is mangled. You mean psychosomatic, do you not? But this is not a psychosomatic condition; one can see the injury here—"

"Injury within," the voice said firmly. "Psychosomatic, yes. That is word. Injury of psychosomatic nature."

"Impossible," Freud said. *Im-poss-ible*. The amplification was unpleasant to profundity; the amphitheater was flooded with terrible sound. "Impossible, you can see the injury, the trauma that has been suffered—"

In the enormous, arching enclosure he knew that he was beginning to sound like the Vegans themselves: *everything* had become alien, all was removed. His mind scrambled in retreat as if the knowledge were a blow, then came slowly to focus again as if it were a blurred pane of glass being wiped clean. The relief at recovering his faculties, at coming to control of himself again, was palpable; he groaned with the sense of restoration. It was the first time that he had felt like himself on this voyage, maybe since Vienna. He could not remember that far back.

"Not psychosomatic. That is a term for an hysterical illness, the inability to perform or function solely by reasons of mind. A functional rather than organic difficulty.

That is the psychosomatic. But it certainly does not enter into the situation; this is a physical injury."

"No," the voice said. Freud thought that he could localize it after all; the speaker was somewhere toward the center of the fifth row, a smaller alien, surprisingly enough. But there still seemed no willingness to be identified. "Is a physical injury not is. We honor your phrase, we your skill in phrase honor as well. He psychosomatic essential is. He must be made then to ambulate again."

"He cannot," Freud said. "This is not a neurotic malfunction, one can see the trauma—" He gestured behind, turned, indicated the injured Vegan twisting against the ropes. "Can you see this?" he said hopelessly. "It is impossible. This cannot be subject to analysis." He had almost said, *This man is in actual physical pain.* How thoroughly he had been drawn into this situation.

"Trauma in absolutely the mind, not the limb. You deal with mind, the limb come along."

Was that it? Was that what they wanted him to do? Freud nodded assent, let new submission run with the blood, infuse every cell. Let it go, then. Protest no more, have no further arguments with the aliens. He could continue, he could fight on, but what did it matter? What would it yield? Was there any more sense to be imposed upon Vegans than humans? Were the aliens gathered there any less mad than the crew of the *Whipperly*? Was this alien any less demented than the captain? The captain had believed in probes; this alien believed in analytic cure of mangling; of the two the captain clearly was in greater command. No, it was *all* bizarre, twisted off-center; the experiences throughout his reconstructions had been uniform in their incongruity, their bewildering absurdity, just as the events in Vienna had been. Everything was of the same inconstancy. He could take these Vegans to be no less strange, no less confluent with himself and his researches, than the crew of broken humans whom he was brought from limbo to service.

* * *

A certain playfulness had infused him when he had shown Dickinson's poetry to Mahler; it was the juxtaposition of this drivel against the serious, ponderous composer which had so amused him. Mahler could not get the joke, it was entirely insular, but he liked to think that Beethoven might. That same playfulness had underlain his decision to tell Jurgensen that there were Venusians, just as, centuries later, he had found it reasonable to tell the crew that the Vegans were coming. Three times, out of a sense of ironic justice, he had warped circumstance in order to gain a desired reaction, appease his sense of the absurd, but this third time it had worked out in a way he could not have foreseen; his playfulness had turned back upon itself savagely.

That would have been manageable; he had always worked from an ironic perspective and convinced of the necessity of the long run, but the expression on Emily Dickinson's face as she had wandered through the spaces of the ship, the plain sense of anguish imprinted upon her features, an anguish which he could barely touch let alone assimilate, stayed with him even now; it made him think about the consequences of his therapeutic decisions. Wherever Emily was, he hoped there was a little more peace for her than had been yielded. There had to be an end to this. There had to be a point, at last, when one would take the consequences of actions regardless of their outcome, but so far he had not found that way. He, founder of the Viennese school, tunneler into the mysteries and confluences of the psyche, *he* had not been able to manage his life.

No, he told himself. It does not matter. It does not matter what is going on here, then; there is no way whatsoever to make sense of this. In all of these moments of ambivalence or stress—and surely this was how he had retained his balance and control—he imagined that he must be lying hallucinating from the impact of McCormick's bullet, that he was on the floor of his office thrashing away the final moments of his mortality, those last instants before the brain wrung itself free of blood, of panorama, and when he perished, which could not, in objective terms, be a long time, all of this would have been wiped cleanly from his consciousness. All of it: Vegans, aliens, McCormick, Venus, vines, Jurgensen, *Whipperly*, colonies, flight, failure, it would be gone, and he would address the more fundamental issues of his mortality.

It must be so, it had to work out in that fashion, because if it did not he was plainly—and as founder of the most innovative school of psychology in all of the centuries which proceeded its advent—completely out of control and plunging toward a tragedy whose most abysmal aspect was that he could not even articulate it, could not find the words to make clear what had happened, and this was something with which he could not deal. It was not an event in any case which should have been forced upon him as this and all of its predecessors had been.

But in the meantime—and how he understood this now; it came at last into focus—there was work to be done. He could function; he could do the best he could. He nodded at the rows in a resigned way.

"All right," he said. "So be it then. Nothing will come of this, but you will see what may happen. I will prove it to you; I will demonstrate my assumptions as they must be." He moved to the table, stared at the crippled alien. The Vegan looked up at him flatly, implacably, little purrs of anguish coming from the bottom orifice. Otherwise there was no affect betrayed at all. Freud put his hands on the restraining ties, began to fumble with their mysterious fabric. He had anticipated great difficulty in what he was trying to do, but the ties came slack in his hand without resistance of any sort. Apparently they were made for release. He pushed them to the side, freeing the alien who lay rigidly on the table, staring at him from shadowy, covered eyes, eyes which parodied human curiosity and submissiveness. Freud sighed, extended a hand, clinically palpated an undamaged limb, felt the slick, moist surfaces become dry under his touch, withdraw toward scaly rigidity. The alien fluttered within his grasp. This was manageable, he could deal with it; the horror was not as extreme as he had thought.

Well, he thought, what is there to lose? What does it matter? It is not as if there are matters of consequence to be decided here. He released the tentacle, ran his hand over the smashed and bruised appendage at the rear. The alien blinked rapidly, squeaked once, was silent. Freud palpated this tentacle as well. It moved easily under his touch. What was there to lose? What difference did all of this make anyway? It was not as if he controlled his fate, and furthermore, since the first moment that McCormick had gotten the idea for an advice column, it had been utterly removed from him. He should have known of this; free choice was an illusion, one was in the thrall of unconscious, unbearable desire.

"Walk," Freud said. "Go on, get off this table and walk."

And walk. There were murmurs through the amphitheater. The syllables boomed. "Walk," Freud said.

"Cannot," the Vegan said. The sound of the word was sharp, contained; there was no ambivalence at all. "Cannot do that," the translator said distinctly. "Pain, cannot walk."

"I think you can."

Think you can.

He took a tentacle, held it stiffly, articulated the appendage through a presumptive radius of some forty-five degrees. See? He remembered this yet from the old medical training; he could do this. There was mild rigidity with some residual stiffness, yes, but an apparent retention of the reflex. It all came back to him. He had an impression of frozen, fascinated attention in the raked seats. Perhaps they had not expected him to get this far. It had to be rather surprising to them. He let the tentacle drop; it slid back into position.

"This looks normal to me," he said. *Normal to me*. "You can support yourself on three tentacles. This is a medical fact. The anterior tentacle is purely cosmetic in function."

He barely knew what he was saying, but it was wholly, remarkably convincing. He found the firmness in his tone remarkable, and so the observers had to; he heard suggestions of astonished murmuring in the distance. "I will tell you about this incapacity," Freud said. "I think that it is almost certainly hysterical in origin."

The alien stared at him bleakly. "Cannot," it said again. "Cannot, cannot. Hurts. Pain."

Freud nodded gravely. "Pain is just as real in those cases as in any others. I know this. I have done many researches into this situation. We know that the mind controls the body to a significant degree. We are not saying that you do not feel pain or that the pain is not agonizing." *A-gon-izing*. "But it has a psychosomatic origin."

"What is hysteric?" the alien said weakly. "What is psychosomatic? Do not understand the meaning of these."

"It is difficult to explain. I don't know if I can do this, if I can enable you to understand." He stared into the haze, the blur of forms. "Is it necessary to go on with this?" he said to the room. "Do you insist that I continue? Is this what you really want?"

There was no response. But then again, at clinics there never was; the student had to carry through right to the end, impelled to do the best that he could. It was immature of him to look for assistance from that direction. The Vegans were there to observe, not relent.

"But you're mishandling this," Freud said. "You're not coming to terms with this properly. It *isn't* a clinic. You can't really handle a situation like this in that manner."

They said nothing. For whatever reason, they seemed determined to let him follow through on his own to whatever unseemly conclusion. Very well. So be it. Let all of this be their responsibility; let it be on them because there was only so far that one could carry a situation of this sort before the responsibility was too much. He did not want to feed off the Vegan's pain, but what could he do?

"I will try to explain." Freud leaned over the Vegan, locked his gaze with those stricken eyes, attempted to establish a posture of some presumptive confidence. "Your colleagues adjudge you capable of rising, walking, moving in a normal fashion. They feel that it is your choice not to accomplish this for reasons of mentality, of secret choice which you conceal from all, including yourself. That you do not *want* to walk but rely upon the appearance of injury to relieve yourself of responsibility."

If this was a misrepresentation of the position taken out in the amphitheater, he assumed that he would hear protests. But he heard nothing at all. "Therefore, the conclusion seems to be that you should arise and walk." *A-rise and walk. A-rise and walk.* Oh if there were only biblical prophecy to resolve all of this!

"But that is not so," the Vegan said reasonably. It articulated in a far more lucid and coherent fashion than any of the others Freud had noticed and, considering that it was a creature in pain, managed to express itself calmly and lucidly through the translator. These were interesting facts which should be considered. The personalities here could be individuated; they were not an undifferentiated mass but appeared to have significant difference. "I have a crushed *mnox*."

"*Mnox*?"

The alien pointed to the instrument, then to the limb. "*Mnox*," it said. "Anterior tentacle. Certain of our terms cannot be translated."

"*Mnox*," Freud said reflexively. "Anterior tentacle."

"It is extremely hurtful. The pain is intense, and the rest of the limbs are locked in response. That is why I am in this condition."

The Vegan grasped the mangled tentacle, showed it to Freud, teased it forward. In this position, so distended, it looked like an enormous, misshapen red penis. "Can do nothing. Injury is actual, you must see that; it is not hysteric, what you call psychosomatic at all."

"You're wrong there."

"No," the Vegan said. It dropped the tentacle, which whisked to its former position, and the alien gave a little cry of anguish, subsided on the table, respiring unevenly, seeming to investigate the matter of its own pain. After a while it said, "So you can see that this is a real situation. Why would I choose not to walk if I could walk? Why would I put myself in such a condition if I were not forced to be in this condition? It is preposterous. You misunderstand. You are not looking at me, at the tearing."

Freud recalled dimly the early days in Vienna. There had been a woman, a pleasant-faced, educated, polite woman who had pronounced herself blind; doctors had found no physical basis, no trauma underlying the complaint, and at last in despair they had recommended Freud to her. He had found her absolutely convincing, the signs bewildering, had been forced to trace the basis of the conversion complaint carefully. An hysterical blindness he had called it. Hours and hours he had spent with the autobiography, slowly unraveling the circumstances, and at the end the secret had come clinging to that rope of recollection, so weak, so inconsiderable, that its presence had mocked Freud's science. Nonetheless, at its revelation, the patient had been able to see again. This had proved then the efficaciousness of his theories.

"Suppose you tell me, then" he said. "Why not advise me why you cannot ambulate, why you have made that choice?"

"*Choice*?" the Vegan said, astounded. "There was no choice. I was performing repairs when the *mnox* was injured. Half the deck fell on me. I screamed and screamed. The pain was terrible. They were able to do little for me."

"But all of them are injured."

"This is true," the Vegan said cautiously. "There are many injuries among us."

"Doesn't that strike you as strange? That so many of

you are injured, unable to ambulate? What does that indicate?"

"I don't know what it indicates. There are many injuries, much crippling, that is all. Terrible pain."

"And nothing otherwise?"

"There is no choice, Professor. Tell me, tell us, what choices are any of us offered now? It is merely fate. Fatefulness."

Fate. Freud pondered this. The issue was not wholly metaphysical; there was some indication from the demonstrated affect shown on this last exchange, the quick defense of the injured *mnox*, that there might indeed be some psychosomatic component to this sympathetic paralysis; the alient had rationalized the seriousness of the injury fervently. This would be a fruitful area to investigate. Perhaps there was some credibility to what he had been told after all; perhaps there was an element of hysteria here. But how could he investigate the issue? Lacking knowledge of the history of these aliens, of their culture, of its modes and mores, lacking comprehension of the inner life of the stricken Vegan before him, how could he be expected to treat any of this? He would be stumbling through, spreading dangerous fire in a dark enclosure whose shape he did not know.

Oh, he could address the assembled out there on the issue. He could speak of the necessity for acculturation and understanding, but he knew, without even attempting this, that it would be hopeless. Nothing could come of it. They would observe and they would further observe until they were past all point of consideration and then, when that was done, they would simply cease observation. They would run out of patience and attention. His outcome— and he had surely known this from the start—was not at all in his hands. It was as fully beyond him as Vienna, as his life, as that one frail and fading sun around which the recollected Earth circled.

But when was it ever? When did he have control, was it ever any different? Freud had to consider this too. When

Jung broke with him, when he and Adler had their bitter parting, when the Wolf Man sank his head and wept . . . as he lived with that intimation of cancer in his jaw and knew that in the fullness of time it would slay him, when McCormick had come into the office . . . did he have any control then? Was it different? His studies, his vision, everything for which he had lived merely prepared him for this understanding after all: that he had no control whatsoever. Fractured aliens, hysterical crew, broken starship, paranoid captain, desperate exec, misguided doctor, the dazzling twenty-fourth itself . . . did any element there possess greater improbability than the others? Where was the center? Where was that which would pull all of this together, make it coherent? There was none. He knew that now, and this fundamental truth had to be accepted: without it there was nothing else at all.

So if this was true, if none of it meant anything, then the solution was to be a charlatan, to lie, to move in the center of misdirection and purpose. If it worked in Vienna, if it had almost functioned on Venus, then it was worth attempting it in that fashion here as well. Dazzlement, tricks, manipulation of event, that was all they understood. That was what they wanted. Nothing else.

"This is what you want," he had said in that horrendous clutch with Jurgensen. "You want the Venusians, you want the disaster, you *want* them to come bring an end to this. Admit it, it's the truth—" rolling and rolling on the ugly ground, the upheaval constant, the drowning embrace, and still he had been unable to stop telling the engineer the truth. "*You want something so bad that you can give up and go away,*" he had cried, and grunting and groaning they had continued in that scramble until at last unconsciousness intervened and he had been dragged away. It all seemed so terribly long ago, and of course it was, hundred of years, centuries extinguished, but it was for him only a matter of few hours. The engineer could

be there, could be witnessing it at the moment, had not
the Venusian darkness intervened.

"Isn't that so?" he cried to the amphitheater. "Isn't
that what you want? Dazzle, enchantment, manipulation?
A little bit of color before the night? You're just like all
of us, there's no difference between Vegans and humans,
you must know the truth no less than I do, that there is
nothing behind the arras."

In front of him there was silence. Perhaps they were
rapt; then again they might have been beyond response.
It did not matter. He held this insight and it was central.
"It never could have been any different. I want you to
know that, accept it just as I have, that there was no other
option—"

O-th-er op-tion. Enough. Enough of this now. The
translators boomed and resonated with the translated syllables. He bent over the Vegan, seized a tentacle in each
hand, pressed them against one another. The Vegan submitted with childlike intensity, bowing its crowned, feath-
ered head. Brief and perfect submission. Freud rubbed
the tentacles against one another, hearing the dull rubbery
sound, feeling the alien flesh glide through his hands. All
right. Done. So be it; there was nothing more he could
do here. The alien sighed in his grasp, shuddered.

"There," Freud said. "There you are. It is done. You
are cured."

"Cured?"

"Yes. Ignore the mangling. It means nothing; you don't
need that limb to locomote in any case. The peritoneum
has been properly disjointed; that will solve all of the
problem. Get up and walk."

"Walk?" the alien said dully. "Now?"

"Yes. Do so."

"Disjointed the what? What have you done here, done
to me?"

"The peritoneal cavity," Freud said rapidly. "It controls the neuromuscular system, the autonomous med-

ulla." Did this sound authoritative? It would have to do. *He* found it convincing. Babbling away, the translating devices seemed to possess a similar authority. "All has been treated in that single gesture of conjoinment, properly recoordinated. Now it is up to you. You will have to deal with the situation. Stand up and walk."

"But I cannot. I do not understand. None of this."

"You don't?"

"Nothing. None of it."

"But you should." Freud felt a magnificent, controlling disdain. "You tell me that you do not understand? You listen here, now, you don't *have* to understand, that has nothing to do with you at all. Where does understanding enter this equation?"

The contempt he felt was remarkable; it was reminiscent of what he had felt so very long ago when he knew, *knew* with that burning of true insight, that he was right and that all of them who opposed or failed to comprehend were wrong. Were opposing because they were stupid or they felt their own prerogatives threatened. The truth had a great and clangorous sound; it was like the tolling of a gong: there were certain small moments of absolute knowledge which could be possessed, and he had had them serially in Vienna; now he knew another. They could not contest. He was strong in precisely that specialty where they were weak; that was why he had been put in this position to begin.

"Get up from that table," he said. "Get up from the table now and *walk* ... go on and ambulate. You know you can do it; you lie to us if you say you cannot. Enough of this foolishness. You must accept responsibility for your life."

"But no—"

"I have," Freud said grimly, "been yanked from the machines, given life after death twice now only to fail, to know utter humiliation, to die once again; I have lived through all of this. I know I can look nowhere else, that this devolves upon me and that whatever I do it will circle

back: on Venus, on Earth, in the fast starlanes, everywhere at all. I accept that responsibility, and you must
also; to do so is to grow. Otherwise there is nothing whatsoever."

No-thing wha-tso-ever. How certain it all sounded. Did
he know this for an absolute, could he believe it? But
there was no choice; he had to follow through to the end,
wherever he was taken.

"It is impossible," the Vegan said frantically. "This is
not an hysterical illness. I tell you that I am in pain, that
it is impossible for me to do as you ask but that I can
only—"

"No more."

Freud struck the alien across its horrendous face, not
brutally but with certainty, a clean harsh bravado meant
to drag an alien to its senses. There were cries from the
rows, but nothing was said. The voice of authority was
silent, would stay silent, he thought. The Vegan collapsed
upon the table with the blow, shuddered. Freud seized
the tentacles once more, felt them rise to heat against his
palms.

Now, he thought. *Now.* There was an unpleasant sexual
tension, a sexual connotation to this act, he knew, but he
would not consider it further. He would rule it out of all
context. Homosexuality could be one of the subterranean
factors in this encounter (assuming that the Vegan was
male; he had never discussed the issue of sex with them),
but it was diminished against what might have been, for
all he knew, the first intimate congress ever committed
by man and Vegan.

"Oh," the alien said. "Oh." It seemed stunned.

Freud kept up the rhythm of palpation, began to tug
the Vegan toward the edge of the table. It lurched in his
grasp, then slowly moved in the direction of that urging.
It rolled upon the table. Freud felt himself beginning to
shake with laughter. The position, the posture, was ridic-
ulous, yet he took it with great seriousness, to say nothing
of what the alien did. The Vegan rolled to the edge, to

the floor; trembling with laughter, clutching the tentacles, Freud fell atop. Clutched in a position much as he and Jurgensen had found, they huddled on the deck of the *Whipperly*. The juxtaposition was no more stunning, no less dangerous, than what he had had with Jurgensen; even the odors seemed similar.

That contact here was shocking yet not sheerly unpleasant. The alien was resilient, its flesh was resilient: the rubbery odor filled his nostrils and transfixed. Freud braced himself in the grasp and then slowly released first one tentacle and then the other, gathered into a protective husk and rolled free. He had a chance to redeem himself; he was reliving Jurgensen in some refractory fashion. Space opened up between them. Similarly, the alien rolled in the opposite direction, came to a stop against a bulkhead. Freud poised, crouched, to observe, felt his attention slowly being drawn on a think line to what was occurring before him. The tentacles were extended. Inch by inch, the alien formulated a crouch which mocked Freud's.

"Now," he said, clenching his fists. "Now you can do it, I know that you can; don't stop, continue. Go on; it's possible, you can do it—"

The Vegan hesitated.

"I know you can; we all know you can."

Know-you-can.

The room seemed to shake. Slowly, the Vegan pulled itself from the crouch, began to come to a standing position. Just as he had known, it was enormously tall; unfolding, it approached the eight-foot mark, its crown grazing the ceiling as slowly, with exquisite concentration and force, it came to the fullest height, stared at the alienist from that height, its eyes clear and full in the off-light.

"Yes," Freud said. "Now you see."

The Vegan seemed to nod.

"I told you it was possible all of the time. It was within your means; nothing held you back."

The alien nodded again. Slowly, determinedly, as if energized by the force of their mutual conviction, it began to ambulate. The alien lurched forcefully past the table on which it had been presented and moved toward the rows. Its stride, hesitant at first, became fluid. It began to move with utter confidence. An entirely different aspect of the aliens was now displayed; they could move with grace, even playfulness. This alien was playful.

The lights seemed to brighten, strobes framed the Vegan, flickered away from Freud as he observed the demonstration. He felt himself becoming transcendent, literally in thrall to that version of himself which he had seen reflected in the alien's eyes. This was different than he had envisioned; it was not like Venus at all. There was a different denouement here. He would not be disgraced. Slowly, the applause began, starting from the background, sweeping down through the rows. That applause came upon Freud in great waves, building, becoming yet louder, filling all of the spaces of the huge room. Assaulted by the applause he felt himself becoming giddy, yet he turned, acknowledged, bathed in it, felt the sound thundering through him. The alien strode confidently around the perimeters of the room, its single damaged limb flung almost insouciantly now over its back as it ambulated. It imposed no hindrance whatsoever.

"Yes," Freud said, hurling the words into the applause, listening to the translators thunder. "Yes, you see now, surely you see it," the amplifiers and translators carrying his message to the Vegans through the ship, to—for all he knew—the trapped and hopeful human crew whose lives depended upon this successful demonstration. "The mind controls everything. The mind in its cunning, its convolution, leaping and possibility, yes, it is the *mind* which triumphs, carrying the corpus along as its willing or unwilling messenger or servant. You must see that now, you must understand all of it. In the beginning was the word—"

And the word was God. They plunged through the aisles to greet him, to touch him. It was a situation which could never have been anticipated; he was surrounded by grateful, insistent aliens. Congratulatory tentacles and limbs were extended, flaps and claws, stalks and extensions, ecstatic mouths crying his name in their language and his; with all of this going on he could not be sure if he had made them understand or not. "In the beginning was the word," he said again, wanting to tell them inevitably what had proceeded from that, but there was no way in which he could be heard, for the Vegans were dancing by then.

They were dancing ecstatically around him; he heard their pagan, joyous cries. It had been a successful demonstration, this. That was clear, he had—oh how long it had taken him and to what endlessly uncertain outcome— indeed proved his essential point. He had given unto them the credibility and the worth of his new science of the mind.

"*You*," one of them said, clutching his elbow, speaking intensely, the translator spitting out the words in a low growl. "You now doctor to the stars, *you* fix now. You fix everybody, you make us good, you make us happy, you make us whole." *Make us whole. Make us whole, Doctor Freud, make us live.*

Oh yes, make them whole. Sigmund Freud feeling the full impact of his mission, then, the first sense of his obligation, rediscovered himself, rediscovered victory, doctor then to the stars, transfixed by ever so much more than light as softly, softly, triumphant Vegans carried him all the way back to his quarters and off then to his more indulgent fate.

CHAPTER TWO

Crazy, Crazy Sigmund

ONCE HE WAS SETTLED INTO THE SITUATION, FULLY acclimatized, Freud cured crippled Vegans in droves. Hordes of them, some with mangling of the greatest severity, others with merely fetching limps and small contusions or impactions in the appendages, came to the luxurious quarters that he had been given in their equivalent of the home ship and were dealt with in precise and symptomatic fashion. He functioned superbly. There turned out to be no problems at all.

Their difficulties—all of them, even unto the most severe cases which were merely cosmetic in their effect— were all psychosomatic. What a vindication of his theories! What terrific proof of their universality! Vegans, it seemed, were highly suggestible, easily victimized by conditions of that sort. It apparently had to do with their history, the nature of their culture, their position as a frail and vulnerable civilization which became timorous when poised on the lip of universal domination. Apparently they were overly reactive to the fear which they engendered in the crew of the *Whipperly*, and this fear had made them timorous, easily intimidated for all of their great technological accomplishment. It was this—and other prevailing factors which were a little less obvious—which had made them take to positions of helplessness with apparently crippling defects, defects which were, however, exaggerated by their own erroneous perceptions.

But once Freud did understand this (and brought the Vegans to that understanding) he was able to effect cures. It was not a matter of treason as he had for a time feared; it had been patiently explained to him with maps, charts, symbols, and exposition that the Vegans were not humanity's enemies at all but their friends and counselors and that in the long run there would be comity between the races. He was merely hastening that time when men and Vegans could live as brothers, that was all. With dispatch and control, Freud could make that time come sooner.

And so he administered standard therapeutic technique in a consultative framework, engaged in some aspects of analysis, probed the preconscious of the damaged with surgical skill, testing the validity of his theories on the aliens. He crouched by them (Vegans were more comfortable if the analyst was in sight at all times, he had learned; they tended to panic in an analytic situation when the context was not clearly established, and they also appreciated the submissive posture which he assumed) and made careful suggestions of subconscious conflict or environmental trauma, poorly sublimated hostility, or blunted sexuality. The translators whirred and glided to his syllables, articulated appropriately alien transliterations. It appeared that the woes of which he spoke were universal. There were certain constants, to be sure, and he had found them.

So he would do what he did best, that was all. He was not betraying humanity; he was simply easing suffering. If he could not deal with the crew of the *Whipperly* (and there was not one who would listen to him, who really cared to hear), he could at least take this group out of their agony. Fearfully, aliens hobbled to his quarters to submit to treatment, hesitantly they spoke to him of their anguish, joyfully at last they leapt from reclining positions after only a brief transaction. The swiftness of accomplishment was almost a parody of the analytic outcome, almost a fantasy rather than an actualization of the process, but he was glad to see it happen. It was inspiring, miraculous really, to see what he had done. If only his colleagues could have seen him; for that matter, if only Wyndham and Hoffman, the captain and the crew, would have observed, they would thus never have doubted his gifts again.

In the early days of his researches, as a very young and naive prophet of the value of his science, Freud had dreamed now and then of the possibility that he would be able to effect instantaneous cure, bypass all the anguished convolution of exposition. He had kept to himself (because embarrassed) how palpable this vision of instant access and cure could have been to him, but now that the actuality had manifested itself, it was so profound, moved him so greatly, that even one as well versed in the hopelessness of paradise as Freud had shifted; he could now be humble in the verification of his desire.

It was this dream of instant cure which undoubtedly had underlain the relationship with Mahler; when the distraught composer had appeared at his door, Freud had thought him an ideal subject, the poetry of Dickinson the proper medium to affect a kind of instantaneous transformation. It was his hope that Dickinson's abysmal poetry would reciprocally confront Mahler with the utter futility, the humor as it were, of his own situation, that the banal poetry would enable Mahler to see how banal was his own suffering, and if this had not quite worked out the way he had desired, well, at the least, he had given it an operative chance. Dickinson's poetry had proved no avenue to conversion at that difficult time, but that did not necessarily mean that Freud had been wrong; it only indicated that he had misapplied the technique. Given sufficient chance on the *Whipperly*, he might have managed to make it work, but the ground had been taken away from him by other events. He had not even had the opportunity to discuss the matter with Dickinson, a lack for which he could not forgive himself.

But Dickinson or not, Mahler or otherwise, Freud persisted in this later context; his thoughts on the matter after all were really irrelevant in the face of the cures that he would manage. This was the best that he could do, and at the least he was being useful.

Freud's quarters were bountiful. He had been placed on the alien ship, an enormous structure without a name, drawn hatch to hatch against the *Whipperly*, given a bounteous suite with magnificent views of the scattered constellations and remarkable facilities: it was, they told him, everything that could be desired. Their own captain had inferior quarters; these were the finest available. Filters cleaned and restored the air promptly; the music of his beloved Beethoven and Scarlatti was piped in through the loudspeakers as if there were chamber orchestras on this ship so close: a miracle. He was granted rich furnishings, enormous meals, concessions of every kind, reading matter from his own time, the satisfaction of every brief whim. All that he was *not* offered was definite word of the crew. The Vegans would not discuss what had happened to them. His inquiries might be persistent but they were turned away with equal firmness. "They are safe and under our protection," he had been informed. "You need have no worry about their condition, but we can tell you nothing more of this." This seemed to be their position, and they were adamant. Lord knew, he had tried to find a way around their obduracy, but nothing seemed to work.

A Vegan had been appointed his particular guide and companion; out of his profound sense of humor—which he liked to feel was metaphysical in these circumstances—Freud had elected to call this one *Alfred Adler*. Alfred was an impressively mottled green Vegan with soaring crest and five undamaged limbs. "I must get more definite word on the matter, Alfred," he said. "I must have more than vague generalities."

"I am sorry, Sigmund," Adler said with equal gravity, "but this is impossible." They were on a first-name basis, of course. Freud had insisted upon it, trying to promote a kind of intimacy with his companion. After all, there was no question of enmity. "We can give no specifics of their condition."

"As you have told me they are alive, Alfred, surely you can tell me something more than that. This is not a matter of specifics."

"Their health and continued circumstance is sufficient, and we can tell you no more. That is a policy."

"The captain . . . is he functioning? I am concerned about this crew, I have responsibilities to them. The captain's condition was so perilous, the paranoid reactions, the suffering—"

"This is of a certainty; they live. They are being cared for. There is nothing of which to be concerned with any, and you should not be preoccupied. Their needs are being serviced."

"Then why may I not see them?"

"Regretfully, no."

"But why *not*?"

"This is policy," Adler said, regretfully but firmly. "It is that which has been evolved. Meanwhile, you have your work to do. You are not to be distracted from this by anything."

"But I already have free time and I am doing the work well. Why cannot some arrangements be made—"

"They cannot."

"I am helping you, you could do the same courtesy—"

"I am sorry, Sigmund," Adler said. He did indeed sound sympathetic. "This work is terribly important, most important, and there can be no distractions whatsoever. Until it is done you must be confined to these quarters and kept in a kind of isolation. Inevitably for your own protection; rest assured that this is only the best for you." The translators had smoothed out since the transfer of ships, the lengthening acquaintanceship, the continuing transaction, the cures, the increasing mutual confidence.

It was remarkable how much more adequately all the Vegans had been phrasing themselves.

"I wish you could explain this to me, Alfred, enable me to understand why you are doing this."

"I wish we could too, Sigmund. But explanations will be for later, after the work is done, after matters have been properly resolved. You are required to be entirely patient."

This left him without further argument. Amiable as Alfred Adler and the remainder of the Vegans might be, he was absolutely obdurate, and Freud had sensed a line beyond which he was unable to push. Freud was under their control anyway, he was at the mercy of the Vegans; crippled or not, they certainly controlled. There was nothing else to be done. He could accept their explanations and quantify as he might or he could for that matter reject those explanations, but objectively nothing was going to change. It was reminiscent of so much else; little had changed since Vienna. Only Emily Dickinson could propound a view of life in which it was rational or could be controlled. True artists like Freud knew otherwise.

But it was frustrating not to know what had happened to the crew. He was concerned, perhaps obsessed, by the matter. Had the Vegans destroyed them, jettisoned them into space, somehow accounted for them at their home base? Or were they telling the truth and were the crew being retained safely somewhere, under guard, waiting to return? There was no way of knowing. Some of these people, particularly the lurking and damaged captain with his confidences (which had turned out to be entirely true) about Vegan probes and the menace of space, had inspired a real if tenuous fondness, and Freud was genuinely concerned about him, that troubled doctor, Wyndham, the enthusiastic men at the meeting who had pounded the furnishings when he had spoken of the need to overcome the aliens. But what was he supposed to do? He had to focus upon the issues at hand; they had given him nothing else. The cures were apparently creating a sensation all through the Vegan civilization or at least the segments touched by this voyage. Freud had, after all, managed to redeem this group, who were known otherwise through the galaxy (he was now willing to accept the word of his captain; the captain knew something that he did not know, was aware of the situation in ways which Freud until the very end could not be) only for their evil, their bestial behavior, their ill temper, their unwholesome thoughts of conquest and of utter dominion.

But now it would seem, in the wake of the accomplished cures (and how ironic all of that was!), that the cruelty and brutality for which the Vegans were well known was simply a result of anatomical dysfunction. They were not constructed for space, it would seem; their bodies, although suited for the gravitational stresses of their planets, went neurologically askew when they went into space, and from that the further damages emerged. But the crippling was a function of the environment, and Freud had made it possible for them to adjust, to come to terms with the trauma. At least this was what they told him and what he was willing to deduce. Ultimately, it was a rather remarkable set of acts that he had accomplished; he should have felt proud of himself. It was the mark of a real spaceman, Adler said; it was a badge of honor.

He wondered: Would the other Freuds, those different versions of himself, have been able to deal similarly? Would any of them have been able to accomplish the wonders with aliens that he had? He did not think so; he felt that he had broken away from all of those unknown multitudes, that he had become truly himself. Dreaming in uneven sleep, feeling the presence of those others almost as palpable as the Vegans, he had seen those other bearded forms, those ponderous, self-important Sigmunds of other ships and galaxies, planets or disasters trooping through the corridors of their scattered nights, and he had known his uniqueness, had felt its weight and consequence, known it moving within him. No, none of the others could have done anything like this at all; he felt torn free, finally, of those other versions of the self, prepared to accept that version of himself which would simultaneously validate and destroy all of the theories and experience of reconstruction.

Separate from the other Freuds who could not understand, set in the channel of his own sufficiency and the resonance of his insight, Freud prepared to go on and on; he would hold out as long as he could until at last all resolution would be achieved. There were no alternates, there was merely, finally himself. That at least he would hold. The heart seeks pleasure first.

It was at some latter point of his service (he had lost track of time and did not care to assimilate it, but clearly it had been lapsed months) when the storms and hordes of crippled Vegans eased to a stately trickle—the latter part of his stay when only the elderly, the laggards, the doubtful, and the superficially injured came, being the detritus of those whom he would treat—it was at this latter point when the cures appeared to have passed through all the dramatically necessitous of that planet who had been funelled like cargo to the great, orbitally locked ship where he performed his work, it was in the latter part of his stay, then, that Freud was summoned and then brought by shuttle carrier and high-speed ground transport to the quarters of him whom he took to be the head of this Vegan detachment and underwent his final interview.

He thought that it might be a kind of royalty with whom he was dealing, judging from the ornate surrounding, the arduousness of the trek, and the reverence of those who surround the glistening, undamaged Vegan creature. Elected or inherited, primogenituer or divine right, ballot or accession by revolution, Freud was not sure of the origins and processes of their ruling clique except that no doubt was left; he was dealing with a controlling Vegan, one of vast influence and central power.

Freud was not a political man, he could not be expected to infer everything about these creatures. Thinking that he could extend insight to know everything with which he intersected was that kind of megalomaniacal vanity which he sought at all cost to avoid, it was the kind of vanity which had almost wrecked the school at the outset. Humility was the proper counsel. But he was sure of his insight here; this Vegan appeared to be a kind of royalty, carrying himself and his undamaged limbs with careful, absent grace, and because he was not unequipped with ironic perspective, Freud elected to address him as *Carl Jung*, just as the guide had been his Alfred Adler. There was nothing better than bringing all of these associations, after all, into closer perspective; parochialism could be truly comforting if it could make the universe a swaddling blanket of familiarity. He was entitled in this nightmare to sculpt out what little resource, what little space was possible.

Jung—or Carl, as Freud decided with a sense of humorous intimacy to address him—bowed when Freud entered the chamber, exuded a kind of royal grace, was similarly gracious as he dismissed the fawning attendants who surrounded him. This was a pleasantly compact alien seemingly of middle years (although who is to know the life span of a Vegan? Freud had never asked) and with an expression which did indeed scatter a kind of benignity. The alien shut off the communicator and gestured toward Freud in what Freud took, anthropomorphically, to be the friendliest of manner. "I give you greetings," the Vegan said precisely, the words perfectly comprehensible. "I have heard so much; reports have been so plentiful, I am delighted to meet you at this very long last." He shut off the communicator with a flourish. "It is a pleasure to talk with you," his unamplified voice pointed out.

"You do not need that device?" Freud said, pointing at the translator. "I can understand you without it?"

"Oh, I absolutely do not need it, Doctor. It is a mark of honor, a mark of our vast respect for you, that I would learn your language, address you on your own terms. I express the highest of regards."

Freud inclined his head. "That is much appreciated, even if I do not quite see the point, the reason."

"You are an extraordinary individual; that is the point. You have done fine work."

"There is no need for flattery. I did what was necessary—"

"Fine work," Jung said more insistently. He hopped up the few steps leading to what Freud would think of as the royal seat and sat gracefully, adjusting his limbs with the poise and assurance of a beautiful woman. "You may think of me as a head of state or as a representative, whatever your wish. It is all the same to us, regard me as you will; our political organizations are sophisticated far beyond the humble capacities of our own situation."

Oh this Carl Jung was gracious and poised, far beyond his namesake in those qualities, and for all of the grace he seemed to be gifted with an equal humility. Surely this was a race capable of being ingratiating. It was remarkable to Freud that he could have initially felt the fear and revulsion for the Vegans that he did. It must have been the influence of the captain; the captain's paranoia sank through everything. In closer proximity, there was a weary and elegant kind of charm here, a charm which was affecting.

"Now, Doctor," Carl said, regarding him fondly. "I want you to tell us what we can do for *you*. We are most grateful, as you can see, highly pleased with your diligent efforts and their great success. You have enabled us to resolve a very difficult situation."

"Anyone would have done it," Freud said deprecatingly. "It wasn't so much for me to do."

"Anyone would *not* have done it; that is precisely the point. There have been many, many failures until your own methodology. This is not an accomplishment to be at all minimized. You should not think of it that way, not after all that you accomplished."

"All right, then," Freud said. "The crew of the *Whipperly*, then, of the ship. This is what I would like to know. Where are they? These were my companions, my comrades, they made their errors but fundamentally had their strengths, they raised me from oblivion, gave me a chance for life again, gave me what they could of possibility and circumstance."

"So what of them?"

"I want to know what happened. Where are they?"

Carl leaned toward Freud, the features smooth, impermeable. "Please," he said, "do not concern yourself with them. I am aware of that concern; naturally, we are most moved by the expressions of loyalty and interest you show, but the crew are not the issue here. Your companions are in custody and good hands, and that is all that should concern you."

"No they're *not*," Freud said. He felt a sudden petulance overtaking along with a more dreadful insight, one which at last he would not push from himself. "They're all dead, all of them. I know the truth. You abducted and you killed these people. And I don't know why."

"This is not so," Carl said with just a hint of affect. The features seemed to concentrate, to grip one another. "They are safe; they are being held in reasonable custody—"

"I don't believe you."

"You have no choice."

"That's unacceptable. How can I believe you? Where are they?" Freud felt a keenness, an edge of aggression, that he had not previously known; the alien's amiability now seemed irrelevant. As the rage knifed at him, he wondered if it was the possibility of death which had energized his response. "Then let me see them," he said, "and I'll believe you."

"You cannot dictate to us. That is impossible."

"Really? I can't dictate. You tell me how grateful you are, that you owe me all kinds of favors, that *we* deserve a favor for what has been done, and then when I ask—"

"I'm truly sorry," Carl said. He made a deprecatory gesture, or then again it might have been one of defensiveness. "Really, on that we can do nothing for you at all. It is policy."

"I want to see them."

"In due course. I tell you they are well, in custody."

"Why not release them?"

"Don't concern yourself with them. Release will be accomplished if we deem it necessary; until then there is nothing to worry about whatsoever. They should not concern you."

"But they do."

"I have asked what we can do for *you* now that your work here is almost at an end. We will return you where you would like, or you may spend the rest of your days as our guest; we can offer marvelous opportunities and call only occasionally upon your vast powers. You may do as you wish, you see. Everything possible falls within your range."

"I don't know *what* I should do. It isn't that easy to decide. I'm not human, you know."

"Of course you are."

"I'm a reconstruction, an outcome of a process, a machine emerged from a cocoon in which I lay for centuries. I have no idea if I'm mortal or immortal or if my circuitry might burn out right now; we know nothing."

"We know of this process, it is mysterious and wonderful. Nothing we have evolved can be said to approximate what you have done. You give yourself insufficient credit. Of *course* you are human, as fully human as any of the others. To us you are indistinguishable. We are here to serve your needs as best as all can be worked out between us."

"I want to see the others. How can I accept your word on this? If I could only see them, confer with them, obtain their opinions—"

"I'm truly sorry," Carl said regretfully. "We do wish to help you; we would like to serve in every way possible.

But I cannot tell you where they are nor allow you to join them, for reasons that are of the highest import. If you are only apparatus, as you claim, then you're overly concerned. What is apparatus to them or they to apparatus?"

"Nonetheless," Freud said, finding that he was amazed by the stubbornness of this leader, his refusal to give ground of any sort, just as Freud was stunned and depressed by his own tenacity, "I would like to know. I have a responsibility for these people; whether or not I am a machine in your estimation, I was enlisted to help them. They brought me back in order to assist with the situation, and I'm not doing a very good job at all if they're abandoned like this."

"They are not abandoned."

"You've made me do that. You will not let me reach them."

"You should not feel that way. You owe them no salvation whatsoever; you need not think of them any more than they thought of you. It is Sigmund Freud who granted us treatment and for whom we wish to render service, not the others. Tell us what you want."

Well, Freud was not surprised. Why should he be? He should have known that events like these would ensue. His guardians—with whom he became progressively intimate as the weeks went on until they were less jailers than associates; well, he had cured several of them too of limps, staggers, or various apparent spinal malfunctions—had prepared him for the eventual meeting with the one who was their leader and the leader's legendary generosity to his subjects and collaborators (so accustomed now to the Vegan hue, the Vegan manner, that Freud scarcely thought of them in that way at all; they were no more alien to him than the damned crew of the blasted boat *Whipperly*), had had ample opportunity to ponder all of the possibilities of the meeting.

"Well," he said, "there are a few things that I might ask. If I must." His guardians had suggested that past a certain point there was no reason to become demanding with the leader; it would get him nowhere, would become contraindicative to a very difficult situation. He was prepared finally, then, to let it go. "I do have a few requests."

"Whatever you want for yourself is yours."

Freud wondered about this large craft, these quarters. Were they perhaps on the home planet itself? There was no way of telling; the Vegans were inscrutable. Ever since he had found himself transferred, he had been unable to understand exactly how they existed there or what the point of it was. Had he found himself a kind of hospital facility for crippled aliens? Or were all of them this way? One thing that he had learned about this monarchical system; it had no bearing upon their technology. King of the Vegans! It was a preposterous concept, worthy of the captain's lunacy, and yet here he was.

"I think," Freud said, pausing to consider the matter further, then deciding that it sounded proper after all, not out of place, credible in the circumstance. "I think I would like to return to Vienna after all."

"The Vienna of your time?"

"Is there a Vienna now?"

"We wouldn't know."

"I wouldn't know either. Yes, the Vienna of my time."

"But that is a long time ago."

"It is the only time I knew," Freud said. "It was the time in which I lived. I would like to continue and complete my work there."

"You could continue and complete here."

"Impossible."

"Your results have been very impressive."

"That is different. Treating Vegans is not treating Viennese; there is nothing theoretical about this. It has no resemblance. Of course you could not understand."

"But we do. We understand very well." Carl shifted on his throne. "But it is not absolutely necessary to go back. You do understand that, of course. There are other and better ways."

"Are you saying that you can't send me there?"

"Why do you think we could? This is a concept of time travel you have raised, not space."

"So you're saying you can't."

"Pardon *me*," Carl said in a somewhat disgruntled manner. "That was not said either. As a matter of fact, we can accomplish that kind of transfer very easily; we have the devices to handle your request, and it is well within our power to return you there. Or anywhere of our choosing."

"Anywhere?"

"Within limits. We cannot, of course, send you to any point in the future. But the past is under our control, and it is manageable. It can be done—"

"Then send me back there. That is what I want."

"But you realize what will happen then—"

"It need not happen." He waved the king to silence with a gesture. "It does not have to happen at all. I do not have to be killed by McCormick. I have been told that this is possible, that circumstances can be altered."

"You have been told a great deal, haven't you?"

"Not as much as I wanted to know."

"Some of us, perhaps, are a little too forthcoming. But yes, it is possible to avert that assassination. We can do this."

"Then I want you to do it."

"It requires, of course, a much larger expenditure of energy. Not that you aren't worth that, of course. You must be advised, however, of some of the difficulties. And the risks. There will be an utter reordering of priorities, of the universe itself, the conversion of energy ... you might implode, there is the possibility of malfunction."

But Freud had heard enough of these abstractions. Like Jurgensen on Venus, this commander, the king of all the Vegans, would ramble on and on unless he was directed and properly controlled; Freud had seen all of the signs, he was quite familiar with that tendency by now. "I want it not to have happened," he said. "Can you understand that? I want to be allowed to continue and complete my work to the maximum degree possible. And that is not all I want. There are other things as well, since you have asked."

"We expected as much. You scientists, you methodologists, are nothing if not demanding." He gave a very human sigh. "We should have expected that this would not be easy for us."

"You offered," Freud said, "and so you are being told what I want. I wish to continue my work. I want that work's completion. I want this too: a world in which poets can be poets, in which the end of their craft is not parody but function, in which symphonists can do their work without hating themselves. I want to feel that there is a twenty-first century which will to some degree be an extension of, a building upon, the twentieth rather than its repudiation. I want the twentieth century, that end of the millennium, to mean something, to have been more than an excuse for the creation of spaceships and reconstructs. This is something of which I have thought deeply, and it is necessary."

"It is very complicated. More complicated than you would think, judging from what we have learned of you. It cannot be quite that simple."

"Poets must be poets," Freud said. "The twentieth century is revered, is the source of the reconstructs, because it was the last in which events truly seemed self-generating, in which people made a difference. But then they flattened it out and tried to change all of that back by making us machines and convincing us that we could be controlled like everything else. I want the twentieth century to be other than the enormous aberration which it has become, that's what I want now."

Carl looked away, seemed to take in the aspect of the royal quarters, their density, their riotous splendor and color. He intertwined tentacles. "Your requests are not unreasonable in full. We have experimented with this situation, you see. We have done investigatorial work, interviewed members of the displaced crew, and have extracted a good deal of information. We have been able to make our own assessments. What you ask does fit within the range of possibility."

"Then let it be," Freud said. "Let this happen. To go back but not to return, then, to be in a world where McCormick did not come, where Dickinson did not drivel, where Clemens himself was granted a little peace, no dreams—"

"I do think I understand."

"*No dreams.* That is what is really wanted; it is the dreaming that wrecked us, gave us a twentieth that was unspeakable, gave us a twentieth in which there were not dreams but only the obliterating machines which took away the underside, that part which gave depth, denied us then—"

The King of the Vegans raised a tentacle. "There's nothing more for you to say now, you're just beginning to repeat yourself. I do understand. We apprehend the condition of which you speak. It is very difficult, what you ask, but it can be done."

"But *will* you do it?"

Carl looked at him; a long, suspiring time went by. "Yes. It will be done."

"Good. I want that."

"You have done well," Carl said, "there is no denying this. You have done very well for us and in pride, and you will be rewarded in that way which we can, for we are honorable. We accept. We accept your request. You will be returned to Vienna, and McCormick will not be there."

"He can be *there*," Freud said in an explanatory way. "I don't mind about that. But I don't want to be shot."

"You will not be shot. We can see to that. There are certain arrangements, certain possibilities, which we can correct. McCormick will not shoot you. He will not be there. He will remain in America and make other plans for his publications. Dickinson, your poet, will not be famous. She will remain secluded within her quarters."

Freud says, "How do you know all of this—"

"We have our reasons," the Vegan said, almost smugly. "We have resources and possibilities for which we have never been credited. Dickinson and Clemens will never meet, and Clemens thus will never have that tragic sense to which you have been exposed. We do not take any of this casually. We have anticipated your request; we have worked upon this far more profoundly, come to understand much more than you will ever know. We appreciate, we understand. We find you to be a most complex, even tormented, but always rewarding circumstance. We take you more seriously than you do yourselves."

Feeling vaguely as if he had lost control of the situation, had lost his own identity, was little more than an accompaniment to the devastating statements of this Vegan, Freud was only able to say, "Thank you. We take ourselves very seriously as well."

"We want you to know that; we want you to understand that this is the eventual message, here, that we take none of you at all casually. This is serious. We are seriously oriented. It is not a frivolous universe nor one so casually arranged but one of great meaning and consequence. You will come to learn this. You will learn it eventually, and it will wholly change your condition; it will cause everything to shift."

"But will it?" Freud said. "Are you sure? Nothing can change our condition. This I must believe, it goes to the core of my own understanding, that in time or released from it, we are beyond that salvation which you so easily promise. But I am grateful; I appreciate what you say."

"You are appreciated too," Carl said. "Everything, everyone, is appreciated. Nothing whatsoever goes to rest or is out of place in these circumstances; some day you will come to see that too."

"I do see," Freud said. "I see everything." This was not, to be sure, true, but it was what he felt had to be

said. He nodded at the Vegan, at his close friend Carl
Jung who had bestowed upon him such wonderful consequence and valedictory, acknowledged the returning
gesture of the Vegan, and then, anticipating dismissal,
walked slowly out of the room, toward the exit. The Vegan
looked at him solemnly, respectfully, as Freud passed
through the door and into the corridor. Outside, his guardians were waiting. They nodded at him as well. He did
not ask them, just as he did not ask Carl, when the expected
recovery of Vienna would begin. This was not within his
right to ask. What would happen would happen, on its
own time. He had to sponsor a form of trust. This was
all they would have asked; this was what he would be
given. He was taken back to his quarters.

Leaving Mahler in the garden, shaking his hand, and
saying farewell preparatory to going back inside and dealing with the less subtle difficulties of his time, he felt that
he could see behind the man's solemn and saddened vis-
age some suspicion of a twinkle, just a hint of humor,
some suggestion that Mahler could understand to what
purposes the poetry of Dickinson had been put. He had
looked for that humorous knowledge, had sought that
intent which would show that Mahler knew to what uses
he had been put, but he was never quite clear, even later,
trying to examine this in retrospect, whether it was indeed
something he had seen or whether he had merely planted
it there out of his own desire. It made a difference, it
made a very great difference as to whether or not the man
would know, but there was absolutely no way in which
he could fasten that certainty, and so he had only let it
slide away from him. He had returned to more onerous,
more immediate tasks. Mahler would have to resolve himself.

The heart seeks pleasure first.

"Do you understand?" he said to Adler when he was
returned to his quarters. "Do you know now why I have

done this? I must do my work in freedom. I must transcend obligation. This is vital."

He paced the length of his rooms nervously. They would do the best for him, he thought. Galactic emissaries of hope, infused with benignity, sickness alleviated, and sickly natures restored to health, these Vegans would begin that series of manipulations and devices which would reconstruct time, reconstruct all circumstance, send him back to that origin where he would be able to do his work in some kind of freedom. "Freedom," he said again. "Without it we are in bondage only to our mortality."

Adler nodded sympathetically. All of them were very sympathetic; he could not believe that there was ever a time when he and the Vegans were at odds. "This is for the best," Adler said. "There is no substitute for freedom. What else can you have?"

"Or responsibility," Freud said, flailing his arms. "That is also very important, to take responsibility for one's acts."

"Oh yes," Adler said. "I agree with you. Responsibility is also very important." He waved a tentacle deferentially, bowed, and withdrew. "I know that you wish to be with yourself now to concentrate," Adler said.

Freud made a motion as if to retain the alien, but Adler was already outside, and Freud thought better of it, of this necessity to plead for companionship. He forced himself to stop pacing, went to the cabinet, removed a small bottle of wine and a glass, poured himself a full red glass of the alcohol, and sipped on it slowly, trying to bring the wine into himself as if it represented a kind of peace. Slightly calmer now, he stared through a viewplate, examining the strange constellations, the unusual formulation and alteration of the sky. It occurred to him then and for the first time since the interview that this might not, perhaps, be the very best course to follow. There were problems back in Vienna with which he could hardly contend, of which he had bare inkling. And he was not even sure that the Vegans *could* manipulate circumstance to get him back there. Why was he so sure that this was possible? Why had he accepted their allegations that they could control time and space, space and time? If they could do this, perhaps it would have been done already.

But what purpose did this rumination serve? He had already made his decision. As he advised his patients, as he told the disjointed and agonized Vegans during the consultations, he had to go forward and not back; he had to enact the endless devices of his life rather than simply replicate. If there was any hope of returning to Vienna and dealing with circumstance, he had to seize upon that possibility and he had to go forward.

Yes, he thought, drinking the wine in greedy, grateful little swallows. That was what he would do. He would deal with them later in a different context; he would contend with this at some time in the future. He would believe that they could send him back there, live upon that possibility. Would they allow him, later, to remember all of this? Would he be granted recollection? Probably he would, although it might be very dangerous indeed to allow such knowledge residence. At an unconscious level, however, he would always retain visions of the mindless and gleaming future, and they would bear upon everything, they would devolve upon all of this. He knew that this must be true.

It had been a job well done. He had at least that pride; he had accomplished much more than any of them would have imagined, and he was entitled to a feeling of great satisfaction. If only there were someone with whom he could discuss all of this, someone other than Alfred Adler and the guardians with whom, however amiable, there was little in common. If only Dickinson were here, Wyndham or Clemens. If even his old enemy Jung, the first, the archetypal Jung, were in these quarters, how gratefully he would seize upon him, seize the invitation to speak!

But he was alone; there was nothing to be done about it. In any event it had been a job well done. He was entitled to feel satisfaction, to derive what he might from the circumstance. Freud put the glass on the floor beside his cot, lay all the way back, closed his eyes, watched the stars spin in fiery circles against the closed lids in that sudden immersion of darkness which had (perhaps like the universe itself, like the starlanes) been self-created, that creation merging into the greater outer darkness, and he thought then of all those latter advantages which would surely someday accrue if he could only get past that sudden flare of shame and equivocation which, for no reason that he could properly assess, so utterly filled him then.

For shame and rage were on their pedestals mocking him; it was not so easy, after all, to shut them off, to consider himself free of those. They looked at him through glinting, heavy-lidded eyes and considered him, and Freud felt himself shriveling under their attention, those disembodied heads measuring, mocking. "No," he said in a whisper. "No, I did not mean it to be this way, I did not want that to happen, I wanted something else entirely." Surely he had other purposes in mind, he thought, but these meanderings, those defenses, could take him nowhere. Shame and rage conferred silently, looked at him with disdain. Freud thought of those defenses, those frail defenses, he could offer which were circular, pointless in all of their convolution, which could only carry him endlessly around and within that tumultuous core of self. It was his own history which he sought, so tentatively and in such trepidation, to embrace.

To embrace his own perished, necessitous self.

And so, at last, all of it slid from him. It passed as if in a great, sighing divestiture, some appropriation of circumstance, some giddy shift; all was taken from him and in whatever equivocal form for however brief a period or then again perhaps for a century (he simply could not hold any longer to conception of time), and Freud lay within that new cocoon of self.

He slept.

* * *

And in that sleep he dreamed; there were no drugs this time to mask the dreams or otherwise restrain him, and so, the unconscious murmuring and hurling the colorful pictures on the screen of observation, he came then to merge with all of those Freuds he had known. Some of them were deep within the trap of the reconstruction chambers, not moving, not thinking. Others were, at this time, conquerors of the stars. One Freud lay in a pit on Aldebaran, hurling defiance at the geometrical beasts of design as on their warped and distorted lines they sniffed at the edges, came ravening toward him. "No more," this Freud shrieked. "You will not have me!" But have him they did, and slowly, violently, he was dismembered. Alert to the end, the Aldebaran Freud held to the image of his death.

Another Freud in a toy Vienna which humorously intentioned colonists at this unimaginable time have made for him on the far ridges of spiral nebula, hums and stalks his way through the mysterious streets alone. He is quite mad, quite broken; he believes that he is surrounded by signs of his destiny. *Freud Street, Sigmund Boulevard.* Natives turn and point at him, laugh behind their hands; there is crazy Sigmund, the alienist, they instruct one another. Crazy Sigmund, he does not care; he has found all of the secrets of the human psyche, he will probe them, explore them to the limits of understanding, and will then *use them for power*. Oh, there is terrific vengeance, terrific possibility, this Freud murmurs to the toy sky, toy faces, toy ducks and geese on the playful lake, terrific reparation. It will not be this way forever, crazy Sigmund says. He has plans. In the observatory, taking all of this in at some great distance, the colonists wink, motion, congratulate one another, then return to the viewing devices. They have never seen anything like this. They have the wit to know they never will again.

Another Freud plunges to his death on Ganymede from the height of a million kilometers, drawn in and in by the perishing, thunderous gravity, jettisoned by the floating ship which has known his devices all too well and which can no longer bear them. He screams as he sinks through the vortex, but there is no one, absolutely no one at all, to hear.

And yet another Freud, this one doomed but earnest, stands with hat in hand in the bedroom at 231 Main Street, Amherst, Massachusetts, and tremblingly faces this red-headed woman in her late thirties who looks at him so levelly, with such a stricken and earnest gaze. "Oh, you have moved me, you have touched me," this least known or honorable of all the Freuds (because of his inability to maintain clinical detachment) says. "You are extraordinary; there has never been anyone like you. Never." The hour's session here is over, and he simply does not know what to say to prolong, but he knows after all these months that if he leaves these quarters without, somehow, telling Emily Dickinson how he feels about her, he will perish; he must tell her then, he must accept, at whatever penalty the consequences, for there is nothing else.

"What is it?" she says to him. "What are you trying to say?"

"I love you," this embarrassing, this stricken Freud blurts. "I love you very much. Don't you know this? Can't you judge? I can't hold it back any longer, won't keep it to myself, I love you—"

She looks away from him. "No," she says. "No, Sigmund, this is impossible. I do not want you in that way."

"I did not ask for this—"

"The heart opens herself once, then turns away, closes forever like stone. It is a mystery."

"You're talking of Lord, of course. I know that. But Emily, Emily, it doesn't have to be only him, your life didn't end there, you're a young woman, truly it is only beginning . . . you must give it a chance—"

"No," she says. "There is nothing to be done for us. The heart seeks pleasure, first, and then release from pain." She moves away from him. "And then all those little anodynes, that deaden suffering." She pauses, looks out a window. "Go away, Sigmund," she says.

"Surely, you can give it a chance—"

"Go away, Sigmund."

"A chance—"

But there is nothing more to say. Nor to be done. She is right. He knows of the anodynes, all the lovely anodynes.

Give it a chance. In the chamber, locked to dreams, hallucinatory images of this last and ruined Freud rejected by Emily Dickinson, the sleeping Sigmund, the restorer of the Vegans, the hero of the Vegan probe now returned to history in triumph, clenched his hands and trembled. He shook and wept, only half-conscious, waves of stupor overtaking him along with a sense of tragedy. The observing Vegans perused all of this with concern but could, of course, do nothing. Small tears were seen to drift from his eyes, the tears cutting patterns on the aged and ruined skin. He was dreaming of Emily Dickinson. The Vegans could not interrupt that process; they were cut off from him as surely as he was cut off from the Amherst Freud, his brother. Surrounded by wire and machinery, he could not be reached, was cut off ineluctably and in some final way.

"I love you, Emily," this plaintive Freud says, wrenching the hat between his hands. "You do not understand, you cannot understand the depths of the feeling that I have—"

He pauses. Drawing upon all of the power and connection that might be available to him, he reaches out for strength as it were, fuses with all possibility to appeal to this poet, this beautiful, damaged figure which stands so tantalizingly near at a gap which he thinks he can breach, but she is unreachable, untouchable through all of this. He should have known it. He can see her sliding away, feel the very edges of this room tilt as if in sympathy, as if in consequence.

"I'm sorry," she says. "I'm sorry, Sigmund, but all of this is in contradiction to what is known. You will never understand."

You will never understand. He, all of his versions, have used this phrase so many times; now the words are being given back to him. It is painful to know such enormous rendering of his own voice, but there is nothing to be done; he must take it. There would have been no other way.

"Ah, Sigmund," Emily Dickinson says. "There is only one reality, one purchase, one possibility, a single life which is given, and everything else; all the rest of it is mystery and an illusion. We lose, we separate, we pass one another never to touch again; this can only be as it is now, and there is no other version. It is gone, it is gone," she says to him, looking at him through the lovely, fading light that clings so softly to her figure. "Oh, Sigmund, it is gone now," her eyes dark and luminous in the spaces of this second-floor habitat that she will never leave, that will be her conveyance through all of time. "It is space-time, we are all gone, all is furnished, all is finished," and Freud backs to the doorway mindlessly. He is at last undone. Finally, there is nothing more to say; she has encompassed everything.

"I loved you," he says. "I want you to know that I loved you—"

She fades before him, lifts an arm in benediction. "Goodbye, Sigmund," she says. "Good-bye."

"I loved you," he says unnecessarily, and then the music and the light overtake him as well; Amherst collapses upon him, implodes thickly, traps him, is gone.

In the tube the sleeping, the primal Freud found himself plunging subjectively further into this, speeding toward some abysmal final knowledge that would give him at last the truth, and in that sleep, unclasped by Emily Dickinson, unclasped by all: unknown, unmourned, untouched, he found for a little while at least some terrific apprehension of that slick and burning history which the aliens had now willed unto him, willed unto them all, unto all the generations of man: forever, forever the fire.

EPILOGUE

The Files of Sigmund

FREUD LOOKED AT HIS WATCH AGAIN. TWO IN THE AFTER-
noon and after this appointment he would be free. He was
looking forward to it, almost desperately; he needed this
time away from the office, from the voices; he needed
this small opportunity to escape the pressure of human
misery and to restore himself. Oh, it ground away at one;
there was no question about it. Perhaps he would go to
the park later in the afternoon, in the evening a concert
(but no Mahler or Strauss, no!), try to empty the spaces
of his mind. Or content himself with a prolonged, solitary
meal, a bottle of wine. The important thing was to get
away from this, from these connections; they were powerful and unsettling in their ability to shift the focus. If
one were to conceive these patients as the world, one
would be reconciled to a parade of human insufficiency
that would be utterly devastating. One would be conniving
with the patients to celebrate the worst implications of
the human condition. This was not what he had sought.

Through all of these musings, the patient had been free-
associating but then stopped, stared at Freud intently,
almost as if these mutterings had some relevance to his
own condition, to some final solution. The patient was a
shabby young man with tormented and debased history;
complaints of impotence obviously masked a deeper and

debilitating rage, but for all of this obviousness, Freud was not very sympathetic, since so much of the suffering, of the dilemma, was self-imposed. More than most of them, this man had brought himself to this.

"I might do something for you," Freud said finally, embarrassed by the stare, trying to focus the attention of the patient elsewhere. "But it would involve considerable application of time, and there would be no assurances of positive outcome. Everything is very uncertain."

"How much time?"

"That is hard to say. One cannot be definite about the progress of treatment. But it would be longer, I trust, than you might think. Any treatment which might yield some results would be complex. I cannot give you anything more than that; nothing is definite."

"Why not?" the patient said. He was imperious, a house painter with only the crudest of educational background, but he carried himself with the spiteful arrogance of a man who felt that he had been denied a more rightful position. It was impossible to imagine how someone like this could even find partners for sexual congress, but the issue seemed to be impotence, not unavailability. "You are supposed to be a famous doctor," the patient continued, "You were recommended to me very highly, everyone speaks of your ability to cure defects and troubles, that you even brag about it—"

"Not so," Freud said angrily. He felt the familiar rage rekindled. Jung must have been misrepresenting him again, creating a false portrait of Freud as an obnoxious, arrogant fool. In this way his failures would be magnified and Jung's own tenuous position would become increasingly unassailable. The man was diabolical.

"Perhaps," Freud said, "you have heard that there are easy cures, easy solutions to problems of the kind which bedevil you. If so, you have been misled, for I promise no easy answers at all."

"I have heard nothing," the house painter said stubbornly. He shuffled his little feet in place, glared. "Nothing whatsoever. I came to you for help because you were highly recommended, because it was said that you were a man who could ease problems of this sort. I don't even *believe* in talking about such things, but I was convinced to see you. That is all I know—"

"The origins of your problem," Freud said determinedly, "are most complex. They have a background in your childhood, your history, many other things. It would take a long time to determine what those origins are, and as we work we must pay the penalty of time. The cure is not easy."

"But you do say that there is hope for me, yes? You are saying, are you not, that something can be done?"

The patient's eyes were piercing; if there was one thing that was clear to Freud, it was that the man did not want to relinquish hope, wanted to believe in the possibility, even the imminence of cure. None of them did, after all; that was part of their curse or condition. "Something can be done, and I wish you were doing it for me, that is all."

"Well," Freud said, leaning forward, trying to look scholarly or at least in control. "That is a step at least. You are able to verbalize your need for help, your desire to cooperate, and this is a most optimistic possibility. We do not have to deal with strong resistance."

"I don't understand. What is *resistance*?"

Yes, Freud thought. I must avoid the tendency to over-intellectualize. It was one of the dangers of his new profession, to throw up a screen of arcane terminology as a means of intimidating patients. He must not do that; it was tempting but played into his worst possibilities. "A technical term," he said, "which you can ignore. Ignore all technical terms; they need not concern."

"Then tell me what you are saying."

"I am saying that it would take a long time, years perhaps, to determine that course of your treatment best suited for outcome. We would have to work very slowly and precisely; these are areas not well understood."

"Ah," the patient said, "but it is embarrassing, this

condition. To be insufficient, unable, with a woman. It is painful and embarrassing. You have no idea, Doctor, how tormenting these encounters can be."

"Yes I do."

"Even when one deals with prostitutes in order to not be known, there is nonetheless a sense of shame—"

"I do know," Freud said quietly. "I know about such things."

"Do you really? Or is this merely something you say to pacify me? You come well recommended, and they say that you can perform miracles, but it is hard to believe that you can sympathize with such as me. Inside you are laughing."

It was the class issue being raised there, of course, but Freud could not deal with that then or ever; it was not relevant to the situation. Nothing was relevant except that one, therapeutic bond which he was still trying to establish. "Don't pursue this," he said. "It is not helpful, not at all. Lie back down on the couch if you will and talk with me."

"Talk of what?"

"Of anything you wish. Anything that comes to your mind. That is the purpose of these encounters."

"I do not have the desire, Doctor. I cannot lie back and talk of this thing or that when I am so filled with shame, when this problem makes me feel that I am not a man. This is what concerns me so terribly, not the matters of which you would have me speak."

"I would have you speak of nothing. It is your decision, within your hands. You see," Freud said, demonstratively, "that is the point I am trying to make to you. Without patience, without the willingness to explore these issues at their own pace, there can be no easy cures; this is not an easy circumstance—"

"No," the house painter said, "Enough of this. *I have heard enough*." He leaned forward intently, stared at Freud. "I am not going to lie back and, what did you call it? *free-associate* for you. This is not possible at all. This is not what I seek. There must be other ways to deal with these demons, and I will find them surely: I will come to find a way—"

They did not understand. As the world became increasingly mechanistic and technological, so did men seek mechanistic answers to their difficulties. They tried to be treated like machines, exposed to a machine's disorders. How could he make them understand that this was not the case, that it would never work, that it was their attempt to *become* machinery in this new and gleaming circumstance that had led to all of those difficulties? The more he attempted to lead them toward that insight, the greater the rebellion. This house painter was not the first. But in his case, because he lacked sophistication and subtlety, the misunderstanding could be seen, perhaps, in its rawest form.

Still, there was nothing to be done but treat the circumstance straightforwardly, as if one could possibly be that way in such circumstances. "I am sorry," Freud said, learning forward, putting his elbows on the desk, trying to address the patient with pure and persuasive honesty. "But there are no easy answers for functional maladies such as yours, there really are not. There is no organic basis to your complaint, that has been indicated. So we can talk, we can probe, we can consider your history in an exploratory fashion as we approach slowly the essence of the disturbance, but we cannot give you an immediate answer—"

"No," the patient said. He shook his head with determination. "*Nein*. I will not accept. I do not want your help."

Does not want his help? What was there to say to this? Freud looked at the house painter levelly, hoping that somehow, at some level, the man would see the compassion, the acceptance, that he was trying to convey. He did not want to turn away from such patients, even the least desirable of them, even though in such situations there often seemed nothing else to do. "If it must be as you say," Freud said, "then I cannot force you to proceed."

"No good," the patient said. "That is no good either. You cannot resolve the issue like that. It is your fault that you will not help me; I must blame you for that."

He stood quickly, rubbing his hands in a nervous, twitching, mechanical gesture. Seen this way, he was a reduced, even a pitiable figure, one of no consequence whatsoever, the kind of shabby, lost defeated youth that Freud saw so often tumbling past him in the streets, ignored in the parks. Sadness, he thought. All is such sadness.

"I am going to leave," the patient said. "I will turn away from you as you have so turned from me." Life from the perspective of this man must have been overwhelming, Freud thought. It must be onerous and difficult: it is remarkable that the little house painter has been able to deal with it at all, even in his sharply decompensated fashion. Nevertheless—

"Nevertheless," Freud said quietly, "I do what I can. I try, I persist. None of this is easy, you know. You have to approach the issue in a spirit of friendship, mutual respect. We must learn how to work together here and to move toward some position of advantage—"

"*Nein*," the house painter said again. He lurched to the door, grabbed the knob, turned to face him. "You have utterly misrepresented your abilities. The truth has not been told of you. They said that you were a man of simple tastes and desires, that you really wanted to help us, but this was not so at all. You do not want to help at all; you merely seek power over others. I think you are a false man, and I do not want to deal with you anymore. A fraud. Everything that was said about you was wrong. But there were other rumors—"

Fraud. How long had it been since he had heard this? But the word always lurked; Jung had waited to spring it on him, and so had the others. Perhaps this patient was their catspaw, perhaps it was all manipulated and this was a means of access to shame him. He had heard of more bizarre scandals than this. Anything was possible with these people. He sat there silently, shaking his head. Who is to tell? Who can know? It is impossible to understand.

"Good-bye," the patient said to him. "Good-bye and good riddance. You stink, as does your stinking city, as do the lies you tell."

The patient left, slamming the door behind him, but it banged open, admitting a wisp of light through which he could see the scurrying, retreating figure, diminished in the access, finally then gone.

And so much for that.

Freud sighed. It was enormously painful, truly this was, but there was nothing to be done. He could not warp his technique, could not misdirect, dared not give them what they thought they wanted. He knew what they must have. This wretched house painter, no less than the rest of them, would have had to take his chances on recall, risked onerous return for that strict plunge, via transfer into the unconscious. What else was there to say?

He could not abandon his science nor his laboriously taken position now. No, all of them were forced to take their chances, knowing then at the end—even in the event of a "cure"—that one would be plunged into a world devoid of history, blown free of that history, functioning now only in terms of its potential connection. Oh, it was too much to bear, really it was too much to assimilate. Freud shook his head, appalled by the bleakness of this vision. So mindlessly one was plunged toward the future, vaulted toward the imponderable; the future then decanted like wine into the eternal emptiness and of no use whatsoever, that memory, than to torment. Enough, Freud thought. Enough of this. It was time for him to leave. There was nothing, at least, to hold him there. The afternoon was over.

Freud skimmed the appointment book to verify once more that he was free. The pages were blank; he sighed gratefully. He found himself nagged by the intimation that he had forgotten something, failed to make a note, that there was some other patient due in now who had made something in the nature of an emergency appointment ... but as he tried to focus on the aspect of this missing patient, dig out that irritating particle from memory (who could it have been?), he felt it beginning to dim. It was a false implant, a false memory. There was no such thing.

No, he was not supposed to see anyone; he was quite sure of this. It must be an illusion, some quirk of recollection as it were, some neurotic distortion of the mind's apparatus as it listed under tension toward the unknown. That future into which lives were decanted. He must be sure of this now; he was not supposed to see anyone at all. No one was due.

Wasn't that so? Wasn't it? This gnawed and nibbled, but it was impossible: he was not that inefficient; he would have made a note. No, there can be no one whatsoever. Freud sat at the desk for a moment, rubbing his hands irrythmically, thinking of catharsis and strength, that which he sought, that he would obtain. He thought of the wretched patient. Poor man. He would go through all of his life dysfunctional, and he would never, ever understand. Understanding in his primitive state, however, would lead only to greater difficulty, more anguish, and what would be the good of that? What difference would it make?

None whatsoever. He shook his hands free of one another to end the ritual, closed the appointment book too, put it carefully in a drawer, and locked it as he had locked all of his files against intrusion. Then he took another cigar, lit it, blew a long plume of smoke determinedly across his empty office. Through the thick, gray smoke he could see the little cracks and spaces, the books and notations that had become all the elements of his life.

So be it. He had made this choice for himself in 1893. No one could change it now. He could only move forward. All of the decisions had been made; one must hold to certainties through the night. No less than Strauss or Mahler, Berg or Jung, he was trapped, but that entrapment at least—for him—was self-selected, and he must always deal with it in that way.

Memory shifted within, regret and recollection joined together, Freud walked quickly, determinedly, toward the door, toward the afternoon. It was his life which awaited outside, nothing less. His life and all of the others, yes, multiply by the millions all of them out there. They waited for him now just as he for them; they were linked, however unknowingly, forever.

Within his mind, knowledge seemed to portend once more, but he pushed that knowledge, for the last time, to one side. The interpretation of dreams necessitates more often than not their negation. His researches, too, had taught him that. He stood poised.

He pulled open the door.

So poised, balanced on the sill for an instant, Sigmund Freud thought of all of this, and then he put it aside, inclined his magnificent head, the jaw containing the nascent cancer that (he knew nothing of it now) would kill him in 1939; he leaned into the Vienna night as if adjusting the cloak of possibility around him, and then—knowing that possibility was all that he had been given, *for unto us a child is born*—he strode into the night, cleaved the night before him, moved into the distant and terrible century, the sound of the charnel houses in the further distance.

He fumbles at the keys, this player of the soul.
Soon to drop full music on.
To stun them by degrees.

1979–1984: *New Jersey and New York*

ABOUT THE AUTHOR

Barry Malzberg is a prolific writer with some twenty-eight science fiction novels to his credit. In 1972 he received the John W. Campbell Memorial Award for the best novel of the year for *Beyond Apollo*—a novel of psychopathology, bureaucracy, and space.

Engines of the Night, his collection of essays dealing with the state of science fiction, received the Locus Award as best nonfiction book of the year.

He lives in New Jersey with his wife and two daughters.